SEPT '93

DOWN BY THE SEA

Also by Bill Kent

UNDER THE BOARDWALK

DOWN BY THE SEA

BILL KENT

St. Martin's Press
New York

Library of Congress Cataloging-in-Publication Data

Kent, Bill
    Down by the sea / Bill Kent.
      p. cm.
    "A Thomas Dunne book."
    ISBN 0-312-09277-6
    I. Title.
    PS35561.E516D69   1993
    813'.54—dc20   93-3519
                                        CIP

First edition: June 1993

10 9 8 7 6 5 4 3 2 1

For Elaine
who should be used to this by now,
and Stephen Leo, our sequel.

Acknowledgements
VIP list: David Slavitt, Art Bourgeau, Greg Frost, Gerald "Ski" Evans, Robin Rue, Ruth Cavin. Special thanks go to members of the Atlantic City casino industry and the Atlantic City Police Department as well as Atlantic City residents and business people, who shared with me their faith in their future.

1

Making a Difference

On a hot night in a stinking, garbage-strewn hollow under the Atlantic City Boardwalk, Vice Squad Detective Louis Monroe arrested Patrolman Reuben Claymore for possession of $2,000 worth of methamphetamine that Claymore had stolen from the police department's evidence room and put in a pizza box.

Officer Claymore thought he was making another routine delivery. He was not pleased when an undercover vice detective tried to take him in. He pulled off Monroe's phony beard. Then he tried to kill him.

Claymore figured he had an edge. He was six feet three inches tall and he was a brawler from the old days, when keeping the peace was a matter of *long-arming:* busting heads, breaking legs, beating up bums, raping and even disfiguring the occasional out-of-town prostitute whose pimp didn't kick back *ice money* to City Hall.

Monroe was five feet two inches tall, having become a police officer when the department eliminated height restrictions in order to recruit more women. He had taken more than five years of elective unarmed combat training classes with Sergeant Vinnie Almagro at the Atlantic County Police Academy in Northfield. He thought that this, and the fact that it was his job to bring lawbreakers to justice, gave him the edge.

He was wrong.

The two members of the Atlantic City Police Department worked out their differences under the Boardwalk, the sharp, sudden sounds of violence disguised by the roaring of surf tumbling in a few hundred feet across the beach.

The Atlantic City Boardwalk varies in height above the dunes. Some sections rest right on the sand, others are held aloft by concrete piers that reach as high as 12 feet. The section in which Louis Monroe had lain in wait for Claymore's delivery was about four feet above the sand. It was known as the Underwood Hotel because it was close to the Convention Hall's hot-water heating pipes where, during the city's unbelievably cruel winter, homeless people could huddle and escape freezing blasts of ocean wind.

Monroe deliberately chose this location so that if Claymore spied a shadowy, bearded figure, he would assume that Monroe was a homeless man. Homeless people were terrified of Claymore because Claymore liked to long-arm them for sport.

Claymore wasn't looking for sport when he tried to club Louis Monroe to death with a PR-24 stick—a baton-like weapon shaped like a lopsided T that, when properly wielded, can shatter bricks. Because the beams of this section of the Boardwalk were four feet overhead, Reuben Claymore couldn't swing his PR-24 stick far. But he had long arms and big hands, and a long-barreled flashlight. He dropped the PR-24 stick, feinted with the flashlight and grabbed Monroe's foot. He pulled Monroe to him, pinned the flashlight barrel across Monroe's throat and started to squeeze the life out of him.

Monroe found himself incapable of movement. He couldn't breathe. He felt the blood pressure backing up in his face. He could hear the surf crashing into the beach, sounding much like the air that used to rush through his lungs.

Then he had one of those moments he never imagined he'd ever have, when you look death in the face and realize that there's nothing much you can do about it, that all the positive exhortations that famous people repeat on talk shows—those homilies about never giving up and fighting for what's right and believing in yourself—are just things that the living tell each other to get them through those days when they're fired from their jobs, their toilets back up, their cars won't start or a slot machine sucks their life savings away in under four hours.

As Monroe faced the imminent likelihood of his death, he realized that it didn't matter that he'd met a woman, pregnant with another man's child, who had accepted his marriage proposal.

When you look death in the face all your good deeds, the few friends you've made, your father in Syracuse, your mother in Florida, your sister still trying to make it as a singer in New York, the people you've tried to treat with dignity and respect, the casino workers, the homeless, the prostitutes and Boardwalk panhandlers whom you've come to trust and even admire, are far away. They can't help you. They don't know how to help you. They have no reason to help you.

Again, Louis Monroe was wrong. James Doochay, also known as Jimmy the Geek, a homeless man, was in residence in the Underwood Hotel.

The Geek said later that it didn't matter that Reuben Claymore had once taken him down by the sea and beaten him half to death. The Geek picked up the PR-24 stick, brought it down on Reuben Claymore's back and saved Monroe's life because, he said, "justice was a participatory sport."

And so, Louis Monroe took Reuben Claymore in, for possession of methamphetamine with intent to distribute, assaulting an officer with intent to kill, theft of state property—contraband, hindering apprehension and related charges.

Officers who make big arrests usually benefit from those arrests, in the form of commendations, promotions, an increase in salary, a day or two of celebrity when your picture is in the Atlantic City *Star* and the article is cut out and photocopied and tacked to every bulletin board in police headquarters, after which your buddies on the shift take you to the Ancient Mariner Bar & Grille and make you drink Sunrise Surprises, Shit Kickers, Mud Sharks and other noxious concoctions until you vomit or pass out.

When Monroe arrested Patrolman Reuben Claymore, he hoped that he'd benefit by gaining a little respect among the officers in the department who insulted him because he refused to accept gifts or deal in favors. Monroe wanted to prove that it was possible to bring down criminals like Reuben Claymore *without descending to their level*, that the difference between cops and criminals is that police officers have the difficult, but ultimately worthwhile obligation of obeying the law, even if the law appears to be on the side of the accused. By living within the letter of the law, police send out a message, not just to law-breakers, but to tax-paying citizens, that it is possible to be better, more honorable and more worthy of respect than the flashy villains who are so eagerly glamorized by the media.

Louis Monroe was about to learn how incredibly wrong he could be.

A few hours after word got out that Reuben Claymore was bawling like a baby in the dingy, windowless Vice Squad office, Lieutenant Larry Claymore, Reuben's younger brother and a powerful aide to the Chief of Police, walked out on his wife and kids and was last seen hopping the shuttle at Atlantic City International Airport, carrying a golf bag that didn't have any clubs in it.

As the plane banked over the floodlit casinos lining the Boardwalk, George Spear, one of the city's wealthiest and most respected criminal lawyers, fled the blackjack pits of the Alcazar Casino Hotel, his gambling fever suddenly replaced with an urge to take his yacht out for a moonlit cruise.

Ellen B. Meade, a former prostitute who had quit her high-class call-girl agency after becoming pregnant with Spear's child, heard the explosion from her apartment on Indiana Avenue. Her first thought was that her fiancé had been killed. Her fiancé was Louis Monroe.

According to Inspector U. O. McTeague of the Atlantic City Licenses and Inspections Unit, Spear was in such haste to depart that he forgot to vent the volatile fumes that collect around engines in a yacht's bilge. The yacht exploded, incinerating Spear and any evidence Monroe had hoped to obtain that Spear was using the boat as a floating bordello, one part of a vast criminal organization that Spear controlled in collaboration with the Claymore brothers.

As Louis Monroe sat at his battered, wobbly, green steel desk in the Vice Squad office, two-finger-typing his arrest report on a white-out-splotched electric typewriter, a black four-by-four jeep—with chrome accents, red leather seats, an overpowered, bass-boosted stereo system, extra-wide tires and various hidden compartments designed to hold the vials and plastic bags that were sold by the jeep's previous owner, a Jersey City crack dealer—drifted up to the rear entrance of police headquarters. A short, scrawny man in a nicely tailored suit emerged from the jeep, identified himself as Lieutenant Commander of the State Police Special Investigations Division, waved sixteen special-release forms at Sergeant Peter Duskine, also known as St. Peter, Keeper of the Keys, and sprung "Officer Roo" from the City Hall lockup. The State Police Commander escorted Claymore to the jeep, giving him a few affectionate slaps on the back right where Jimmy the Geek had hit him.

Monroe didn't hear about this until 8:30 A.M., when Vice Squad Commander Captain Marty Gant put his hand on Monroe's shoulder and gently shook him awake.

Monroe hadn't been aware that he had fallen asleep on the typewriter. He moved his head and felt his neck cramp. He raised himself, felt a numb soreness in his throat.

"Ascertained on the whereabouts of your suspect recently?" Gant asked. He was a 64-year-old South Philadelphia–born rowhouse cracker with a nose that had been broken so many times it was squashed flat above his upper lip. "If you ain't hurting now, you'll be hurting later."

Gant occasionally got in moods in which he liked to pretend he was the sheriff of Dodge City. He stood before Monroe in full western regalia of blue jeans, inlaid boots, a red-and-orange plaid shirt with pearl buttons, and two holstered, long-barreled Colt revolvers hanging from a dung-brown cowhide belt. Seven days a week at precisely 8:30 A.M. Gant arrived at the Vice Squad office, unlocked the box, removed the vials, packets, the bagged-and-tagged assortment of pills and hypodermic syringes that had been seized. He'd take them back to his office, weigh and photograph them, and then have them sent to the department's evidence room where, unless Reuben Claymore resold them, they would await laboratory analysis.

"Officer Roo has got himself BWS'd," Gant said as he crossed to the bulky, padlocked street mailbox that stood in one corner of the Vice Squad office. Contraband seized from narcotics arrests that night went into the mailbox. "He's now property of the Bureau of Witness Sequestration. It's like the Fed's Witness Protection Program but without their budget."

Monroe was dazed and bewildered. "You mean he's not . . . here?"

"Nope," Gant said, fiddling with the combination lock.

Monroe was still dazed and bewildered. If Reuben Claymore wasn't in the lockup, where *could* he be?

Gant unlocked the box. "How's the bride to be? She holding that baby okay?"

Monroe's head cleared. "She's due next month. We're planning on her moving in with me sometime this week."

"Powerful thing of you, son, making an honest gal out of Ellie. Not that she ain't as honest and decent as they come already. What is it about working vice that inspires the men to fall for working girls?"

"Ellie quit the service, sir," Monroe said testily.

"An exception to the rule," Gant said, dropping the contents of the mailbox into a plastic saltwater taffy bag.

Monroe rubbed his eyes and brushed some grit from this eyes. The Vice Squad office was unusually empty for 8:30 P.M. He squinted at the arrest report, pulled it out of the typewriter and handed it to Gant, who refused to take it.

Gant said, "You might want to hold on to that, as a souvenir. Go home to that bride-to-be of yours, marry her damned quick or you're going to spend the rest of your life explaining."

"I *am* marrying her damned quick. You're invited to the wedding," Monroe said.

"That's kind of you, considering." Gant went to the wall of cubbyholes for departmental mail and memos. He pulled a memo out of Monroe's box.

"Says here 'As of this date oh-five-hundred hours IAU will process, evaluate and disseminate any and all information regarding ACPD Patrolman Reuben R. Claymore and ACPD Detective Louis Monroe. IAU will clear all media contact. Evidence of unauthorized media contact or dissemination of information will be viewed as insubordination and will be acted upon in accordance with procedures as specified by IAU. In addition, Detective Monroe will make himself available to IAU at all times for investigation in accordance to procedures as specified by IAU.' Signed and initialed in his goddamn royal purple ink, Ephrum Traile, ET, Inspector, IAU."

IAU was the Internal Affairs Unit, a squad within the police department assigned to investigate violations of procedures and criminal activities committed by other police officers.

"Nice to see that Inspector Traile is involved," Monroe said. "They should be figuring out how to give me a medal for locking Claymore up."

"Traile's going to figure out how to bust your balls, is what he's going to do," Gant said, eyeing Monroe from afar. "You ever hear of a Lieutenant Commander Wayne Zimmer of the State Police?"

Monroe shook his head.

Gant smirked. "You're going to. There's a saying that floats around the fifth floor here: When Zimmer's in town, the mayor's going down."

"What's this have to do with me?" Monroe asked.

"I was saying the same thing myself when I saw the memo in my box. I'm less than a month from retirement and I'll be goddamned if the Extraterrestrial is going to screw me out of my pension just to save the mayor's ass."

7

Then he narrowed his eyes on Monroe. "Why in God's hell didn't you tell me you were going to bust Officer Roo?"

"Because," Monroe said righteously, "you would have tried to talk me out of it."

Gant sat heavily in one of the battered office chairs. "As I should have done. Lou, I was aware you didn't like the man. I was aware you'd run up against him. I was aware your old man went to jail on corruption charges, so you're sensitive about being honest and upright and moral. And I know you feel you're on some mission from God to stomp anybody you think is using excessive force."

"That's not quite true, sir—"

"Don't disagree with me when I'm angry. I changed your goddamn diapers one too many times to let you tell me what I see in front of my face ain't true when it is."

Monroe stood. "I'd be the person I am regardless of what happened to my father."

Gant heaved himself to his feet. "Let's move."

Monroe followed Gant through the lobby of City Hall and into the nauseating lemon-yellow and swimming pool–blue corridors of the police department. Their destination was Fort Knox— Gant's narrow closet of an office with its multiple door-locks and antique steel safe.

On the way Monroe noticed Gant walking slowly, his paunch parting the flow of uniforms, plainclothes men, secretaries, court personnel and bureaucratic drones. Gant smiled at everyone, muttering first names, nicknames and "How you doin' " at the hacks Monroe knew Gant despised.

"Sir," Monroe said, "don't tell me what I did was wrong."

"Don't talk to me when I'm doing Pension Preserving Procedure." Gant muttered through his teeth. "The shit a man will do for money."

Gant gushed happiness at one of Atlantic City Mayor Bernie Tilton's many gainfully employed relatives, then unlocked the five deadbolts on his office door. He pushed it open, tossed the taffy bag on his desk, growled at Monroe to "batten down the hatch."

Monroe closed the door and locked one of the deadbolts, found his eyes wandering to one of Gant's collection of posters of jet fighter aircraft.

Gant put sheets of white paper on his desk, dumped the contents of the bag on his desk blotter, grouped them on the paper by category, then retrieved a Polaroid camera from a closet.

"Okay," he said, while photographing the contraband, "I'll admit what you did was right by you. You took a beloved but repulsive officer, who is now probably getting his hair cut, getting all made-over and pretty so that Zimmer can use him to get the mayor."

Monroe was dazed again. "Claymore is a small-time cop gone dirty."

"Claymore is also a link to the city's past. Anything Reuben tells a grand jury about our Mayor Bernie Tilton, especially stuff that ain't true, will get picked up by the media. Bernie's up for reelection in November and he wants four more years as much as I want my pension. With Zimmer in town, he might as well start planning his retirement. Operations supervised by Lieutenant Commander Zimmer of the State Special Investigations Division have put five Atlantic City mayors out of office or behind bars, starting with Uncle Sam Claymore in the early '60s. Sam, as we all remember, was Reuben's daddy."

"Sam Claymore deserved to go to jail," Monroe said. "I read about him somewhere. He was the last of the city's political bosses. Corrupt in every way."

Gant examined the photos as they developed. "Corrupt but consistent. It takes an extraordinary leader to run a town whose business is giving folks a good time, legit or otherwise. It's like a machine whose parts are always changing. You need somebody at the center who doesn't change, who's predictable and dependable. Our current mayor is inconsistent, unpredictable and, beyond putting too many relatives on the payroll, not corrupt. But he's made a big mistake, coming out about how he thinks the city has too much low-income housing that is in bad shape and we should fix what we have instead of building new slums."

"It's not my problem," Monroe said. "All I did was get a corrupt cop off the street."

"All you did," Gant repeated, shaking his head. He crouched beside the looming, dark combination safe near his desk and spun the dial. "All you did was force Wayne Zimmer and Reuben Claymore, two men that might have otherwise hated each other's guts, to derive some benefit from each other's company. And, given that the mayor can't get to Officer Roo, he can use the Extraterrestrial to get you."

"Why me?" Monroe said.

Gant locked the contraband away, sat down at his desk, picked up a pen and began to doodle on one of the sheets of paper. "Because you started it. Because the mayor's pissed and he wants to beat up somebody. Because after all this time, with legal casinos and five billion dollars capital investment in the casino industry, the city still looks like shit, has the highest goddamn per capita crime rate in the state and is currently getting its ass whipped thanks to a dead economy and Las Vegas."

Gant almost spit. "Jesus, Lou, don't ask me for reasons. Bureaucracies aren't reasonable. They're like big dumb animals that don't do nothing but sit and eat and shit. Anything that bothers them, or anything that *causes* someone to bother them, is the enemy. If you hadn't gone after Roo, it would be business as usual. Inasmuch as business is now unusual, you're now the enemy."

Monroe was suddenly too tired to talk, to think or even to be angry. He found a chair next to Gant, forced himself to smile and said, "Sir, it's *my* job . . . *our* job to protect anybody in this city from those that would harm them. I can't do my job if every time I spot a serious offender I have to look over my shoulder at who he might know or have a relationship with."

"Exactly," Gant said.

"So you're telling me I shouldn't be doing my job."

Gant stopped doodling. "I'm asking you, could you arrest your brother-in-law?"

"Ellie's an only child," Monroe said.

"Could you arrest your sister? Let's say she took a knife and killed the sum-bitch who raped her, way back when."

Monroe sat up straight. "Sir, that's personal and private and you have no right—"

Gant threw down his pen. "As your superior I have every right to question you as to matters of competence, and I am sure as hell doing that now. Answer me—if you found out your . . . wife's father was doing something very, very wrong, something that affected the lives of thousands of innocent people, some of who you might know personally, could you go up to him, read him his rights, cuff him and throw him in the lockup?"

"Ellie's parents live in West Virginia," Monroe said.

"What if they didn't?" Gant demanded.

"Sir, this is hypothetical. In reality—"

"Don't you tell me what's hypothetical. I'll be the judge of what's goddamned real or not in this town. You answer my question."

Monroe hesitated. He closed his eyes.

"I'm waiting for an answer," Gant said.

"I don't have one," Monroe said after a minute. "I guess it would depend on the severity of the crime, or crimes."

"What it depends on is the relationship you have with people who are important to you. What you failed to consider is that everybody's got somebody who is important to them, somebody they want to protect, believe in, maybe even love *no matter how rotten that person might be*.

"In the future, before you nail *anybody*," Gant roared, "you will do background and make sure that that whoever you're going to nail does not have slightest importance to those who might be displeased at the consequences."

"But sir, that means the only people I can bust are people I don't care about, who don't . . . know anyone, who are poor or stupid or weak." Monroe's eyes shut and it took effort to open them.

He saw that Gant had become paternal again. "That is your job. That's always been your job. The rest you have to give up on. You can't change the way this town is. No one can. This town is too complicated. Loyalties and blood ties run deep, deeper than anybody'd want to know."

Monroe pushed himself to his feet. "Sir, I will bust anyone, and I do mean anyone, who is . . . breaking the law."

Gant's smile faded to disgust. "You let me know when Zimmer contacts you. And he will contact you. Until then," Gant picked up his pen, "I suggest that you resign."

2

A Good Enemy

Monroe went home, took a long shower, tried to sleep and failed, tried to run on the Boardwalk, came back and passed out. Then he spent most of the afternoon replacing the glass windowpanes in his apartment that were shattered when George Spear's boat, anchored a hundred yards west on the opposite side of Clam Creek, had exploded.

It was early evening when Monroe got a telephone call from his extremely pregnant bride-to-be, Ellie Meade, a former prostitute who Marty Gant had hired as a part-time youth counselor at the police department. She said that if he had the night off—

"Who told you I had the night off?"

"I had a little notion, like one of those tingles you get when the slot machine is about to pay off."

"You had a tingle about me?"

"More than that. I mean, I felt *something*. Then Marty Gant called me, said that you were probably going to spend the rest of your life moping around, so I should keep you busy."

"You and that baby are going to keep me busy enough."

"Might as well start. You can help me move."

He was tired from his run. He was tired from what had happened last night. Suddenly he had energy.

Must be love.

He told her that there was no way he would permit her to lift a single box, or anything heavy.

"You are so wonderful," she said.

As he moved her considerable possessions into his dank, one-bedroom second floor apartment in a subdivided former guest-house overlooking Clam Creek, Ellie asked him how things were at the department. She'd heard about this Vice Squad officer who had fallen in love with this former working girl who might be getting himself in trouble.

Monroe said he didn't want to talk about the department.

After carrying what felt like the hundredth box into the living room, he collapsed on the frayed, sagging, brown-rust-and-beige striped living room couch that he had bought at the Salvation Army. He let his head fall so he could look down the hall, past the bathroom where the bedroom door was open and Ellie stood, hands on the shapeless sections of her maternity dress that hid her hips, staring at the pile of laundry, running shorts, running shoes and soggy martial arts uniforms in his bedroom closet.

She said, "All of this stuff has got to go."

She told him to take the night off.

"I already did."

"Go out with your buddies. Get drunk or something. I have to organize this place."

Monroe was about to tell her that with his former partner, Sergeant Darrell "Bad Day" Pratt, in bed in Atlantic City General Hospital recovering from gunshot wounds, his only other friend was Jimmy "the Geek" Doochay, who didn't have a phone number. He wanted to say that, in the entire city, she was his only friend—the only one he felt he could trust.

Then she said, "Before you go bring me that box of garbage bags."

"I'd, um, like to see the stuff you're going to throw out."

"It's better if you don't." She put her a hand in the closet then quickly withdrew it, as if she'd been burned. "Some of these . . . these *things,* you must have had them for years."

"As a matter of fact, I—"

"We'll give them to the Salvation Army, if they'll have them. Everyone has dignity. You can't just dump things on people."

Then Monroe saw that day's paper rolled up on top of one of the boxes. He saw his picture, and Reuben Claymore's, side by side.

She said, "While you were bringing up the cartons, your casino friend called. Raleigh, the one who smiles all the time. He said he wants to give you a casino job."

"Dan Raleigh is not my friend and I won't take anything he wants to give me, and I don't need a casino job."

"He says he knows some people and you know some people and everybody's saying that you're going to need a new job."

Monroe was silent for a while. "And what do you say?"

"If it were me, I'd make sure I was getting better money, decent medical benefits and a contract that says they can't fire you, lay you off, or change your job title, description or duties for eighteen months."

"You don't want me to stay in the department?"

She came to him and held his hand and said, "I want you alive."

For a while they sat on boxes. She put her arm around him and held him, saying nothing as the sunlight faded outside and the room became dim and dark.

Monroe met Dan Raleigh in Zack's, a stucco-encrusted rubber-sombrero Pacific Avenue Tex-Mex bar near the Alcazar Casino Hotel where Raleigh, an ex-biker who became an ex-cop, ex-casino security chief, ex-casino host, was working on being the ex-director of player development.

"Wherever you are is a step to somewhere else," Raleigh said. "No way I could stomach what I have done and what I continue to do if I wasn't certain something ten times better was waiting 'round the bend."

As he loosened his midnight-blue painted tie, unbuttoned his indigo silk shirt and smoothed the lapels of his black silk sport jacket, Raleigh mentioned that his new position paid ten times Monroe's detective salary.

"At least we have something to celebrate," Raleigh said. "Your first big bust. Possibly your last. And this time, I'm paying."

He hoisted a shot of Ambassador scotch aloft, clinking it against Monroe's margarita. Monroe looked at the green liquid in his glass and sighed.

"Don't fade on me now, Lou," Raleigh said. "I'm figuring you for four or five rounds at least, and given that we are in the only municipality in the state of New Jersey in which bars never close, that should take us until dawn."

"It just might," Monroe said, thinking of the closet being organized back in his apartment.

"Down in the dumps already?" Raleigh raised his glass again. "Did you really expect that your own people would adore you after you arrested one of them, and forced them to see how awful they can be?"

Raleigh smacked his glass down on the bar and glanced at Monroe, pleased that it took Monroe longer to swallow liquor. A thin, animated talker with tightly cropped red hair and a tendency to check his reflection in mirrors more often than necessary, Raleigh had the ability to get along with anyone—even shy Louis Monroe, who he met five years ago while attending the Police Academy in Northfield. Upon taking the oath, both rookies were given the Boardwalk beat. Monroe had the 8 A.M. to 5 P.M. shift, Raleigh came on after him. Raleigh quit after a few weeks to get a job as a security guard at the Alcazar Casino Hotel.

"Put yourself in my shoes," Raleigh began. "Every day, I am paid very good money to manipulate, seduce and plant in the hearts of ordinary folks—many of whom are truly disgusting and despicable individuals—that they *deserve* to win money. How long do you think I'd last if I informed them that they're just greedy sons-of-bitches falling for the oldest con in the book?"

Monroe asked, "But would you do this for your sister?"

"I don't have a sister."

"Would you do this for your father-in-law?"

16

"I wouldn't do a damned thing for my father-in-law. Felicia and I are divorced."

"Would you do it for a friend?"

"What are friends for?" Raleigh grinned, winking at himself in the mirror behind the bar.

Monroe watched him preen. For as long as Monroe had known him, Raleigh always had to have the edge. Raleigh indulged their friendship, Monroe realized, not because he appreciated company, but because Raleigh needed someone he could be sure he was better than; if not better, than ahead of in terms of salary, status, clothing, cars, sexual conquests—so many things that competitive men use to measure themselves.

Against those things, Monroe was a loser in a town that thrived on losers. Raleigh's salary was immense, he had extraordinary power over the running of the Alcazar, his clothes were always flattering and perfectly tailored, he drove a Porsche 928S and carried on numerous affairs, sometimes even with the wives of high rollers.

Monroe's detective salary was low to start, even lower after being raped by federal, state and municipal taxes. With the exception of one gleaming, white Italian suit purchased at an overpriced men's shop and his costly running shoes, Monroe's clothes came from discount department stores out on the mainland malls. Monroe's influence in the police department was at an all-time low. The air conditioning in his rusting, robin's-egg blue Datsun 280Z had quit for the fourth time.

And there was only one woman who mattered in his life.

So why did Raleigh have to keep his edge with Monroe? Where was the race? Who was competing? Why did Raleigh try so hard to prove to himself that he was having such a great time?

"Sometimes I wonder why I meet people who don't even know me and they immediately despise me," Raleigh said. "When I go on marketing trips to Chicago, New Orleans, New York, wherever, I say I'm from Atlantic City and I work for a casino and, unless they're gamblers, people put their hands over their wallets like I'm going to pick their pockets, for Christ's sake. I may *drag* horses to water, Lou, but I can't make 'em drink."

Monroe looked at his margarita and drank.

Raleigh leaned back. "I have two suggestions for you, Lou. The first is open your sails. We have an empty suite . . . Actually we have several empty suites and Mr. Z suggested . . . Well, you don't have to hear about Mr. Z. Let's say, we have an empty room so why not take it?"

"Keep it. Ellie used to work in places like that. She's got a lot of bad memories from places like that. Who is this Mr. Z?"

"Just somebody."

Monroe drank again. "Dan, you know me better than to buy me with anything. Police officers can't accept gifts from a casino, or anybody."

"Who's going to find out?"

"Every comp that gets written out, every freebie goes on your computer."

"Just because it goes on the computer doesn't mean you're in bed with us, Lou. We have ways of covering a trail."

"Give it up, Dan. You're not going to buy me."

"Nobody wants to buy you, Lou. It's the people around you that are so interesting." He clapped Monroe on the back. "Ellie told you about the job—a job that I can get you at a time when the industry is hurting and we are laying people off. You should be grateful, buddy boy, for what I can do for you."

"I have learned never to be grateful for anything you do for me because anything you do for me you do for yourself."

"Not true. Anything I do, I do for the greater benefit of all, which includes the industry, the state of New Jersey and this wonderful city."

"Since when are you so concerned about the city or the state of New Jersey?" Monroe said.

"Hey, Lou, we're all in this leaky boat together," Raleigh said. "Now that Vegas is beating us, the shuckers in the Casino Control Commission and Division of Gaming Enforcement have realized that it's the industry that pays their salary. They need us more than we need them. So we're getting along fine now. The hatchets aren't exactly buried, but everybody's doing everybody else little favors, favors that we wouldn't have dreamed of doing years ago. To be frank, I've grown fond of the antagonism. A good enemy teaches you a hell of lot more than a mediocre friend."

Monroe thought of Claymore menacing him under the Boardwalk. "Like what?"

Raleigh glowed with nostalgia. "Like who you can *really* depend on. You can trust your enemies to try to do you in. Your friends . . . they aren't so predictable."

"And you want to give me a job." Monroe gulped his margarita.

"It would give me the satisfaction of making somebody else happy."

"My wife?"

Raleigh smirked. "Always had a terrific business sense, that girl. When she was working, she was so popular with our more elite clientele. Oh, sorry, I shouldn't dwell on the past."

Monroe took in a little bit too much of his margarita, coughed, felt some of it come up through his nose. "Ellie has a new life with me," he said, feeling awful. "What she had before that is over."

"We have so *much* to celebrate," Raleigh said as he ordered another round.

By the sixth round, Monroe felt himself wavering. Raleigh said there was a goon named Hadruna he wanted to get rid of so Monroe could have a job at the casino as a security captain, which was a desk job three days a week. Two days a week he would have to wear a purple Alcazar Casino Hotel jacket and walk the casino floor making sure that when money was taken, the casino took it all.

"It's easy and it's indoors," Raleigh said. "You don't get wet, cold, hot, rain on, shit upon by seagulls. You might have to handle a cantankerous customer or two. Show 'em the door, politely. Easy."

"When's it hard?"

Raleigh blinked. "What?"

"You told me the job's easy. When is this job not so easy?"

"Well, you have to realize that you represent the house, and everybody is playing against the house. There is an adversarial element that takes getting used to."

"Like, gamblers are my enemies?"

"Your best enemies," Raleigh beamed. "The casino makes its money off gamblers, but money isn't what's going on. When the risks are high, when the percentages guarantee that the longer you play, the more you lose, the secret to survival is getting the player to stay in the game."

"You mean not to quit?"

"Absolutely. Wise up and admit it, Lou. Everybody has to lose more often than they win. So you try to minimize your losses. You admit that being a cop shit isn't for you because you're not a team player and nobody wants you on the team. You stay in this game and you're going to get ground down until you have nothing left. And it's your own people who are going to do the grinding. You are more of threat to them than anything that could be on that street."

"That's bullshit," Monroe said.

"It was until you womped Reuben Claymore. Remember what they used to tell us when we were on the Boardwalk? There, you smile and you keep the peace, and if you come down on anybody, you come down on whoever can't fight back. You don't fuck with anybody who is bigger, stronger, richer, more powerful than you. You work *for* them, not against, because they will destroy you, if they want."

"Only if I let them," Monroe said. He reached for his wallet and slid money toward his glass.

Raleigh put the money back into Monroe's pocket. "Lou, we go back, you and me. I know people and you know people and some of the people we know are the same people, and they *all* want your ass out of this. Quit now. You're not exactly ahead, but you're not too far behind, either."

Monroe slipped off the barstool, grabbed the bar to steady himself while he chose his words. "Dan, I have only one reason for staying in the game. It's the one you didn't mention. It's this hunch that nobody who is in the game really wants to stay in it. These people you say are bigger, richer, more powerful than me don't want to be in it at all. They're just like all the millions of people coming into your casino, they're like you—looking for the next step that's going take them somewhere else. I'm not looking for anything to do that. I don't need to go anywhere else. With Ellie, the baby coming, and this job I have, I can be happy with things as they are. If I quit, I'll never know that happiness."

Raleigh said, "If you quit, you'll know better."

"I'm *not* quitting because I know better," Monroe said, heading for the door. "And I know worse."

3

Insurance

Monroe was awakened that morning, early.

"You turned him down," Captain Gant said to him on the phone. "I bet you didn't even ask him about the pension plan."

Monroe saw Ellie on her side, the sheet draped over her enormously pregnant middle. She was huddled around it, curled beneath the air conditioner's chill blast.

Monroe was hung over, so he looked at the phone in his hand to make sure it was a phone and in his hand. It was a cheap thing of bright green and purple plastic that the Alcazar Casino Hotel gave away for three dollars to drive-in customers who clipped a coupon from the *Atlantic City Star*. Monroe didn't gamble, but he needed a bedroom telephone when he had moved to the apartment, so he clipped the coupon and got his $3 Alcazar Casino Hotel Luck-E Fun Fone.

"He didn't mention the pension plan," Monroe said.

"You did right. He's going to contact you again. Next time you're going to tell me when he does."

"Raleigh?"

"Zimmer, through any one of a variety of agents."

"Why would a state police investigator want me to get a job with a casino?"

"You ask him when you get the chance. I have some theories, one of which is that casino employees need a state license to get a job with a casino. When you apply for a state license you have to sign away your constitutional protection against unauthorized search-and-seizure. So the Division of Gaming Enforcement does an amazingly thorough background check on you, as well as your close friends and relatives, and anything in your background—and I do mean *anything*—can be used."

"For what?"

"Blackmail, coercion and extortion, to name the less imaginative personnel manipulation techniques."

"There's nothing in my background that could be used against me."

"All Zimmer has to do—through the Division of Gaming Enforcement—is *say* there's something nasty in your past, and suddenly your license is suspended, you have to figure out a way to pay for a lawyer and make a living until your hearing comes up. My other theory is maybe it ain't you he's interested in."

"Who would he be interested in?"

"I'll let you use your imagination on that one, for the time being. But when he contacts you, or your wife, you let me know."

Something about Gant's voice cut through the post-alcoholic indulgence. "Why are you so concerned?" Monroe asked. "It isn't *your* pension."

"I'm concerned because I've never approved of law enforcement officers who manipulate the media to accomplish their aims. Everything I've heard about Wayne Zimmer makes me sick."

"There are plenty of people you don't approve of, who make you sick," Monroe said.

"Which brings me to my next situation. The Extraterrestrial has sent me another memo. Though I am in charge of partnering in my unit, Traile has it in his heart to match you with Detective Sergeant Ray Deegan."

When he heard Deegan's name Monroe shuddered. "Sergeants don't require a partner," he said.

"Traile has just made it a requirement for him," Gant growled. "Frankly, I can see some wisdom in it. Deegan's in a rather compromising situation. He's fallen for one of his prostitution suspects. Maybe the Extraterrestrial wants you to throw some cold water on him. It's goddamn embarrassing when my men fall in love with whores . . ."

"Sir—"

". . . that ain't quit yet."

Ellie was awake when he put down the phone.

Monroe said, "Uh, hi."

"You're still drunk."

Monroe averted his gaze. "I guess I should make breakfast."

"Stay away from anything sharp," Ellie said and moved slowly until she sat, then reached for a frayed blue terrycloth bathrobe. Monroe couldn't keep his eyes off her belly.

She belted the robe above her belly, lifted herself out of bed and disappeared into the bathroom. Monroe waited, found himself drifting off to sleep, remembering the way Ellie had smiled at him when he first saw her. When he opened his eyes he saw her rummaging through the closet.

Monroe stood, gently put his arms around her. "Ellie," he began awkwardly, "The life you had before, it's not going to . . . I don't know how to say this, but . . ."

She turned in his arms, her huge belly touching him. "Say it."

He couldn't say anything.

"Oh, Lou, how could you think this?"

But he hadn't told her what he was thinking. "Okay, forget I, uh, thought it." He lifted the robe and spoke to her belly. "You, too."

She broke from his embrace. "Louis, this child means that we have to put the past behind us. Your past, and my past."

"What was so bad about my past?"

"Who said anything about the past being bad?"

"I, um," Monroe fumbled. "You never seemed to like it. Yours, that is."

"There were times I *loved* it. I mean, compared to the girls on the street, I had it made. As long as I could forget what I had to do to earn it, the money was sweet. The three-bedroom condo on

24

the Boardwalk was sweet. The clothes. The meals in all the fancy restaurants, the wines I drank, the time I had to myself. All of that was fine by me. Until I had to go to work. Then it was awful. And just about everyone connected with it was awful. And everything became awful, though I was pretty good at putting on a smile for the clients. But then I'd come home and I wouldn't know what to do with myself. Some girls just go into the shower and turn the water on so hot it's like it's burning the skin on your face. Or they drink, or they snort something, or they shoot up. I couldn't think of what to do. I'd go out on the terrace and I'd see those ocean waves rolling in, and if it was daylight there'd be some people on the beach and maybe some children in the water having a good time and I'd start to bawl my eyes out."

She sat on the edge of the bed. "Once, it was years ago, I felt so hopeless. I was living in the condo but the other girls were out. I took the elevator down to the lobby in my sweet black dress and my sweet black handbag and my sweet high-heel pumps and my sweet bright-red jacket—oh, how I loved that jacket, it was so big and roomy—and I walked across the Boardwalk to the steps, onto the sand and down by the sea I started taking my clothes off and throwing them into the water. Then some poor girl in rags and a T-shirt came up to me and said, if I was just throwing them away, I could give them to her so she could sell them and use the money to feed some children that had nothing to eat."

Monroe said, "You gave them to her?"

"I wanted to give her everything I owned, but I couldn't. It was the way she wanted it, the way she jumped into the ocean and fetched my jacket out, wrapped it around herself—she couldn't have been more than sixteen or seventeen—and ran off, I knew she wasn't going to sell it. She might've been young but she knew what I was, what I did to get that jacket, and she wanted it, because I had it and she didn't, and I could tell from the way she went into that water—it was March or April and that water was *freezing*— that she would do anything to get that jacket and be where I was.

25

I got so spooked I turned around and ran back to my big sweet bed and cried myself to sleep.

"Try as I did," Ellie continued, "I could never put the memory of that girl behind me. Times I'd look out on Pacific Avenue and see the working girls down there, with silly dreams in their heads that would never, ever come true. I only had one dream that stuck, through all those years. Only one thing I ever wanted to have happen to me, only one wish I wanted to come true."

"What was that?" Louis asked.

Ellie hugged her belly. "You're looking at her, front and center."

At a-quarter-to-five on an unusually dry Friday afternoon Louis Monroe steered his rattling, wheezing, rusting Datsun 280Z past a NewsWave 64 remote TV-news truck that took up two visitor parking spaces beneath the big black cube of City Hall.

He skirted the truck and walked quickly through the side entrance to City Hall, through the lobby. Though the entire building had been declared a smoke-free zone, it had developed that arid, late Friday afternoon stench of stale cigarette smoke, bad coffee and the vague, unnervingly sour reek of human beings whose underarm deodorants have failed the torture test of government work.

The Vice Squad office was empty because most vices in Atlantic City don't begin until sundown and nearly all the detectives, sergeants and squad leaders who are not part of a specific operation tended to arrive as close as possible to the twilight hour.

In Monroe's mailbox was a memo from Captain Gant stating Monroe's new orders. Until further notice, Monroe was to assist in any and all police operations conducted by his new partner and squad leader, Detective Sergeant Raymond Deegan. Monroe and Sergeant Deegan were to confine themselves to Pacific Avenue, the sad, gloomy "casino strip" running parallel to the ocean and the Boardwalk.

He wondered when Deegan was going to show up. He looked

up, past the lockers to the badly adjusted color TV set that Darrell Pratt had taken from a crackhouse during a dawn raid, and had enshrined above the rusting cabinets holding the Kiss-Off (Known/ Suspected Offender) files. The set was tuned to Channel 64, the South Jersey–shore UHF TV station based twenty miles to the south in Wildwood. Channel 64 consisted mostly of local news and reruns of ancient sitcoms. Monroe sat in a ripped swivel chair and watched an episode of "Gilligan's Island." He watched another episode of "Gilligan's Island." Then the news came on and the NewsWave 64 Atlantic City reporter, a former Miss New Jersey, was standing in front of City Hall talking about how the sudden arrest by Atlantic City Police of the New Jersey State Police under-cover informant Reuben Claymore might have been a last-ditch attempt by the city police, under orders by the mayor, to thwart Operation Long Spoon, a state police probe into corruption in Atlantic City government.

Monroe tried to laugh. Reuben Claymore, an undercover infor-mant? Please.

The camera cut to a previously taped press conference with the Deputy Attorney General.

"We have accumulated more than enough evidence for grand jury indictment of several significant members of Atlantic City and Atlantic County government. Those people know who they are."

Back to the reporter, who said that representatives of the city police department refused to comment about the arrest or Clay-more's status as a state police informant, but that it was only a matter of time before the indictments were served.

"To rule is to serve," said a snide voice behind him. "Tennis anyone?"

Sergeant Ray Deegan was a spare, unathletic, unremarkable man in his early forties with thinning brown hair, a soft face and murky brown eyes that could narrow to suggest unnatural appe-tites, or open wide to show a coward's reckless regard for his own skin. He wore loose, baggy black pants, deck shoes without socks and a faded black sport coat. Under the coat, he wore a gray cardigan sweater with white piping pulled down over his belt-holstered 9mm automatic.

He sniffed, eyed the chair, then peered into his mailbox. He glanced at his copy of Gant's memo, crumpled it into a ball and tossed into a trash can.

"Um," Monroe said. "Hi."

"That's it? Just hi? You can't think of nothing better to say to your brand new partner?"

Monroe shrugged.

"This is how we're going to work it," Deegan said, checking the bulletin board. "We're going to fuck around for awhile and then I'm going to see my forty-nine, during which time you will make yourself scarce. If I feel like working after that, I'll let you know."

A *forty-nine* was police radio code for a person-seeking-rendez-vous. It was also department slang for a girlfriend.

"My forty-nine," Deegan announced, "is a casino cocktail wait-ress, one of the few that isn't in her thirties with a kid in the cradle and some guy who said he'd be true to her forever who is currently hiding out in Saskatchewan. She's gorgeous and young and dan-gerous as hell."

"Didn't she, some time ago, work Pacific Avenue?" Monroe asked.

"Let us not get bogged down in details," Deegan answered, popping a portable radio out of its recharger unit and clipping it to his belt. "What she *works* now is the top floor high roller lounge, the one you need a special card to get into. Anyone who works that lounge is supposed to keep her mouth shut about what goes on but who does what they're supposed to do? Doing what you're supposed to do is so boring."

"That all depends," Monroe said.

Deegan sat on the desk beside Monroe. "She doesn't keep her mouth shut with me. Seems the state police have taken over most of an entire floor of rooms at the Alcazar and everything they're getting is comped. Unlimited food, booze, the works.

"And there's this one old, fat, battered, brand-new guest who is alternatively crying his guts out while knocking back the Dom Perignon and stuffing his fat face on lobster, caviar, shrimp, filet mignon. So this new guest, during a quiet moment when they're changing the porno tapes in the VCR, asks this friend of my friend where he can get a woman—no, make that a girl, a real *young* girl—from out of town, some piece of meat that nobody cares about so he can punch her around, and how much she's going to cost."

Monroe opened his mouth but before he could say anything Deegan added, "Now, my forty-nine knows that, unlike some municipalities that have had to brave the transition from a manufacturing-based economy to a service-based economy, Atlantic City has always been based on service. My forty-nine quotes the most outrageous price she can think of and this fat fuck just says, 'He'll take care of it,' and points to one of the suits. So now she's got to ask the suit, and this is the kind of suit that doesn't look like he parts with money easily, but before she can drop the hint that she might have a strategy to service this need, the fat fuck calls the suit over and says if he can't find an outlet for his frustration, he just won't be an effective witness. Those were the words he used. Effective witness. This bothers the suit. The suit gets all shaky and mean, as if the fat fuck said this to get under his skin. And the fat fuck says, 'You want her first?' "

Monroe couldn't believe this. "There's no way in hell the state police would ever use a casino hotel for a base of operations."

"Then this," Deegan beamed, "must be heaven. Lieutenant Commander Zimmer likes the high life, and he likes it very neat and proper. The best equipment, the best wine, food, a pretty girl on his arm, so people will think he's a really neat dude. Makes it real easy for me to hate his fucking guts."

He winked. "I hope I'm not making myself too clear?"

Monroe went to the rack beside the bulletin board to fetch the keys for an unmarked police vehicle and found none except the set for the Mobile Crime Lab, a huge, absurdly expensive recreational vehicle filled with obsolete computer equipment that the department was forced to buy with state grant money.

He turned around and saw Deegan dangling a set of unmarked car keys in his fingers. "One step ahead of you, partner of mine."

Deegan motioned Monroe out of the Vice Squad office, through the lobby of City Hall, out the side exit and into the hot, steamy, fading sunlight of early evening. The air had already begun to stink of diesel fumes from casino buses and their cargo of slot machine junkies.

Deegan paused in front of a dented, unmarked Dodge. He gazed at Monroe, evaluating the younger detective as he might size up prey. "Let's meditate upon the possibilities," he said slowly, opening the driver's side door.

Monroe got in beside him thinking, remembering that the state police traditionally despised Atlantic City and everything in it. If, as Dan Raleigh suggested, the Division of Gaming Enforcement, an arm of the state police that acts as a watchdog on the casino industry, had become friendly with the industry to the point that favors could be done, then why *not* a casino? The state Bureau of Witness Sequestration was probably feeling the budget crunch afflicting other state government divisions. Casinos were good at keeping some things secret, such as the identities of high-rollers. Casinos were also good at disguising funds spent for illegal purposes, for those gamblers whose business was good enough to warrant it. Why *not* give Claymore the high-roller treatment, if the state wanted a cooperative witness?

Deegan slammed the car door. "Gant probably told you something about me busting my forty-nine, and then falling in love and slacking off, right? He probably said something about you throwing cold water on me."

"He mentioned it," Monroe said.

Deegan laughed. "I know Gant better than his own children. Before you came along, I was Gant's boy. So, when it comes to Gant, I can call every ball he's going to shoot without even looking at the table, hear me?"

"I hear you," Monroe said evenly.

"The thing about this forty-nine is, you see her, and you can't think of her anyplace but in the sack. Now, I could've come down on her, no problem. But, I got this feeling, this hunch, like the gamblers get—"

"A tingle?" Monroe said.

Deegan paused. "Not that. It's like, you know, in your gut. She and me have this thing in common. We don't like Wayne Zimmer. We come up with a way to blow him out of this town so bad and ugly that he'll never come back. What a service that would be to the mayor and his friends, and their friends!"

He held the car keys in his hand, admiring them as if they were something precious, valuable, unique. "But we can't do it alone. We need a front man. Somebody who is stupid enough to take on the really big bad guys. Last night I asked myself who, among the all the police officers in City Hall, would be feeling so victimized, so despised, so outcast among the brothers in blue, that he would be grateful for my . . . involvement in his life? Who would might be sufficiently inspired to lend assistance, and yet have such a dumb-fuck sense of honesty and integrity that he would not want to share in any of the enormous financial and political rewards that are waiting to be reaped, and yet be in a perfect position to be blamed for anything bad that could possibly happen?"

"You *requested* me?" Monroe blurted.

"Requested? Demanded. And guess what?" He started the car, gunned the engine. "I got you!"

With the exception of Monroe's former partner, Darrell Pratt, and his new partner, Sergeant Ray Deegan, no other Atlantic City police officers wanted to work Pacific Avenue. Prostitution and petty drug arrests were either too easy or too depressing for an officer to derive any satisfaction from his job.

There were far more glorious beats, such as the city's Inlet section located north and west of the casinos, where ruined slum tenements and a disaffected, impoverished, black and Hispanic underclass accepted, as a cost of living, regular police narcotics raids which were held not so much to "turn the tide of drugs," as Mayor Bernie Tilton claimed, but to provide favored officers with the opportunity to make hundreds of easy arrests. Arrests generated paper, which generated promotions for the officers and statistics for the department, which used statistics to qualify for state and federal drug enforcement funding, most of which was spent by the administrative inspectors on five- and ten-day drug enforcement seminars at sunny hotels in the Bahamas and Hawaii during Atlantic City's winter.

Narcotics arrests also generated property, which generated money. Upgrades in the federal controlled/dangerous substances statutes permitted police to seize the property of a drug dealer during the arrest. Cars, houses, boats, clothing—virtually everything a drug dealer owned—could be confiscated and, if the drug dealer was convicted, sold at auction, with the money going to the county and state government. Drug busts in Atlantic City tended to net small-time street-corner mules who owned little more than clothing, sneakers and an enormous stereo system. But every once in a while a dealer was nabbed in his car, or in his condo or beachfront home. Promotions came rapidly to those who cracked those cases.

Prostitution arrests earned no promotions. Monroe's previous partner, Darrell Pratt, had told him that prostitution was a necessary evil in a resort town and that officers were supposed to arrest the out-of-town girls, who tended to be infected with a variety of diseases and arrived with abusive, violent pimps who used them to roll johns. Out-of-town girls were considered a menace, while the PARAtroopers—the Pacific Avenue Regular Army girls who had worked the street for years and could be depended on to do what the johns wanted and nothing more—were to be protected.

Deegan and Monroe found Pacific Avenue to be one long wall of buses waiting their turn to unload passengers into the casinos. Monroe saw few faces behind the tinted glass windows. The casinos were experiencing their worst summer ever and, with fewer gamblers coming to town, summer traffic on Pacific Avenue was so light that it was possible to exceed the twenty-five mile per hour speed limit.

Deegan did so with the joy of a man who disobeys laws because it gives him pleasure. He veered past an empty jitney, almost sideswiped a station wagon filled with sunburned tourists. It wouldn't grow dark for another three hours but, because it was Friday the PARAtroopers, wearing tight, skimpy clothes, were already out along Pacific Avenue, standing with one leg bent under motel awnings near the entrances to restaurants, bars and back alleys. Every race and physical type was represented. Some of them were overweight, overage, overdone in their hideous orange or copper wigs and matching eyeshadow. Monroe waved at the few he knew. They didn't wave back.

There were few pedestrians on Pacific Avenue: a prematurely busted-out gambler stumbling back to his motel room, some drunken tourists staggering toward a bar, a group of PARAtroopers leaning into a car window, and—

"Ain't she the *biggest?*" Deegan said.

He was referring to a huge PARAtrooper who stood on the east corner of Mount Rushmore and Pacific, under the awning of the King Arthur Motel. She glared at them, or rather, *through* them, as Deegan stopped short at a red light.

Unlike the other PARAtroopers who were beckoning, teasing and enticing the passing motorists, this one radiated disdain from the corner of Mount Rushmore and Pacific. She stood tall, large, incredibly wide, her brown hair piled up in a rhinestone-encrusted cone, her bloated arms and mottled breasts trussed up in what resembled a black leather hammock, her enormous derriere packed into black leather short-shorts from which her thighs descended like twin funnels into wide, red, flat shoes.

Sunk in her deep navel was a tiny red flashlight that blinked on and off.

"Fatsie Morgan," Monroe said.

"Six-feet even, dark brown hair when she ain't frosting it or wearing one of those beehive wigs, three hundred and sixty pounds when the wind is dry," Deegan sneered. "You'd just love to hump her."

Monroe said, "No."

Fatsie Morgan supposedly didn't have sex with her johns. A provider of degradation, her johns typically sought her wearing wigs and fake beards. She was notorious for stealing their wallets and neckties.

Monroe set his jaw. "We should take her off the street."

"No way, José. Long time ago, I get the word, hands off Fatsie."

"Who gave you that word?"

"Gant."

"He didn't say anything about her to me," Monroe said, turning back to catch a glimpse of her.

"You didn't ask him. You ask him, watch what happens. He gets all huffy and mean and sad at the same time. Then he'll come up with something like," he imitated Gant's plonky Philadelphia accent, " 'As long as an individual in business on Pacific Avenue fulfills a function sanctioned by the powers that be, it's your function to keep her functioning.' "

"Theft is theft," Monroe said. "We don't do something about it, then we get in trouble."

"On the contrary, we do nothing about it, we stay *out* of trouble. That woman's what I call an insurance policy. You want to be a cop and keep your job and stay alive, you gotta find yourself at least one. You're marrying Ellie—that's insurance you wouldn't believe. The stuff a high-class call girl like her has in her head could put sergeant stripes on your sleeve in no time."

Monroe counted to ten. "You shut up about her."

Deegan cackled. "So sorry. What'd I do, partner-of-mine, bring you up short?"

Monroe put his fist, the middle finger knuckle extended, next to Deegan's ear. "Partner-of-mine, what I have against the side of your head is called a short punch. *Short* punch, you hear me? Remember what Sergeant Almagro used to say in the advanced unarmed combat class about this kind of punch? How it doesn't matter how big or strong you are, you put your body into it, and you can go through a wall? If you say anything I don't like about my wife, I might want to put my body in it."

"I didn't take the advanced class," Deegan said. "I'm not into violence."

"Well, neither am I. But it's a violent world out there, with all these assholes in it that think they don't have to show any respect or decency for people. So I've had five years of every unarmed combat class that Vinnie Almagro teaches, with the assumption that I will never, ever have to use any of this stuff that I learned. But somehow, I find myself using it more often than not."

Deegan pulled the car into an abandoned parking lot, turned the key, rolled down the window to let a blast of diesel fume–scented sea air roll in. "You got a problem, partner-of-mine," Deegan muttered, his eyes straight ahead. "You *and* Reuben Claymore. Any excuse for busting heads is just an excuse. When it came down to it, he didn't give a shit about the law anymore than I do. He just liked busting heads. Me, I like finessing things."

Monroe lowered his fist.

Deegan leaned back his seat. "My mom used to be a secretary in the County Solicitor's Office, and she used to pay me a dollar or two to straighten the place up, sweep the floor, clean out the old files and answer the phone while she and Wayne Zimmer were going for rolling-chair rides on the Boardwalk. I used to read the deeds, wills, adoption papers and it didn't take much smarts to see that half the shit coming in had been so thoroughly fucked up that all these pieces of paper were doing was covering up crimes.

"I became one of the brothers in blue, just like you, because I wanted to uncover some of those crimes. Ran into Gant—he was a sergeant at the time. But he had his insurance policy. I went out to get mine."

"What is this insurance you keep talking about?" Monroe said.

Deegan checked his watch. "Let's talk about insurance." He started the car, roared into the street and drove again past Fatsie

Morgan. "The way it works with Fatsie is, she takes a john's wallet, which is what the guy wants her to do anyway, because if she's got the john's wallet, she's got his ID and the john gets to suffer long-distance, in the privacy of his own home surrounded by his wife and kids, wondering if this big whale on Pacific Avenue is going to trash him for good, or will the wallet come back, minus the cash. You want to get yourself insurance with her, you volunteer for wallet delivery detail."

"Like you?"

Deegan ran another red light. "The rumors I hear on this street, the last guy that did it wanted to move on to bigger and better things. As for a rookie dick such as yourself, it's cake work. You get this stack of wallets, with all kinds of credit cards and photo IDs in them. Chances are the guy cancels the cards—though the real hard cases, they don't cancel the cards because they wonder what it is she'd buy with the cards *just to hurt them more*. But a photo I.D., that's solid. You can't cancel that. You find the guy's phone number, no problem. As a bona fide law enforcement officer, you have access to the unlisted directory You call the guy's home right at 1800 hours, you know, when they're sitting down for dinner. It's great when the wife answers. 'Scuse me, Mrs. Chillytits, this is Sergeant Raymond Deegan of the Atlantic City Police Department and we have located a wallet containing credit cards and identification materials that bear your husband's name.' Usually the wife doesn't know her lover boy hasn't been in town, and that causes all kinds of grief which makes the guy suffer even more. But, you can't let it go at that. You have to give a little zinger at the end. You say, 'Tell your husband that his necktie has not been recovered.' Fatsie's supposed to have more than six thousand neckties nailed to the wall of the room she keeps in that motel."

"You're telling me you do this?"

"I'm telling you the secret of survival in this town is you can't just be useful to people. That's *required*. You can't just be useful to somebody, like you consider yourself useful to Gant. You got to be useful to everybody, and you got to do it with that smile that

says, 'This is the best seagull shit I ever did eat.' But most important, you got to find yourself an insurance policy—some kind of
deal, action or situation you can get a slice out of that's important
enough so that anybody who's going to fuck with you is not going
to *want* to fuck with you. Then you can work a scam or two and
if you hit the right one, you're out of here."

He did an illegal U-turn, zoomed past Morgan, giving her the
finger. She screamed obscenities back at him.

"Must be love," Deegan laughed.

Monroe shook his head. "Somebody's got to take her off the
street."

"Not until somebody in the department retires. I'm not saying
who it is, but he has a case of permanent hots for her. One clue:
he loves to lose."

"You have to tell me," Monroe demanded.

"I found my insurance policy, partner-of-mine," Deegan snick-
ered. "You get yours."

CHAPTER
4

The Look

"We don't have much chicken out tonight," Deegan said. "You like young chicken?"

Monroe ignored the question, repeating what he had been told about underage prostitutes. He regarded the thin waif. "They're underage, we take them in on vagrancy and have Ellie talk to them. Ellie's got some of them to give up the life."

Deegan ran a red light. "What a crock of shit this counseling is. Nobody gives up nothing. The situation changes, but it's still service for service. The reason Gant put your Ellie on the counseling gig had nothing to do how good she was at what she was supposed to be doing."

"I want to hear nothing about her, is that clear?" Monroe said firmly.

Deegan waved to a group of giggling PARAtroopers. They waved back at him. "They love me," he confided. Monroe recognized one he remembered from his days cruising the street with Darrell Pratt. The body was right but the teeth, so bright and pearly under the flickering streetlights. Those teeth were not natural.

They passed an especially miserable looking PARAtrooper—fat, flabby, in soiled green leotards and striped halter. She had sores around her mouth and the dazed look of drug addiction.

"You want to go into business for yourself?" Deegan asked. "Get to know that girl. Some guys—rich, poor, indifferent—have a thing for really that kind of street hooker. The dirtier and smellier, the better. These are the kind that wouldn't make it past casino security but, if needed, can be shooed in through the loading docks or employee entrances, and set up in rooms away from their john's family and friends. It's all very confidential."

"And you provide this?"

"I'm just talking about a business opportunity. But you have to consider, if people are going to come all the way to this town to spend money on something that's against the law, they might as well come to you."

"They come to me and I'm taking them to jail," Monroe said.

"How boring . . ." Deegan drove ten blocks to stop in front of a green neon arrow pointing to the Alcazar's parking garage. "Time for you to fade, partner-of-mine. You're going to meet me in the casino lounge of the Alcazar, what do they call it, the Topkapi, at 2100 hours. Until then, go to the Boardwalk. Look at the ocean. Take a walk. Buy yourself a soda. Go into the casino and put a quarter in a slot machine. Avoid anything that has to do with law enforcement, at least until I can come along as a consultant."

"You're going to see your girlfriend," Monroe said.

"I'm taking lunch, okay? Just know this, partner-of-mine: Anything you do, anybody you talk to, anything you're *thinking* when you put a foot on Pacific Avenue, I'm going to know about."

He nosed the car onto the concrete ramp and began to climb the spiral. "I know you're a little envious of me. I have to accept that. You're the shy type, so you wouldn't understand."

"I understand enough," Monroe muttered.

"Not nearly enough," Deegan went up to a level empty of cars, found a space between two concrete pillars that blocked the television cameras mounted near the garage's elevator doors, and shut off the car. "Get out of the car and out of here, now, fast. Consider that an order from a superior officer."

Monroe opened the door as slowly as possible, yawned, stretched his right leg, then his left, wiggled to the edge of the seat, stretched his right leg again.

"Move it!" Deegan said.

In the distance near the elevators someone approached the car.

"I said, get out of here!" Deegan yelled.

He wouldn't move because he had to see her. Deegan's forty-nine was worth seeing. She was of medium height, which meant she was taller than Monroe, and thin, with long legs in dark stockings ending in the blue Alcazar Casino Hotel cocktail waitress high-heels with the toes curved up. Monroe noted the proud, arrogant, deliciously assured way she held herself, could only glimpse the bemused curl in her lips under the mop of loose, blown all-over-the-place hair.

His eyes dwelled on her jacket. At first Monroe thought it was just another ordinary linen or denim jacket that is then bleached, washed in gravel, ripped and shredded so it becomes destroyed. The closer she came, the more Monroe saw that the jacket she had been wearing was about five years out of fashion, and that the injuries had not been inflicted, but had accumulated over time until, with a weird irony, times had changed and what might have been an eccentricity became the height of fashion.

She smiled at him and he felt a weird blast of heat that didn't come from the faint breeze rolling through the empty parking deck.

"Listen Ray," she said. "They're coming in the bus—"

Then she stopped, and saw that Deegan was still in the car and it was Monroe standing there.

"Uh, hi," Monroe said.

"It's okay, Nita," Deegan said. "He's my new partner and he's harmless. He just doesn't know it yet."

She gave Monroe a look that went straight through his eyes and into that reptilian corner of his brain that didn't care that he was going to marry a warm, supportive, intelligent woman who needed him so much. Nita's look threw a switch that Monroe wasn't aware had been built into him. For a few brief seconds, he turned into a machine that was willing to do anything, risk everything to possess this hot, simmering and utterly dangerous woman in a torn red jacket who was all that his fiancé wasn't; who let him know, with that one look, that what she had going with Ray Deegan would be *nothing* compared to what she wanted with him.

It was like looking death in the face, but a different, more powerful kind of death—one that made you want it more than anything else.

Monroe was terrified. He did a fast fade.

He took the elevator down, asking himself, why is it so wrong to see someone for five seconds and get instant hots? It's natural, right? Men and women are supposed to be attracted to each other and they are also supposed to be able to keep cool, stay in control, acknowledge that there are bigger, better, more important, honorable, trustworthy passions than absolute lust.

It was with that attitude that Monroe had fallen in love with his bride-to-be. The woman who had thrown out everything he adored in his apartment was moved by bigger and better passions. She wanted to love deeply and unselfishly, to seek what was best in him, in herself, even in the city they lived in, and commit all of her effort to bring that goodness into its own. You meet a person with that attitude in a place so barren of virtue as Atlantic City, well, you want to hold on to that person.

Knowing that such a person exists, and that this person was going to be his wife, gave a quiet sense of purpose to Monroe's job. The prostitutes and petty offenders with whom he worked aroused in him, at best, feelings of sympathy and at worst, disgust at the levels to which a human being could sink. Since meeting Ellie, he had never felt any kind of attraction to these people, or anyone else, until tonight.

He went down to the street, looked at the long row of casino hotel towers rearing up between Pacific Avenue and the Board-walk, the lights in the guest rooms twinkling on. Then he walked south, down Pacific Avenue, passing a few out-of-town girls who, miraculously, did not recognize him as a vice cop. Though he didn't fit the vice cop profile, he was astonished at how quickly the PARAtroopers had learned to spot him.

He didn't bother to make an arrest. To do so would require that he pretend he was a john. Then he'd have to obtain a fee from the women for a specific sexual service. Once informed of the fee, he would have to detain the woman while calling for a patrol car to bring the woman to the lockup at the police station.

In order for such arrests to work, the patrol car had to arrive fast, so fast that on larger sweeps the arresting officer would just hold up his hand and the patrol car, usually hiding in an alley with its lights out, would rush up in seconds.

Reuben Claymore had been a patrol car officer who had, on occasion, waited *hours* before answering the call from a detective he didn't like. There are few fates worse than standing on the sleaziest street corner in Atlantic City, having identified yourself as a police officer who must prevent a prostitute from running away. Out-of-town girls are typically brought into the city by pimps, who lurk nearby to make sure that they get paid for every trick the girl turns. Out-of-town pimps, especially those from New York, tended to be better armed than the average Atlantic City vice detective, and would use "butterfly" knives, MAC-10 automatic machine pistols or any of the other macho weapons to show his girl that he can handle the situation.

Yet the out-of-town girls *had* to be controlled because they tended to victimize the johns, some of whom were Atlantic City taxpayers whose money was going to Monroe's salary. Monroe developed a powerful urge to prove himself, to do *something* on his shift tonight that would make him feel as if he'd done his bit to make the city safer.

He passed dark alleys where bums lolled, an empty parking lot where a car that had evidently died was no longer a car, just a pile of wreckage too big and rusted to be worth carrying away.

He passed a brightly lit snack bar whose neon OPEN 24 HOURS sign buzzed like an angry greenhead fly. He hadn't eaten dinner but his mouth was locked shut. He pressed on, moving under a weatherworn hotel awning. Graffiti was scrawled over the hotel's once-shining entrance sign: THE WINDERMERE.

The next block down was the Pacific Avenue entrance to the Lucky Shamrock Casino Hotel, a wall of glass, brass and green marble that seemed to absorb sound.

Two blocks ahead he saw Fatsie Morgan, hands on her hips, glaring at the passing traffic from under the awning of the King Arthur Motel.

He tried to affect a casual walk, as if he were just another normal guy in a sweatshirt and jeans out for a twilight stroll.

A block from Fatsie he stopped in his tracks. It seemed as if she was staring at him, the great turret of her body had swiveled toward him and was sending waves of revulsion his way.

He pressed on until he was close enough to catch the aroma of bathroom deodorizer. He looked up and felt as if he were a rabbit or deer or something to be hunted, and had just glimpsed the sheen of the rifle barrel that would blow away all five feet two inches of him.

"Uh, hi," he said. He flashed his badge. "I'm Louis Mon—"

"Go fuck yourself!" Her voice was like the chilly, briny gust that Monroe had once smelled blowing up from beneath a rotting amusement pier.

"Listen to me," he began, "I'm a police detective, and I know this other police detective, Raymond Deegan, and the way he reacted, and the way my old partner, Darrell Pratt, ignored you when we rode on this street, makes me wonder if there's—"

"I SAID GO FUCK YOURSELF!"

"A reason . . ."

"I'M GOING TO KICK YOUR GODDAMN HAIRLESS ASS!" she roared, and took one single heavy step that sent vibrations rolling through the concrete, up Monroe's ankles into his brain.

Monroe stood firm. "Maybe you don't understand what this badge means. It means you have a choice," he said. "You can talk to me decently and treat me with respect, or I will do whatever I can to take you off this street."

He caught a flash of something in the dark, eyeshadow-smeared hollows under her forehead and guessed that it might be amusement. But with that, he also saw lines, wrinkles, layers of age. Fatsie Morgan was probably the oldest PARAtrooper working, but you had to go close to her to see it.

She lowered her voice and that shocked him. "You get the fuck out of my face and off my street, asswipe, or I'll pick you up and throw you into that bus over there."

Monroe had learned from previous encounters that when you're five feet two inches tall and threatened with physical violence, it does no good to tell people you've been taking unarmed combat classes, giving you the equivalent of at least a brown belt in karate or the other martial arts.

"I want to ask you something else—"

"The answer is FUCK NO!" She turned away.

Monroe looked wildly around Pacific Avenue, and just across the street, saw the dark maw of Mount Rushmore Street.

"Is that your final—"

She turned back, as slow and inexorable as a great, wide hurricane wave crashing in, the kind that grabs boats, piers, whole sections of the Boardwalk and smashes them against the sides of buildings. Swinging with her was her black patent leather purse aimed at Monroe's face.

Monroe saw it coming and managed to hop backward. His hop turned into a step, which turned into a run and he was running again from another woman, and he became instantly enraged at himself for being afraid.

He was a cop. The badge in his pocket meant Monroe had the law on his side.

In taking a swing at him, Fatsie Morgan had broken the law.

As Monroe ran the mile and a half back to police headquarters, he told himself that it was time for the law to make its presence known.

5

Going Inside

As Louis Monroe ran toward the back entrance of the police department, he made sure that the Mobile Crime Lab was resting in its usual berth and that no ineptly parked cars were blocking its exit.

The Atlantic City Police Department acquired this dinosaur a few years after the last gasoline price crisis. A politically connected Essex County recreational vehicle dealer, stuck with too much stock on his lot, leaned on a few state representatives who gave him a grant to install out-of-date computers, a stereo tape system, police radios and a few poison control suits in a closet inside the largest, fuel-inefficient RVs he had. Then the state issued anti-crime funding to various police departments specifically for the purchase of the vehicles, at the inflated markup set by the Essex County dealer.

The MCL was almost never used officially, though it had a way of disappearing from its corner berth in the fenced-in City Hall parking lot across Baltic Avenue. It was typically missing during December hunting season.

Over the years the police department markings on the MCL's side and front panels had been obscured by graffiti sprayed on by children from the housing projects near City Hall. Because the Chief of Police had a thing about graffiti, the wild paint designs were immediately removed. The caustic paint thinners also erased the police department markings. The Atlantic City Fine Arts Foundation then pressured the Chief of Police to give the Mobile Crime

Lab "to the creative community, where it would be transformed into a permanent art exhibit."

The Chief refused. Then a clever motor pool mechanic noticed that, as long as police markings were left off the MCL, the neighborhood kids left the vehicle alone. The motor pool mechanic was promoted to assistant supervisor and the MCL became the police department's largest unmarked vehicle, virtually indistinguishable from the bulky, somewhat battered camper vans and RVs that rumble into Atlantic City, their cabins crammed with feverish families of good old boys and girls who only wanted to believe that everything worth seeing in America could be glimpsed from the side of a road.

Monroe dashed into the department, trotted to his locker and pulled out the motley, drunken tourist ensemble he had used when he had disguised himself to arrest Reuben Claymore. In the back of his locker was some stage makeup and accessories that Monroe had bought at a party supply store on Tilton Road.

He took out a packet of beard hair and a vial of spirit gum. He then went into the small lavatory adjoining the Vice Squad office, washed and dried his face, then dabbed the spirit gum over his upper lip, cheeks and chin. He unraveled the beard hair, stuck it to the rapidly drying spirit gum, clipped and shaped it with scissors. Then he slipped into the touristy jeans and T-shirt, shrugged on the denim jacket over the shirt. He transferred his badge and wallet to his pocket, clipped on his gun, handcuffs and portable radio, and put his street clothes in his locker.

He found a rubber band and scissors in his desk drawer. The day's edition of the *Atlantic City Star* lay wilting in a trash can. He cut the newspaper to scraps about the size of a dollar bill, stacked them up until they were about a half-inch thick, then took two twenty-dollar bills from his wallet, put a bill on the top and bottom of the wad, and bound it with the rubber band.

He put the flashwad in the front pocket of his denim jacket, with the twenty poking up like a green pocket-square.

Because the MCL had been intended for inter-unit use within

the department, copies of its keys hung in every squad room and unit command post within the department. And because it was occasionally used for nonpolice purposes, it was made sure that such uses did not create the tedious paper trail required before requisitioning an unmarked police car.

Monroe took the MCL key set off the rack and stuck it in his back pocket. Then he went to the lavatory mirror.

He looked ridiculous.

He put a pair of cheap sunglasses and a blue, green and purple Alcazar Casino Hotel Silver-Liner Club cap on his head.

Perfectly ridiculous.

Monroe had once had a summer job driving delivery trucks along the flat, angular rural roads of Galloway Township, but the MCL was larger than any truck he'd been near.

He leaned against the cool flank of the beast, saw where the briny air that corroded everything from bridge girders to computer guts had created cancerous pockets of rust that mottled the vehicle's skin and had eaten into some of the fixtures holding the windows and the doors. He noted that, like a bus, the van had only two doors. One, like a bus, was opposite the driver, the other was in the very back.

He checked the tires. They seemed thick and high enough to withstand the debris on Mount Rushmore Street, the narrow alley that opened in front of Fatsie Morgan's corner. The wide van itself appeared to be just narrow enough to make the trip.

Before he made that trip, he'd have to test the disguise. Before he made the test, he had to make sure the van would start.

Before he could start the van, he'd have to deal with the alarm system. Though an alarm going off in a police parking lot would not bring the police, he'd still have to find some way to disable it before he left the lot.

He put the key in the front door lock, waited for an alarm to go off. It didn't. He opened the door and, over the reek of spirit gum, caught a scent that reminded him of a used motel room.

He found a switch and turned on the cabin lights. With the exception of a old gray TRS-80 computer bolted to the galley table, the MCL was more RV than PD. Finished in luxurious teak, it could sleep six. It had its own narrow toilet and shower, television set, refrigerator and freezer. A stale pot of coffee, its edge mottled with mold, was held on the galley stove by metal restraints. A champagne bottle stood up-ended in the small garbage pail and a bed had been opened in the back. It was unmade. Strewn across the rumpled, stained sheets were withered flowers. A card attached to the flowers said, "To my love bucket."

Monroe checked the escape hatch, made sure it was locked tight. Then he sat in the dark leather throne-like driver's seat, stuck the key in the dashboard and jumped as Elvis Presley screamed at him from the speakers.

The tape player was hidden somewhere above and behind the computer. It took him one whole song to find a volume knob. It came off in his hand. He tried to twist the bare shaft down and was able to reduce the volume by only half. The second song arrived and he remembered something about Elvis Presley having recorded a ridiculous Christmas album. Monroe listened to it and decided it was just perfect.

He went back to the driver's seat, turned the key one more notch and the MCL groaned, sputtered, coughed and roared to life. Monroe adjusted the mirrors, looking to see if anyone from the department would notice that the beast had awakened. No one seemed to.

He set the air conditioner at full blast, then backed out of the lot as Elvis wished for a white Christmas.

It took him several wide turns to get the hang of driving the van, but Monroe noted that one characteristic of overpriced, over-loaded, overpowered gasoline vehicles with automatic transmissions is that they tended to be easier to drive than cheap, underloaded ones.

He turned onto Pacific Avenue and gazed down from the van's

high front seat and saw, standing below motel awnings, in front of all-night pawn shops and greasy cafes, the PARAtroopers out in all their finery. A few even waved at him.

Time for the test.

Looking lost and somewhat stupid in front of an all-night greasy spoon stood an emaciated woman in a white halter, a waist-length down jacket and blue leotards and black leather boots. She was a PARAtrooper known to the Vice Squad as Gnarly Marlene.

Monroe pressed the power window switch and rolled down the window, trying on an old boy accent.

"Uh, howdy," he said. "I just made me a score in the casino and I'm looking for some . . . head."

Gnarly Marlene looked at the van, looked at Monroe, who rocked in his seat so she could see the flashroll.

She saw it. "You want it delivered or I got to meet you somewhere?"

"You can come on in if the price is right."

"Can you make me a cup of coffee in that thing?"

Monroe said, "There's a pot on, but it's kind of old."

"Seventy-five bucks and a cup of coffee, and I take double cream, double sugar."

She stepped into the side door. Monroe awkwardly squeezed around her as he closed and locked it, identified himself, showed her his badge, charged her with soliciting for prostitution, recited her rights and asked her to relax in one of the plush captain's chair seats.

She whistled. "Monroe. The short one. What you doing in a beard?"

"Oh, the usual," Monroe said in his normal voice. "You didn't recognize me? You didn't smell the gum holding my beard?"

"You know I got no sense of smell. If I had one, I couldn't deal with this work." She went down the aisle. "This is the most awesome vehicle I ever see. Looks like an airplane or jet or something." She glanced at the coffee pot, and before Monroe could stop her, put her lips to the edge and took a gulp.

"You say it was cold?"

"That, too."

"Oh, hell, all I care about's the jolt."

She finished the pot on the way back to police headquarters, where Saint Peter, aka. Sergeant Peter Duskine was delighted to have company.

"Night like this, I'm about to doubt the purpose of my existence," Duskine said. "Glad to see somebody on the job, keeping the streets safe for democracy, even if it's a rat that busted a cop. Cops don't bust cops."

"The cat's away, the rat's going to play," Monroe said, signing Marlene into the lockup.

Duskine bit a chunk from the edge of his styrofoam coffee cup and spit the chunk into the trashcan beside him. Before Marlene could be put in the lockup, she had to be strip-searched. Duskine called over "Queen" Ida Hoffetz, a police woman who read Shirley MacLaine books and was absolutely certain that, in a past life, she had been one of the queens of the Nile.

"You ever been to Egypt?" Queen Ida asked Gnarly Marlene.

Marlene thought about it. "Which one?"

"Just checking," Ida sighed.

Back in the van, Monroe cleaned out the coffee pot and made himself a fresh batch. He laughed to himself as Elvis sang "Pah-rumpa-pum-pum." He was having fun, the same kind of fun he had had when he had dressed as a high roller, borrowed a limousine, and with Darrell Pratt at the wheel, yanked twenty-three women off the street in a single night. Fatsie Morgan hadn't been among them.

He thought about doing a sweep. He'd certainly rack up the paper—make enough arrests so that it would seem as if he was doing the job.

But doing a prostitution sweep is like skipping through a dozen casinos in two hours. The first casino is a dazzler, an eye-opening sensory barrage. The second gives you an opportunity to compare and contrast. You notice the differences between a light-patterned day casino and darker night casino floor. By the third you are evaluating the efficacy of pink marble versus white marble, red-and-gold carpet patterns versus paisley swirls of blue and silver.

After a while, your senses become dulled from too much cheap stimulation. Soon everything bothers you: the lights, the noise, the smells of spilled alcohol and stale cigar smoke. You feel as if the adventure has taken more from you than you have received, and you want to quit but you can't because you're still curious about what the next one will be like. It seems so easy to keep going.

And that's when you screw up.

He decided to try one more, just to be sure. He cruised until he saw the girl with new teeth. He honked the van's horn, pulled over, let the window whirr down and looked into the pearliest set of white teeth he had ever seen.

"Uh, how—"

"Why Mr. Monroe," the girl said, "what you all bearded up?"

"Hello, Sunshine," Monroe said.

"How you like the profile?" Sunshine Stevens leaned back, her white sequinned short-shorts and orange bathing suit top swaying on her stringbean body. "The mouth, the mouth!"

The last time Monroe had seen Sunshine Stevens her mouth had been punched out. Now he saw a brand new set of pearly whites, perfectly shaped.

"I am impressed," Monroe said.

"With that nasty old Pizzaman off the street, I figured I could invest in a good set."

The Pizzaman was one of Reuben Claymore's street names.

The teeth glistened under the street lights. "So," Monroe said, "business must be good."

"Business sucks, Mr. Monroe, and I don't mean that lit'rally."

Horns began to honk behind him. He asked Sunshine in. "I smell some coffee in there. You buying?"

"You want to talk?"

"You not arresting me for nothing?"

"Can't," Monroe said. "You're too good."

"My mother always say, be a good little girl and stay out of trouble." She sashayed in, shaking her rear for the cars behind them, setting off a chorus of honks.

While he drove to an abandoned parking lot, Monroe thought that if Sunshine Stevens could spot him and Gnarly Marlene couldn't, then his chances of roping Fatsie Morgan were fifty-fifty *until* he got her into the van. Then he would lock the door and throw the key out the window, if necessary. The only way the both of them could leave would be for Saint Peter to fetch another set of MCL keys. He could always use the police radio in the MCL, or the portable radio clipped to his belt, to alert Duskine of his special cargo.

The cream had spoiled in the refrigerator. "I just use the extra sugar," Sunshine said, dumping a stream of sugar into her cup. "Man that fix my teeth, say I got the deluxe kind. No cavities as long as I floss."

"They look great," Monroe said. He turned the motor off and the ghost of Elvis, crooning about seven lords-a-leaping, died. Then he sat beside her in a captain's chair.

"Ain't done much for business, though. I mean, girl has a nice smile, she get the kind that like a nice smilin' girl. Used to be, girl could do ten, twenty, sometime thirty tricks in a good night. Now the only way you make ends meet is in the casinos, but the shit you gotta go through to get into casino lounges or show up at the parties, it's criminal. Girl can't just walk in. They throw you out."

"Because the casinos want every bit of money a gambler brings in. Why should they let you get any of it?"

"Because sometimes it's me that they wanting for!" She huffed. "Girl's got a right to repeat business."

Monroe nodded. "So who fixed your teeth?"

"Just because business is bad don't mean a girl can't get lucky every once in a while. Remember that convention of dentists at the Lucky Shamrock? There was one sneaking out for some street trade. Used to be we'd get 'em sneakin' out all the time, but with this AIDS shit and all the stuff in the papers about the streets ain't

52

safe, most of them stay in. But Myron, he was a sneaker, and he and me worked something out." She ran a gold painted fingernail beneath her upper set.

"It almost worth it," she continued, "for Officer Roo to punch them out. What I got is better'n what I was born with. Like I says to all the new girls come to me asking for advice, you gots to let the cops do what they want. Cost of doing business, though there be times you might not wants to be payin' it."

Monroe asked, "Did you ever have any business expenses with the other officer that's been patrolling around here?"

"You mean that Deegan dude? He's okay." She made a show of drinking the brew.

Monroe waited. "Okay?" he asked.

"That's what I said. Okay. Okay?"

"You don't want to tell me anything that would get him in trouble?"

"I don't want to tell anything that would get *me* in trouble."

"What could he do to you?"

"I don't want to find out. Not that he'd get nasty. He's not like Officer Roo. He's all business."

"What kind of business?"

She looked at his flashroll. Monroe peeled off a twenty and gave it to her. "This is awful cheap for me telling you stuff that's going to get me in trouble."

"He won't know it's you."

"But if he's in trouble, I'm in trouble."

"Maybe not," Monroe said. "If you tell me . . ."

"If I tell you, you do something about him and I lose business."

"He gets you business?"

Sunshine brightened, relieved that Monroe had guessed so that she didn't have to feel responsible for telling him.

"Sure! He comes around, and you want to work the casino lounges, or meet up with some friend of his inside, he sets it up. Sometime his friends tie me up a whole night, and he never pays me nothing for it. That's what he calls them. Calls them friends-of-mine."

"You don't get paid for this?"

"Sometimes I get a tip from the friend if I do something extra. But there's no money changing hands unless I gets it from doing extra."

"So he sets you up with his friends, who get free sex—"

"Or whatever they want. I had one guy just wants to lick my teeth."

"And all you get is a tip?"

She became quiet.

"Let me guess. Deegan gets you into the casino, through the employee entrance, right?"

She looked into her coffee cup. "This is empty."

Monroe refilled it, then brought her the sugar and a spoon. "You're in the casino, you meet the friend, you do what the friend wants, and you get nothing for that, maybe a tip if he's feeling generous. But there's never a discussion of price."

She pointed to the other twenty. Monroe gave it to her. "I'm supposed to act like it's natural we met in the elevator or the lounge or something."

"You work for a tip in exchange for not busting you?"

"Shit, anybody can get busted. It's no big deal. Pay some money and you're back in business."

"You say this friend uses you all night?"

"I don't mean that exactly." She make loud, slurping noises. "If he's got friends . . ."

"So you have to work for whoever it is who says he's Deegan's friend. After that?"

She shrugged. "You know. I just . . . go."

"Home?"

"Girl gets in a casino past all them guards would put her out, has to be crazy to go home. You do what you can."

"So the deal is, Deegan gets you in, you service whoever he tells you to service—these are only gamblers or employees?"

She frowned at him. "I don't make a man fill out a questionaire."

"But some of them are wearing uniforms?"

"They ain't wearin' much when we go to it. But, yeah, some of them has uniforms."

"And when you're done, you're free to solicit whatever business you can find. And you keep the money you get from that."

"That's the way it works. Long as I'm not too obvious about it. I mean, girl in a casino dressed like me, she get the wrong kind of attention. I dress it more large if I'm going inside."

"What about drugs? Is he a source?"

"Everybody's a source, they want to be. Deegan never offered, never said yes, never said no. There could be girls takin' off him, but ain't me."

"Does he set you up in all casinos, or just some?"

"Pretty much all. Different casinos got different folks controlling access. Used to be we'd hang in the casino lounges, and nobody cared much 'cause they was enough dads with money for everybody. But now we gets put out unless we cut the access man a slice and even then it don't promise nothing. I'll cut anybody a slice if it does me good, but most of them that's in the casinos, they just take and take and they 'spect you should be grateful. You know what I'm saying?"

Monroe thought of Raleigh. "I know exactly what you're saying."

"Deegan handle the access men. All you gots to do is be nice to his friends, and you don't get no hassle. That's why he better not get in no trouble that gets me in trouble." She put down the cup, made a show of looking at her wrist, though there was no watch on it. "Now, if you not be minding, I have appointments to keep."

Monroe didn't move. Sunshine stood, stepped to the back of the van, slipped past the empty bed, saw the flowers and giggled. She tried the back door. "You gonna open this thing?"

Monroe said, "No. The front door's open."

She marched past him. "One of these days, I get rich, any

55

coming and going I do, be by the front door." She opened the door, felt the blast of humid August heat, and turned back.

"You make trouble for me, I put Fatsie on you."

Monroe said, "Who?"

"Ain't no man can stand up to Fatsie. A girl in trouble, they say it used to be Darrell Pratt could help her out. But Pratt only helped those he want to help. You can't get no help from nobody, there is always Fatsie. Any problem a girl has, Fatsie has the answer. She been on this street the longest of anybody, and she gonna be on this street after I bank it out of here."

She stepped down and Monroe followed her. "Is this Fatsie Morgan you're taking about?"

Sunshine kicked an empty bottle into the gutter. "Now you should do something for me."

Monroe smiled. "Have I forgotten something?"

"They be bringing in some out-of-town meat tonight around 10:30," she said. "Word is one of them is downed out. Meat that's downed out is set to get herself hurt. You know, like what was done to me, but worse."

"Sunshine, there are at least a hundred and fifty prostitutes of both sexes that pass through Pacific Avenue every night. Nearly all of them are intoxicated, most with drugs. How am I going to find this girl?"

"She's chicken, is how. I don't like no young chicken getting hurt. But don't you worry yourself. Fatsie can take care of the girl. You find what's looking for her."

"What *is* looking for her?"

"They say he been coming around in a jeep, some kind the posses like to ride around in. All black and nasty and done up in stereo. You find the man and take away his jeep. Fatsie'll do the rest."

"What do you mean take away his jeep?"

"Only reason Pizzaman did what he did, was he did it to girls dumb enough to get into his car with him. Fatsie can't do nothing when a girl get into a man's car. But she find him on the street, she can do plenty."

"Like what?"

"You take his car away, you find out." Then she was off walking, as fast as she could.

6

Christmas with Elvis

The alley called Mount Rushmore Street was a dark, cruddy, pitted, pot-holed, one-way eastbound trench connecting Atlantic Avenue, the city's forlorn main street, to the bright casinos, motels and parking palaces along Pacific Avenue.

Just wide enough for garbage trucks and delivery vans, Mount Rushmore attracted out-of-town gamblers looking for a sneaky shortcut past the rush-hour traffic snarls on Missouri Avenue.

Some shortcut. The casino-crazed shoobie—Atlantic City slang for a penny-pinching day-tripper who, instead of enriching the local economy, packs his lunch and brings it to the beach in a shoebox—would drive down Mount Rushmore for about ten yards, trying to ignore the burnt-out street lights, broken glass and gathering gloom. He'd then stop dead in front of a pile of trash, or a dumpster that was supposed to have been chained to one of the narrow strips of sidewalk but had somehow become loose and rolled into Mount Rushmore Street to block his car. The car would be surrounded suddenly by underage scumbags-in-training, who rolled a few garbage cans behind it and then crammed as much menace as possible into their gangling 12-year-old frames as they sauntered up, greasy rags and crusty squeeze-bottles in one hand, bricks and monkey wrenches in the other, thrusting their faces into the windshield, pushing their noses and tongues on the bug-spattered glass, leering at the suddenly mortified shoobie. "Five dollar washer window, mister?"

At the beginning of the summer, Mayor Bernie Tilton called the kids "vicious parasites" and declared war on them. A memo went around the department instructing all vehicular-assigned officers to patrol Mount Rushmore at least four times during their shifts.

But, as Sergeant Vinnie Almagro liked to say in his police academy bump 'n' thump unarmed combat classes, "those who declare war tend to lose more than they win." Mount Rushmore soon had its own traffic jam of disabled police cars whose thin tires inevitably blew from the glass that the vicious parasites threw into the street. Once stranded the cars would be pelted with rocks, bricks, clam shells, broken bottles, anything that the scumbags-in-training could drag up to their perches on the rooftops of the restaurants, shops and apartments that backed up to Mount Rushmore.

No one in City Hall bothered to replace the burned-out street lights, which would have made the street less inviting for scumbags-in-training who, because they were juveniles, associated darkness with safety from police. No one thought of putting uniformed men on foot patrol and sending them down Mount Rushmore every few hours. Some war.

Monroe steered wide and hard to slip the MCL off Atlantic Avenue onto Mount Rushmore. He put on the cheap plastic sunglasses, pulled the cap low over his eyes and, as, soon as the MCL was safely tucked in, he put it in park and replenished the flashwad with his last twenty dollar bill.

He shifted into drive and slowly rolled foward. The van's tires were too thick and hard to be foiled by the glass on the street. Perhaps the size of the MCL intimidated enough of the neighborhood punks to keep them away. Or maybe it was past their bedtime on a Friday night when they had better things to do.

Despite the MCL's overpowered headlights, the sunglasses Monroe wore darkened his vision so that the backs of the old buildings were reduced to sharp, harsh, weirdly angled lines, edges and planes that didn't intersect. The structures that framed the narrow street seemed broken and, as Monroe moved the MCL forward, it looked as though shattered edges were moving toward him.

Just before reaching Pacific Avenue, he saw a dumpster jutting out a little too far. He put the van back into park, opened the front door, checked carefully for people outside and around the van, and saw no one. He stepped down and wind blowing off the ocean pushed his beard in his face. He put both hands on the dumpster and shoved. Its wheels squeaked loudly and, about a hundred feet ahead, where Mount Rushmore met Pacific Avenue, a face below a pile of rhinestone-wrapped hair rotated toward him.

She crossed the street. Monroe told himself to be calm.

"You're in my way," she said.

Monroe scurried back and she stepped heavily into the van, moving her bulk sideways through the front door.

"Where the fuck is he?" she demanded.

He snuck in behind her and closed and locked the door. He said, "Howdy."

She said, "Fuck you."

"I was hoping, if you wouldn't mind."

"Fuck off and fuck you!" she bellowed. "Where is he?"

"He's right here," Monroe said. He felt his sunglasses slide down and pushed them back up his nose.

"You mean *you*, dipshit?"

"Uh, I got lucky in the casinos tonight," Monroe said. He put his hands on the flashwad. "I think I have what you would—"

"It'll cost you three hundred dollars for me to piss in a pot and you to drink it."

That she had taken a swing at him an hour ago was a violation of the law, but without a witness he'd have no case for the prosecutor. What she had just mentioned was somewhat disgusting, but nothing that would make a case against her. Monroe needed her to quote a price and describe a sexual, or even perverse act. "Well, what about some, umm, head?"

"I'd cut your weenie off 'fore I let you near me."

Terroristic threats? No, he'd need the price and the description.

"We can do it right here."

60

"We'll do it wherever I want to do it, and there's nothing I want to do with you, dipshit."

"But—"

"I SAID FUCK YOU, DIPSHIT!"

"Well," Monroe shrugged, stuffing the flashwad back in his jacket pocket. "I guess I'll just have to spend my money elsewhere."

Then Elvis began singing the "Jinglebell Rock."

"You're not going to spend it," she said, turning on him. "You're going to give to me. Right now. You're going to go down on your hands and knees and lick my shoe and then you're going to give it to me, you little dipshit."

Monroe backed toward front of the van. "I'd rather not."

"In that case, you're gonna lick the *bottom* of my shoe after I step in some squishy dog dirt. Squishy, squishy. Here squishy! You'll like that. Give it some flavor. Like that, wouldn't you, dipshit."

"I—"

"DIPSHIT!"

Monroe took refuge behind the driver's seat. "Why don't you make yourself comfortable?" he said nervously.

"Make this, dipshit!"

As Elvis rocked, she began to shake herself. The skin, gelatinous and globular, trussed like an overstuffed goose, strained against black leather straps.

Then Monroe lost it. Absolutely. He looked at the mass of tied blubber and started to laugh.

She stopped, stared in astonishment, and then became enraged. "WHADDERYOOO laughing at?" she roared, hurling her purse at him.

Monroe ducked. "I'm sorry," he said.

"That's better."

"It's just that—" he couldn't help himself again. "I've never seen anybody so damned ridiculous—"

She took a swing that snagged Monroe's beard, pulled it off and away, knocking off his sunglasses and ripping away the hairs that had been glued to his skin.

He covered his face, staggered back, ducked under the bed in the back of the van.

"You want to be fucked, I'll fuck you," Morgan snarled, waving her fist. "I'll shove this up your asshole and then I'll sit on you till you choke, dipshit! Fucking bastard dipshit!"

Finally an act had been described and, with the previous price quoted for degradation, the soliciting charge could be applied. Now all Monroe, still cowering under the bed, merely had to do was subdue her, handcuff her and bring her in.

Morgan leaned over, grabbed the edge of the bed and grunted. Monroe heard a twisting, ratcheting sound as the bed's aluminum frame buckled and ripped off the wall. She shoved it back and Monroe shrunk against the back door.

"Like that, dipshit? Like a strong woman, dipshit? Now, you say you're sorry, or I swear you won't have a mouth to say it with."

Monroe leaned against the back door, felt for his gun with one hand, the key for the back door in the other, saw her looking at him. "Dipshit, did I see you before?"

"Uh, as a matter of fact—" Before he could bring out the gun she smacked him across the face, then grabbed him by his jacket, pulled him up, threw him against the back door, grabbed him again, threw him back, was about to grab him a third time when she saw the flashwad.

She reached for it and Monroe shoved the key into the door handle, twisted it and fell out and back, slamming hard on the cool, pitted asphalt. He had tucked in his head, as he had learned when practicing break falls, but the impact knocked the wind out of him.

The light from the open door seemed to fold up, diminish. Monroe was sure that he hadn't hit his head, so there must be something wrong with the door and then he saw that what had been an open door was now filled almost completely by the leather-strapped Fatsie Morgan, wedged sideways, her white, sagging right arm still groping for the flashwad.

Monroe saw her arm retract, the hand plant itself against the door frame. The arm pushed and the door framed groaned but it didn't move. Nothing moved.

The hand changed its position, pushing from the top now, against the aluminum lintel, which bent outward but stayed.

She said, "What the fuck." Then she said it louder. Then she screamed, "DIPSHIT, YOU HEAR ME DIPSHIT?"

She glared at him, flailed her arm as Monroe blinked, rolled over, stood and backed away. He touched his face, felt another tender spot, brought his gun out, and then noticed that Morgan wasn't going anywhere.

"I hear you," Monroe said.

"Get me the fuck out of here, right now, this instant."

"Uh . . ." He folded his arms. "No."

"You hear me, dipshit! I'm stuck, get me out of here or you don't get nothing from me."

"I, um, not quite sure exactly what I want from you," Monroe said. He held his gun in his left hand, took his handcuffs out, saw that the cuffs wouldn't fit around her wrists.

"You're under arrest for soliciting for prostitution, making terrorist threats, assaulting an officer and criminal theft. . . ." He laughed again.

"THIS ISN'T FUNNY, DIPSHIT!"

"No, I guess it isn't." He recited her rights.

She squinted at him. "You're not a real cop, are you?"

"I'm Detective Louis Monroe of the Atlantic City Vice Squad," he said, showing her his badge. "I'd like to talk to you about what's been happening on this street. Specifically, a police officer named Dee—"

She gaped at him. "NO!"

"I can do something—I want to do something about the street crimes happening around here. Perhaps as a condition of your plea, you could ask to serve so many hours community service and maybe we can make it better for those that live and work around here."

She smiled. She even laughed and it was a new and different light breaking through the twilight. "Them local punks turned Mount Rushmore into a trash pit. What can a loser and dipshit do?"

"I get inspired sometimes," Monroe said.

"And I perspire sometimes," she said. "Want to sniff my pits? Want to get me out of here, dipshit?"

"Soon. You're still under arrest."

"You better let me go or you're really and truly going to get fucked."

"Right now I'm trying figure out how I can take you back to police headquarters."

"I ain't going to police headquarters."

"You'll have to," Monroe said. "I'm going to need help pulling you out of there."

"Fuck *you!*" she said, and began to flail her arms.

Monroe squeezed around the side of the van and entered through the front door. As long as Morgan was wedged in the back, she was about as subdued as she was going to get.

He wandered back to make sure she was stuck. She turned her face at him and Monroe suddenly saw terror there, not fear of what might happen to her, but the fright of a helpless animal. It was oddly familiar, too. Where had he seen that face before?

He went back to the driver's seat.

"GET ME OUT OF HERE!" she screamed.

He shook his head.

"I'LL KILL YOU IF YOU DON'T GET ME OUT OF HERE!"

He put the van in gear, rolled forward a few feet and heard a terrible, wrenching sound.

He looked back and saw she had put both hands against the back door frame and heaved against a spot where the rust had eaten through. The frame had buckled. She heaved again and the frame popped out of the back body panel and she went out the door, making a wet slap on the street.

He stopped the van, ran to the back but saw nothing. He stuck his head out and ducked just before a brick came flying toward his face.

He staggered toward the front while stones, garbage and debris seemed to follow him. They hit lights, the bathroom door fixtures, the TV monitor on the TRS-80 and the coffee pot with the new brew. With the computer monitor shattered on the floor where Monroe had been standing, the tape deck was revealed. An empty Thunderbird wine bottle found it and Elvis died again.

Monroe scrambled to the driver's seat, put the van in gear, floored the gas pedal, heard the brakes of cars screech as he almost drove straight into the King Arthur Motel awning before he turned and brought the van back onto Pacific Avenue, careening through a red light, swerving around a jitney, putting nothing but speed between Fatsie Morgan and himself until the unlit City Hall lot came into view.

He eased the van into its space, turned off the engine, turned off the air conditioner, turned off the lights and listened. Through the open hatch in the back he heard the sounds of vehicles roaring through the night, and under the sound, faint but steady, the distant rumble of the ocean.

Monroe would have sat in the van, motionless, until the sun came up, had he not looked up and caught the gleam of streetlights on chrome, and saw the chrome attached to a black, four-by-four jeep with tinted windows, its license plate light out, running the red light in front of City Hall.

He looked at his watch. He still had time. He was out of the van and halfway across the street when he recalled that the back door had been broken. Anyone could go into the van and take anything. There was only one thing worth taking and Monroe couldn't understand why it had been left there.

He crept through the back door, removed the "love bucket" card. It had been written in purple ink. Only one person in City Hall wrote in purple ink.

Ephrum Traile.

He put the card in his jacket and thought that if this wasn't an insurance policy, it was the next best thing.

He tiptoed into the police department, restored the MCL keys on the hook, removed what was left of his beard, changed his clothes and ran out.

The cab found him on Atlantic Avenue, on his way to the bus terminal. The cabbie had his window down. He called out, "Hey, you in trouble?"

"Most of the time," Monroe said.

"A ride going to help?"

Monroe stopped running, looked at his watch. The New Jersey Transit bus from Philadelphia was due to arrive right now. He said, "Yes."

In the front seat sat a German shepherd so large that Monroe could barely see the driver.

"In the back," said a pale, bearded man with thinning hair and a broken nose. "I don't normally solicit business, but, the way things been, with the economy and all, somebody needs help, you just got to do it."

Monroe flashed his badge and identified himself.

"What is it, you gotta problem with me taking Patrocles here?"

"I just need you to take me to the bus terminal."

"What's a cop need a ride to the bus terminal?"

Monroe turned around and saw the black jeep two blocks behind them. "So somebody doesn't get into any worse trouble than she's going to get into."

"That's okay with me. You mind we put it on the meter?"

Monroe said he didn't mind.

"So I got two cops with me," the driver said. "Patrocles's a cop, too. Was a cop. He was a K-9 dog until the mayor cut the budget back and they said they were going to destroy some of the dogs. I figured I'd give him a retirement job."

"You did right," Monroe said, keeping the jeep in sight. "He still know the basic commands?"

66

"Some words you don't want to say around him."

Monroe gave Patrocles a deep scratch around his back. "What do you feed this guy?"

"Am I putting on the meter?"

Monroe nodded. "And I'm paying cash."

"Good," the cabbie said, punching the meter on the dash. "Then we can buy Pat some weenies."

At the word the dog barked, turned around and slobbered on Monroe's face.

"He likes weenies?" Monroe asked.

The driver turned up Michigan Avenue, then made a left to come around and behind the bus terminal. "He'll do anything for 'em. Run, jump, dive. Say, where we going? You want me to take the cab stand, or I let you out front?"

"Go around to the front," Monroe said, guessing that a doped-up out-of-town girl who had never been to Atlantic City would do what most visitors do on their first bus trip—go straight through to the front of the terminal, instead of wandering to the cab stand at the corner.

"Slow down. I want to talk to those these people right outside the front."

The cabbie pulled into traffic. "If it's that mother and daughter, they look like they're waiting for somebody."

The jeep was still two blocks behind them. "They are," Monroe said.

The mother wore a red, fake fur coat. Beside her was a girl who was no more than twelve, in white leotards and a short, scarlet T-shirt.

The cabbie said. "If you're going to do what I think you're going to do—"

Monroe leaned over, rolled down the window. The mother sized him up.

"You're here to see someone at the Alcazar casino?" Monroe asked.

"Finally," the mother said. She opened the door, pushed her

doped-up daughter in beside Monroe, slid in and shut the door. Monroe saw the blurry makeup on the girl's numbed face and he wanted to kill the mother.

"What's the dog for?" the mother asked.

For making me not strangle you, Monroe thought to himself. Patrocles barked.

"I ride in a lot of cabs and this is the first time I got a dog," she said.

"He's protecting me," the cabbie said.

"The gambling element attracts some dangerous types," Monroe said. He watched the black jeep pull up behind them. "Let's go," he told the cabbie. "Make a left onto Arkansas. Then make another quick left."

"I do that, that puts me in with the buses."

A horn honked and a maroon Dodge had slipped in between the cab and the jeep.

"Is this how you go to the casinos?" the mother asked.

"Casinah!" the girl said. She had the vaguely sweet aroma of barbituate intoxication. Monroe touched her arm and she didn't move.

"Don't mind her," the mother said. "With what she has in her, she won't feel a thing. They said the client likes 'em docile."

Monroe could barely restrain his contempt as the cabbie made the turn fast, too fast for the maroon Dodge to follow.

"Get lost in these buses here," Monroe advised. They quickly found themselves squeezed between a pale blue-and-white Greyhound and a grumbling striped New Jersey Transit bus.

Monroe took out his badge and turned on the dome light so the mother could see it. "I'm Detective Monroe of the Atlantic City Vice Squad. I should arrest you but I . . . can't." He gave her his last twenty dollar bill. "I want you to get back on that bus to Philadelphia, or whatever bus you came in on. It's going to turn around and if you leave now, you can just make it."

The mother said, "No way. I got five hundred dollars waiting for me in that casino hotel and nothing is going to stop me from getting it. Now they said the cops in this town cooperate and, if you're trying to take a slice—"

"I don't know if this girl here is your daughter, or just some *friend*," Monroe seethed. "But you're feeding her to somebody who's going to beat her up."

The mother patted the girl on the head. "Sally likes it, don't you, Sal?"

Sally said, "Casinah!"

"Either you take us there or I find my own way," the mother said, her hand on the door handle.

The jeep would be closing in now, Monroe thought. If the truth wouldn't work, a lie might. Monroe said, "The client has AIDS. They bring in women for him because none of the local girls—"

"AIDS!" the mother stiffened. "Fuck that." She had the cab door open in a flash and dragged her daughter toward the bus, without a look back. She didn't even take the twenty dollars Monroe had been holding.

The cabbie watched them go. He tapped the meter as the Dodge pulled up behind the cab.

Monroe gave the cabbie the twenty dollars. The cabbie held the bill, looked at Monroe. "You a real cop?"

Monroe nodded.

"That how real cops work?"

Monroe suddenly felt vulnerable and afraid. *Had* he done right to let them leave? Shouldn't he have taken them in and tried to make them tell him who set up the deal before the lawyer showed up and had everything they said made inadmissable? Should he have filed the papers, made appointments with the social workers, rolled all those boulders up the hills so that the girl would be put in a drug rehabilitation program that probably wouldn't work and a juvenile home, where she'd never get the love and tenderness she'd need to find a normal life? Even if he managed to get Ellie assigned to talk to the girl, that couldn't take away the revulsion crawling through him.

Monroe asked himself if he put them on the bus because what

he had seen had so enraged him, and the thought of what was about to happen to the girl had so horrified him, that he could do nothing but find a way to get them as far away from it as possible.

"I honestly don't know," he said finally.

The cabbie pocketed the bill. "I think, maybe, if something bad was going to happen, it won't happen tonight. I think, maybe, you—we—did okay."

Monroe took a breath and nodded at the driver. Then he heard the door of the Dodge open and shut behind him. He said, "Give me your card. Maybe I have a job for Patrocles tomorrow."

"Patrocles don't come cheap. And I have to chaperone."

"Meet me at 221 Clam Creek tomorrow at eleven A.M. He gets all the weiners he can eat."

"That's a lot of—" But Monroe was out, with the door closed, running to stop Deegan from entering the bus terminal.

"Let them go," Monroe said.

Deegan turned around slowly, his fists clenched. He forced a smile. "And I asked for you."

"Just keeping the peace," Monroe said. "You shouldn't be getting girls for him."

"I was going to stop that," Deegan said, distraught and trembling. Monroe looked past him and the unmarked car. The black jeep had begun to back out of the terminal. The Philadelphia bus was backing out of its berth between them. Monroe stepped back as the wall of white-striped metal passed. He looked up and saw the drugged girl waving at him. He waved back.

Deegan watched the bus go. "You did exactly what I would've done."

"Really?"

"I swear to you, I didn't bring them girls in."

"But you do bring them in."

"Not *young*." Deegan said. "Not that way. Whatever I'm involved in, I make sure it's done right. I was coming here to send them back."

"Sure you were," Monroe said.

Deegan strode back to the unmarked car, paused at the door. "As your superior officer, I order you to get into this car."

A bus horn blared at him. "Why?" Monroe said.

"We have an operation scheduled. It's our job."

"I've done mine."

"One *lousy* prostitution arrest? You could have been suspended if not for me."

The horn grew insistent.

"Tomorrow the *Star* will have a small feature on vandals striking out at police property," Deegan continued. "There will be no mention of the extra miles on the MCL's odometer."

He smiled. "I just did you a favor for you, whether you like it or not. Now you owe me. Get in the car."

Monroe thought about it until the hot fumes of a bus almost choked him. Then he got in.

Deegan put the car in drive and backed out of the bus lot.

"You did this favor for me?"

"You and somebody else. There's always somebody else."

"Somebody who writes in purple ink?"

Deegan held out his hand. "Give me the card."

"I'll wait to see the story in the *Star* tomorrow," Monroe said.

"Whenever," Deegan said, taking the car around the bus terminal, then heading north toward the Inlet. "You'll want to hand it over sooner or later."

"If it's my insurance, maybe I should hold on to it."

"It's not important enough for insurance. Some of the other stuff you've seen and heard and done tonight, if you knew how to add it up, might be insurance. The card is just something somebody forgot. If I come back with it, we—both of us—might make somebody very happy."

Monroe despised the man, but also found himself admiring him. "How sure are you about what I've done tonight?"

"I told you, anything that happens on the street, I hear about it and I act. Fast, if I have to."

"That card is important?"

71

"Everything is important to someone."

"And you trust me to give it back to you?"

Deegan said. "I know people who know people who will destroy you if you don't."

"Threats don't mean anything," Monroe said, aware that he didn't sound as convincing as he wished. "People have threatened to kill me. I'm still here."

"Who said anything about killing? I know people, they want to destroy you, they let you live."

7

Pi Man and Mr. Maybe

Deegan drove slowly across town, away from the casinos into Inlet Park, a section of Atlantic City near the fishing docks. Unlike most neighborhoods in Atlantic City north of the Albany Avenue, tree-shrouded Inlet Park had not experienced neglect and decay. The small, tidy houses with tiny porches and trim lawns housed fishermen, old-timers, even the mayor of Atlantic City, who invoked Inlet Park as proof that the city wasn't as bad as everyone said it was.

And it wasn't that bad at all. Monroe saw a few dilapidated boathouses that needed renovation, but most of the houses were little suburban fantasies, with a rusting swing set in the back and a plastic pink flamingo planted out front.

"That bust you did," Deegan said. "I want you to think about it. Think about all the work you did, just to get Gnarly Marlene."

"I'm thinking," Monroe said, but his thoughts were trying to puzzle through what things he had experienced that could possibly be construed as insurance. If anything, he was on Fatsie Morgan's shit list, and if she included Ephrum Traile among her clients, then Monroe would need some more significant insurance fast.

"I want you to see how a pro makes paper," Deegan added, as he picked up his police radio, ordering patrol cars to transport suspects from an address in Inlet Park.

"But we haven't arrested anybody yet," Monroe said.

"So I just made a reservation."

"An officer has to be able to ascertain necessity before ordering any diversion of manpower."

"Is that the Code of Conduct?" Deegan laughed. "Last time I opened that book I'd run out of toilet paper. Don't worry about necessity. There'll be plenty of that."

Monroe stared at the safe, secure houses as they passed by. He thought about the fact that, through his negligence, police property had been damaged. Through his partner, the negligence was being "fixed."

He regarded the man. "Why did you fix the MCL for me?"

"Why? Why not, partner-of-mine?"

"I've done nothing to help you. But you helped me."

"I wouldn't call it help. Internal Affairs is out to barbecue your butt. That requires major charges. If you'd trashed the MCL off duty, *that* would be major and, I can assure you, if you hadn't been smart enough to bust Gnarly Marlene, and came back with the MCL in that condition, you'd be dead in the water. But, because you made one scrap of paper tonight, you could argue that the damages occurred while in the line-of-duty. Then there's the juicier fact that nobody, but nobody, wants to bring grief to who did the damage."

"Why? Why is she so protected?"

"She's ultimate insurance," Deegan said, turning down a street ending in a row of boathouses. "Not because of who loves her though that, too, is significant. If you look at this town like some big poker game, she's a hole card that nobody is quite sure how to play, except maybe Gant. Gant could have played her a while ago. He should have played her and, dammit, there were a lot of people who wanted him to, but he didn't. He gave up. He gave up because as long as Gant doesn't play her, he's secure right where he is, which is where he wants to be, which is where he's always wanted to be, especially now. He's retiring in a couple of weeks and there is no way he wants his pension taken away from him."

"But why would he, or anyone, want to play her?"

"Because she has something on Zimmer that could ruin him.

74

Utterly, totally. She . . ." and Deegan went grim for a moment. "But she's not the kind to sway a grand jury. And neither am I.

"Understand me, partner-of-mine," Deegan continued. "You see before you Marty Gant's former best boy, a not-that-much-older, not-that-much-wiser version of yourself who went sour along the way. You haven't. You're perfect grand jury material. Or almost perfect. Keep your eyes open, mouth shut, and maybe you'll get your time in the sun. Me, anything I pull has to be behind the scenes. I'm never going to amount to anything. I'm the kind that gets used, stepped on, glossed over. There's no miracle, no Santa Claus, no pot of gold waiting for me at the end of the rainbow. So I do my little favors, work my deals, try to keep the job interesting."

"What would happen if you had a miracle? What if something happened and you made a big score so you could leave?"

"Big things don't happen to me," Deegan said. "It's the little shit that matters."

"But if something big happened anyway?"

Deegan became uncomfortable. "You mean, if I got rich overnight, like some uncle I never knew left all this money to me?"

Monroe thought of his wife and how she would see, in the ruins of the city, possibilities, opportunities, fortunate accidents, "miracles waiting to happen for anyone that wanted to take the first step."

He tried to put that into words. "What I'm saying is, what would happen if you found out that it was really possible to do something decent with your life and that, all along, instead of pulling all these scams, you could have made a difference?"

"I don't buy this idealistic shit," Deegan said.

"But if you did?"

"No way I ever would," Deegan said, grinning, as if proud of his understanding. "My mother got shafted by my father. She got shafted again by Wayne Zimmer. I got shafted by Gant. Everybody gets shafted. There are no miracles. Things don't get any better. They don't get any worse. If I can rake a little bit off the misery and happiness of my fellow beasts, so much the better. Take too much and the beasts turn on you. Take too little and they eat you. Anything else is bullshit.''

''But—''

''No buts. For what you're saying to be true, it would have to be a different city.''

''What if it's the same city, seen differently?''

Deegan eased the car beside a boarded-up boathouse. ''It would only go to show that I never should've been born.''

He turned off the car. ''Time to make paper.''

As Deegan pocketed the car keys, a pair of patrol cars swooped in behind them. He got out of the car, said hello to Officers Jerry ''Lad'' Ladzinski and Tony ''Bigfish'' Filmont, who came out of their cars with cans of insect repellent and cheap cologne.

''Glad to see you guys got with the program,'' Deegan said.

''Fuck the program,'' said Officer Filmont, six foot seven inches tall, with a surprisingly tiny nose and mouth, like the snout of a bluefish. ''We gonna catch some fish or catch some fleas?''

Deegan turned to Monroe. ''You hear this abuse? You hear the conditions I got to work under?''

The Lad squinted at Monroe. ''Since when is the Deeg hangin' with the prick that ratted on Claymore?''

''Since now,'' Deegan said. ''Now boys, I want you to treat my new partner with the same disgust and contempt that you reserve for all senior officers.''

The Lad picked something out of his nose. ''We don't find you disgusting, Deeg. You got us laid three times since we started on your shift.''

Deegan pointed to his ear, then pointed to Monroe. ''Boys, I haven't inculcated my partner in all the mysteries of the Deeg. So let's keep it quiet about the fringe benefits. Ya Deeg?''

''We Deeg,'' the Lad replied. ''But, seriously, Deeg, this rat is not worthy.''

PI MAN AND MR. MAYBE

"Monroe is what the Deeg used to be, before the Deeg became the Deeg," Deegan said. "Hard to believe?"

The Lad said, "Hard."

The Bigfish said, "Hard *on.*"

Deegan came around to Monroe's side of the car, reached in through the open window, patted Monroe on the head. On the second pat, Monroe moved his head back. He reached up and grabbed Deegan's wrist. Deegan withdrew the hand.

"Someday, you're going to think back on this, and remember how it was when you saw the Deeg in action."

"You're going to do something?" Monroe said.

"I'm going to do nothing. A whole lot of nothing. And nobody's going to get hurt, nobody's going to get in trouble, everybody's going to go home happy and content."

He swaggered off toward the boathouse, banged on a sagging rotting door. "Yo, Pi Man? Time to bring 'em out?"

Monroe stepped out of the car, immediately feeling the warm, briny dampness from the stagnant waters around the North Inlet.

The door to the boathouse creaked open and out staggered a thin, wispy runt of a man with matted, kinky black hair, a broken nose, five days of stubble on his cheeks, dark hiking boots on his feet, filthy tan corduroy shorts showing bruised and battered knees, an even filthier Hot Dice—Atlantic City T-shirt, and a studded and chained black leather jacket hanging down from his shoulders.

"This here," Deegan said to Monroe. "Is the Pi Man."

The Pi Man grinned and Monroe saw about five greenish-brown teeth. "Thass me," the Pi Man said. "Pi. The number, not the food."

Deegan put his arm around the leather jacket, squeezed it. "The Pi Man is one of our finest citizens. Calls himself Pi because—"

"Issa number that go on and on." The Pi Man shook, or rather vibrated, his puny head. "Thass me. Long as I gemme some crack, I go on and on."

77

"What you get, you get," Deegan said, "when you deliver the goods. How many tonight?"

"There be two, maybe three."

"There are supposed to be a dozen," Deegan said. "At least a dozen. And what's this maybe?"

The Pi Man vibrated his head again. "Not so many along and about. I be takin' what's left. Had to go out offerin' it. The maybe, well, he's a maybe."

Officer Bigfish Filmont stepped forward, raised a spray can. "Maybe I should give Pi Man a shot of Bug-a-Boo, so's he's more sure about his junkies."

"He always dissin' me, Deeg," the Pi Man complained, his voice rising to a squeal. "Muthafuck be wantin' junkies, ness time, muthafuck get his own."

In one hand, Filmont had the can one inch from Pi Man's open, running eyes. In another, he had a canister of mace. "You take that back, you pipe-sucking scum, or, I swear, I'll burn the eyes out of your skull."

"Gentlemen," Deegan said. "Let's just take what we have and be grateful. Pi Man?"

The Pi Man spun around and did what Monroe originally had thought was a stagger, back into the boathouse. Pi Man's spastic, jerky step was in fact one of the signs of a crack cocaine addiction so severe that the hyper-stimulating drug had already begun to erode the Pi Man's motor cortex.

Bigfish and the Lad followed him in, holding flashlights and spray cans of insect repellent as if they were weapons. Monroe turned to Deegan. Deegan nodded his head toward the door.

"You're the junior partner. Care to supervise?"

"What am I supervising?" Monroe asked warily.

"A raid on a shooting gallery. You heard Pi Man. There should be two or three crackheads inside. We make the arrests, Bigfish and the Lad take them back to police headquarters, we write them up, they get a bench warrant and the choice of a nice night in jail and a free meal before they go back on the street. We make the paper, which racks up statistics for the department so the department gets more funding to buy shit we don't need and the fat-assed inspectors on the fifth floor can go to drug enforcement seminars in the Bahamas."

Grunts of anger and surprise came out of the boathouse's doorway, as well a sweet, burning aroma of crack smoke and a weirdly chemical odor of something like paint.

"But this isn't a shooting gallery," Monroe said. "The department has had no complaints about addicts in a boathouse, at least, not in Inlet Park. This is one of the last decent neighborhoods in the city. We're more than a mile from any corner where an addict could buy the stuff. Crackheads don't walk any farther from their sources than they have to."

Deegan opened his hands. "That's why we have the Pi Man. He rounds them up, gets them where we want them, sets them up so they're pleasantly roasted by the time we arrive. The insect repellent is necessary, by the way. Addicts are usually infested with anything that creeps or crawls. You can't blame Bigfish and the Lad for wanting to keep as much of it out of their cars as possible."

"What about the cologne?"

"Crackheads don't bathe regularly either."

"So who wants them here?" Monroe said.

"The crackheads?" Deegan put his finger on his lips. "Oh, you just never know where undesirables will pop up."

"But you do."

"If the city can prove, through the police department, that a property has been used for sale or consumption of illicit substances, the city can seize the property in lieu of fines," Deegan said. "This particular piece of property is like hundreds in the city. It was bought by an out-of-town speculator who is just sitting on it, waiting for waterfront prices to go up. Prices were up for a while, now they're down and this particular out-of-towner isn't paying his taxes, fixing up his property or contributing to the general welfare—"

"You mean making payoffs?"

"It's all the same. Used to be, when my mom worked for him. Before he hitched himself into the state police, good old Wayne Zimmer worked in the County Solicitor's office, and my mom was his secretary. If the city wanted a piece of property, the Solicitor got a hundred dollar bill and Wayne would lose the deed, or do it over with some technicality that rendered it void. Same with wills, birth certificates, same with anything he handled. Wayne was one of Sam Claymore's little fixers, the kind who would do anything legal or illegal, just because he wanted to be useful."

What appeared to be a screaming, swearing whirlwind of arms and legs tumbled out of the boathouse door and collapsed between Monroe and Deegan. Bigfish Philmont came out, aimed the nozzle of a spray can over the pile and let fly a stream of insect spray into the addict's face.

The addict, evidently a woman, squealed as she jumped back and slammed into the wall of an adjacent boathouse.

Bigfish laughed and searched his belt. "I dropped the can of no-stink. Yo Lad," he called into the doorway. "You see a can of no-stink?"

"I don't see nothing, I don't hear nothing, I don't feel nothing, but I sure smell something disgusting," the Lad said as he kicked an older, bedraggled man out of the doorway. He threw a pair of dishwashing gloves at Bigfish, who dropped the spray can and flashlight and donned the gloves to pat their suspects down.

"What they're doing is unnecessary force," Monroe said to Deegan. "These are addicts. As long as they're high they'll cooperate."

"You can never be sure with the hardcore cases," Deegan said. "They get to a point where their brains are either on or off. On, they're revved up to maximum. Off, and they're just out there."

"Hey, another Zippo!" Bigfish exclaimed as he removed a cigarette lighter from his suspect. "You got another? These crackheads, they always got all this fire on 'em." He pocketed the lighter and became a little too friendly as he patted the woman's breasts.

She lowered her head, snagged a finger with her open mouth and bit down, hard.

"Bitch!" Bigfish yelled. He whipped back his hand, kicked her in the leg and then, as she fell, kicked her in the head. "Fucking bitch." He turned to Monroe. "You so smart about force, you go in there pull the last one out."

"Yeah," the Lad smirked. "The 'maybe'."

Monroe reached for the Lad's flashlight.

"Get your own, Rat," the Lad snapped.

Monroe turned to Deegan, who shrugged his shoulders. Monroe looked in the unmarked car and found a flashlight whose batteries were so weak the bulb glowed like a feeble ember.

He went to Deegan. "You expect me to go in there with a known offender waiting, without even a light?"

Deegan folded his arms. "The electricity was turned off a month ago," he shrugged. "I'd give you my lighter but I don't smoke."

Monroe regarded the boathouse and the open door. He saw the door's handle had been broken off recently, as if with a brick. The door was next to a larger set of padlocked wooden double doors, presumably wide enough to wheel in a boat or fishing equipment. If he could open the double doors, the glare from the streetlights would shine in.

The padlock was thick and mounted solidly enough so that it would not be easily pried off. Monroe didn't have a pick, or a pin that might open it. A course of grimy windows ran above the doors. Monroe jumped up and tried to wipe some of the filth off the panes. A bit of light came in, illuminating rows of stout metal drums or canisters. He wiped off a few more panes and saw writing on the canisters. In the dim light, he could make out one word.

Tolulene.

So *that* was the other odor. Tolulene was a highly flammable solvent used in paint applications and fiberglass manufacturing. Whoever owned this boathouse might have bought it with the hope of building or repairing small craft.

He ran to Deegan. "Call the fire department."

81

"Get this. The fucking rat smells smoke," Bigfish growled as he snapped handcuffs on the unconscious woman and hauled her toward his car.

"That boathouse is loaded with leaking tolulene canisters," Monroe said, bringing up his portable radio. "That's enough of a fire hazard without you moving crack addicts in there. One spark and the whole block could blow."

Deegan put his hand on the radio. "Seems to me, partner-of-mine, that there have been plenty of sparks already, and everything's just fine. Those assholes *smoke* that shit." He shook his head. "Nobody said anything about a fire hazard."

"Nobody said anything because nobody bothered to look," Monroe said. He thumbed his radio. "Monroe to Dispatch—"

The radio erupted in profanities, mostly mangled, obscene variations of Monroe and rat.

Deegan smiled. "The price you pay for busting your brothers. If we just mosey on along, get Pi Man and Mr. Maybe out of there, we can call it a night. Get the fire department out here and there just might be some questions you, me, Bigfish and the Lad might not want to answer."

Monroe switched channels, trying again to make an emergency call, and heard different voices jeering him.

"Your fellow officers would rather express their feelings about you than let you to use the radio," Deegan said. "Get the hint?"

Monroe switched to the fire department's private line and Deegan knocked the radio out of his hand, kicked it away and stomped the recharger unit at the bottom. "These things, they can be so fragile. Don't worry, partner-of-mine, the armory sergeant is a good buddy. He'll get this fixed up by next week."

Monroe wanted to put his fist in Deegan's smiling face. Deegan just shook his head, nodded at the looming bulk of Bigfish, who had come around with his yellow dishwashing gloves still on. Then Monroe saw a flicker of flame coming from inside the open door. He tensed. No matter how confident Deegan was, Pi Man and Mr. Maybe had to be removed from the boathouse, fast.

He went to the door, smelled the sharp, acrid smoke of smolder-ing crack-cocaine and heard Pi Man mumbling, "On and on. On and on. On and on."

He raised his voice, "This is Detective Monroe. It's time to move it out."

Pi Man made a gagging sound.

"Come on, guys," Monroe repeated. "Time to go."

A wet, gurgling, oddly pitched voice said, "*You* go, Five-Oh."

"The deal is, you're coming, or . . ." Monroe trailed.

"No no, Five-Oh."

Five-Oh was street slang for police. Monroe saw another flare of light. He stepped in and caught sight of boxes, bins, shelves of tools and the Pi Man's legs jutting from between two tolulene canisters. Monroe had his hand on one of the Pi Man's slimy ankles by the time the light went out. He pulled.

"Easy, man," the Pi Man said. "Easy on me, man." He pulled his leg away. Monroe held on until he felt the nick of a knife on his wrist. He yanked his hand back, touched blood.

The wet voice said, "Go go, Five-Oh. Deal's been changed. You go 'way, you live another day."

Monroe reached for his gun, knowing that he couldn't risk a shot, but hoping that the sight of a gun might do something.

He heard a high, moist laughter. "Five-Oh flappin' steel, but he ain't gon shoot. He shoot, we blow, blow, blow.

"On and on," the Pi Man mumbled. "On and on and on and on."

Then the long jet of a lighter flame bathed the end of a bent glass crack pipe and Monroe saw a dark shape, lean and angular, the face dim, the jaw marked with the dark ribs of a ragged scar extending from the mouth to the ear, the skin slick with sweat, mucus pouring from the nose, drool oozing from the lips, the hand holding the lighter also holding a curved, glistening fish-scaling knife.

The light went out, leaving the impurities in the tiny coal of crystalized cocaine glowing like a reddened eye, and Monroe moved. He felt the wind as the knife slashed in front of him.

"Listen to me," Monroe said, staring at the glowing coal. "This place can explode. We have to get out of here right now."

"You go," the wet voice said. "We stay, all night, all day."

"I try to get him to . . ." the Pi Man pleaded. "Reason. But he say maybe he like it here."

"No go, Five-Oh," the wet voice said. "You fry, Five-Oh."

Monroe thought fast. He could break some of the windows, let out some of the fumes and—

Then he saw the lighter spark and flare again. Mr. Maybe had the lighter in one hand, a deodorant spray can in another. He saw Mr. Maybe's face, the scars stretching from his lips becoming a ludicrous, crazed grin as he brought the nozzle of the spray can close to the flame.

Put a flame in front of an aerosol deodorant spray and you get a flame thrower that can spit out a tongue of fire two- to four-feet long.

Monroe's face was a foot from the lighter. With his free hand he reached for the lighter and slapped it away, pulling his hand back as Mr. Maybe's knife came down, snagging the edge of his sweatshirt, pulling him in, toward stink and smoke. He felt something slimy rake his cheek, struck blindly with the hand holding the gun, heard the Pi Man cry out and start to jabber curses.

Then he was alone. He moved backward and bumped into a stack of tolulene canisters, which wobbled and fell around him.

Another lighter flashed—this one with an even longer flame. Mr. Maybe was standing, a narrow, black leather-clad figure, the fish-scaling knife thrust into his belt. The lighter flame touched the end of the crack pipe, and Mr. Maybe sucked and strained as if to take in the last of his supply as the Pi Man crawled toward the back of the boathouse, toward the water.

Monroe holstered his gun as Mr. Maybe dropped the pipe and the lighter and staggered backward into a forest of rotting wooden fiberglass forms. Monroe jumped forward, collided with the Pi

Man, who was still spouting curses, grabbed him and wrestled him toward the door.

They tumbled out. Monroe put cuffs on the Pi Man. Then he went up to Bigfish Filmont and before the officer could move, snatched the flashlight out of his belt and ran back into the boathouse.

He shined the proud, white, wide beacon into the pile of fiberglass forms and was almost overwhelmed with the chemical stench of tolulene. He shined the light on the walls, on the rotting wooden floorboards and saw a glistening trail leading to the back of the boathouse. He brought the light up.

Mr. Maybe stood against the boathouse's two wing doors. The doors had been so battered by weather that they sagged on the hinges, the cracks letting in large slices of dark night sky and enough air, perhaps, to reduce but not eliminate the explosive potential of the tolulene fumes.

He held a can of liquid that he let spill on his head, on his face, letting it run and course down his neck, his sunken, grime-streaked chest, cracked and ripped black leather pants. Monroe took a step forward and Mr. Maybe brought up the lighter.

"Is it?" Mr. Maybe crowed, the slick liquid making his scarred grin more hideous and twisted. "Is it go blow? Or is it not go blow?"

Monroe couldn't afford to find out. He lunged and grabbed the slippery length of Mr. Maybe as the lighter sparked. The impact pushed them backward against the rear doors, which groaned and strained and flew apart.

Monroe felt a strange, queasy moment of freefall, then a smack of stinking, foul water in his face, in his mouth, running into his nose. Its heaviness claimed him, pulling him down into the murk where the flashlight he dropped still shone.

He wasn't aware of letting go of Mr. Maybe. The shock of hitting the water, the repulsive taste and odor of it, threw him into a panic. He coughed and flailed about, spitting out water as he discovered that the real reason that prices of waterfront property facing the North Inlet canals hadn't gone up.

Years of silt and debris and the kind of sewage that you don't want to think about had so clogged the canal that the water was no more than two feet deep. Monroe tried to stand in the muck, fell forward and managed a sitting crouch.

Then he heard a shriek that made jump again and saw Mr. Maybe tumbling in the water, his arm a rolling torch of blue flame that would not go out. The flames crawled up his arm and snaked out over the water, following the tracings of the fluid, winding back toward the glistening, glass-like rod of liquid, climbing up the liquid toward a can that was somewhere up in the boathouse filled with one too many leaking canisters of tolulene.

Monroe tried to run but the water rushed up and hit him in the face, went back into his mouth, up his nose, in his ears. This time he welcomed the violation. His eyes were closed but the awful orange light seemed to shine through him. He struggled, grasped the fact that he had to breathe and came up for air as the second explosion shot flame out of the back, collapsed the second floor and the sides of the boathouse, just as the third blast curled back the roof and shoved it into the sky.

CHAPTER

8

Kiss-Off

Sometimes you wake up and you know somebody is going to call you. Monroe was up at 8 A.M. but nobody called.

He left his sleeping fiancé in the bed, tiptoed naked down the hall to the window that faced the street. Wedged in, beside a row of garbage bags that contained most of what he loved and valued from his closets, were the water-fouled remains of his clothing from last night.

His running shoes were in the apartment house's basement, drying on the hot water heater. He had two other pairs that Ellie hadn't thrown out. The parts of his disassembled Smith & Wesson .38 special lay on a towel on the kitchen table, beside the oil and brush applicator. On another towel were his badge, his I.D., his wallet and its contents. The license, registration and credit cards had survived but the picture of Ellie and the "love bucket" card had become a mess of flaked paper.

Scabs were forming over the cuts on his wrist and his arm. His gums were still raw from last night's frantic brushing to remove the awful taste of the canal water. He had bruises on his back and arms, and an overall stiffness that only a long run would cure.

He opened the refrigerator door and decided that he wasn't hungry. He saw that the package of frankfurters he had taken out of the freezer before going to bed were defrosting gradually.

Then he sat at the kitchen table, too tired to run, too tired to go back to sleep. He heard the distant churning of fishing boats on Clam Creek and the louder, angrier roar of pleasure boats, the big floating fiberglass icebergs leaving the state marina for a day on the water.

Water. He smelled only soap on his fingers—the long shower had washed away the sulfurous, briny stench.

He closed his eyes and saw the boathouse going up again. He remembered the angry pops of the tolulene canisters exploding one by one, and the sirens of fire engines wailing in the night.

He waited for the call. He went downstairs and picked up the newspaper. He saw the headlines.

He waited until 8:45 A.M. Gant would be in his office, photographing the crack vials, pipes and other "evidence" Sergeant Deegan had procured. He dialed Gant's office line.

"You were going to call me," Monroe said.

"Thought I'd give the lovebirds a morning's sleep," Gant said. "With that baby coming, you won't be getting much more. Seen the paper?"

Monroe said he had.

"Read the paper?"

"No."

"Says the vandals were busy last night," Gant said. "They broke into and ransacked the Mobile Crime Lab *and* set fire to a boathouse, and Sergeant Deegan is up for a commendation for saving the life of a homeless individual named Simon Piper. Says here, Deegan went into the burning building to drag him out."

"The Pi Man was out before the boathouse blew. I put him out."

"Says here it was arson, but they can't be sure who did it."

"It was stupidity."

"The question you must be asking yourself is, did you make it any better. Better yet, ask yourself if you made it any worse."

"The question I'm asking, sir, is why I was hooked up with Deegan."

"Wrong question. I also hear you had some girl trouble last night."

Monroe closed his eyes, saw a face. "Why are you protecting Fatsie Morgan?"

"Ask Deegan. Ask Deegan how Fatsie introduced him to his girlfriend, and ask him why."

"Sir, I can't believe anything he tells me. I think he's just as much a menace as Reuben Claymore was. But I have to admit one thing."

"What's that?"

"He's happy."

"He's not," Gant said. "He's angry at me, and himself. He thinks he has something in common with that girl. He does, but it ain't love. When you work on a regular basis with the most disgusting, repulsive members of the criminal element, you gradually identify with these scum. You start seeing the street through their eyes and find yourself capable of any evil that they do. You eventually develop a need to believe in the unquestioned goodness of someone else. This need can be dangerous and destructive, if the person you believe in is not what you want that person to be. Or it can save your life, give you something to hope for, live for, a light in the darkness, that kind of thing."

Monroe listened and thought of how quickly he had fallen in love with Ellie. He asked, "Why do you care about him?"

"I feel sorry for him," Gant said, a tone of annoyance building in his voice. "I'm hoping you might have an effect on him."

"What kind?"

"The motivating kind. You're a challenge to him. You're trying to do what he once tried to do—play by the rules and use your smarts to make job work the way it's supposed to. Something awful happened to Deegan, something damned horrible, when he was too young to understand it. It made him give up trying to make himself or his situation any better. So now you come along, doing the same thing he once did, and he's going to have to make you give up, to prove to himself that giving up is still the smart thing."

"He says he wants to use me to get to Zimmer."

Gant's tone became urgent. "Deegan say anything else about him and Zimmer?"

"Only about him setting up shop in the Alcazar, and that I was the type who would pursuade a grand jury—"

"Deegan's just playing with you. Time for you to play with him. Ask him about the woman who's going to be your wife."

"What about her?"

"Just mention her name. Watch what happens."

"Nothing had better happen."

"If nothing happens, ask him how he really met his girlfriend."

"Sir, I'm not playing games with him. My job is—"

"Your job is saving that man's soul and persuading him that he *alone* can bring down Zimmer. He's got it. He's got everything. You know how rare it is in the life of a police officer when he has a legitimate case that can really rid the world of an abusive, criminal menace? Deegan's had one on Zimmer for a long time but he just won't take that step to do it."

"What's stopping him?"

"Love," Gant said, and hung up.

Monroe slowly put down the phone. Then he made himself a cup of instant coffee and stared out the kitchen window at the boats moving through Clam Creek. Near the kitchen phone was his wife's address book. He dialed a number on the book's first page.

The first time he had called Carlton and Annmarie Meade in West Virginia was to tell them that he had given an engagement ring to Ellie. Annmarie answered, and cried when Monroe told her, and then said she couldn't speak and hung up.

Ellie and he each made up lists of people to invite to their wedding. Monroe had invited his mother and father, knowing that neither would come for fear of running into the other. He invited his sister, knowing that she would come just so she could be a pain in the ass. He put Ellie's parents on his list.

Now he wanted to find out why they hadn't answered the invitation.

"Good morning." Carlton Meade's voice had the guarded reserve of a man who had been awake since dawn.

"Uh, hi, Dad."

"Who is this?"

"Louis Monroe. Your future son-in-law."

Flat, toneless: "Yes."

"Am I disturbing you?"

"What is it you'd like to tell me?"

"You know that Ellie and I are getting married and I was going over the list of people we'd invited and—"

"We are sorry but we will not attend."

"If it's a problem with getting up here, I can get you plane tickets—"

"I did not say that we would not be able to attend. I said that we will not attend."

In the address book was a creased Polaroid photo of a round man in a red cap and golfing jacket standing beside a shorter, rounder woman in a matching red cap and yellow raincoat. Behind them was the White House—the one in Washington, D.C., not the one in Atlantic City. Monroe searched their faces for some of the beauty he saw in his wife.

He found nothing. "Sir, I was hoping to meet you and Mrs. Meade," Monroe said. "Getting married means a lot to me, to Ellie and me. My parents split up, divorced, when I was a kid and I've always wanted . . ." He stopped himself. He couldn't admit that he always wanted to belong to a family. He just couldn't. He added, "Ellie said you always liked coming to Atlantic City."

"We found what we wanted in Atlantic City. We promised never to return. We did everything conceivable to enforce within Ellen solid Christian values. That she would run from our house was more than her mother could bear. That she would go to Atlantic City and let herself sink into sin is more than I can bear. She is not our daughter. She never was. I am not ashamed to say this. I hope you have a good life. Good-bye."

He went to the bedroom and looked for a while at his fiancé. She

91

shifted slightly in the bed, opened a sleepy eye and asked if something was wrong.

"I'm going to need another picture of you for my wallet," he said.

Anthony Andropopolous was in front of the apartment house, honking the cab's horn at precisely one o'clock. "You mind telling me what I'm in for?" he said.

"Weenies," Monroe replied. He held the defrosted package of franks in a soggy paper bag. "I want Patrocles to ride in my car with me, then I want you to follow me. If I get in any trouble, call the cops."

"Cops make trouble for other people," Andropopolous grunted. "What you doing it for yourself for?"

"Fun," Monroe said.

Andropopolous shook his head sourly. "Patrocles is not into fun. He won't leave my cab."

Monroe took a frank out of the package, tossed it into the tiny backseat of his 280Z. Patrocles leaped out of the cab, shot across to the car and dove in.

Monroe drove to Atlantic Avenue and turned down Mount Rushmore Street. He drove slowly.

When the dumpster mysteriously blocked his path, he pulled the passenger's side seat forward, he told Patrocles to "go low," the police dog command for make-yourself-small. Then he rolled down the driver's-side window, and quickly got out of his car.

The kids rushed the car. Monroe, who had deliberately dressed like a tourist, in a pale blue linen jacket, blue polo shirt and tan pants, was pleased to note that the biggest scumbag-in-training was a foot taller than he was. The scumbag swaggered up, wearing dirty black-and-gold sweatpants and a fashionably ripped gold pocket T-shirt. He held a brick in one hand and the rag in the other and before he could say "wash—" Monroe said, "No."

The kid looked incredulously at Monroe and said, "No?"

Monroe leaned back on his car, folded his arms to hide the one hand that held a fistful of hot dogs and said, "I don't need my windshield cleaned, and I don't think anybody that comes down this street needs a window cleaned, and I think you kids have better things to do than scare innocent people and rip them off on this street."

"Oh, you thinks?" The kid nodded, absorbing this information. Then he winked at the mob of smaller fry around him and hoisted the brick. "Then, first, we gonna break your face. And after we break your face, we gonna break your windshield. And maybe, after we break your windshield, we trash your car, 'less you give us what you got and get the fuck out of here."

Monroe unfolded his arms. "You want what I got?" He quickly slipped one of the hot dogs in the kid's T-shirt pocket, another in the pocket of his sweatpants. Two other menacing types standing near him received strategic hot dogs, too.

Before they could question why they were getting hot dogs, Monroe said, "Food!"

Patrocles shot out of the driver's-side window, jaws open like an alligator's. He chomped down on the hot dog in the big kid's shirt pocket, taking some of the shirt with him and then dove for the kid's sweatpants.

Monroe was impressed at how fast the kid moved, but Patrocles moved faster, biting a chunk out of the kid's pants as he ran behind the dumpster. Then the huge beast turned, demolished the trousers of the two menacing types, one of whom was trying to shinny up a lightpole; the other had dived into the dumpster.

There was no escape from Patrocles, who had played the "find the food" game as the first part of his police training in sniffing out narcotics.

The kid in the dumpster yelped and Patrocles, his jaws closing with a loud snap, poked his head up from the dumpster. He looked expectantly at Monroe, who held the remaining hot dogs overhead and asked, "Anybody else want what I got?"

When the kids didn't move, Monroe tossed a hot dog at the group standing in front of his car. They fled as if the hot dog were

93

a hand grenade. Patrocles leaped from the dumpster and gobbled the hot dog before it hit the ground.

The kids ran screaming. Monroe called out, "The next time I see any of you here, it'll be you that's eaten."

Then he said, "Easy," the command for quiet down, put his hand on Patrocles's neck, gave him a few deep scratches, said, "Good boy," and let him finish the hot dogs at his leisure.

Andropopolous pulled up. "You in any trouble?"

"Do I look like I'm in trouble?"

"You look like you are the happiest man alive."

"I am," Monroe said.

They looked at Patrocles, who was ripping the bag apart with his paws.

"He eat all those weenies?"

"I didn't see any escape."

"We'll call it even. No more money, unless you want to."

Monroe gave Andropopolous another twenty. Andropopolous sighed, accepted it under duress. Then he stuck out his hand, shook Monroe's, paused long enough to examine him as if for the first time, in the afternoon sun. "You *sure* you're a cop?"

"Positive," Monroe said.

"How come you don't arrest nobody?"

Monroe gazed down Mount Rushmore at the awning of the King Arthur Motel and said, "Sometimes you just want to be useful, you know?"

Andropopolous nodded, as if it were a secret shared between them. "I know." He beeped his horn. Patrocles jumped in his cab, and he backed out.

Monroe watched him go and drove to the police station, feeling good all over.

Deegan was late. Monroe didn't want to watch the news. He turned down the sound on the television set in the Vice Squad office and opened the Kiss-Off files.

Data on Known/Suspected Offenders were in a single huge,

wall-to-ceiling cabinet, and were surprisingly orderly, having been regularly pruned and updated by Vice Squad detectives who didn't feel like going more than a few feet from their desks.

Each file had a photo, either a black-and-white mug shot or a color TOA (Time of Arrest) Polaroid taken by the arresting officer. After an hour he found a photo of Simon Piper and someone who could have been Mr. Maybe. Both Piper and Evan James Navarro were listed as AUK—address unknown. Piper had done time on possession of low amounts of various controlled/dangerous substances. Piper was a mule, a drug runner loosely affiliated with the Inlet-based criminal organization run by Pieto Soladias. Though Piper had been arrested more than a dozen times over the last ten years, those arrests that led to convictions were made by Patrolman, then Detective, then finally Detective Sergeant Raymond Deegan.

Navarro had five outstanding bench warrants on charges of assault, illegal possession of firearms and three charges of arson. He had one previous employer: the Atlantic Natural Gas Company.

Monroe was about to close the book when his right hand, accustomed to leafing the pages, kept leafing. He saw photos of two former members of the Soladias organization with "happy faces," also known as "coke smiles"—jagged, horrifying scars made by knife cuts from the corner of the lips to the base of each ear.

He looked up from the book and saw a TV commercial with a baby in it. He found himself thinking of the baby Ellie was carrying and suddenly all the faces in the Kiss-Off book became babies, born in blood and pain and innocence. He had heard the arguments that some offenders had a genetic bent toward antisocial behavior. But when you look at them as babies, you wonder how the hell they change from someone who just wants to be fed and loved to scumbags who will take a knife and rip open somebody's mouth.

His hand stopped on a photo of a youthful, defiant, flirtatious grin, complicated by heavy eye makeup, bright red lips, darkly rouged cheeks.

Juanita Ivas's date and place of birth were unknown, as were her parents. Her last known address was Sea Park Plaza, a hotel in the north Inlet that had been converted to a low-income housing project. She was first seen on the streets about seven years before, when she was taken in on charges of vagrancy by Vice Squad Detective Raymond Deegan.

Monroe's previous partner, Darrell Pratt, had used a vagrancy charge to take underaged prostitutes off the street. The idea was to keep from starting them off as juvenile delinquents with a prostitution rap. Vagrancy was a misdeamnor offense that gave the kid a taste of a night in jail, and could be easily expunged after the kid was remanded to his or her parents or guardian.

Nita's guardian was listed as a Miss Ramona Drew, living in Sea Park Plaza. Drew's occupation was listed as "vocalist."

Detective Deegan arrested Nita Ivas two other times on prostitution charges, but then DC'd her. A DC was a dropped charge. This meant that Deegan either botched the arrest by making a procedural error, or that he dropped the charges in exchange for something.

A police detective who makes an arrest can't merely drop charges on a whim. Beside each DC was an initial. Monroe saw Gant's initials on the first; Ephrum Traile's, in purple ink, on the second.

Attached to the file was a recent clipping from *Rolling Chair,* a monthly magazine distributed free within the casino hotels. The article, "Swizzle and Sizzle," was about the top casino cocktail waitresses and mentioned Nita, among "the handful who have become favorites of entertainers and high-rolling players alike."

The article mentioned that Ivas had joined the Alcazar as part of community employment effort designed to find and place Atlantic City residents in the casino industry.

He noticed one more item in Nita Ivas's file: an annotation in

Marty Gant's low, flat handwriting. "Seen by EM for counseling." And a date.

Monroe thought about the date. Then he remembered the time of the year when his fiancée had quit being a high-class call girl and had turned to counseling working girls who wanted to give up the life.

Nita Ivas had been Ellie Meade's first client.

Deegan's dark blue sportjacket was pressed, his khaki pants creased, his yellow polo shirt without a wrinkle.

His face was swollen, puffy, and haggard. He said, "We had a fight."

He stood at the door to the Vice Squad office, addressing the battered furniture, dented lockers and flickering television set like Marc Antony telling friends, Romans and countrymen that all he wants to do is bury Caesar.

"I hate to fight and I hate to fight on the phone."

"About your girlfriend—" Monroe said.

"I don't want to talk about her." He rubbed his eyes. "I really wish this town weren't so goddamn small. Too many people know too many people. You know what I mean?"

Monroe smiled. "I think so."

Deegan pointed a finger at him. "You owe me another."

"I don't owe you anything."

"That bullshit you were doing on Mount Rushmore this afternoon. One of the kids that dog almost ate up belongs to the mayor's secretary."

"He shouldn't have been there."

"No, *you* shouldn't't've been there. But I fixed it, so you owe me."

Deegan stomped into the small lavatory and began to wash his face. "You have to check these things out *before* you fuck with them."

"Like last night? Did you bother to check that among the crackheads Pi Man rounded up was a known arsonist?"

"He is being taken care of. Both of them." He looked up, remembered. "The card. I want the card."

"It got wet," Monroe said.

"So?"

"You can't read it anymore. The purple ink is gone. Inspector Traile is off the hook," Monroe said.

"He was never on the hook. Returning it to him would have been a gesture of respect."

"He's the only one in the department who uses purple ink. The MCL was a department vehicle," Monroe said. "And I don't have any respect for people who use department property that way."

Deegan rinsed his face. "Your way was so much better." He patted his skin with a paper towel. "Anyway, you owe me." He combed back his hair. "There's something I need and you're the only person who can give it to me."

Monroe smirked. "What can you possibly want from me?"

Deegan smirked right back. "An invitation to your wedding."

CHAPTER

9

Respect

"You invited Gant, didn't you?" Deegan said as he took the Dodge out of the police parking lot.

"Ellie and I have a lot of respect for him," Monroe said. "Why do you want to go to our wedding?"

Deegan ignored the question. "Where we're going, you ask Miss Ramona about Gant. I found out from her that when Gant was a rookie on the Boardwalk, he got into this major, major scam. They used to call it baby-makes-three. Some of the whorehouse madams would tap Gant if they lost a customer and figured they could squeeze a little bit more money out of them. They'd finger some john that comes to town often to screw around, some guy that's married, successful, nice house with neighbors that can't keep their eyes off his business, and then they show up on his doorstep with a blanket and a baby.

"The baby does the crying and the cop does the negotiating," he continued. "The goal is go-away money, no more than a few hundred dollars, but you go after the guys that carry that around in their pockets.

"It sort of went out of fashion when the lawyers took over. If the kid really is the guy's, you get more out of him if you find a lawyer and sue for support. But that involves blood tests. Not that you can't find somebody to screw up tests. But with most girls using rubbers now, it faded.

"But back when Sam Claymore was the mayor, the scam was common enough. Ramona Drew used to rent the kids."

"What happened to the money?" Monroe asked.

"If you ask Gant, he'll tell you he gave it to Miss Ramona to help support the kids."

"What's wrong with that?"

"What's wrong? It's not fair to use kids that way. It's not fair to use kids anyway."

Monroe regarded Deegan. The man was a bachelor—why was he so sensitive about kids?

Deegan headed into the Inlet.

"It's a Saturday night," Monroe said. "There are more prostitutes on Pacific Avenue on Saturday night than any other night of the week. We should at least take a look at the street."

"We'll do more than that," Deegan said. "But I have a fight to win, and it's got to be in person."

He parked the Dodge beside a grassy, litter-clogged vacant lot on Mediterranean Avenue.

Monroe looked around. "I don't see anything anybody would live in."

"That's the idea," Deegan said. "We leave the car here because if we park in front of the projects we don't have a car left."

Monroe followed Deegan along an unlit, cracked, broken sidewalk toward the crumbling colonnade of what was obviously an old, grand hotel. Deegan scampered up the chipped, weathered stairs to the portico. Monroe paused on the landing and thought he saw a black jeep lurking on Mediterranean a few blocks away.

What had been in Atlantic City's golden years an airy imposing lobby was now a dim passage lit by buzzing, flickering fluorescent light tubes, walled in with cheap plywood painted a sickly institutional green, streaked with spray paint and spotted, in the corners, with urine stains and fly-flecked manure.

Monroe looked up and saw the mountings of missing smoke detectors. He passed a row of elevators that didn't work, a hall lavatory whose door hung askew. A steaming rivulet of water trickled out of the lavatory. It darkened the industrial carpet into a black, stinking stain of mildew. A rat scuttled out from the bathroom, stopping to regard him. The roaches crawling up the walls seemed to be in a hurry.

He heard noise, television sets and music played loud enough to offend, to insulate, to keep people away. He heard dogs barking, voices shrieking and speaking so fast that they seemed to be a kind of audio graffiti, markings in his ears that were as incomprehensible as the painted scrawls that covered every surface he could touch, and a few that seemed impossibly high overhead.

No one threatened him as he passed the stairwell. Three kids, no more than four years old, played with filthy, broken plastic toys. They stopped when they saw him, stared at him with dull curiosity.

"Uh, hi," Monroe said to one, a boy who covered his eyes with his hands, one of which appeared to have been crushed, a long time ago, and had set into a crippled claw.

Monroe wanted to ask him what had happened to his hand. He tried to find his voice. He opened his mouth and the boy peered at him through his fingers, then slowly backed away, up the stairs and out of sight.

"Down here," Deegan said.

Monroe continued down the dark, cacophonous tunnel of threadbare carpet. In a few places the linoleum beneath the carpet had worn through to the wood planks that had been pushed out, leaving holes through which he could see pipes, and a basement area, below.

The corridor was quiet when he came to Room 1G. Scrawled in the paint was the word: Drew. Deegan rapped politely on the door.

A young, scrawny girl with dirt on her cheeks asked them if they had an appointment. "It's Raymond."

"I see that."

"Nita hasn't left for work yet?"

"If she has I didn't see her."

She looked at Monroe. "He wants to see Ms. Drew," Deegan told her.

"She on the porch."

"Then he'll see her on the porch."

They passed through a narrow hallway that reeked of mildew. Floorboards groaned beneath them and Monroe thought he could see lights from the basement shining through, the glare seeming to push up odors of gas and rot. Children ran past them, screaming, laughing—impossibly happy, one of them grabbing a tongue of peeling, dingy green wall paper and pulling it away like dead skin.

Deegan went through what could have been a dining room, a place of soiled, stained mattresses and broken plastic toys. The walls were covered with posters of singers, musicians, pop idols in sweaty poses of power and sexual heat. He paused at a door with an Alcazar Casino Hotel Do-Not-Disturb card hanging from the knob.

"The woman you want is out on the fire escape," he said. "She might act a little crazy and that's because she is. Ask her about Gant."

Deegan knocked lightly on the door. "Nita, it's me."

Monroe heard a muffled voice tell Deegan to go fuck himself.

"I have something I want to give you."

The voice told him to fuck that, too.

Deegan opened the door and Monroe caught a sight of Nita's long, curving back. She was leaning in front of a mirror, wearing only a pair of very small lace panties. In the mirror Monroe could see her breasts.

Deegan caught Monroe staring. Monroe blushed. Deegan gave Monroe the look of two men who are suddenly equals in their admiration. He wagged a finger. "Naughty, naughty." He slipped in and shut the door.

Monroe heard them yelling at each other. He moved away from the door, back into the dining room, where the evening breeze slipping past the ragged curtains was uncharacteristically cool for steamy August. He saw a figure sitting on the fire escape. He stepped over the window sill.

She wore a billowing, blue robe, with white towels wrapped

around her hands, neck and hair, and a pair of sunglasses on her eyes.

"Miss Ramona?" Monroe said. He reached the step below her landing, stopped and leaned against the railing.

Her ruined lips were moving. Monroe caught the faint lisps of melody.

"A minute," she said. "Have to finish my song."

Monroe waited until the lips stopped moving.

"I'm done," she said. She turned her head toward him.

"Miss Ramona?"

"Is me."

Monroe perched himself uncomfortably on a railing. "I'm Detective Monroe. I work with the Vice Squad."

"Marty Gant work with that. You know him?"

"Yes," he said, inhaling the faraway odor of ocean brine which, in this ruined, run-down place, seemed pleasant, cleansing, oddly pure. "I think I do," he added.

"How's my babies?" she asked. "I can't see my babies no more, but I gots to watch 'em."

"They look fine," Monroe replied, noticing that a few kids playing on the street had stopped to look up at the fire escape.

"Gant got something for me?"

"He's not here right now."

"He always got something for the babies."

Without taking his eyes off her, Monroe took some money from his wallet and put it in her hand. She fingered it as if it were a silk scarf.

"Who brings your babies to you?"

"They find me. I find them. It no matter. You just gotta be for them. You gotta be for everyone, whether they be for you or not."

A scrawny child with chocolate-stained lips tumbled out on the fire escape. "That you, Anselmo? Say your name to the officer."

"He's a five-oh," the child spat.

"You be respectful of your elders," Miss Ramona said, feeling the boy's head with her hand. She stopped at his lips. "You messed yourself again, Anselmo? How you grow up to be President of the United States you mess yourself all the time?"

Anselmo regarded Monroe suspiciously. "I no be president," Anselmo snarled. "You can't be President 'less you rich and white. I gon' be a crackjack. Drive big car. Rip you face."

"You be dealin' in drugs you be dead, Anselmo. Some things they kill you while you still livin'."

He broke away, aimed a finger at Monroe and started shooting. He shot at the kids below the fire escape. He jumped back through the window and continued shooting.

"You gotta give 'em love," she said. "That's the easy part. Givin' hope is the hard part." She turned to the breeze. "Cold spell. I can feel a cold spell coming. I can smell it. Smell it coming. Time to close the windows. Batten them hatches."

She buried the money in her dress. Monroe also turned into the breeze and saw past the alleys, vacant lots, shadowy slums and pitted streets of the Inlet to a sparkling path of moonlight on the water.

Her lips curled. "You heard my song yet? Maybe the gentleman wants to hear a song. I used to be in the show. Old breakfast show from the Cabana Club."

Monroe remembered the name. "Wasn't that a nightclub on Missouri Avenue?"

"What you sayin' was? It still there. Las' thing I know'd they said they'd found someone new for the show and the show must go on."

Monroe was about to tell her that the Cabana Club had been torn down to make a parking garage for one of the casinos when Miss Ramona moved slightly. "The world need music. They say one day the casinos are gon' come and be legal and anybody can go inside. I say, what about the music. Time was, people come to Atlantic City for music. Why is it, only music I hear is my babies and my own."

"How many children do you have here?" Monroe asked.

"They so many. I been pickin' up stray children all my life.

Started when I was singin'. The first one, come with a song. You listen now. I'm gon' do the Cabana Club revue again. Some folks missed it. Some folks wan' see it again. Lord, it makes me feel good to sing it. You listen now."

Her lips started to move. Monroe felt the rusted metal of the fire escape digging into his rear. He shifted and Miss Ramona stopped.

"Uh, sorry," Monroe said.

Her lips moved again, though Monroe couldn't hear anything. They continued for several minutes. "There," she said. "I done my song. That the song I sung the night I found her. Done the song."

Monroe waited.

"It happen, it was in August, I remember it was hot everywhere and the Cabana Club had the air condition but it was still hot. We was drippin'. I went off the stage with the rest of the girls, down to the room behind the kitchen to change my clothes and I was to go out with them, and the mens that was waiting. There was always mens waiting after the breakfast shows, waiting around 6 o'clock in the morning."

"Tell Detective Monroe why they used to have breakfast shows, Miss Ramona," Deegan said at the window.

"They have 'em 'cause the white folks have a union and the union say they can't play more'n so many hours a night, but they have no union for the black folks, so the black folks have to play all night and into the morning."

"Mount Rushmore Street is behind the Cabana Club, right, Miss Ramona?" Deegan said. "You were out on Mount Rushmore Street at 6 o'clock?"

"Sun was up. Way up. It was later. I was hangin' out, talkin' to the boys. Tommy Fugari—he's white but they let him play with the black folks. Him and I talks some."

"You may have met him," Deegan said to Monroe. "He's paralyzed from the chest down. Sits in a wheelchair on the Boardwalk and plays the xylophone with a spoon in his mouth. Calls himself the Maestro."

"I've met him," Monroe said.

"So you're not sure exactly when you left the show," Deegan continued.

"It was when the garbage trucks were coming down. I was standin' where the back of the Cabana sort of stuck out a little, so you could hide there, but I wasn't hiding. I was having my smoke and some folks, they don't like seein' a woman have a smoke."

"So you were having your smoke."

"And them trucks make so much noise. Right away I see this man come out down Mount Rushmore, something in a bag, like one of them supermarket bags and he just stands there for a minute, holdin' the bag. I could see he was thinkin' to put the bag in with the trash, and that he was waitin', maybe he should put it in the back of the garbage truck, or maybe he should just leave it. So he leaves it in with the other trash. I just felt a pulling, a calling inside me, that I had to go out and pick up that bag. Find that was a baby. And I take the baby out, was all wrapped up in plastic so it was almost dead of suffocation anyway, but I tore that plastic off and took that baby away and she breathed and she opened her mouth and sang that song I just sung for you."

"And what did you do with the baby, Miss Ramona?"

"I did everything with it, just like I do with all my babies. I found Tommy and we took her home and we fed her some warm milk with an eye dropper and we tried to keep her warm while Tommy did some checking to see whose it was."

"And what did he find out?"

"All I knows is Officer Gant comes by and says we have to get rid of the baby fast. Tommy, he was playin' the ballroom at the Windermere and he overhear some couple on a visit, goin' hand in hand and talkin' about how they want to have a baby but they can't have one, and we all go and give it to them, and Tommy says to them you gots to promise to never come back. And ever since then, I been takin' in babies, children, whatever they age. I been takin' in, as long as they stay."

Deegan looked Monroe in the eye and said, "You ever ask Tommy Fugari how he got himself in a wheelchair? The Claymore brothers took him down by the sea, beat the living shit out of him, broke his back and just left him there so that greedy Gant could take him to the hospital."

"Don' be sassin' on Marty Gant," Miss Ramona said. "But Gant, he always bring me food and money for the babies. When the Cabana Club close and there be no work for the showgirls, the babies keep comin'."

"The baby should have been brought to a state home," Deegan said. "Gant wanted to make a buck."

"But," Monroe began, "it was for the good of the people here."

"Was it? Was it really? You still don't get it about Gant. You think you know him, but you don't."

Monroe said, "Like you know your forty-nine?" Monroe asked.

"Nita and I are . . . different." Deegan shook his head and left the window. Monroe sat and felt the breeze tickle his hair.

"A lot of folks say what should and shouldn't be," Miss Ramona went on. "Sometime it comes out right. Nita was a bad one, come here. Now she work in the casino, she give me money for the babies. What happen to Tommy . . . Tommy once said to me, he can't play, he might as well be dead. So he dead now. Everybody dead now but me and my babies."

"You ever hear from those that were adopted?" Monroe asked.

She sighed. "Ain't that many get out. The first one, she was white. White folks want white babies. The couple that take her live real far away anyway. They was hill people, from the south. They said they couldn't believe they find a baby here. Marty Gant say they had to promise never to come back."

Monroe sat up straight. "Do you . . . do you remember their names?"

"Was no time for introduction. I just brung the baby and we all say how cute she was and the woman, she don't want to look at me, she say it time to be headin' back. I was born down Charlottesville so I know from how they speak. They was hill people. West Virginia hill people."

Monroe sat on the railing for a while longer. He listened to the breeze. Finally the sounds of Deegan and Nita Ivas arguing inside grew louder. More doors slammed.

"At least let me take you to work!" Deegan shouted.

Nita snapped, "I got a ride."

"You can't be seen with him."

"I can be seen with anybody I want to."

"They always be fightin'," Miss Ramona said.

Deegan appeared at the window. "Let's move. Now."

"Miss Ramona—" Monroe began.

"You remember the babies," she said. "I be dead soon, but don' forget to be there for the babies."

"I won't," Monroe said.

Deegan ran through the apartment. Anselmo burst from the kitchen, aimed a plastic MAC-10 gun at Deegan, who shoved him away and rushed down the corridor.

"It's not nice to shoot people," Monroe called back to Anselmo, feeling like an idiot as soon as he said it. He wondered if he would be saying these things to his kid in a few years. He caught up with Deegan on the street, where a black jeep was speeding away toward the glowing towers of the casino hotels.

Deegan swore and kicked his foot against the battered curb. Then he started to walk back, silent and dejected, to their car.

Monroe saw that a mob of kids were following them, some holding rags. Deegan glanced at them. "Dumb shits, you can't change them."

"Why do you want to change them?"

"I don't. It's Nita. She has to . . . she has to understand." He paused at the car.

"Give her up, Ray," Monroe said.

"I can't," Deegan said. "She's not like the rest. She can do something with herself. She and me . . . She'll come around. She's coming with me to your wedding."

"She is?"

"She says she's busy." He got into the car. "You're still letting Gant come?"

"I respect him even more now," Monroe said.

He started the car. "You'll find out more about Gant. Then you'll see."

He rolled the car forward and then, perhaps because he was depressed, he inadvertantly stopped at a red traffic light. As soon as he did the kids who had been following them suddenly swarmed around the car. One rubbed a greasy rag over the windshield while another hoisted a brick and said, "Washer window?"

Deegan and Monroe were out of uniform. There was nothing to indicate that they were police officers and, given that Inlet kids often throw rocks, stones, and trash at police officers, and even pull guns and fire on officers, Deegan just scowled, "Look at these two-bit cheats." He reached into his pocket for some money.

Monroe recognized one of the boys from the Mount Rushmore Street gang. He opened the car door, stepped out and reached for the kid he remembered.

The kid saw Monroe, stepped back and said, "You the Dog-man!" and the group flew apart, with kids fleeing in every direction just as the light changed.

Monroe watched the last one disappear behind a ruined grocery store and then got back in the car.

"You idiot," Deegan snarled. "Those punks are armed and dangerous and they could've kicked your ass and trashed this car and maybe sprayed you with a real MAC-10 on full auto. What the hell did you think you was doing?"

"They should respect their elders," Monroe said.

10

Put on a Happy Face

Fatsie Morgan was on her corner, but this time, as they drove past the intersection of Pacific and Mount Rushmore, Deegan's eyes roved to the corner opposite the King Arthur Motel, where a woman—the mother of the drugged girl that Monroe had packed off on a bus the other night—was pacing with short, worried steps in front of a boarded-up snack bar near Mount Rushmore Street.

"What's she doing there?" Monroe said.

"She thinks she's selling."

"But they went back—"

"And now she's here."

"With—"

"Without her daughter," Deegan said firmly as he ran a red light. "Somebody thinks she's going to get taught a lesson."

"Who's that?"

Deegan beamed. "Nothing for us to worry about. Some kinds of justice, if police get involved, it looks bad. The way this is set up, pieces are going to cancel each other out."

Monroe looked back at her. "It doesn't matter how bad something looks. We have to show people on this street that we can be relied upon."

"We *can*," Deegan said. "We don't do anything and let things work themselves out."

"Who's set her up?"

Deegan pulled into an empty parking lot. "Does it matter? She was going to give her daughter to . . . to *him*. Now you see concern on her face. Fear, even. She must be in some kind of trouble. What if I told you she rolled her johns? Would you still leap to her rescue? What if I told you her pimp's pissed off that she didn't tell him about the five hundred dollars she was going to make on her daughter's hide? What if I told you there was nothing you could do to change anything?"

Monroe jumped out of the car and ran toward Mount Rushmore Street. Deegan slipped the car onto Pacific Avenue and screamed, "Asshole!" at Monroe as he drove past. Monroe watched the car zoom through two red lights. He neared the corner and became aware that Fatsie Morgan's eyes were on him when he crossed the street, making for the girl in the red coat. He groped for his portable radio, remembered that Deegan had smashed it last night and that it would be a week before it was fixed.

"What's going on?" he asked.

She glared at him, as if this was *his* fault, and turned away.

"Whatever's happening," Monroe said, "I'm here to help. You look like you're in trouble and I—"

"Fuck off!" she snapped.

Monroe took a breath. "If there's no problem then what are you doing standing here?"

"I'm here because I have a right to do what I want with my *property*."

Monroe remembered the woman's daughter and wanted to leave. But he stood by. "I told you, I want to help," Monroe said.

She looked up the street and it seemed as if something in the shadows stirred. She began to move slowly up Mount Rushmore Street.

Monroe hesitated at the corner, then followed at a distance, observing her quick, deliberate stride, that kind that street people use when they want you to keep away from them.

Monroe stopped when he heard feet behind him. He heard someone giggle. "On and on and *on!*"

He turned around and saw the narrow, shuddering silhouettes of Pi Man and Mr. Maybe. They were in black leather jackets, caps turned backward, black pants and boots. Mr. Maybe's right hand was bandaged in white filthy wrapping, holding a knife.

"Look who it is," Mr. Maybe hissed.

He picked up an empty glass whiskey bottle and threw it at Monroe. The bottle hit the side of a dumpster and shattered.

"You might want to get on out of here," Pi Man said.

Mr. Maybe shook his head. "Maybe he want to stay. Maybe he wants to put on a happy face."

"Maybe not," Monroe said. He let his hands fall loosely to his sides.

The knife indicated deadly force and gave Monroe the legal right to use what Sergeant Vinnie Almagro called the Blue Cross, Blue Shield and Major Medical unarmed combat techniques. When properly applied, these techniques "insured" the victim a long, restful stay in Atlantic City General Hospital.

Monroe feinted back and, at the last second, decided not to send Mr. Maybe into the hospital. As a police officer, he was required by law to use only enough force to subdue and apprehend, not injure, the suspect. So he lightly sidekicked him in the solar plexus. The kick knocked Mr. Maybe backward into a doorway. Monroe then spun around to face the Pi Man, who was wobbling toward him with a smaller switchblade sticking forward in his hand.

Monroe didn't have time to go for his gun. The Pi Man lunged and Monroe kicked the hand holding the knife, hitting it hard with the edge of his shoe. The kick didn't break the Pi Man's grip on the knife but it knocked him sideways. Monroe moved in, put both hands on the Pi Man's arm and shoved the knife, the hand and the arm, and the rest of the Pi Man into the side of the doorway. The knife pried itself out from the Pi Man's fist and dropped to the ground.

Monroe was about to pick up the knife when he heard a shoe scrape inside the doorway. Mr. Maybe was now on his feet, head low, crouching, arms jabbing and swinging as he charged.

You pray for attacks like this when you train for hours and hours in unarmed combat. Monroe moved to the side, stuck his left leg out and swept it back, tripping Mr. Maybe, whose scarred happy face smacked wetly into the asphalt.

Then the Pi Man's studded leather sleeve came around, streaked across Monroe's face, rolled down to choke his throat and pull him down. Monroe struggled to pry his fingers under the sleeve. Then he saw the knife come up, aimed at his gut. Monroe stuck out one arm, attempting to redirect the knife, but it was coming in too strong. The blade was inches from Monroe's gut when he caught the aroma of bathroom deodorant. Then the knife stopped and Monroe heard the Pi Man grunt as a huge, white hand clamped around his wrist. The grunt became a scream as another equally huge hand clamped around the Pi Man's fist and yanked it back, making a brief snap of breaking bone. The Pi Man screamed as the great white hands pulled on the wrist. Then he howled from a blow so strong that it sent both the Pi Man and Monroe stumbling forward. Monroe twisted and was on his feet in time to see the Pi Man describe an arc that ended some ten feet away, with the Pi Man's head hitting the asphalt with a loud pop.

Monroe saw the immense rounded shape step in front of him. Mr. Maybe raised his head from the ground and before he could move away, the heel of Fatsie Morgan's flat black shoe came down on his bandaged hand.

He howled as she raised her the foot and brought it down again. He made a horrible gargling sound as he pulled his shattered hand away, rising up on his knees when she planted a kick so deep in his stomach that it lifted him backward and sent him tumbling into a row of plastic garbage cans.

"My hand," Mr. Maybe wailed. "You . . . killed it. You killed my hand!"

Morgan took a step toward him. He tried to hide among the garbage cans but Fatsie Morgan was on him. She grabbed the back of his jacket, raised him up, slammed him head first into a brick wall, and then let him drop.

He didn't move. She turned, saw the whimpering Pi Man clutching his broken wrist. He wasn't moving much, either.

She turned around, grabbed the Pi Man and Mr. Maybe by their jackets and began to drag them toward Pacific Avenue.

"Uh, hi," Monroe said.

She peered down at him.

Monroe said, "Wait," but she kept going. He looked for the mother but she was gone. He ran to catch up with Morgan.

"You can leave those guys with me," he said.

She crossed Pacific Avenue with a slow dignity, as if she owned it.

Monroe put his foot into the street and a bus lumbered by, followed by a taxi and a jitney. He scurried after her. "I'm going to arrest these guys. I want you to corroborate the assault."

She ignored him and kept walking.

"If you don't help me," Monroe said, "I can't make a case."

She said, "They don' need no case."

"But I do," Monroe said, almost running to keep up with her. "And I need as many witnesses as possible or those guys will walk."

"Walk," she said. "They can still do that."

"But if you help me arrest them—"

"I don't help people," she said, not looking at him.

"You helped me!" Monroe said.

She said, "You were in my way." She walked down a narrow alley beside the King Arthur Motel.

"Where are you taking them?" Monroe called to her.

"Rowing."

He took a step. She turned and said, "Don't."

"Don't what?"

"Follow me."

"Why?"

She turned, stopped him dead with a gaze of wrath and power, "You want to go rowing, too?"

He hesitated, then he remembered that the mother was still somewhere near Mount Rushmore. He told himself that she could still be in danger and that the reason that he was running back across the street was not that he was terrified of a hideous old, fat and powerful woman.

Back on Mount Rushmore, it was as if the mother had become absorbed by shadows. The backdoors, dumpsters, piles of trash and debris stood silent, impenetrable. A sudden breeze blew trash around his legs. Monroe banged on doors, upended boxes, shoved dumpsters aside, began to check the doorways.

He stood motionless as the street became darker. Then he felt the unmistakable chill of a kiss against his neck. He turned around, saw nothing.

"Where are you?" He turned around, ran up and down the street again. Once, he thought he heard her laughter.

He glared at the dark, empty street. He searched the doorways again. He touched his neck where he had felt the kiss.

Then he looked at his watch and realized he'd better get some sleep. Five hours from now Ellie would be waiting for him in a church and he'd better be awake for the occasion.

11

Like a Clam

The party immediately following Sunday's wedding of Ellen Meade, resplendent in her final month of pregnancy, and Vice Squad Detective Louis Monroe was held in a back room at the Ancient Mariner Bar & Grille, a shot-and-beer joint just off the Boardwalk at Utah Avenue.

Captain Marty Gant, Commander of the Atlantic City Police Department's Vice Squad, began his toast to the bride and groom by comparing Atlantic City to a giant clam.

"Correct me if I'm wrong, ladies and gentlemen," said Gant, his squashed nose ruddier from having consumed his fourth Irish blitz (a mug of Harp lager spiked with a shot of Jameson's whiskey), "but on some days, I get the feeling, that I am, along with the illustrious bride and groom, an inhabitant of one vast, big, stupid clam that just stays put, going nowhere, doing nothing, while the ocean flows itself in, and the ocean flows itself out, and—correct me if I'm wrong ladies and gentlemen—isn't it a fact that with the exception of the illustrious bride and groom, the shit does definitely stay?"

"Absolutely," said Clark Wells, a blackjack dealer at the Alcazar.

"Nahhhh, some things just be's that way!" roared Monroe's former partner, Soon-to-be-Sergeant Darrell Pratt, who was still in his wheelchair, having taken three bullets below the belt. The most of the small crowd agreed that the shit definitely stayed.

"As a professional," wheezed Jimmie "the Geek" Doochay, a

homeless man in a rented black tuxedo, "I resent the comparison."

Ellie kissed Doochay on the ear. Monroe put down a bottle of cheap champagne and blurted, "But if the shit stays there long enough, it turns into a pearl."

Everyone but Doochay booed him. Monroe's sister Lisa, in a high-necked blouse and ankle-length blue cotton granny dress, blushed and retired to the ladies' room.

"Now I do believe that you believe that," Gant said, hoisting his fifth Irish blitz at Monroe. "I want you to find me one. Find me one of them pearls. 'Cause every time I'm down there, all I see is lot of dead clams, garbage and some gooey, nasty-ass pollution-type foam riding above the water which is so disgusting it makes me queasy to think about it."

He raised the mug, slopping gooey, nasty-ass pollution-type whiskey-soaked beer foam over the edge. "To a couple of pearls if there ever was one, Mr. and Mrs. Louis Monroe!"

Monroe once again kissed his bride, a lingering, slurping movie kiss that brought another round of cheers. Ellie started laughing and was the first to break away. Monroe then caught his breath and looked back on the narrow room filled with friends: his friends, her friends—people who had little more in common than the fact that they knew the bride and groom, and were willing to forget about scams and schemes. Everybody wanted to have a good time.

Or so he thought.

Dan Raleigh strutted up in a sky blue suit, pink shirt and tropically hued tie. At his side was Nita Ivas in flaming red lipstick, her hair permed into dark shoulder-length spirals cascading toward a strapless skin-tight black spandex cocktail dress cut to a point about two inches above her navel.

"Uh, um, hi," Monroe said.

She waved her fingers, then came toward him, touched his neck, ran the hand down the side of his white Italian cut suit, along his chest, stopping somewhere below his waist as she brushed his lips with hers.

Monroe backed away.

"I don't get to kiss the groom?" she whined.

He looked at her, found his eyes drawn to her breasts and the breathtaking sweep of her hips, and then he remembered that this was his wedding and that he shouldn't be looking this way at anyone but his wife.

"Uh huh," he said, more to himself that her.

She planted a kiss below his ear.

"I can't believe this!" Ellie shouted behind them, opening her arms. "You look *smashing!*" They hugged, Nita patting her hand on Ellie's stomach. "Oh Louis, this is so wild. Remember the girl on the beach I told you about—"

"We've met," Monroe said.

"You got somebody looking after you," Nita said. "I got somebody looking after me. There are a lot of somebodies is town, you know?"

"This is so wonderful!" Ellie exclaimed.

Raleigh elbowed Monroe. "So, how about a room at the Alcazar for a honeymoon? I'll even send you a bill."

"We couldn't afford to pay it," Monroe said.

"But it's nice of you to offer," Ellie said. Then, as if on a signal, Nita, claiming that they *must* talk, moved her away.

"Your little lady is a gold mine," Raleigh said.

Monroe agreed.

Raleigh chimed in. "In more ways than one. You thought much about the future?"

"I think about it all the time."

"Aside from whatever reasons you had for marrying her, in the area of customer relations, Ellie could be a very valuable—"

"You'd better shut it off right here, Dan. We're going to have a family."

"Have a great big happy family then," Raleigh said. "And when you want to pay the bills, we set Ellie up as a private contractor, which means she only needs a fourth-class license. The DGE doesn't investigate fourth-class license applications because, when gambling was legalized, the casino industry had to give work to New Jersey construction companies, suppliers, vendors and private contractors, half of which were either directly linked to the mob, or used labor unions that were under mob control. So they came up with the fourth-class license and it's worked wonderfully. You'd be surprised—hell, astonished, at some of the people we got working for us under a fourth-class license."

"I'd be astonished if Ellie did anything as dumb as that," Monroe said.

"You just got married," Raleigh boomed, pounding Monroe on the back. "Prepare yourself to astonished, kiddo."

Monroe slipped away, grabbed a bottle of champagne, took a swig from the bottle and leaned against the jukebox. He got down a few gulps when his sister Lisa marched up to him. "I don't like any of these people," she said.

Monroe took in his sister's severe face, saw the wrinkles around her eyes and mouth, wanted to tell her not to be so damned serious, to go to the service bar, pop the top off a bottle of champagne and chug the stuff, as he had been doing for the last half hour or so. He wanted to drop his arm around his sister and hug her, but Lisa didn't like to be touched.

"Let's see," Monroe began. "We got some top-shelf whores, some bottom-shelf cops, a casino executive and a blackjack dealer and at least one guy that's been living under the Boardwalk going on twenty years. What's there not to like?"

"That Ivas woman *says* she's an entertainer."

"So?"

"So she isn't dressed for this affair. This one . . . we see them in New York all the time. They dress a certain way because they think that men will do what they want, but men aren't so stupid."

Monroe took a long gulp from the champagne bottle and said, "They are."

Lisa sniffed. "You're lucky Mom was too sick to travel. She would have . . . I don't know *what* she would have done."

"Mom hasn't been sick in fifteen years," Monroe said. "I think it's about Ellie being pregnant."

"She just didn't want to risk running into Pop," Lisa said. "If you had assured her that he wasn't coming, she would have been here."

"I couldn't assure her because our parents have the right to be here, even if they can't stand each other."

"Some family we got," Lisa said.

"Some family we both got," Monroe said, putting his arm around Lisa. "Now you loosen up and relax, okay? It's been a long time since you left—"

"Since I was raped, you mean."

Monroe walked her over to a less noisy corner of the room. "Lisa, the reason I wanted you down here was so you could sing at my wedding and we could say good-bye to our lousy childhood. If I could I'd change it all, come up with a completely different life for you and me, in which there was no divorce, no rape, no jail for Pop. So I'm doing that now. Every once in a while, you have to move on, and I'm moving on."

"Moving in is more like it. Honestly, Louis, what attracted you to this woman?"

Monroe gazed at his wife who was talking rapidly with Nita Ivas. "She has a nice smile. The real kind. And she has a head on her shoulders and, unlike most people in this town, she likes the town for what it is and wants to make it better. With all the shit that spins around, she's has a way of being above it, like she's—" He was about to say innocent and stopped himself.

"You had to go and marry a native?"

"She's from West Virginia," Monroe said, hoping his face didn't betray his confusion. "She came here because she wanted to get a job as a dancer in the shows and got sidetracked for a few years. Then she got pregnant and decided to marry me."

"You make it sound so easy."

"Some things are. I find it kind of nice, actually."

"I hope you do," Lisa said. "I find it all embarrassing."

"She's decent, Lisa. If it makes you feel any better, Ellie's parents didn't come either. She has problems on her side, too, I guess."

"I noticed."

Monroe changed the subject. "Everybody liked what you sang at the wedding."

"Do you have a name yet?"

He paused. "A name? My name—"

"For your daughter! You know it's a daughter, right?"

Monroe blinked, remembered tears falling down his face as he saw the swimming image of the child in Ellie's womb on a video screen. "Yeah. We did the ultra-something. Ultrasound. They said it was a girl. Gave us a picture of her in there."

"But you don't have a name."

Monroe shrugged. "One'll suggest itself. I mean, we'll come up with something."

"That's what Mom and Pop did and look what they did? L-names! Lisa and Louis. You talk about boring! Important people, when they see a name like Lisa, they assume automatically that you're from the suburbs. They look at that on my pictures and resumé and you'd be surprised the work I don't get because I have such a mediocre name. You had better come up with a name, and it had better not begin with an L."

Monroe saw Darrell Pratt on the other side of the dance floor and said, "Later."

"Who'd've thought," Pratt said, "I just gave the best bride to the best man and now I got nothing left."

"You got plenty left, Darrell," Monroe said, noticing, as he dropped his second bottle of champagne into the trash, how Pratt's hugely muscled chest had shrunken since he was shot.

"What I got is a desk job, coming down, nice and simple," Pratt said, an open bottle of Johnny Walker Red tucked between his thighs. "I'm not exactly admiring my good fortune. But I can use the pay. Five kids, I can use it."

Pratt put the bottle to his lips, demonstrated from the way the whiskey went down that a man recovering from a bullet in his belly feels even *more* pain when he chugs the strong stuff, but some men are born to feel pain and that means you drink like you can't get enough of it.

Pratt dropped the bottle and said, "I do love it when it burns."

"Darrell," Monroe began, "when you were on Pacific Avenue, why did you stay away from Fatsie Morgan?"

"Politics," Pratt said.

"What does that mean?"

"It means that some people you see and some people you don't see. She was invisible to me, hear?"

Monroe looked at his former partner, the one person he thought he could trust, and saw that the man was lying to him. "Darrell, you never used to care about politics."

"Well, I care now. The desk I want to sit at is public information. Public information means interfacing with the public, and that means paying attention to politics."

Monroe saw Pratt's body and the withered, shrunken, once mighty muscles that had grown soft. Pratt had been feared and admired in the department, despite his open contempt for the department's bureaucracy, the courts, prosecutors and prisons.

His hands were still strong, powerful, the knuckles scarred and knotty from so many fights.

But his eyes were soft, wet, worried, and he spoke in whispers. Monroe had never, ever heard Pratt whisper. He never thought the man was capable of lowering his voice.

"You listen up to me, Lou-boy. I been nine years givin' bad days to pimps and drug monkeys, and that's nine years too long. You take a bullet, you take three bullets as me, you start understanding the street gonna be out there forever and you ain't. So, when the Chief comes to you, fucking big Chief of Police himself, in the flesh, comes up to your hospital bed with all his aides and flunkies scurrying around him like flies on fish gut, and the Chief says the mayor is sick and tired getting his ass kicked over him bein' a racist 'cause there ain't enough black folks in the upper ranks of the department, says to me he need someone up front to make the department look like it's equal opportunity time, someone who took three bullets and therefore can say he served his time on the street—I say, I give it a try, Mr. Chief. And then he says, 'Soon as you get the chance, I want you to talk to that boy of yours, that boy who was your partner, that Monroe boy. Find out who he and his wife are really working for and tell me.' "

Monroe leaned back, surveyed the party. "You tell the Chief I'm working for anybody that wants to take a walk on the Boardwalk, or Pacific Avenue, or any street in this city, at any time of the night or day, without getting robbed, mugged or scammed," Monroe said. "And you tell the Chief if he has any more questions, he can ask me direct."

"You know the Chief don't do nothing direct. If it's sensitive, or if it's politics, he don't want it to look like it's coming from him."

"Then tell the Chief that Ellie and I are working for . . . the baby. The baby's the boss."

"I'll tell him that, Lou," Pratt promised, not at all at ease.

Monroe was into his third bottle of champagne when Clark Wells, a casino dealer who Monroe had met when he worked undercover in the Alcazar, knocked him gently in the ribs. "I'm looking at one stewed oyster," he said.

Monroe took another swig from the champagne bottle. "Ellie's not supposed to drink, with the baby in her, so I figure . . . I figure I can do for the both of us."

Monroe dropped the champagne bottle and was amazed that it didn't break. He watched it roll on its side, away from the jukebox, under the buffet table of salads and snacks. No champagne came out of the bottle, which meant that Monroe had drunk most, if not all of it.

He smiled. He felt proud. He felt good. He looked at his wife. His world was growing stronger. His wife was dancing with Nita Ivas to some song about french fries and what was it, oh God, it was

123

Under the boardwalk
Down by the sea
On a blanket and my baby
That's where you'll find me.

That was the best beach song ever written, even if it was written about Coney Island.

Ellie caught his eye and blew him a kiss. Then she tilted her head toward the entrance as Nita stepped back and ducked into the lavatory.

Sergeant Raymond Deegan stood at the entrance to the room, giving him the eye. He was wearing a black iridescent sport coat, gray T-shirt, baggy beige pants and black canvas loafers, worn without socks.

He staggered up to Monroe. "Partner-of-mine!"

"I don't think you were invited," Monroe said.

Deegan's eyes were on the dance floor. "I came to say hello."

"Nita's got a date," Monroe said, taking a small sip from the neck of a bottle of champagne.

"He isn't a date. He's a beard."

"A beard."

"A substitute for another man, so you don't think she's going with the guy she's going with."

"You?"

Deegan seethed. "No. Not me."

"Well," Monroe shrugged. "It must be over."

"It's just beginning. Pi Man and this punk named Navarro—"

"Mr. Maybe."

"They washed up on the Longport beach this morning. Dead. I figured you were too busy to listen to the news."

Monroe said, "I'm thinking about dancing with my wife right now."

"Go dance. First, tell me where Nita's hiding."

Monroe stared into his eyes. "I don't want any trouble, part-

124

ner-of-mine. I want you to do what everybody wants me to do."

"Nothing?"

"Nothing."

"Too late for that," Deegan said. "Either she comes back to me or I bust her."

"What are you going to charge her with?" Monroe said.

"Whatever appeals to me."

"It would appeal to me if you and her took it outside."

"You want to try to stop me, don't you?" Deegan smirked. "You want to save her ass."

Monroe shook his head. "I want to dance with my wife."

Deegan glowered at Raleigh. "This morning I got a message from one of the Alcazar security goons, a Mr. Hadruna, that I'm no longer needed there. She's with Zimmer now. She's sucking up to him, trying to play him."

"Zimmer?" Monroe blurted. "I don't want to hear about him. The guy wasn't invited."

Deegan looked down at him. "What're you, five feet tall?"

Monroe counted to ten. "Five two."

"Your wife's taller'n' you are. Wider, too. She's all set to drop, ain't she?"

Nita Ivas emerged from the washroom. "Look, Sergeant-of-mine," Monroe said, "you want to say hello, say it. But don't try to piss me off. You could succeed."

"I already have," Deegan grinned. He stomped across the dance floor, and in doing so shoved Lisa Monroe so hard she slammed against the wall and fell to the floor.

Nita rushed up and seemed to touch Deegan's chest and his crotch, and he went flying backward toward the dance floor, falling flat on his ass, one hand in his crotch, another holding his throat. He looked up and saw Marty Gant, hands on his hips, staring down at him.

"You don't want to embarrass me or the department, now, do you, son?" Gant said.

Deegan stumbled to his feet, coughed, sputtered. "You *know* why I'm here—"

"I'll be ready for an explanation in my office, tomorrow morning, 8:30 sharp. Until then, I don't think I have to advise you to get your shiny pants out of this establishment."

Deegan staggered to his feet, glared at Nita Ivas and lunged for her, but he never quite reached her. She smacked him across the face with her purse and he collapsed instead, falling in on himself, then back on down, his head bouncing on on the dance floor.

Gant picked Deegan up by his collar, hoisted him over his shoulder, took him to the door and tossed him out.

Louis Monroe picked up his sister. She was blushing, embarrassed, flustered, "These are your friends? I—I want to go home. Is there a late bus or train out of here?"

"Sure there is," Ellie said. "But don't you go running out just yet. You're supposed to be spending the night. We laid out the couch for you."

Nita stared at Lisa Monroe with pity. "So what you want to run away for?"

She shuddered. "I'm sorry, but, I just can't. You . . ." She couldn't face Nita, and turned to Ellie. "I'm sorry, this is your wedding and all, but, I really . . ."

Ellie put her arms around her. "Please stay with us."

"On behalf of the department," Marty Gant began, "I want to apologize, Ms. Monroe. I also want to tell you that we all enjoyed hearing you sing for us at the ceremony."

Lisa shook her head. "I thought I could sing. I'm graduating from Julliard next year and . . . then I heard her." She pointed at Nita. "She was doing *Ave Maria* in the bathroom and I . . ." A tear trickled from her eye. "I should never have come back. I'm sorry. I'm sorry for all of this."

"I wouldn't be sorry," Marty Gant said, become courtly and polite. "The man had it coming and, I might add, assault charges are not necessary. I am capable of addressing the problem and seeing that Sergeant Deegan is adequately disciplined."

Lisa said she didn't care what was done to Deegan. She just wanted to leave. "I'm so sorry. I just can't . . . will somebody tell me why *they* make us do this? Why do women have to fight back?"

"Because," Nita Ivas said, "there's no time to get somebody to do it for us."

Gant nodded at her, and Monroe saw something familiar passing between them. "I was powerfully impressed with your technique, Ms. Ivas. Was it perhaps a sword hand to the groin with a rising punch to the solar plexus?"

She gave him a seductive wink. "I don't give nothing away for free."

Gant's face went red. "Well, now. I was just wondering . . ."

An hour later Monroe was spectacularly drunk, sprawled against the jukebox with his fifth bottle of champagne in his hand. Marty Gant had driven Lisa to the train station. Most everyone had left except for Ellie and her friends, and Clark Wells, who was doing serious damage to the anchovies.

"You can't understand the pleasure of eating something that is going to totally, positively, completely wreck your breath for three hours," Wells said. "When we come on shift, the shift manager, Major Domo, sniffs our breath to make sure we don't burn the customers. I have to come up to him and go *hah* right in his nose. Domo's got colds all the time. I pity the guy because it's all for show. A player who's ahead at blackjack will stick with a dealer if the dealer's got five-days body odor and an eyeball hanging out, as long as the player stays ahead."

Wells finished the bowl. Among casino dealers, he was known as a mechanic, a person adept at intimidation, false shuffles, and dealing from below the top card, so that he could make gamblers lose, or win.

"The guy that got decked," he asked, licking his fingers. "One of yours, wasn't he?"

"I don't want to talk about him," Monroe said, yawning.

"It's okay. I know who he is," Wells said. "At the other casino hotels, I think it's the Savoy and the Shamrock, they call him the

Trashman. The players that want a street jizzy, you know, a real cheap-shit whore, they call him. He either brings the girl in, or takes them out. And they trust them, because he's a cop."

"I don't want to hear about it," Monroe said.

"It's not just players," Wells continued. "I could never understand it, but there seems to be a crowd that likes things as awful as they can get them. Real low-down. I've heard that he's picked up trash for the big players. I guess being rich and successful gets boring after a while, so you try to pretend that you're a poor, broken-down, dirtball loser."

"Clark, this is my wedding. All I want to do is—"

"Bust him? I know somebody, not a player, but . . . middle management at the Alcazar. He's slightly peeved that the Trashman has been leaning on him to truck his street jizzies into the Alcazar's lounges. He might be willing to help you set him up."

"Clark, some other time—"

"Sure. Why do you want to fuck around with a loser?" Wells continued. "Listen, I didn't bring you a gift, so some Saturday night at around 11:30, when it's real busy, you come to my table, and I'll make sure you win. Not a lot of money, but enough to make you and Ellie and the baby happy for a while. Least I can do for a friend."

Monroe rubbed his nose. "Don't."

"It would feel really good," Wells said. "I mean, what else am I going to give you? You want to bust Nita? She used to be down in the Topkapi lounge, close enough for the slot junkies to barf on her. The minute the state police set up on the nineteenth floor, she's promoted to the private lounge they have up there, the Alhambra. Which means she has big juice, I mean big juice, either with management or a player." Wells paused. "I could find out."

"You'll excuse me," Monroe said to Wells, "but I'm about to make a damned fool of myself."

He pulled himself to his feet, staggered toward his wife, opened his arms, said, "Let's dance," fell on his face and passed out.

chapter 12

The Extraterrestrial

They took Monday off. They didn't talk about the wedding, Atlantic City, relatives, friends or enemies. Monroe disconnected the telephone and let the mail and the newspaper sit in the box on the creaky subdivided guesthouse's first-floor landing.

It was one of the best days of Monroe's life. On Tuesday, Monroe made the mistake of putting the phone back on. It rang a half an hour later. "Dangerous" Delores Lipatto, so-called because as administrative assistant to the five inspectors who ran the department she had the ability to so thoroughly screw around with an officer's paycheck, paperwork and other important records, telephoned him to tell him of an OTR in his mailbox.

An OTR was an official Order to Report, a commandment requiring an officer to be someplace at a specific time. That time was 3 P.M., an hour away. The place was the office of Inspector Ephrum Traile.

"I think I have to do this," Monroe said to his wife.

She giggled. "Then do it."

She was naked, on her side, on the bed, her middle so preposterously large that when she giggled it stayed firm.

"What's so funny?" Monroe asked.

"You look so serious."

"I have a feeling it has to do with . . . your friend, Nita Ivas."

"My word, she's grown up so gorgeous. And tough, too."

"You knew her all these years?"

"I wouldn't say I knew her. We had a way of running into each other, mostly in the casinos. It was nothing planned, or it didn't seem to be. We got to talking. She never said much about her life, but I could tell where she was coming from—one of those places where any way out is better than where you are. I used to sit and think to myself, after I'd seen her, that if I could do something decent with my life someday, I'd find girls like her and show them a better way of getting what they want. She showed me that I could do that. She was my first success.

"I can't take credit for getting her her job. That Deegan character knew people at the Alcazar. They hired her under a fourth-class vendor/private contractor license, so there wouldn't be a problem about her background. You look at her now, and you can be sure she's made it right."

"Have any idea why she would get promoted last week to the high-roller lounge?" Monroe asked.

"Because she's probably the best person for the job," Ellie said. "That's one of the things I love about Atlantic City: the way, all of a sudden, people can change, or things can happen to them to make them change. I remember my folks telling me that was why they came here. I guess that was why I had to come here, too."

"You told me they were on one last fling before you were born," Monroe said.

She touched her face, caught her reflection in the bedroom mirror. "People need a place where they can pretend to be something else. They want to believe that if they pretend hard enough, whatever they want to happen will happen. One of my clients used to say that the key to this city was not the beach or the Boardwalk, but in the rolling chairs. You could ride on a rolling chair and dream that you were the kind of person who deserved the rich life."

She shifted position again on the bed, holding her middle. "She just gave me a little tap, right there."

"I still have a month to figure out how I'm going to pay for her college," Monroe said.

"I wouldn't worry," Ellie said. "Your friend Raleigh was talking to me. You know there just might be a job for me in marketing at the Alcazar? Part-time, choose my own hours, good pay and benefits, and a chance to do what I've always wanted to do, make the casino industry treat *everybody* right, not just gamblers."

"Ellie—"

"I know. You'd rather be the big strong man and earn the money. But isn't it just great that I have this opportunity? I think it was fate that I left home and came here, and I think it was fate that I sunk low enough so that I could become part of a system that only wanted to drain money out of rich high-rollers. And now I think it's fate that I can get into the system and make it work better."

"Ellie, the casinos don't want to change. They just want to make as much money as they possibly can."

"And half of them are bankrupt or close to it, so they're going to do something different now, and maybe I can have a say in that."

She saw his expression.

"Oh, Louis, it's just a dream. Nita used to tell me, when you're on the bottom and everybody seems way ahead or above you, all you can do that's any fun is dream. She'd say, the real criminals are those that take your dreams away."

Monroe sat on the bed. "Ellie, Nita Ivas might be someone you helped, but I have a feeling she . . ." He paused when he remembered that a feeling was all he had, a feeling that Nita Ivas wasn't what she seemed to be.

"That she needs more help? We all do. She told me what her dream was." Ellie grinned, assuming a dramatic pose on the bed. "She wants to be a singer."

"That's a nice dream," Monroe said, "but if she's involved with something illegal . . ."

"Oh, just lay off Nita for a while. There are more than enough crooks to keep you busy. I want you to promise me that you'll let her make her own mistakes, and learn from them."

"But if she is breaking the law, and I don't go after her, that can be used against me."

"Louis, *everything* you do can be used for you, or against you. It all depends on who's doing the using. Marty Gant will protect you. You can depend on him."

Monroe closed the bedroom door and started the shower going, and had a feeling that—about some things—the person that you love can be dead wrong.

The Foambutts were five administrative inspectors who ranked directly below the Chief of Police. They had a deluxe suite of offices on the fifth floor of the big, black, magnificently ugly cube of Atlantic City's City Hall. These offices were the most lavish in the building, far more elaborate and impressive than the mayor's or the Chief's, whose sixth floor offices were seen almost daily by reporters and power-brokers from Trenton. Therefore, they had to be modest and even austere, with the hope that the reporters and power-brokers would believe that tax money that would normally go to decorating these offices was instead being spent on projects that would eventually result in a city free of slums and crime.

The Foambutts were so-named because, with one exception, they had very fat behinds, acquired from years of sitting on plush, foam-rubber cushioned chairs. It was rumored among the uniformed men that the Foambutts would gather in the deluxe fifth-floor lavatory (installed by a mob-linked developer as a way of saying "thank you" after a joint police/Bureau of Codes and Licenses investigation found no evidence that the developer had been negligent in permitting raw sewage from luxury condos to gush directly into the ecologically fragile bay between the city and the mainland) where, in the midst of so much polished brass and Italian marble, the Foambutts would drop their pants and use yard sticks to determine who had the largest butt, and most capacious asshole.

The exceptional Foambutt was Inspector Ephrum Traile, the Extraterrestrial, who by right shouldn't be called a Foambutt at all.

Unlike the other inspectors, whose paunches, summertime yachting stories and wintertime vacation stories seemed adequate, justifiable compensation for a bureaucratic life well-lived, Traile was rail-thin, an ascetic, a St. Anthony immune to every temptation.

Monroe arrived at the Foambutt floor, and went to the glassed-in reception area where Dangerous Delores Lipatto labored over a computer keyboard.

"He's in," she murmured.

Monroe saw that she didn't look up at him.

"And you shouldn't keep him waiting."

Monroe scurried past her into Foambutt City, a cluster of walnut-paneled offices where colorfully dressed secretaries applied cruel attention to beige computers and humming office machines. Men and women in blandly dark suits strode purposefully past him. The soft, soundless, dark blue carpeting, the plush, slightly worn upholstered waiting areas, the scuffed tables with thumbed magazines about boating, hunting and exotic guns, suggested the mood of an old, prosperous construction company.

The Extraterrestrial's office was past these, a simple black walnut paneled door set in a blank white wall. He had no secretary, no waiting area, no glass wall to give the illusion of open government.

Monroe tapped the door and it swung open into a dim chamber in which the vertical blinds were tightly drawn. Near the blinds were a dormant television set and VCR sitting on a dull brown metal cart. In the center of the room was an immaculate, featureless desk with a single-bulb desk lamp burning over it. Monroe saw two identical hardbacked chairs, one for the desk's occupant, and the other for a visitor. Under the buzzing glare of a fluorescent desk lamp was a single legal-sized pad, a purple felt-tip pen and a telephone.

"Enter and sit," said a parched, emotionless voice behind the door. Monroe took two steps in and heard the door close, and lock, behind him. He sat in the chair facing the desk, noticing immediately that the chair had no cushions, which forced him to sit up straight.

Ephrum Traile went behind his desk. He was in his late fifties, reedy and stoop-shouldered, in a gray, short-sleeved shirt with an annoying pink-and-brown tie that dangled from his neck like a wilted tongue. His badge and identification card hung from the shirt pocket. He kept his hands in his lap and looked at Monroe for several minutes, his bleached, pale blue eyes motionless behind heavy trifocal lenses.

Then he leaned forward, the light glancing off his bald, blotched head and bloodless lips. He folded his hands and said, "Before you comment, I want to warn you that this is an informal meeting. You are not obligated to answer any of the questions I put forth. If this were a formal administrative hearing you could request an attorney or suitable representative to advise you. Because this is an informal meeting, you cannot make such a request. However, any information you supply can and will be used against you, if an investigation of your activities is initiated, and that investigation takes an adversarial direction. Have I made that clear?"

The office was not hot, but the lack of sunlight and the dryness of the air unnerved Monroe.

"Sir, I—"

"Answer the question."

"Yes, sir."

He unfolded his hands. "This meeting is to address your behavior up to this point," Traile said.

"Sir, I . . ."

"You have an idea, vision or some such understanding of your role as an officer that is inconsistent with that of the department."

Monroe felt himself shrink in his chair. "You think I haven't noticed?"

"That is a question. I do not have to answer your questions. I ask. You answer."

Traile picked up a purple pen and a list of questions from his desk. Monroe thought of saying something about the "love bucket" card, but held the words in.

Traile began, "My first question is, have you ever heard of Operation Long Spoon?"

Monroe fidgeted. "No."

"My second question is, are you happy in the vice squad?"

Monroe sat back. "Am I happy? Am I supposed to be happy? Yeah, I'm happy. Delighted. Overjoyed."

"My third question is, have you ever accepted gifts or funds from Juanita Ivas?"

"No. Absolutely not. One hundred percent no. She was at my wedding. That's it."

"Obviously the social event of the season. My fourth question is, have you at any time observed your assigned partner, Sergeant Raymond Deegan, make contact with Lieutenant Commander Wayne Zimmer or other representatives of the state police unit investigating the mayor?"

"No."

"My fifth question is, have you now, or at any time, had any contact, or exchanged any information, with State Police Lieutenant Commander Wayne Zimmer?"

"No, sir."

"My last question is, can you recognize the person on the videotape I'm about to show you."

He pushed his chair back, wheeled the television and VCR cart forward, turned on the ensemble.

On the screen Monroe saw the words "Property of the New Jersey State Police, Division of Special Investigations."

The words flicked off and Monroe saw a bright orange, green and purple couch with a man sitting on it. The man wore smartly tailored black pants, a gray sport jacket and a blue shirt buttoned at the top. He was old with the gaunt, pinched face of someone who had recently lost weight. His hair was trimmed, eyes wet and shiny from what were apparently contact lenses.

A muffled off-camera voice said, "Look at the camera."

The man on the couch looked into the camera and Monroe suddenly remembered where he had seen a couch like that—in a suite at the Alcazar Casino Hotel.

"Begin," the off-camera voice said.

The man opened his mouth. His low, rumbling speech was uncertain, afraid. "I, umm, did some bad things, and then I found Jesus."

The screen jumped, indicating that the camera had been stopped. The same man was in a taupe leather jacket, blue corduroy pants, a gold chain around his neck. "I was prescribed pain killers, lots of pain killers and when I took them, I just couldn't control myself, even when I wanted to."

The screen jumped again. The man was in a dark blue, conservative business suit, blue shirt, red tie. "I made some mistakes. We all make mistakes, but I didn't do anything wrong."

The screen jumped a third time. The man wore a brown sport jacket over a tan sweater, white pants. "Up until the time I was arrested, I was working in an undercover capacity, investigating corruption within the Atlantic City municipal government with respect to links to a criminal enterprise known as the Soladias Organization."

The screen jumped a fourth time. He was in the gray sport jacket again. "The Lord wants me to help people."

Then, in the business suit: "I feel a need to make a positive contribution to society."

Brown jacket: "The only way Atlantic City can get back on its feet is if it gets rid of these crooks in city government before it's too late."

Traile froze the image, with the man's mouth closed, jaw set, a look of determination on what was still an apelike face.

He said, "Answer the question."

Monroe said, "Yes."

"Who is it?"

"Reuben Claymore."

"Officer Reuben Claymore, of the Atlantic City Police Department, now under the protection of New Jersey State Bureau of Witness Sequestration, whom you arrested on charges of possession of methamphetamine with intent to distribute, an arrest you made single-handedly and without any corroborating witnesses other than a Mr. James Doochay, whose address you've listed as homeless?"

"Yes, sir," Monroe said.

Traile turned off the TV set and cleared his desk. "You are now, from this point on, transferred into the Internal Affairs Division. I am making this order on an oral basis. This transfer is confidential and will not be revealed to anyone, including members of Atlantic City Police Department, or your family. You will continue to report to Captain Gant and behave as if my order to you was not issued. I am making no official, unofficial or otherwise written record of this order. Your transfer to my command will be made known only by me, when I see fit. You will report to me at times and places determined by me, outside this building. We will communicate in person only. You will call a telephone number once a day, every day, from different public telephones, before 1700 hours and act on any directions or statements you hear. Follow all instructions precisely. Memorize this number."

He recited it.

Monroe stared at him.

"Have you memorized it?"

"Sir, before I memorize anything, I want to know why I'm being transferred."

From a drawer Traile removed a file folder marked DEEGAN and opened it. "Seven years ago, Captain Gant unofficially assigned Detective Raymond Deegan to gather information that could be used to discredit State Police Lieutenant Commander Wayne Zimmer, who was then conducting an investigation against Mayor William DiFenistre. The nature and extent of the information gathered is unknown, though Captain Gant indicated to me that it would have forced Zimmer to remove himself from the investigation. What is known is that the information was not used and Mayor DiFenistre was indicted during an election year, and was not reelected. Lieutenant Commander Zimmer is currently investigating Mayor Tilton—"

"And you want me to find out what Deegan has on Zimmer," Monroe said. "I guess I can't ask why you didn't go to Deegan or Captain Gant."

"That is correct."

"But I can *guess* that because it was an unofficial investigation, you can't make Captain Gant tell you anything he doesn't want to tell you, and Gant doesn't want to tell anything because he's retiring in a few weeks and doesn't want to rock the boat. You could force Gant to tell you by making him the subject of an official inquiry, but that would require a hearing and lawyers who can stall for time. Mayor Tilton's up for reelection in November, so you have to find out pretty fast if this information will do what you want it to do."

Traile tapped his pen on the pad. "Continue guessing."

"You might have asked Deegan. Deegan probably refused to tell you. And you can't make him tell you because . . . he has insurance."

Traile leaned forward. "All officers in this police department are covered by union-managed copayment plans regarding hospitalization, surgery and major medical expenses, as well as life insurance."

"The other kind of insurance," Monroe said. "You can't get to him because he can get you back. So the only reason I'm in here is that you can get to me, or the mayor's on your back to find something to get him off the hook and you're desperate."

Traile silently studied Monroe, then made some notes on his pad.

"Sergeant Deegan's days off are Sunday and Monday," Traile said. "Tonight he is scheduled to commence his tour of duty at 5:00 P.M. You are to go out with him. That is an order. If you fail to carry out this order I can suspend you immediately for insubordination."

Monroe told himself that next time he took the phone off the hook, he should leave it off the hook.

"You are to acquire evidence that will be used to suspend or otherwise discipline him. Any conduct he displays that is, to your knowledge, in violation of departmental codes of conduct, will be noted by you and passed on to me. Furthermore, you must keep Sergeant Deegan out of the Alcazar Casino Hotel. His presence there is no longer desired."

"Why?" Monroe asked. "Is it that somebody's cut him out of the procuring business? Sir, if you're going to blackmail him—"

Traile closed his eyes, shook his head minutely, as if to clear the question from his view. "Any statement Sergeant Deegan makes concerning information about himself, Captain Gant and Lieutenant Commander Zimmer will be relayed to me. You will wear a wire and you will submit tapes of your conversation to this office at the end of your tour. Failure to comply with any of these instructions will be construed as grounds for suspension. If you are suspended the department will withhold your pay until a hearing determines your guilt. I am capable of stalling that hearing for quite a while." He folded his hands.

Monroe gaped at him. "Why the hell are you doing this to me?"

Traile stood, went to a small file cabinet in the rear of his office, took out a tape recorder, microphone, a stack of microcassettes, rechargeable batteries and duct tape. He put them on his desk and said, "Because it's your job, Detective."

13

American Made

Deegan swaggered, three hours late, into a Vice Squad office empty of everyone but Monroe. His burnt orange jacket was stained, his copper pants wrinkled, his loafers scuffed and dirty.

"Do you take me, to be your ever lovin' partner . . ."

"You're drunk," Monroe said.

"*Was* drunk. I've since sobered up." He walked into a desk, slid into a chair, put his head on the table, popped his head up and said, "How come you're not surprised?" And laughed so hard he fell off his chair.

Monroe watched his partner, feeling the weight of the portable tape recorder strapped to his body. He wondered if he should tell Deegan he was taping him. He wondered if it would make a difference.

Deegan stopped laughing and leered at Monroe from the floor. "You wearing a wire?"

"Why would I be wearing a wire?"

"Because the Extraterrestrial has them in his office and gives them out like dentists give out lollipops," Deegan said, pushing himself up so his eyes hovered over the filthy green-and-yellow linoleum. "That, and disguises. Traile has this box of wigs and moustaches, likes to go out at night and play let's pretend."

"Dentists don't give out lollipops," Monroe said.

"They do, to kids. It's one of those weird bits of pure evil in life. The kid goes to the dentist because he has a cavity, which comes from eating too much crap with sugar in it, and the kid's reward for the dentist drilling and filling, and billing Dad for his pain, is a lollipop, which sets the whole process in motion again."

"One lollipop isn't going to make a difference," Monroe said.

"Say it loud so the microphone can pick it up," Deegan said. "If you have on the mike with the little red spot of paint on the edge—it goes out if you sweat."

Monroe felt a drop of sweat forming in the small of his back.

"So Traile's sicced you on me. My very own partner, the kid who busts cops, is going to bring the Deeg to justice."

Monroe said nothing.

Deegan rolled into a crouch, slowly stood up. "But you're not going to bring the Deeg to justice. You're going to give Traile some bullshit that he thinks he can use to force me to . . ."

He giggled.

"What?" Monroe asked.

"Bastard. Fucking, fucking bastard. Gave the department the worst goddamn years of my life, and for what? For what?" Deegan whirled around and pointed a finger at Monroe.

"You think I don't know what it's like?"

Monroe was confused. "What are you talking about?"

"The end. The bitter, fucking end. You give something your life and, all of a sudden, it's over."

"What's over?"

He steadied himself. "Traile wants it. Gant wants it. The goddamn mayor wants it. What I got up here," he tapped his head. "But you get what I got up here, and you use it, or assholes like Traile try to make you use it, then you have incidents, accidents, un-for-tu-nate fatalities."

"If you're so worried about something happening, maybe you should call it off for tonight," Monroe said.

Deegan put a black capsule in his mouth and swallowed. "Methamphetamine, which, when taken in sufficient quantities, can induce a state of steel-brained sobriety."

"You're on speed, too?"

"You want a urine sample, partner-of-mine?"

"You mix amphetamines and booze, you can give yourself a heart attack," Monroe said.

Deegan rubbed his nose. "Nah. Don't want to cheat the Extraterrestrial out of phoning me home." He took a deep breath. "You'll see. Half an hour, I'll be raring to go."

"Let's call it off, tonight."

"Let's not and say we did!" Deegan said. He shot up, grabbed the keys to the unmarked Dodge and took off.

They were in the unmarked car. Monroe, having wrested the keys out of Deegan's hands, was driving randomly, thinking only of the tape recorder attached to his body.

"I feel like making a statement," Deegan said, aiming his voice at Monroe's middle. "Verbal and visual."

"I don't see a camera," Monroe said.

"I mean a public display, something that people will remember, something I can shove up Gant's ass."

"Lay off about him," Monroe said. "He's a decent man."

"He's the worst. Traile must've told you what happened between Gant and me."

"Partner-of-mine, I'm wired," Monroe said.

Deegan popped another pill. "That makes two of us." He rolled down the window, waved at a working girl on Pacific Avenue.

Monroe paused at the chaotic intersection where Atlantic, Pacific and Albany Avenues met. He went left onto Atlantic, heading downbeach.

"Gant fixed you up with me to make me tell you," Deegan said.

"Tell me what?"

He shook his head. "About Nita."

"He said maybe I could talk to you about it."

"More than that. You ever work with juveniles, partner-of-mine? Not toss hot dogs at 'em but, like, be there when you find a four-year-old boy with his eyes blacked out, a broken collar bone and third-degree burns from a cigarette all over his behind, and listen to his parents tell you the kid was playing with matches and then he fell down."

Monroe shook his head.

"I *wanted* to do juvenile work. It was the reason I got into the department. I figured I could, with my . . ." He stopped.

"With what?"

He rubbed his face, as if he were in pain and the rubbing would make it go away. "The sickest thing about it, partner-of-mine, is that, as much as the kids suffer, as many times as they get kicked and beaten and burned and raped, they want to go back to their parents. They think their folks love them. They learn to equate violence and inflicting pain with love because . . . because it's something they know. It's familiar. What do you think of that, partner-of-mine?"

Monroe thought of the drugged-up girl at the bus terminal.

"Makes you want to vomit, eh, partner-of-mine? So I want to vomit, now, right here in this car. I want to vomit my entire life out, because I have seen someone I love go back to the bastard who did things—"

"Did what things?"

Deegan slammed his hand on the car's windowsill. "I'm not going to tell you because it's sick to even repeat it!"

"Nita Ivas was an abused child?"

Deegan put his mouth an inch from Monroe's ear and said, "She still is. You never *stop* being abused, ASSHOLE! If somebody isn't doing it to you, you do it to yourself."

He became quiet after that. Monroe turned right onto Jackson Avenue, the southernmost street in Atlantic City, which formed the border between Atlantic City and the cramped, crowded beach burg of Ventnor. Jackson Avenue was about a mile south of the nearest casino, part of a neighborhood called lower Chelsea.

Monroe was always amazed, when he ran the Boardwalk down to lower Chelsea, or when he drove downbeach toward Ventnor and Margate, how the people who lived here could pretend that the grim sections of Atlantic City didn't exist. As he paused at the light on Jackson and Ventnor Avenue, lower Chelsea's weather-worn but faithful copy of a 1930s Main Street, Monroe experienced a momentary dislocation, as if the drunk, drugged-up detective sergeant sprawled beside him was a ghost, a disembodied shade who had sold himself to a devil buried far below the carefully swept beaches, tidy lawns, narrow driveways leading to four-car garages and sun decks with their all-important beach views.

Monroe was about to make a right turn to go back north, toward Atlantic City, when Deegan told him to turn left on Ventnor Avenue. As Monroe drove south, passing the slumbering seashore lanes, Deegan pointed out apartments, houses, towering condos slathered in virginal white stucco. He named politicians, businessmen, doctors and professional people, entertainers, Philadelphia mafiosi and a director of a local convent.

"That bungalow over there—I brought three girls for what they told me was a fraternity party, only the youngest guy at the party was old enough to be my father. I sold a twenty-shot bag of crack vials to a bunch of psychiatrists having a barbecue. I guess they were dissatisfied with what they could get from the pharmacies. I showed up with two girls to that French chateau on the corner—it's a married couple and they wanted to sit there and watch me screw the girls."

"Did you?"

Deegan shrugged. "The things you gotta do to make people happy. Sometimes it's pathetic. Those girls were not my type."

"What type is that?"

"Listen to me, asshole," Deegan growled at the tape recorder. "I provide a lot of sex and a little bit of drugs for people with money who don't want to get their hands dirty. I do it because I, because it's . . . what I do.

"I became a cop because I wanted to work with juveniles. I wanted to set their lives straight and I wanted to do something decent with my life. Naturally, every blue-suit in the department immediately hated my guts, except for Gant. He was like the father I never had."

"What happened to your father?"

"He and my mother had a fight, he blows out, I never see him again. Then I found—well, I didn't find, it was more like . . ."

He seemed to go blank for a minute. "And Mom was Wayne Zimmer's secretary back in the County Solicitor's office. But, when . . . after he fired her, she never did anything about it. Or maybe she was afraid. Or maybe she just gave up.

"So I was hanging around with Gant, and then Mom died and I had to bury her. You ask yourself a lot of questions when you have to bury your parents, especially when you really only had one. I put her in the ground up in Pleasantville but I couldn't deal with her stuff. I shoved it into storage and forgot about it, and jumped into the job. Tried to be the best goddamn cop there is. Decided to do more than just bust people. I was smart enough, like you, to realize that busting people just feeds this system. You want to do good that's permanent, you have to get to the root, find out why it is that there are so many scumbags out there and if there is a scumbag-making device out there, turn the fucking thing off. I was stupid enough to think I could do that. Until Gant said no."

"What was that about?" Monroe said.

"It was one of those situations when it just drops into your lap. Gant said he'd help me. I had a case. I made a fucking case. I had it in my hands and then . . . he just said no. He let me down." He rubbed his forehead. "Then it became real easy to give up, give in and spend the rest of my time working angles, making deals, pulling scams, making some bucks for myself, making some insurance, making people happy."

Deegan hollered out the window, "Is everybody happy?"

A kid in roofless Ferrari shot through a red light and said, "Yep!"

They crossed into Margate and passed plantation-style Greek revival mansions, French chateaus with bright-green copper roofs, enormous whitewashed Spanish colonial villas, and even a few medieval stone castles, each lording over a precious quarter-acre of beach block turf. So tightly did these houses cram together along the oceanfront that they became a wall that shut out everything but the salty odor of the ocean beyond them.

Monroe's stomach began to grumble. "I feel like getting some food."

"Not now," Deegan said, sitting up and restlessly drumming his fingers. The traces of Deegan's alcohol binge had disappeared. He patted his gut. "That's the great thing about crystal meth. All energy, no appetite. Gets rid of pounds of ugly fat."

"Also causes liver damage," Monroe added, "as well as capillary ruptures and hemorrhages, muscle spasms, paranoid delusions. And it fries your brain."

"Like I have to worry. Right now the only thing that's keeping me alive is you."

"Me?"

Deegan flashed his goose-bump grin. "As long as you're in this car recording my wicked, wicked ways, no one's trying to do anything worse. Then it would be down by the sea for me."

"What the hell is that?" Monroe steered the car into a bug-lit custard-and-burger stand in Margate, an anachronism on the block of painfully chic boutiques pretending to be Beverly Hills' Rodeo Drive. "I've been hearing about it, like it's some kind of thing people do to you and there's nothing you can do but take it or watch."

Deegan drummed his fingers on door panel. "You can be sure, partner-of-mine, we're both going to find out."

Before he returned with his late-night lunch, Monroe changed the tapes behind the hamburger stand. Back in the car, he unwrapped the greasiest cheeseburger he had ever seen. He took a bite, thought of how much it cost, and asked Deegan how much money he takes in from his scams.

"I never kept track," Deegan said, sneering at the food Monroe was eating. "Whenever the FBI bust a major scumbag, what's the first thing they get? The record book. Who keeps records? Who gives a shit? I wasn't in it for the money. I was in it because it was fun to have these upper-classy creeps be so grateful to me, a cop that they would spit on, for getting them their little piece of candy. And it was useful, too. You can fix all kinds of problems with sex and drugs, partner-of-mine."

"But not solve them," Monroe said.

Deegan shook his head.

"So tell me about this thing that dropped into your lap," Monroe said.

"You would ask that." Deegan closed his eyes, took a breath. "One night I saw this girl. Ten, twelve years old. She was the right age for some of the guys that like them before they, you know, start to bloom. Found her on the street wearing this brand new red coat, which looked stolen.

"When she saw me she picked up and ran, but she tripped and fell and when she just lay there and cried and didn't get up, I went over to her and saw she'd been worked on. There were bruises that I recognized. You could almost see where she was gripped, on her shoulders and her neck. We started talking and it was the strangest damned thing, but she started coming on to me. She was frantic and I couldn't deal with it. I just wanted to talk, but she wouldn't, so I took her in on vagrancy just to make *sure* that it wouldn't happen."

"This was Nita Ivas."

Deegan flinched as if Monroe had hit him. "It doesn't matter what she was then. The girl had no parents. She needed somebody and Gant suggested I put her in with Miss Ramona. So I did. When I came back to see her a few days later, she'd run off to be with the guy who worked her over."

He shuddered. "Some time later, I found her again, on the street. Same bruises. Same blood dripping from her legs. I had to run to catch her. But this time I took her back to Miss Ramona and got her cleaned up and took her out for some food. I told her I'd meet her again the next night and I did. She tried to come on to me and I wouldn't let her. It took weeks but we started to talk. I mean really talk. Share things about who we are and what we were doing. We had a lot in common, her and me."

He paused. "It took a while and she told me who did it to her, and it wasn't some scum who lived in the projects. It was a white male, aged forty to forty-five, hundred and eighty pounds, educated, sophisticated, respected, admired, who likes girls *and* boys just before they bloom . . ."

He raised his fist. "I wanted to nail him. I knew who he was. I knew how evil he was. So *many* people would be happy if I nailed him. I made the case. I could've had the guy but Gant said no way, José."

"Why? He must have had a reason."

"He did, but what can be reasonable about a guy who sodomizes children who are too young and helpless to do anything about it?"

Monroe couldn't believe this. "There must have been——"

"There *was,* and he said I had no case. No case. Can you believe that? After I promised Nita I would do something. After I convinced her that I could help her." He rubbed his face again.

"I know it sounds kind of silly, for a guy like me to just give up over that but . . . what is it that we're supposed to do, if not wipe these scumbags off the map? Nita worked the street for a while, was gracious enough to let me arrest her a few times——"

"And the charges were dropped. Why?"

His face clouded over. "Because Nita is an abused kid, it's in her to like to be, to want to be . . . used. She sucks up to people and can be incredibly seductive, and then she's got you, and if you go along with her, things are okay. She turned in some drug dealers who were working Sea Park Plaza, so Gant dropped one set of charges."

"And Traile?"

"After I began to indulge my wicked, wicked ways, I busted her and she went right up to Traile and threatened to turn me in, so he let her go, just to be rid of her," Deegan said. "I learned a lot from her. I learned that you can't let her fight you because the only way she can fight is to hurt, deeply, to inflict the kind of pain that takes your life away."

"But you fell in love with her?"

"It didn't happen overnight. I felt I needed to make it up to her. She deserved better. And there was a lot that we . . . shared."

Monroe was incredulous. "What could you possibly have in common with this girl?"

"A desire to destroy Special Investigator Wayne D. Zimmer," Deegan said.

"He was—"

Deegan said, "Gant said I had no case. Gant said this when Zimmer was in town to bust Mayor DiFenistre, who was demanding that all the low-income housing projects be brought up to code in one year, or be closed down. Sound familiar?"

"DiFenistre was indicted for embezzling city funds to pay his campaign debts," Monroe said.

Deegan smiled. "And don't you think Mayor DiFenistre would have *wanted* something on Zimmer? Zimmer was on TV, standing behind the state attorney general, who was making statements about how he was cleaning up Atlantic City. I was screaming at Gant, why don't we come down on Zimmer? The guy's a monster, a beast. If what we had could blow Zimmer out of the state police, why can't we just do it?"

He shook his head. "For a moment, I thought he was going to do it. I remember, we were out on the Boardwalk, right at Kentucky Avenue, him and me. He was eating a slice of pizza and I was begging him to give me the documents back and let me go to the newspapers. I saw him frown and set his jaw, as if he was getting ready for a big fight. Then he turns and sees Zimmer coming down the Boardwalk in a rolling chair with some girl on his arm, and Gant gets so twisted I think he's going to barf up the pizza but he manages to hold it down. And Zimmer rolls right by. Doesn't even see us. Zimmer fucking rolls right by."

He took a breath.

Monroe asked what had happened after that.

"Nothing. DiFenistre was indicted but there was never a trial. They didn't need a trial. The people of Atlantic City will let you get away with just about anything," Deegan said. "They love great scoundrels even more than they love saints. Mention Uncle Sam Claymore to anybody over the age of fifty-five and they'll shed a tear about what a wonderful guy he was. A real character.

"But what the people of this town won't tolerate is a bullshit scam. Embezzlement of public funds is bush-league. There's no challenge to it. DiFenistre went down the tubes. The day after the election Gant mumbles about how I didn't have enough evidence, and that I needed a *reliable* witness and that people would get hurt unless I did what I was supposed to do. What was I *supposed* to do? What would I need, a picture? A picture with Zimmer and his little chicken boy in it? No way I could part with that kind of insurance. No way, José."

Monroe felt as if he'd been doused by cold water. "What was that? A picture?"

"Picture," Deegan seemed to go blank for a moment as he checked his jacket pocket. Then, as if to sweep the remark under the rug, he said, "Talk about pictures. I never thought about it until now, but that girl Zimmer was with in that rolling chair? I remember she was smiling like she was living inside an Atlantic City postcard, like nothing could please her more than to be on Zimmer's arm. Reminds me of the way your wife was looking at you at your wedding."

He sniffed. "Women sure can be stupid about men, eh?"

On the drive back to the city Deegan mentioned he had a forty-nine to meet at 10:30, and would Monroe mind if he indulged?"

Monroe said, "You're asking me?"

"You're in the driver's seat."

"Where?"

"Pacific Avenue."

Monroe didn't know what to do. He was trying to make sense out of Deegan's confession but the parts weren't fitting together. And this thing about Ellie—where did that come from?

He drove and Deegan sank into a nervous gloom, giving strange, circuitous directions that Monroe followed. They were soon on Pacific Avenue, close enough to the Alcazar to make Monroe ask if Deegan's forty-nine was someone special.

"This forty-nine," Monroe said. "Is this somebody special?"

"Every forty-nine is special. Tonight, on my last night alive, I am going to make *you* happy."

"Don't," Monroe said. "Just tell me why you are so sure somebody's going to kill you."

"They might do worse and let me live. That's what it means when they take you down by the sea. Something they used to do way back when in the good old days when the town was really loose. The goal, not always achieved, was to let the victim live, barely. As for me . . ." He knit his hands behind his head. "One of the rules of the road is that people who live for fun have short lives. I figure I have time for one more blast."

Deegan checked his wristwatch. "He should be getting into that jeep just about now to pick her up and take her to the casino."

"Who's getting picked up?"

"I want you to go slow, real slow. There she is . . ."

He began to sing the Miss America theme song. Coming into view was Fatsie Morgan, standing tall and wide in a shapeless white gown, under the awning of the King Arthur Hotel.

"That's your forty-nine?"

"No way, José."

"You said you—"

A wall of black metal swerved past them. Deegan sat straight up. "Time for you to have some fun, partner-of-mine. We won't settle the score, but we may make him shit his pants."

"What—"

"Nothing scares a scumbag who's got himself off the hook more than the seeing the guy that put him on the hook."

Monroe was about to say something about hooks when Deegan reached over, took the wheel and stepped on Monroe's foot, shoving the accelerator down. The unmarked Dodge lurched behind a tall, black, four-by-four jeep—with tinted windows and a matching black cargo compartment—which was stopped at a red light.

Before Monroe could stop him, Deegan hit the brakes, throwing both of them almost into the windshield but stopping the car close enough to the big black jeep to kiss the bumper. The jeep jumped through the red light, dodging a jitney, and roared south on Pacific Avenue.

Almost sitting on top of Monroe, Deegan piloted the car, following the jeep as closely as possible. Above the roar of the unmarked car's badly tuned engine, Monroe could hear, and even feel music from the jeep's overpowered stereo pounding at him. The beat was slow, bombastic, familiar. Monroe found himself humming the tune . . . it was . . . it was *Frank Sinatra*.

"I want it," Deegan said, banging his hands on the wheel in time to the music. "I want that jeep *my way*."

He cut off a jitney to remain behind the jeep.

Monroe struggled and fumbled under the man. He thought of using a few joint locks and other pressure point applications he had learned in Vinnie Almagro's unarmed combat classes, but not on a man pumped up into a paranoid methamphetamine rage who was driving a police vehicle from the passenger seat at sixty-five miles per hour in a twenty-five mile per hour zone.

Deegan screamed. "He's the bad guy. We're the good guys. Let's roast his ass!"

"Deegan, get the hell—" Monroe said.

Deegan put the red blinker on the roof of the unmarked car. "Fucking asshole's going down."

"Deegan—"

Deegan stomped on Monroe's foot again, kicking the car past seventy miles per hour, stuck his head out of the driver's side window, and yelled, "PULL THE FUCK OVER, ASSHOLE!"

Through the jeep's darkened glass Monroe saw a head turn. The jeep turned to the right, rode up on to the curb and the sidewalk. Deegan followed, hitting the curb so hard that Monroe felt the top of his head brush against the car roof's mildewed foam.

Sidewalks in Atlantic City are wide, deliberately so, a zoning code relic from the grand old days in which the wide streets and boulevards of an ocean resort were meant to contrast with the narrow, stinking, claustrophobic alleys of Philadelphia and New York. The two cars careened between street lamps, no-parking signs, fire hydrants and, of course, pedestrians—night-walking tourists, busted-out gamblers, PARAtroopers, juvenile punks looking for an old lady to rob.

At least they got out of the way, Monroe reflected. At least they were smart enough to avoid trouble. At least they didn't have the sweaty armpit of a drug-crazed cop in their face.

The jeep bounced off the curb and stopped suddenly. The Dodge's brakes weren't so good. Nothing on the car was, and so it was almost excusable that Deegan, in his bloodlust, did not stop in time and slammed the car into the back of the jeep. The car seemed to bounce upward as Sinatra warbled about strangers exchanging glances. Monroe felt himself crash into the steering wheel, heard the dull crump of metal meeting metal. Deegan threw the car into park and said, "PERFECT!"

He opened the passenger side door and had his foot out when the jeep jumped forward, dragging the unmarked car with it. In a second Monroe saw that their bumpers were locked, and the jeep had an engine to match its sound system. The jeep was strong enough to drag the car behind it.

Deegan fell back into the car as the jeep roared up New York Avenue, swerving on and off the sidewalk, through traffic lights, shuddering, shimmying from side to side, trying to shake them off.

In the front seat Monroe pumped the brakes and heard the back tires screech. Loose objects in the front seat bounced and flew around when the jeep skidded and slammed the unmarked car into a streetlight, snapping the light at the base.

"YABBA DABBA DOOOOO!" Deegan roared. He had his gun out, tried to hang out of the passenger's side window to aim, but the jeep swayed from one side of the avenue to another, slid against another car, ripping paint and metal, then shrieking into a bone-crushing turn. Deegan howled and discharged his 9mm Gloch through the roof of the car.

For a moment Monroe couldn't hear anything. He realized Deegan must have a police radio. He would pull it from him and call for backup.

Monroe smacked himself into Deegan, felt a thick wad of paper in Deegan's jacket pocket, smelled the man's scorching, vaguely acidic "meth breath," found the radio clipped to Deegan's waist and yanked it out. The car slammed into the curb and took out another lightpole. The radio bounced out of Monroe's hand. Deegan screamed obscenities at the jeep. Then he turned back at Monroe. "Is this rich, or is this rich?"

The car skidded to the right.

"Deegan, we are fucking up public property! We have to stop this before—"

Deegan pulled the blinker off the car. "There! Now nobody'll know it's us."

"We have to call for backup!" Monroe shouted, as the jeep roared onto broad, wide Route 30, heading out of the city, blasting through stop lights, roaring into a stream of buses at Martin Luther King Blvd. Monroe saw his death as the jeep fishtailed and threw the car into the front of a bus. The bus halted with a screech of bad brakes and Monroe heard a *crump,* saw Deegan cover his face and as the driver's side of the car split and crunched and folded toward him.

The jeep didn't stop and went past the bus, through the stream of traffic, heading for the broad median that divided the boulevard. The jeep ran its left side on the median. The bumpers clanged and the jeep made a hard right turn; the black metal ripped away from them, and kept going, its left wheels swimming into view as the jeep rolled on its side and kept rolling, onto its roof, over and back onto its wheels.

The jeep stood there for a second, its rear bumper twisted into a sneer, its sides dented and crushed. Its tinted side-windows were shattered into spiderwebs of broken glass, Sinatra billowing out.

A hand punched through a shattered side-window and in one precious, perfect moment, Monroe saw the new-and-improved Reuben Claymore holding his neck, groaning. Claymore's carefully styled hair was in disarray. His eyes were wild and went wilder when they locked into Monroe's.

Then Monroe saw Reuben Claymore stare at him with the same fear that Monroe had had when he had confronted Claymore under the Boardwalk. It was the look you see on small animals that freeze and tremble in front of your car's headlights as you speed toward them. It was the look you glimpse on a fish as you reel it in through the last remaining inches of water. It was the look Monroe had received after he chased a young teenaged arsonist through the Inlet to New York Avenue, where the kid collapsed, exhausted and terrified, on the street.

It is the expression that living things show when they look death in the face.

Claymore broke the stare and grabbed the jeep's steering wheel. He raced the engine, bounced into traffic and sped toward the mainland.

Deegan gaped. "Did you see that? What a vehicle! American made. You can always tell."

Monroe couldn't speak. Deegan slapped him on the back. "Feel good, partner-of-mine? Feel like you did something *really* decent for the first time in your life?"

"You . . . crazy asshole," Monroe said. "You almost got us killed."

"Fuck that. You're alive. And you're probably feeling better now than you've felt all night."

Monroe remembered the look on Claymore's face and something about seeing that look on the face of his enemy made him feel very good indeed.

Then he thought about the car.

Deegan reached over, tapped the accelerator with his foot. The car jumped forward and Deegan howled, "American made!"

CHAPTER

14

As Luck Would Have It

Monroe was outside the car, shaking his head at the damage. Departmental procedure demanded that they call in a report immediately.

Deegan had his portable radio on. There was no mention of what had happened.

"We have to file a report—" Monroe began.

"Fuck it," Deegan said. "We're working for ourselves tonight. You've had your fun. Time for me to have mine."

He slid into the driver's seat, gunned the engine and tenderly guided the unmarked car over the median, off the curb. Monroe stood stupidly for a moment, watching him, and then ran after him. Deegan slowed the car, Monroe hopped in.

Deegan turned right on Arctic Avenue, and left on Montana Avenue and headed for the Alcazar.

"You're going to see her again?" Monroe asked.

"As I always do," Deegan said. "This time, it's different. This time, I'm going to walk right into her lounge. She told me she didn't want to see me again, but that's her way of telling me she wants to see me again. She drops hints like that all the time and you have to be sharp to pick them up."

"Maybe she wasn't hinting," Monroe said.

"She's been working that high-roller lounge, sucking up to Zimmer, while she was telling me what was going on. That's how I knew Claymore would be in that jeep. It's also how I know that

Zimmer doesn't approve of her seeing me, which is why I think she went to your wedding with that casino sleaze."

"You think? You're not sure?"

He smiled. "That's what's so beautiful about her. She never tips her hand, never tells you everything. Just enough to keep you fascinated."

"At my wedding, she clocked you."

"She did it because she had to show your casino sleaze that she and me weren't an item."

"I thought she did it because you were a pain in the ass."

"That was an act," Deegan insisted with the frantic energy of a man obsessed. "She can't show her true feelings, not even to me. She couldn't let on that she really does need me."

"For what?"

He grinned. "Fun."

Deegan tossed the keys of the battered automobile to a skinny parking valet with a runny nose, who mumbled about having to fill out an "as is" certification so that the casino couldn't be held responsible for. . . .

Deegan didn't stop to hear the explanation. He didn't even pick up the valet ticket. Monroe snatched it out of the valet's hand and followed Deegan through the Alcazar's mirrored entrance, past the blinking trailing lights, the swirling pink-and-purple paisley vortices in the carpet, the beveled mirrors cut with their angles pointing, pointing, pointing down the low-ceilinged concourse with its enlarged pictures of smiling, smiling, smiling entertainers stationed against the walls like guardians of the temple.

Deegan didn't walk the corridor as much as he ricocheted along the concourse, moving his feet unevenly as his attention was drawn by the glitzy facets of the corridor. He passed a few wilted, somnolent gamblers affecting that slow shamble of deep, irrevocable loss, then went under a swirling art nouveau arch of green, purple and brass hues where a sign of glowing red letters said "Casino."

As awkwardly as Deegan moved, he was fast. At best, Monroe could stay a few feet behind him. He noticed that the concourse, which would normally be thick with gamblers heading toward the games, now had only a few. The casino's peppy music-track high-lighted the lack of warm bodies. Monroe saw no security person-nel. Security guards are the first to be laid off when casinos tighten their belts.

Deegan paused at the casino entrance. To his left was the casino gift shop, a gaudy little hutch stuffed with overpriced tourist shlock and astronomically expensive watches, jewelry, gold medallions, pieces of exquisitely carved jade and ivory and, against a wall, leather jackets, purses, hats, lingerie. Upper Crust Gift Stores, Inc. ran this shop, and two more in other casino hotels. Special custom-ers were presented with gift catalogs that showed women modeling the gifts. The customers asked for the gift, got the woman, and the casino paid for the gift as a comp—complimentary service—to the gambler.

Ellie Meade had been one of Upper Crust's most popular gifts. He tried to put that out of his mind as Deegan slipped to the right, skirting the casino that was nearly deserted. The orderly rows of twinkling slot machines were disquietingly empty. The rhythm of the place was off. Instead of the churning, vibrant pulse of money changing hands, the casino was oddly gloomy under so many bright, focused lights, like a department store decorated for Christ-mas after Santa Claus has gone. Missing was the cacophony of bells and buzzers, the roar of craps shooters on a roll, the manic crunch of slot machine handles, the rat-tat-tat jangle of coins spewing out, the fluttering whirr of the Big Six wheels, the subtle chatter of a roulette ball finding its slot.

The Alcazar had followed other casinos in trying to solve the problem of lack of gamblers by ignoring the source of the problem. Instead they toyed with their marketing programs, dreamed up an elaborate series of T-shirt, hat and sunglasses giveaways and tin-kered with the ambience of the casino floor itself.

The most obvious kind of tinkering was with the slot machines. Claiming hardship, the casinos lobbied the New Jersey Casino

Control Commission, and won approval for credit card slots—machines that didn't require a coin input, just a credit card.

Another trick was a change in the "mix," the geographical positioning of the slot machines. Traditionally, casinos placed the absurdly oversized "Big Bertha" slot machines near the entrances, in an effort to deprive gamblers on their way out of the last few coins in their pockets. The Big Berthas tended to have slightly higher payout odds than other machines, and their metal coin hoppers were tempered specially to make a loud, percussive jangle.

Because so few gamblers were wandering into the casinos, a new, even bigger array of Big Berthas were moved into the center of the casino floor. These machines, dubbed by the Alcazar the "Serendipity Seven," were linked progressives. That is, they shared a common jackpot that increased arithmetically with every coin played. In Atlantic City's early days of casino gambling, slot junkies lined up ten and twenty players deep to get a crack at progressive slot machines. They were driven to a frenzy as each coin and pull drove the jackpot, spelled out in red sports stadium numbers above the machines, higher and higher. Progressive slot machine winners were given the same flashbulb-blinded celebrity treatment as state lottery winners: a complimentary, all-expense-paid night or two in the casino, their photos in the morning *Atlantic City Star,* as well as their hometown newspaper, accompanied by an article in which the dazed winner invariably said, "We don't expect this will change our lives one bit."

These gimmicks, and a computerized chorus of come-on voices that squeaked, "I'm lucky" and "You're lookin' good," were supposed to turn the tide. They hadn't. Without a constant flow of losing slot junkies, there could be no more than a few spectacular winners. Despite a jackpot of $3,826,592.25, Monroe could see and hear, from fifty yards away, the lonely Serendipity Seven chattering to themselves like burnt-out crazies on the Boardwalk.

Elsewhere on the casino floor, dealers stood idle, their hands motionless over the purple-felt playing fields of the blackjack, roulette and craps tables.

One of the blackjack dealers seemed annoyed at the lack of business. Gaunt and reedy, his purple-and-green uniform clashing with his expertly blow-dried blond hair, Clark Wells must have felt Monroe's eyes on him, because he turned, pointed a finger at his nose, made a pinching motion, then gestured to the spangled, mirrored entrance to the Topkapi Lounge.

Dealer's sign language arose so that dealers could communicate with each other across the broad avenues of noisy chatter, loud carpeting and velvet ropes. Unwritten gaming industry rules forbade dealers from speaking when they weren't dealing a game, and demanded that they speak only to customers when a game was in progress. Dealers also had to keep their hands in view at all times. They could not touch any part of their body, especially their faces, because too many dealers had been caught palming chips off the felt and tucking them in their mouths or uniform.

So all the gestures had to appear as if they were casual or unconscious. If Wells hadn't taught Monroe the nuances of this language, Monroe would have assumed that Wells was stretching his fingers or making awkward gestures to relieve his boredom.

But Monroe didn't need a knowledge of the lingo to pick up that something stank in the Topkapi Lounge.

Monroe tilted his head to his right, toward the lounge. The room was perched on a platform overlooking the casino floor just high enough so that patrons inside could slouch over a drink and never forget that, a few steps away, the wheels of fate were waiting. A band of five men in baggy purple tuxedos, with a short, sweating, rhinestone-drenched female singer out front, banged out pop tunes with mechanical haste.

Wells pointed again at his nose, then opened his arms—stink, large, big stink. Something big was stinking, no—something big was—

Deegan went past the lounge, toward a bank of elevators that led to the Alcazar's hotel tower. The entrance to one of those elevators was trimmed in gold, blue, purple highlights, and a very, very obvious television camera set in an inlaid, vaguely Egyptiod sun-disk. This was the express elevator to the Alhambra Club, a "private" lounge for high-rollers on the casino's penthouse level, where, Monroe remembered, Nita Ivas worked.

Monroe had never been to the Alhambra, but remembered from Dan Raleigh's description that, because it was in high-roller country, you needed a special key card to get anywhere near it. Deegan obviously didn't have a card, because he was searching for a button to push. When he didn't find it, he began banging on the doors.

While the public areas of the casino suffered from a lack of security guards, the casino floor had a special plain clothes "thumper" division. Five appeared in seconds and surrounded both Deegan and Monroe.

Thumpers were heavies, security guards who spent their off-hours pumping iron until they had the shoulders, arms, balding crania, acne-speckled skin and twitchy eyes of steriod injection–molded beefalos. Their purpose was to intimidate through physical size, and as Monroe stared up at a column of high-density, low-IQ muscle rising as high in front of him as one of those Serendipity Seven, he developed a powerful urge to be somewhere else.

"You fellas are gone," the thumper said, in a steriod-scented falsetto. "Out of here."

Deegan touched his jacket and the thumper was on him, a broad, thick and oddly hairless meat-paw clamped on Deegan's wrist. "Easy," the thumper said.

Deegan's nerves were on a methamphetamine overload, so the thumper's touch, which probably wasn't more than a sweaty tap, made him jump back against the elevator doors. Deegan slid to the carpet, a bundle of sweating skin, bones and overpriced clothing.

"Assault," Deegan squealed to Monroe. "That asshole assaulted me. Arrest the son of a bitch, *Detective* Monroe. That's an order."

Monroe felt the attention of the five thumpers, as well as the

Egyptoid sun disk above the elevator, focus on him. "Uh, hi," he said. "We're cops."

The thumpers didn't react.

"Let me show you," Monroe said. He slowly put his hand on his pants pocket, where his police ID lay. He was about to take it out when he saw the thumper lean forward and the meat-paw descend.

Among the less spectacular, but insidiously effective unarmed combat techniques taught by Sergeant Vinnie Almagro in his bump 'n' thump classes were joint locks, in which a finger, wrist, fore-arm, elbow, leg, shoulder, hip, ankle, or neck, is grabbed or bent, ever so slightly, and made to go where neither God nor evolution had intended.

Because Monroe was five feet two inches tall, the thumper had to lean forward to place his paw on Monroe's hand. Because Monroe had taken five years of bump 'n' thump, he saw the movement, sensed the direction of the thumper's weight and intention, touched the paw so that the thumper's wrist turned backward and the knuckles of the paw, not the palm, grazed against Monroe's hip. Then Monroe put his hand on the wrist, pushed his hip forward, crunching the thumper's paw, the wrist, the forearm and elbow into a "N" shape.

Monroe gave the paw a slight twist, shooting excruciating pain from the thumper's wrist to the steroid-reduced brain. Monroe stepped lightly out of the way as the thumper continued forward, falling to hit the carpet and skid, nose down. The polyester fabric in the thumper's green-with-blue-piping security jacket brushed the synthetic weaves in the carpet, creating a series of static electri-cal discharges that made visible sparks. His descent resembled a dramatic emergency landing by a wide-bodied jet whose landing gear had failed to operate.

"Ank," the thumper said.

The thumpers around him were too surprised to move. Then the fallen guard was on his feet. By then, Monroe had his ID out and open and in the thumper's red, synthetic-carpet-fiber-streaked face.

"No cops," the thumper boomed, trying to reassert his dignity. "We got an arrangement. No city cops in here, for no reason, not tonight."

"Except when you need us, right?" Deegan said, standing. "It's very important that we gain access to the Alhambra Club at this very moment so that I can assist a resident of this city in her quest to bring a slumlord to justice."

Then Monroe heard a familiar voice say, "No way, José."

"Dan."

"Louie baby," Dan Raleigh piped, "how *is* the honeymoon?"

The thumpers moved aside and Raleigh positioned himself between Monroe and Deegan.

"They say they're cops," the head thumper said, aware that whatever was going to happen next would not be any fun.

"But they wish they were somewhere else," Raleigh said. He told the thumpers the situation did not require their presence.

"But Mr. Raleigh, he—"

Raleigh looked at the thumper who had fallen. The carpet fibers had entered the thumper's nose. The thumper was trying not to sneeze. Monroe almost felt sorry for the man, a person who had designed his body, and his life, around physical intimidation, to lose it all to a sneeze, and then to sneeze tremendously on the lapels of Raleigh's midnight-blue silk jacket.

"Mr. Hadruna," Raleigh said, with the measured, patient delivery of a man who enjoys having his victims tortured before they're killed, "kindly take yourself to the Topkapi Lounge. Make sure the VIP in the lounge doesn't look this way."

"But—"

Raleigh smiled and the thumpers fled.

Deegan watched them go, then stepped forward, his hand out with a handkerchief, ready to wipe the goo from the casino executive's jacket. "Mr. Raleigh, Sergeant Ray Deegan, ACPD, I know you remember me from my partner's wedding and I really have to get up to that Alhambra Club you have up there and—''

"No," Raleigh said.

Deegan stopped, regrouped. "You don't understand."

"I don't have to," Raleigh said.

"I know what you're thinking," Deegan resumed. "You're thinking that you can tolerate a state police investigator who is going to cause more harm—''

"Please, shut up." Raleigh took the handkerchief, dabbed his lapels, put it in Deegan's palm. "Let's be cool about this, okay? I want both of you out of here. You can come back in an hour and do whatever you have to do then."

Deegan was about to explode. Raleigh put up a finger and silenced him. "All I'm asking for is a little patience. We happen to have a player, a significant player, with us right now who doesn't much enjoy himself when in the presence of police officers."

Deegan folded his arms. "He's wearing a wig and he's into you for a quarter million."

Raleigh frowned. "How did you know?"

"Doesn't matter," Deegan said. "I have the law on my side and the law says that in the course of police activity, casino personnel will grant the police access to all public areas, and the Alhambra Club is—''

"Private." Raleigh gazed at Deegan as if Deegan were a sand flea.

"Private?" Deegan exclaimed. "Private, my ass. Anybody who gambles can get in there."

Raleigh said. "It is limited to special customers of the Alcazar."

"You don't have to tell me what makes them special," Deegan said.

"As the director of player development, I determine what makes them special," Raleigh said.

"So," Deegan said, a methamphetamine-induced St. Vitus dance vibrating his arms, "if I go out there and gamble, you'll let me up."

"That's not special enough," Raleigh said. "Now I want you two boys to take yourself out of here, before I call Mr. Hadruna to escort you . . ."

But Monroe had stopped paying attention. He was staring, instead, into the Topkapi Lounge where, at the bar, a woman, a very, very large woman was sitting next to a scrawny man with thick dark hair and a bushy dark moustache. He wore a navy-blue blazer, madras-plaid pants, pink button-down shirt with a green tie hanging loose below his scrawny neck. He had one hand on the woman's hand, which was inside his open zipper. His other hand was raised, finger extended, signalling the bartender for another round.

Fatsie Morgan was doing an impressive job of pretending to be her companion's best friend. Her face was rouged, creamed, perfumed, oiled and powdered. She sat with a big gold purse on the bar before her wrapped in cascades of rhinestones and fake jewels, her hair piled into a blond beehive. Beneath that was a white Roman toga-like gown that left one jiggling, powdered shoulder bare. Her wide, stump-like ankles ended in gold platform shoes, and when she threw her head back to laugh, she giggled enough to make Monroe seasick. Some portion of her must have rested previously on the man's shoulder, for a whitish smear lay above one of his dented blue shoulder pads.

Monroe couldn't glimpse direct evidence of indecent exposure, but the man was obviously savoring Fatsie's coddling grip. He watched her other hand wander toward the man's pants pocket and hover over the wallet that bulged within.

Monroe strode purposely toward the pair. Raleigh called out and Monroe ignored him. He was up the stairs and ten feet from Morgan when his way was blocked by Mr. Hadruna.

"Turn around and leave," Hadruna said.

"I have to speak with this lady, here," Monroe said.

Monroe saw Fatsie slip the wallet out of her victim's pocket.

"No way," Hadruna said.

"Get out of my—"

Hadruna frowned, seemed to look over Monroe's shoulder, then shoved both hands forward, hard. Monroe let one touch his chest and then faded to the side. Hadruna stumbled and fell face-forward into a circular green formica lounge table.

"Excuse me, sir," Monroe called. "The woman sitting next to you got your wall—"

He felt a hand grab his ankle and Monroe exploded. It was as if the tension, confusion and frustration of this night, and so many others, had grown inside him, building pressure until something cracked and this was it. Monroe raised his other foot and brought it down on Hadruna's wrist. Hadruna swore and rose like a bear rearing up on its hind legs, and the man at the bar was watching, *amused.*

Fatsie Morgan popped the man's necktie out of his collar as she slipped his wallet into the folds of her toga below her open shoulder.

Monroe stepped beside Hadruna and had his hand out toward Fatsie when he felt a blow hit deep in his stomach. This told a distant part of his mind why it was that Hadruna was not a professional with unarmed combat training. A professional would have hit Monroe in his solar plexus, near the center of his chest. Such a blow would have knocked Monroe's wind out and thus made it easy for him to be subdued.

Monroe felt the blow go into his stomach. It pushed him back and he tripped over one of the green plush lounge chairs.

It hissed as he fell on it. He came up on one knee and saw, out of the corner of his eye, Hadruna bringing up a shoe to stomp his head. Monroe backed away and the shoe missed him. Hadruna took a step and pulled back his foot to kick again.

Monroe shoved a cocktail table in the way and Hadruna's shoe slid into Monroe's thigh, midway, where the muscle is wide and if you're the slightest bit tense the impact causes a screaming, spasmodic pain called a charley horse. Monroe got a charley horse and paused to clutch his leg.

Hadruna seemed pleased with himself and was readying a third kick when Monroe brought his unharmed leg in, rolled on his side. Hadruna was coming down when Monroe scrambled aside, reached back for his revolver, sprung off his good leg and buried the gun into Hadruna's crotch.

He had been aiming for Hadruna's stomach but he aimed too low. Because Hadruna was in motion, the pain from a blue-steel thirty-eight caliber two-inch gun barrel propelled into testicles took a second to reach Hadruna's brain. His eyes opened and his mouth opened and he roared, but the wind left him, his physical coordination ceased and he fell forward onto Monroe, the gun digging deeper (the safety on, Monroe noted), the barrel grabbing and ripping cloth, and coming free as Hadruna hit him like a tree falling.

Monroe fell backward into a lounge chair, taking Hadruna's weight on his shoulder. They went down. Monroe pulled his arms in, made himself small in time to see Fatsie, her gold purse swaying as she waddled down the steps from the lounge when he said, "POLICE, FREEZE!"

She kept going.

Monroe pulled one foot under him, forced his numbing, paralyzed charley-horsed thigh to push him up and forward. He crawled out from under Hadruna, who grabbed Monroe's shirt, ripping it around the collar, ripping it even more, before Monroe turned around and pistol-whipped Hadruna across the nose. Hadruna let go.

Always hold on to your weapon with both hands, the voice of Sergeant Vinnie Almagro, Monroe's police academy unarmed combat instructor, echoed in his head. *A pistol-whip is another way of giving your weapon to the enemy. As long as you can maintain control of your weapon, you have no problem!*

Monroe promised himself to hold on to his weapon with both hands as he hopped over an upended lounge chair and felt his charley-horsed leg nearly crumple beneath him. He managed to stagger forward, down the stairs, out of the lounge and into the hotel's grand concourse where he caught a glimpse of Fatsie Morgan's toga.

"POLICE, FREEZE!"

Fatsie was a pure professional, moving slowly, almost gracefully, as if it was her right and privilege to leave the casino. She didn't change her pace, didn't send any signal that the battered man in the ripped blue sport coat behind her had any possible business with her.

Monroe pulled out his ID, slipped it, badge out, in his jacket pocket. The few people in the concourse glanced at him when he stated, "Police! Everybody out of the way, against the wall!"

They shrunk back, leaving Fatsie Morgan alone under the glittering lights.

Monroe limped forward, holding the gun in both hands. "You're going to give that wallet back or I'm going to arrest you," he said.

She slowed, turned, flashed Monroe an expression of cool indignation.

Monroe stepped carefully, both arms straight out, the gun aimed at Fatsie's massive, quivering bosom where he could make out the faint outlines of a rectangular object about three by four inches—the wallet.

"I am Detective Louis Monroe of the Atlantic City Vice Squad," Monroe said, "and you are under arrest for theft, criminal trespass, resisting arrest, public lewdness, leaving a crime scene and—"

"Saving your goddamn life," she said.

Monroe held the gun on her. "Move over by that wall."

She didn't move.

"Drop the purse," Monroe said.

She didn't move. Monroe tightened his grip on the gun, moved closer and was about to pull the purse away when she swung it up, knocking his gun and the two fists holding on to it, to his right. Monroe kept his hands on the gun, turned his head, kept his eyes on her as he saw her wide, fleshy fist, studded with rings just below the knuckles, racing up to slam into the left side of his face. Monroe felt his jaw pop as he went backward, one foot going off the floor. Then the purse came back and caught him just below the ribs.

She wasn't a professional, Monroe decided as he fell flat on his ass. A professional would have kicked him in the—

He coughed, choked, the pain jolting from his crotch making him contract into a ball, his knees coming in. He took one hand off the gun, reached upward to block the purse that was swooping down for his face. His fingers found it, tangled in the handle, grabbed it. Using all of his weight, Monroe twisted and pulled down on the purse.

The purse didn't go down and for a moment they were locked together, the bathroom-freshener smell of Fatsie's perfume invading his nose, the gasping nose-whistling wheeze of her breath somewhere overhead, and then he opened two fingers on the hand holding the gun, reached up to the bulge of the wallet, grabbed it through the cloth and yanked.

Her toga ripped and his fingers snagged the isthmus of a terrifyingly large white fishnet bra that dipped and then flew apart. Her white, shapeless flesh poured forward, the wallet tumbling ahead, bouncing on the purple, blue, green, pink, rose, fuchsia, black and gold carpet.

Then Monroe saw little twinkling colors that weren't on the carpet, or on the ceiling. He turned his head to see her fist slam again into his eye. He loosened his grip on her purse, slipped to the carpet and put his hand on the wallet's moist, warm leather, and pulled the hand in as the gold heel of her shoe came down where his hand had been.

He had the wallet, and having it was far more important than the jarring impact of the purse on his head. He rolled out and away, saw Fatsie hovering over him, a fast shadow of shredded clothing obliterating all light. He felt her fingers using an extremely professional grip release, his fingers using an even more professional grip release and then, a sliding, ripping sound, of paper this time, and he saw above his head an explosion of money, health insurance card, long-distance telephone service card, dry cleaning claim check and what looked like an Atlantic City Police Department ID card.

Monroe scrambled along the floor but found himself enveloped in a grasping tangle of arms and legs. More people than he had seen all day, all week, were fumbling around, grabbing the money, and anything else that was loose.

And then they were gone. Monroe put his elbow on the carpet, propped himself up, looked around. The concourse was empty. Fatsie Morgan was gone, the wallet was gone.

He looked. He still had his gun in his hand.

No problem!

Then he put a hand on the carpet, pushed, tried to get up. His body wouldn't move. He put both hands down, then a knee, then the other knee.

His lips were wet and one side of his face seemed to be ringing, a bell that had been struck repeatedly. He pulled himself to his feet, saw the garish green, gold, red, purple, pink, blue, black and orange carpet swim under his feet, saw a scrap of noncolor on the carpet: the laminated police department ID.

He picked up the ID, saw Ephrum Traile's picture on it.

He coughed, rose painfully, looked down the concourse and saw no sign of Fatsie Morgan. He put the ID in his pocket, hobbled back toward the Topkapi Lounge, and saw that Mr. Hadruna and the rather badly disguised Ephrum Traile had also left.

That Traile was one of Fatsie Morgan's customers explained why Traile didn't want police officers, especially Deegan and Monroe, in the Alcazar tonight.

He felt his face begin to throb. Leaning against a mirrored column he saw, in the reflection, a flash of movement on the casino floor near the Serendipity Seven slot machines.

He had to squint and force himself to ignore the pain. He moved forward until he saw the back of Dan Raleigh's sport jacket. He moved to the side and saw Raleigh furious but perplexed. Of course, Raleigh was perplexed. Just ahead of him, Sergeant Raymond Deegan clung to the broad, spangled surface of a Serendipity Seven slot machine, one hand holding a credit card in a slot, the other pumping the handle. Deegan's drug-crazed eyes were on Raleigh's, not on the seven "reels" as they appeared to spin on each machine's color television screen.

"Am I gambling now?" Deegan roared. "How much longer I have to do this before you let me in your goddamn private club?"

Then Monroe thought his ears had decided to quit. The sound that filled them was not a ringing, or a buzzing. It was more like sirens. Sirens.

The cheeseburger in his stomach made a renewed effort to leave as Deegan turned around, dropped the handle and saw the front of the monster machine flashing and shimmering, the red stadium letters hanging above, alternately blinking $3,826,598.50 (the amount had increased thanks to Deegan's credit card input) and the word JACKPOT.

"Son of a *bitch!*" Deegan bellowed.

Sergeant Raymond Deegan had just become a multimillionaire.

There was, Monroe decided, no justice in the world.

CHAPTER
15

Is This a Miracle?

When a big slot jackpot hits, nothing happens for a few seconds. Then a cordon of security guards, some in plain clothes, some in uniforms, appear from nowhere and surround the machine, and the person who pulled the handle. Slot technicians are summoned. The slot manager calls the shift manager, who calls the director of slot operations, who calls the president of the casino and the casino's director of public relations, who calls a photographer. The casino president calls the chief operating officer of the casino. If the casino is owned by a colorful, mercurial, obnoxious and typically publicity-hogging personality who can't let a photo opportunity pass him by, this personality's twenty-four-hour secretary is called, who then tries to determine exactly where the personality is.

If the personality is with an equally vulgar publicity-seeking mistress, or involved in an embarrassing, unmacho or banal activity that might offend the high-rolling gambling clientele (such as making an obligatory, discomfiting, legally mandated visit with his children from his previous marriage), the secretary calls the personality's twenty-four-hour public relations consultant, who weighs the mood of the gambling-oriented public that tolerates, and even admires, the exploits of such personalities. The public relations consultant will then invent a more attractive ("contacted on his cellular phone while skiing on the slopes of Aspen"), flattering ("informed while making one of his characteristic unannounced visits to a hospital for terminally ill children"), perhaps

IS THIS A MIRACLE?

even ironic location ("I was in deep concentration in my gold-plated bathroom, which was designed by one of the top European bathroom designers for a member of royalty who went broke and gave me the whole shebang to pay off his marker") for the personality to inhabit when the great news is then delivered.

Fortunately the Alcazar was not connected to such an obnoxious, egocentric figurehead. It was owned by a corporation headed by monotonous, low-profile, thick-necked corporate types who, while not linked to organized crime, shared organized crime's goal of wanting to bleed as much money as possible from the enterprise without interference from the government, suppliers, labor unions or shareholders. The benefit of having greed-crazed upper management is that they tend to spend all of their time misleading government, suppliers, labor representatives and shareholders so as to maintain the bloated salaries, disproportionate benefits and parasitic indulgences that are, at best, paltry rewards for investing effort in the heroic salvation of Atlantic City.

With upper management too distracted by the noble task of covering its collective ass, middle management types, like Dan Raleigh, who worked an eighty-hour week, could transform events that could be beneficial to the Alcazar as a whole, into opportunities for personal gain.

At least, that's what Monroe thought was going on when, during the precious formative seconds of nothing that followed Sergeant Raymond Deegan's $3,826,598.50 pull on the fourth Serendipity Seven linked progressive slot machine, Dan Raleigh removed a portable radio from his jacket and assured the Alcazar's collective mind, in a tone loud enough and certain enough for Monroe to hear, "Raleigh One, Raleigh One. Cut the noise. No calls. No publicity. Everything on hold. I'll handle this."

Then Raleigh put the radio away, straightened his suit, rocked back on his heels, put on a Boardwalk smile and said, as the sirens shut off, "Well, well, well."

Deegan hadn't heard him. He still gripped the machine's handle. He couldn't take his eyes off the machine which, for all its lights and noises, had suddenly reverted back to what it had been before he had played it. The jackpot numbers overhead still read $3,826,-598.50, but they weren't flashing.

The security guards surrounded them, though without Mr. Hadruna.

"I won," Deegan said to the machine. He turned around, saw the security guards facing him, saw Raleigh and Monroe. "I won," he said firmly.

Raleigh smiled. "You've given us some things to do. Formalities. We have to check the machine, to make sure that everything's on the up and up, that there wasn't any tampering—"

"I *won*," Deegan said, more firmly. "I fucking won!" He looked at Monroe. "You saw it. I won."

"I seem to recall you wanting to visit the Alhambra," Raleigh said. He raised the radio again. "Raleigh One. Prepare the Alhambra for VIP priority visit. Clear all . . . unessential personnel and customers."

"She's going to be up there," Deegan said. "You'd better make sure she's there."

"Sergeant Deegan," Raleigh replied, gesturing with his hand. "We need to check the machine so, for a few minutes at least, why don't you and me and your partner have us an elevator ride to a more comfortable place."

For a moment a shadow of doubt crossed Deegan's face. Monroe could read his thoughts, or thought he could. He watched Deegan bring his eyes down from the machine, to the handle itself, knowing that handle had changed Deegan into a different person, and that once Deegan let go, the change would be complete.

"I won," Deegan said to the handle.

Raleigh glanced at a pitifully small crowd of gamblers who had left their machines and tables to peer at the new winner through the cordon of security guards.

"It appears as if you have," Raleigh said. "The law requires that we—"

"She'll be there," Deegan said, his eyes on the handle. "I can finally . . . get what I want."

Deegan let go of the handle and Raleigh gestured toward the elevator to the Alhambra lounge and said, "You're going to get everything that's coming to you."

The elevator cabin was a simple, narrow box of gold mirrors trimmed in green, blue and purple glass, whose arrows pointed down.

Only Deegan spoke on the ride up, repeating to himself, "I won, I won, I won, for the first time in my life, I won . . ."

The doors opened to small landing, where a young, tuxedoed maitre d' stood and moved to the side, his eyes down, as Raleigh, Deegan and Monroe passed.

The landing opened into a surprisingly small arrangement of overstuffed chairs in loud, blue-and-gold patterns around cocktail tables adorned with white-and-gold telephones. To the left was a broad, fully stocked bar with two stools. To the right was a wide-screen television, and a black baby grand piano where a man in a tuxedo sat, playing tranquilized pop tunes.

But what dominated the room was the view, seen through a floor-to-ceiling wall of glass, of the floodlit tops of a row of casino hotels, their signs glowing red. The view looked south, and Monroe could see glistening lights along the Boardwalk, stretching like a string of pearls against the inky, evening black of the beach and the ocean. The Boardwalk ended amidst the spangled lights of Ventnor and Margate, with the narrow fragment of Longport curving to the left, and the northern tip of Ocean City, the next barrier island town, rolling into the horizon.

To the right was the city itself—all lights, lines and shadows that concealed everything that didn't glow. Slums, boarded-up shops, and trash-strewn vacant lots were invisible from this height. Hanging just under the crescent moon, the blinking lights of an airplane drifted lazily on to Bader Field, the city's small airport. Just beyond it, the flow of headlights from the Atlantic City Expressway gave Monroe the illusion that he was gazing down on some vast, vibrant, healthy machine.

Moving against the view was Nita Ivas. She appeared delicately thin, without the harried, stone-faced, perpetually annoyed stare that most cocktail waitresses have after an hour or so of wearing a costume that doesn't quite fit, over three layers of pantyhose. Add to that painfully high heels and so much makeup that it would crack and fall off in chunks if she tried to smile.

Nita Ivas looked fabulous. Her wink included the three men in such a way that each felt he was getting her complete attention.

Monroe tried to project confidence, until he glanced in a smoky mirror hung near the bar and saw a leering idiot reflected back at him. He blushed but his eyes went back to the Nita's face and he couldn't help but notice the ringlets of Nita Ivas's tightly curled black hair, her bright-red lips, her marvelously shaped legs, hips, waist in a ridiculous blue, purple and white cheesecloth belly dancer ensemble that left her midrift bare, and showed enough of her breasts to make Monroe yearn.

She pointed to a small cocktail table. Resting on the table was a double scotch, a margarita, and a glass of orange juice.

She swooped past another table, scooped up one glass ashtray and put a clean one in its place. Monroe smelled cigarette smoke. The lounge had been occupied.

Raleigh took a seat in front of his scotch. Monroe sat in front of his margarita. Deegan stood, picked up his orange juice and stared at Nita Ivas. Monroe wanted to tell him to sit down but he saw on Deegan's face the mooning, completely un-self-conscious stare of an infatuated man.

She fluttered toward the bar. Deegan watched her for a few more seconds, then downed the entire glass.

The bartender immediately put another orange juice on the bar. Nita was by Deegan's side, settling the glass down, her eyes refusing to look into his. She smiled briefly and went back to the bar. Deegan stared at Nita as if he didn't recognize her.

"Perhaps Ms. Ivas would care to acquaint our new player with the more intimate facilities," Raleigh said. He tilted his head at a door set in the wall between the bar and the elevator. A discreet gold plate on the door said SALON.

Deegan's eyes seemed to go blank. "Why?" he said innocently.

"If you have to ask—" Raleigh began.

Then he said with unnatural calm, "I don't have to ask. I don't have to do anything anymore. I'm rich now. I won."

He looked at Monroe. "Right?"

Monroe nodded.

Then he said to Nita, "I have something to give you. A picture that I thought would explain everything. I don't need it anymore. I don't need to explain anything anymore."

"Anything you want," Nita said.

Deegan set off for the Salon. He had his hand on the knob when he said to Monroe, "Is this a miracle, or is this a miracle?"

He held the door open to a room lit in warm, suffused, amber, pink lights. Nita strode in as if she owned it.

The door shut, Raleigh lifted his drink and said, "Strange night."

Monroe's aches and pains had once again begun to make themselves known. He looked at his drink.

"Might as well, Lou," Raleigh said. "It's not going to get any better." He lifted a telephone on the table, called down to the marketing department for an empty suite "to put the victim in."

He hung up the phone, took another sip of scotch. "I know what you're thinking," he said to Monroe. "Why him, of all people?"

"I'm thinking that it's been an awfully long time since you asked to have the slot machine checked out," Monroe said.

Raleigh pointed to Monroe's ripped sweatshirt. "If you'd be so kind as to remove the little device you're wearing?"

Monroe lifted his shirt, and saw that, not only was he wearing the microphone with the red dot on it—the one that wasn't supposed to work when the operator perspired—but that, in addition to the fact that he was sweating, the little spindle inside the tape recorder had stopped turning. He shut the machine off, opened it, pulled out a microcassette encased in a bush of crinkled tape.

"Wonderful how technology can let you down when you need it the most, eh?" Raleigh said.

"You don't seem surprised," Monroe said.

"Fuck-ups never surprise me. Fuck-ups create losers and we do need our losers. It's the winners that always throw me. You'd think there'd be some reason or rationale to it, that the guy who hits big is a saint and never cheated on his wife and has a mother on a kidney machine and needs the money. But it never works out that way. What works out is: the people who win, no matter how low they are, no matter how disgusting, no matter how many times they did wrong, are the first to think they deserve it."

Monroe took a slow sip of his margarita. "So what's going to happen to him?"

Raleigh shrugged. "That all depends."

"On the machine checking out?"

Raleigh took a big, deep, sad breath. "Lou, I wish that Ray Deegan was just some normal, ordinary, desperate dipshit who wandered off the street. We could handle that. We're experts on turning dipshits into winners. But everything I've heard about Deegan says to me, this boy is up to his ass in so much shit, we take his picture and put him in the paper, somebody connects him with the property and . . ." Raleigh took a big gulp of scotch. "So we have to check the machine."

"He won. I saw that. There was no way he could've jammed that machine."

Raleigh touched his ear and nodded toward the salon room. "Did you hear that? Sounded like a grown man crying. We have a hot tub, shower and massage table in there. It's supposed to be soundproof, but I've had moments when I've sat here and imagined that I'm hearing a human being *actually* having a good time."

He brushed his lapels. "When Deegan's finished his business, there'll be a keycard in room 1802. There's a spiral staircase behind the elevator column. He can take that down to the eighteenth floor.

There'll be four suite rooms. The door to 1802 will be open. You can tell him that if he wants to spend the night, the room is on us. Room service he'll have to cover from his own pocket. You hanging around? No matter, I'll tell the bartender to catch him on the way out."

"Dan, he won."

Raleigh turned toward the window. "Some people can't, Lou."

It was late and Monroe was throbbing and buzzing and probably bleeding but he couldn't help but lose himself in the view. He became astonished at how beautiful and mysterious the slum sections of the city appeared when seen from a height. The streetlights and the backglare from the floodlights illuminating the casino towers gave the streets an almost magical moonlit glow. In the same way that a fresh snowfall rounded out the harsh, lifeless edges of a winter landscape, so did the evening light transform the scars of greed, poverty and despair into inviting, luminous shadows that hid—not muggers, drug dealers and prostitutes—but possibilities, opportunities, potential for great and wonderful change.

He looked down at his drink and wondered if it was the alcohol, or the long night that had given him this vision. He asked, "What's going to happen to him, Dan?"

Raleigh stood. "Machines can have problems," he said. Monroe imagined that Raleigh was looking at the same view, but seeing it differently. "Sometimes, we solve one problem by finding another, you understand?"

Raleigh went into the elevator, punched the button that said DOWN.

16

Down by the Sea

The next morning Ellie Monroe was in the bathroom when her husband painfully extracted himself from the bed, tiptoed into the kitchen, ran the hot water and made himself a cup of terrible tasting lukewarm instant coffee. He drank it while watching rain slash against the window, reducing the view of the fishing boats and sagging boatsheds to a rippling blur.

On the kitchen table was a five-page list of things they had to buy before the baby came.

He went downstairs, retrieved a soggy edition of the *Atlantic City Star* and saw an item about Reuben Claymore, on the front page above the fold. EX-COP AIDS STATE.

An unnamed source "within the State Police organization" told the *Atlantic City Star* that Claymore, an Atlantic City patrolman who was charged with possession of methamphetamine with intent to distribute, was assisting a special state police investigation that was going to implicate "highly placed individuals in Atlantic City municipal government."

The article went on to say that Claymore had been an active informant with the state police's Department of Special Investigations up to his arrest.

There was nothing about the new millionaire.

Monroe sat at the kitchen table, watching the rain until the doorbell buzzed.

The mailwoman had a damp package and a wet card with a

dotted line for Monroe to sign. "Who's it from?" Monroe asked, hanging back in the shadows so she wouldn't see his face.

She read the return address. "Upper Crust Gift Stores, Inc. c/o Alcazar Casino Hotel. Looks like one of those gifts they send out." The package was addressed to Ellen B. Meade.

"She didn't order anything from these people," Monroe said.

"Don't you want to find out what it is?" the mailwoman said. "I've delivered some incredible stuff for them. They ain't no run-of-the-mill outfit."

"It's a front for a high-roller call-girl service that's run out of casino gift shops," Monroe said.

The mailwoman shook her head. "You say that? I say I'm sick and tired of people pinning all kinds of organized crime and Mafia stuff on the casinos. My brother washes pots at the Frontenac and he don't know anybody named Luigi or Nickie or Carmine or anybody like that. You can flap your mouth all you want to, but my brother has to own up to loose talk like yours."

"I didn't mean to hurt your feelings," Monroe said to the mail-woman. "But my wife can't accept this."

Then he heard Ellie call down, "What is it?"

Monroe saw her at the top of the stairs, her face pale and gaunt, her eyes sunken, her hair matted from sleep. She was wearing a mottled pink bathrobe that showed wear from too many washings.

Monroe pulled his bathrobe around him. "A package from . . . Upper Crust Gift Stores."

She was delighted. "Really!"

"Really. And we're sending it back."

Ellie came down the stairs. "Not before we find out what it is."

Monroe saw that she was barefoot. "We can't send it back if we open it."

Ellie put a thin, delicate hand on the glossy black-and-gold wrapping paper. "If we don't like it, I can always run it back."

"You aren't going near that place again," Monroe said. He was about to give the package back when Ellie lifted it out of his hands.

"But I want to see—"

The mailwoman said, "You can see all you want, but somebody's got to sign for it."

"It's for me," Ellie said. "I'll sign for it."

Monroe glared at her. "Did you order anything from them?"

"Of course not—"

"Then we can't sign for it. If you or I sign that piece of paper, it means this has been accepted, and police officers and their wives are not allowed to accept unsolicited gifts."

"I'm unemployed and pregnant," Ellie said, smiling as the mailwoman's eyes dropped to the bulge around her middle. "I can accept anything I want." She took the pen from the mailwoman's hand.

"But Ellie, it's from—"

"I know who it's from."

"And—" He stopped as he watched her sign her beautifully neat, legible signature.

She handed the pen back to the mailwoman. "Sorry about the fuss. We don't get many packages."

"I can see that," the mailwoman said. She regarded Monroe. "So, you're a cop, huh? Atlantic City police? Is it true what they say, about that officer, the one busted for drugs is going to bust the mayor?"

"The papers always get it wrong," Monroe said.

Then Ellie shrieked. "Oh my *Lord!* He remembered!"

She was sitting on the stairs, the package open, a luxurious black-and-burgundy silk robe in her arms.

Monroe became afraid. "Who remembered?"

"My *birthday!*"

Monroe wanted to disappear, better yet, jump in a time machine, go back two days, buy *something,* wrap it, have it waiting to avert the explosion that was about to come.

The mailwoman was triumphant. "Now, see what I told you? It's not so bad, is it?"

Ellie hugged the robe. "Oh, it's wonderful!" She looked at her husband. "And you forgot."

The mailwoman shut the door fast.

"I, um—"

Ellie stomped upstairs, slammed the door so hard it bounced open. Monroe waited a few minutes, slowly mounted the stairs. The door was open. He was halfway up the stairs when he peered through the open door, down the hall and saw the bedroom door closed.

He looked under the couch and found a pair of running shorts that Ellie hadn't thrown out, beside a rather stiff, smelly pair of socks. He decided to forego the T-shirt.

He was out of the apartment almost before he knew it, taking slow, awkward, excruciating strides, forcing his damaged muscles to work slowly, repetitively. The rain turned his running shoes into squishy sponges.

A few minutes later the rain lessened, as if its purpose in soaking Atlantic City was merely to make Monroe's first mile difficult. He wasn't quite running until he passed the rotting remains of Captain Starn's Pier, the northernmost point of Absecon Island, where the Atlantic City Boardwalk began.

As he raced up the ramp and tore along the Boardwalk's northern edge, he felt the pain fade and his body wake up. To his left, ocean chop tumbling through the Absecon Channel crashed beneath the Boardwalk, dousing sections of the Great Wooden Way with angry blasts of seawater. The rain seemed to retreat from the surf, and finally ceased as he passed the first ruined, storm-shattered Boardwalk pavilion.

The pavilion was at least a century old, but had been destroyed less than a decade ago by a hurricane and had never been repaired. The ruin, and the Boardwalk's flimsy, warped, sea-battered planks gave anyone who was brave enough to walk this far the impression that City Hall would rather that this stretch of the Boardwalk, and the North Inlet in general, did not exist.

Because the Boardwalk was built above street-level, Monroe could look down the long avenues and see through the morning fog groups of drug dealers standing on corners that, a little more than fifty years ago, hid speakeasies and backroom casinos. The dealer's mules—young gang members barely in their teens—ran out to the drivers of expensive automobiles who were lined up for a little something to make the ride back home go a little faster.

It took Monroe about twenty minutes, just about when the Boardwalk curved around the old, blue glass, former senior citizen enclave turned condo, for his body to grow comfortable with the run. Then gravity seemed to let go of him and the springy planks of weathered yellow pine and jarrah wood began to fly beneath his feet.

After half a mile he found himself trotting the section of the Boardwalk that had been his beat as a patrolman. He worked for five years on the four-block stretch from Brighton Pier to the Alcazar Casino Hotel. He remembered standing outside in worse storms, when the wind and rain ripped into him, soaked him to the bone, and always seeing people.

He saw a few rolling chairs, their pushers positioning themselves near the entrances to the casino hotels. The pizza stands had yet to open their doors so there was only the sharp odor of sea brine blowing across the beach. Monroe saw, across from Brighton Pier, the Pizza Pit, where a month ago, the right kind of customer—a casino blackjack dealer in uniform with a few thousand dollars cash—could get a plastic bag of illicit drugs when he ordered a pie for delivery.

Officer Reuben Claymore had been the Pizza Pit's unofficial delivery boy. Monroe wondered if he could still get a large pepperoni with extra cocaine.

Monroe looked down the Boardwalk toward the Alcazar Casino Hotel, and saw that the top of the tower seemed to end in fog. His mind drifted to last night, to Deegan emerging completely naked from the salon, a wild, happy, delighted grin on his face, strutting down like a paunchy peacock to his opulent room.

"Things are going to be different now, partner-of-mine," Deegan had said to Monroe as he shut the door. Monroe had walked him to his hotel room. "There's nothing like coming into a lot of money to make you realize what you don't need."

Monroe passed a few joggers, morning walkers and shambling, stumbling losers, who, in the way of some of the down and busted-out, believe that if they keep moving, they will not have to face the enormity of their losses. No one said hello, good morning, or how's it going.

In the distance a man sat in a wheelchair, his scrawny upper body wrapped in a frayed, oversized tuxedo. Shielding him from the elements was a broad, red and white umbrella tied to the chair's frame. Suspended above the chair's armrests was a child's xylophone, the metal keys tinged with rust from the sea brine. On top of the xylophone sat a long, silver spoon.

The man, who took in as much as five thousand dollars a day during the big holiday weekends of Memorial Day, Labor Day, the Fourth of July and the Miss America Pageant weekend, was paralyzed from the neck down. He stationed his wheelchair in front of Brighton Pier, or near a casino hotel's Boardwalk entrance, and played the popular classics, "The Star Spangled Banner," "Semper Fidelis," "White Christmas," "Luck Be a Lady," or the classic Peaches and Cream song—"On the Boardwalk in Atlantic City," by gripping the handle of a spoon in his mouth and tapping the spoon on his zylophone. Few strollers could pass such a pathetic display of virtuoso talent without digging deep into their pockets.

While on the Boardwalk beat, Louis Monroe wrote begging citations against this man and was astonished to see the city do nothing about them. Then he learned that the man who called himself the Maestro Toccata N. Fugue was no mere beggar, but the wealthiest man on the Boardwalk, thanks to his enormously lucrative loan-sharking operation. The dollars donated to what appeared to be a poor, sad-sack musician tended to go into the pockets of busted-out gamblers desperate for one last chance. They got their chance, and then they got a visit from the Maestro's bodyguard, Big Mike McKue, who stood behind the Maestro like a sentry in a leather jacket. When passersby claimed that they

wanted to fill the Maestro's cup but "couldn't break a twenty," Big
Mike stepped in and, with a voice sufficiently low and menacing,
announced that he could make the change.

The Maestro waved his spoon and Monroe found himself stopping. "Do I know you?" the Maestro asked.

"I think you do," Monroe said.

"I feel behooved to express my 'preciation," the Maestro
wheezed. "The business climate hereabouts is improved with Officer Roo removed. I consider this as payment of debts between us.
I'd also provide for you a tip." Monroe saw Big Mike reach into
his leather jacket. "But you don't work for tips."

"No, I don't," Monroe said. He looked at Big Mike and wondered how a person as powerless as the Maestro could command
a bodyguard so huge and imposing. Big Mike held all of the
Maestro's cash. Big Mike did the Maestro's collection work. Big
Mike drove the Cadillac stretch-limousine, parked out of sight
behind a moldering motel, that the Maestro used to commute from
his home in suburban Linwood to the spot on the Boardwalk he
called his "recital hall."

The Maestro hoisted his spoon in the air and plunked out the
wedding march. Before the final note, he tossed back his head, let
the spoon drop to the key that resolved the musical phrase. "How
is your lovely bride?"

"Ellie's still one of your fans, Tommy."

"You are not referring to me correctly."

"Your name's Tommy Fugari."

"Is it?"

"You and Marty Gant saved a baby's life."

"For what reason?"

"The only decent one there is."

"What a lovely world it is," the Maestro announced. "That two
men can exchange courtesies in the light of day." He bent his head
forward. "If you need my services, don't hesitate to beg."

Monroe regarded Big Mike again, watched Big Mike throw his
shoulders back, square his chin and smile proudly.

The Maestro lifted his spoon and began to play "Under the Boardwalk." Big Mike mumbled the lyrics.

Monroe said, "What happened to you when they took you down by the sea?"

The Maestro dropped his spoon. "Nobody needs to know."

The ocean had been the attraction that brought millions of people hundreds of miles east. But few people went near it. It was almost an act of courage to step off the Boardwalk and put one's foot on the sandy grit. Tourists would glance at the beach, make some comment about fresh air and perhaps toss some uneaten pizza crusts at the seagulls, and then move on.

Monroe had heard that it was possible to run along the tideline, that zone of sand between the ocean and the dry beach that was neither wet nor dry, moist enough and firm enough to support a runner's shoes without soaking them.

So why, having been born and raised a mere ten miles from the Jersey shore, had he never done it? Perhaps being born close to the ocean had prevented him from enjoying it.

Ellie had never tired of telling him that, because she was born in West Virginia, she got tired of mountains. Mountains were there before you were born and they'll be there when you die, and there won't be much difference for anybody to see. But an ocean, she told him, an ocean is changing every second of the day. Look at it once, blink, and it's a different world.

So why did he feel so rotten for forgetting her birthday? Or was it because he was beaten up by a prostitute who had just been in the act of coddling and robbing the man responsible for integrity in the police department? Or did it have something to do with watching Deegan become a millionaire? Why couldn't he just blink and make it a different world?

Monroe took a set of weatherbeaten steps leading toward the sea. The sand was covered by a crust of dried, sunbaked grit that broke as he ran. The soft powder beneath swallowed his shoes up to his ankles. He felt the sand slipping around his socks, but he kept going, his feet sinking deeper into the sand as a breeze tumbled toward him from the water. He heard the waves—no more than a whisper from the Boardwalk—begin to roar.

Down by the sea the beach was a collection plate of seaweed and shells, as well as cigarette butts, rotting soda cups, corroding beer cans and shards of glass, soiled paper plates, Styrofoam cups. It was a filter that took from the ocean astonishing varieties of junk discarded by Boardwalkers on land, boaters at sea, and the overloaded sewage treatment plants hidden in the back bays.

He saw a sickly yellow foam rolling over the pale brown grit like fluffy yellow detergent suds. He remembered reading in the *Atlantic City Star* that this was a perfectly natural phenomenon based on the presence of tiny living organisms, natural organic chemicals, wave motion and wind currents.

The waves rushed and covered his path, tumbling broken, fist-sized quahog clam shells. He tried to run along a four- to eight-foot wide stretch of moist, firm sand that was free of broken clam shells and man-made trash.

He had to watch his steps. He had to avoid the slipping, sliding motion of the waves. The tide appeared to be coming in, pushing the waterline higher up the beach. He turned around once, and saw his footprints erased by the rushing water.

The sighing, crashing sounds of the waves began to merge with the inner sound of his breath. He looked up and saw, burning through the fog, a blurry, golden orb hanging grandly in the sky.

If this city is a clam, then there's the pearl, Monroe said to himself, feeling the light on his face.

Just below the sun, at the edge of the tideline about fifty yards in front of him, was a sky-blue jeep with big tires and a flashing yellow emergency light on top of the cab. He saw two men, one muscular in a black wetsuit, another frail and shabby in a collection of ragged clothes, wrestling an orange, inflatable liferaft out of the back.

Monroe recognized the guy in the rags.

In front of the jeep he saw, slumped along the tideline, a fat, dark, slick tube, fat in the middle, narrowing at the ends. Monroe thought first that it was man-made, a gray metal piece of a ship that had gone down some miles out, or maybe an old torpedo from one of the World War Two U-2 subs that had sunk somewhere off the Jersey coast.

He approached cautiously and then stopped when he heard breathing that wasn't his own. It was a wet, rasping, tortured sound, louder than the crashing surf, coming from that dark tube. He moved closer and saw water spurting out of a darker hole at one end of the ten-foot-long thing. At the other, half submerged, a tail flicked in the rushing foam.

And along the edge of the thing, cuts, welts, running sores of ruddy red blood.

"It's alive!" Monroe shouted.

"Aren't we all," muttered the guy in the wetsuit. He said, "*Kogia breviceps*. Pigmy sperm whale. Stranded."

The fellow in rags said, "That means he ain't where he's supposed to be and he can't get back unless we do something about it."

Then he recognized Monroe. "Good morning, Officer. Is the weather pleasing today?"

Monroe smiled at Jimmy "the Geek" Doochay. "It is, Geek, it's just fine."

The Geek pulled his Phillies cap down tight over his long, tangled gray strands of hair, as he helped the guy in the wetsuit put the liferaft on the tideline.

Monroe glanced at ten feet of helpless, dark gray, shuddering, bleeding, rain-spattered whale.

The guy in the wetsuit introduced himself as Don Havenshead, of the Marine Life Rescue Station in Brigantine. "Go into the back of the truck and get some gloves," he added. "Whales don't strand themselves unless they're frightened or sick. We don't know what's wrong with this one and we don't want to catch whatever it is."

"What could we catch?" Monroe asked, hesitating. Then he

saw the rage in Havenshead's eyes—rage that wasn't directed at him, but at a world in which animals suffer.

"Anything that can make him sick, can make us sick," Havenshead said. "He's a mammal. He breathes air. His internal organs are virtually identical to ours. The only thing he can't do is tell us what's wrong."

Among tackle boxes, coils of rope, and other rain-soaked supplies, Monroe found a pair of scratched and pitted scuba diver's gloves. They felt wet on his hands.

"How do you know it's a he?" he asked.

"You want to see?" Havenshead called back as he laid the liferaft beside the whale.

Monroe held up his hands. "No, no. That's okay. I was just curious."

"You might want to take those shoes off," Havenshead called. "If you hang around with marine mammals, you're going to get wet. There are some wetsuit boots in the back there, too. Put them on. The jellyfish aren't too bad today, but there's no need to get stung."

Monroe glanced back at the Boardwalk and saw a few spectators had stopped to stare. He wrenched off his shoes and socks some distance from the tideline, then pulled a pair of clammy orange mid-calf boots over his feet.

"Come down here and hold this in place," Havenshead said.

Monroe fit in between Havenshead and the Geek, put his hands on the waterlogged, uninflated liferaft and a wave came up, splashing between his legs. The water went up, doused his stomach and seeped into his crotch. He yelped and laughed and the Geek, whose filthy pants and shirt were somewhat improved by the sea bath, laughed with him.

Havenshead went back to the truck, opened the cab, began talking into a CB radio.

Monroe asked, "Where's he go—"

Another wave slammed into him, splashing his stomach and

flinging brine into Monroe's face, nose and open mouth. His face, especially the side that had been hit, sizzled with pain.

"Gotta watch that," the Geek said.

Monroe spat out water, looked up at the shuddering, blood-streaked bulk of the whale. He tried not to think of whatever in the water had made the yellow foam.

Havenshead said, "There's a problem with the boat. They're getting a weird cross-current in the Absecon Channel, so I'm going to have to take it out."

"Maybe that's why Moby paid us a visit," the Geek said.

Havenshead blinked the rain out of his eyes. "No way. This baby's in trouble. Some of those lesions could have come from abrasions, but not the rest. He's sick. Too sick to go back. We have to get him to the tank."

"They gotta tank they can put 'im in back in Brigantine," the Geek said. "Gotta get 'im there first."

Havenshead turned to Monroe. "You and Jimmy are going to stay here while I drive back and bring the boat, if you're okay."

Monroe said he was okay.

"We normally have a lot of volunteers on call, but sometimes you can't get anyone to answer the phone. Fortunately for me, Jimmy doesn't have a phone."

"I keep a lookout," the Geek said, the stained lips behind his beard frowning in discomfort. "Sometimes I'd rather not see what I see."

"I offered him a job," Havenshead said, "but he wouldn't take it."

The Geek brightened. "Don't want to rot behind a desk."

Havenshead turned to Monroe. "You ever make a sand castle?"

Monroe said, "Not in a long time."

"There's a snow shovel in the back of the truck. Get it and I'll do the digging."

Monroe found the shovel, gave it to Havenshead who, after telling Monroe to hold the liferaft, used the flat shovel to remove sand from under the whale's middle. As he removed the sand,

Monroe and the Geek shoved the deflated raft into the cavity he'd made.

"Moby's a little too heavy to lift," Havenshead explained, "And we don't want to drag him any, because the sand will take his skin off. The idea is to put the raft under him, right in the middle here, then we inflate the raft. The raft lifts him about an inch or two off the sand, and then we pull the raft and Moby back into the water."

"He must weigh a ton," Monroe said as a wave swamped his legs.

"Not a bad guess," Havenshead said, panting as he shoved wet sand away. He went around to the other side of the whale and began digging. "We would have had a problem if the tide weren't coming in. By the time we get the raft under him and inflated, the tide will give us about four to five inches of water to work with."

Monroe pushed the raft under the whale as chilling waves smacked into his legs. The Geek was at his side. "Shouldn't've happened," he heard the Geek mutter. "What they did to him."

Monroe saw the Geek more troubled than he'd ever seen him. "Geek, what are you talking about?"

"He couldn't do nothing but give up," the Geek said. He wiped the spray out of his beard. "They took it away from him, like they took it away from so many."

"*What* did they take away?"

The Geek raised his voice. "What it is, what it is that makes you want to keep livin'."

"These are living creatures," Havenshead said. "They breathe the same air we do. They live in the water we dump our trash in. And they can't figure why they have to die any more than we can."

Havenshead centered the raft under the whale, pulled the stops on the compressed-air tanks, and the raft hissed to life. He dug away the sand on the seaward side of the raft as Monroe, shivering in the light breeze, grabbed a rope tied to the front of the raft and followed the Geek into the surf. They stopped when they stood in two feet of water.

Havenshead shouted, "PULL!"

Monroe tried to find traction in the sand below the water when he was hit broadside with a wave and went face down into the surf.

"Time out," the Geek called. He grabbed Monroe's arm and helped him to his feet. "The way we do it is, we pull just a little, when the wave is coming back. Let what's working do the working."

Havenshead held his hand in the air. "Okay, get ready. I'm going to count it down now."

Monroe and the Geek stood side by side, holding tightly to the rope. A wave slapped against their legs and rushed toward the beach.

"One . . . two . . . three. . . . PULL!"

They pulled and a ton of gray, bleeding whale slid a few inches toward the ocean.

"Now we wait 'til Don tells us to pull again," the Geek said.

After a dozen yanks the raft, its center submerged under the weight of the whale, was floating freely. Havenshead waved them back to the tideline and said, "Now you hold on to him while I get the boat. Figure a half an hour. Wet him down but keep water out of the blowhole."

Monroe noticed that the whale was breathing, too, and that their breaths seemed to move together.

Havenshead climbed into the jeep, gave a thumbs-up sign, backed the jeep away from the tideline and toward the Boardwalk.

The Geek assumed an authoritative pose. "Now we take turns holding the rope, so our hands don't get cramped up much. We make sure Moby don't float away and we throw some water on him."

Holding the raft's rope in one hand, he picked up a boat bailer with the other, scooped some seawater and gently poured it over the whale. "Somebody in one of the casinos spotted him, called for Rescue. No matter what it is, no matter where it is, somebody's always watching, whether they want to or not."

"Geek, what did you see last night?"

The Geek shook his head in broken movements. He bent over and threw some water on the whale.

Monroe glanced toward the Boardwalk. The call could have come from several casinos, though the Alcazar was the closest. He stared directly at the Alcazar, searching the windows for some movement, a face, a figure. But the fog had shrouded the casino's upper stories in mist. If anyone had called about a whale, that person would have had to have been walking on the tideline, or close to it, to be able to see the creature.

The Geek poured more water on the whale and tugged on the raft until its corner rested on the sand.

"You think he'll live?" Monroe said.

"If he don't give up," he put his hand on Monroe's arm. "You can't do that. Folks look at me, they think I gave up, but I never."

Monroe knew the Geek could be exasperating at times, and this was one of them. "Gave up *what*, Geek?"

The Geek poured more water on the whale and said, "Hold on, Moby. You just hold on." He turned to Monroe. "Don says they can be afraid of what's coming after them, or sick, or lost, or they make a mistake and forget about the tide going out."

"Natural causes," Monroe said.

"And then there was the time we found a sea turtle that had its neck cut up from a boat prop, and a seal that strangled on the rings they put around six-packs of beer, and a sea lion that suffocated when it swallowed one of them campaign balloons the mayor let go when he announced he was running again. The sea lion was dead when Don found it, and when Don did the operation to find out why, you could see the mayor's name still on one of them balloons. If they get the mayor like they say they're going to get the mayor, there's the ghost of a sea lion out here that won't mind."

Monroe tried to smile. "That would be an unnatural cause."

The Geek again wiped spray from his beard. "Unnatural, natural, it's all the same. World's more mixed up than it's not. Sometimes it's the ocean itself does the killing. The ocean can take a living thing and do a lot before it throws it back. Makes you wish you never seed it. Makes you wish you got no memory, so you don't have to know what it used to be."

"Geek, what the hell are you talking about?"

"Can't say, Officer. The day's too nice, and we got to take care of the livin'."

He said nothing until heard the sound of a motor and saw, coming through the last filaments of fog, Havenshead fighting the surf in an open launch. The Geek waded out into the surf and tossed the rope to Havenshead, who tied it to the boat.

He went back to Monroe. "I'm going to ride back with Don and Moby. Don says you can come along if you want. Or you can go down a little further, see what it is you came to see."

"I'm just out for a run," Monroe said. He thought he saw a blinking red light in the mist ahead. "What's going on down there?"

The Geek asked for the boots. Monroe tossed them off, handed them over and hurriedly yanked on his socks and shoes.

The Geek saluted. Monroe saluted back. The Geek waded out to the boat. Havenshead hooked a ladder to the gunwales, then moved to the opposite side of the boat as the Geek heaved himself aboard.

Monroe tied his shoelaces and then raced for the flickering red light. As he ran closer, he saw red lights from the cherrybars atop police and emergency vehicles.

They were clustered around a stone jetty. Monroe counted three police cars, one ambulance and the broad, white bulk of the Mobile Crime Lab, its rear door hanging like a dead wing from its broken frame.

The vehicles were positioned so their headlights shone on the jetty. A group of figures, mostly uniformed men, were milling about, soaking up overtime as two men wearing what looked like spacesuits crouched over a gray corpse that had been snagged and jammed into a crevice in the jetty.

The spacesuits were Anti-Contamination Gear, part of the Mobile Crime Lab's complement of overpriced equipment.

Standing before the rocks, his belted khaki raincoat and floppy fishing hat almost shining in the headlights, was Vice Squad Commander Captain Marty Gant, who turned around with uncanny instinct, as Monroe ducked past a blue-suit and stopped in Gant's shadow.

"You get the message I left with your lovely bride?" Gant said. "The message was to stay away. You got a birthday to celebrate."

Monroe felt a coldness creeping through his body, freezing him as he took in the colors of the corpse's skin which, under the lights, were a dark, waterlogged blue, alternating with great patches of purple bruises.

"What was that?" Gant asked.

A few fingers on one of the corpse's hands had been either eaten, or ripped off by things in the water.

Monroe was unaware that he had said anything. He saw that the corpse was barefoot, one foot twisted horribly into the crevice, the other projecting against a rock as if the corpse had woken momentarily and tried to kick free. The face was missing its jaw, eyes, and portions of its ears. The rest of the skin was flayed and shredded. The clothing, made of inedible, unrecyclable industrial fibers, remained on the limbs and torso, and helped Monroe fill in the absent parts of Sergeant Raymond Deegan.

"I'm afraid we are looking at a suicide, or accidental death due to drowning," Gant said, his face long and ashen. "We must defer to the coroner, of course."

"This is not a suicide," Monroe said. "Nothing would have made him kill himself."

Gant spat on the sand as Deegan had from the unmarked car last night. "There's plenty. Sometimes suicide is the only thing you can be sure of. The rest is just a mess of parts that never fit together. Like what happened to your unmarked vehicle. Dispatch got a call from those distinguished officers Big Fish and Jerry Lad at 0122 hours about how an unmarked police department vehicle was found vandalized in the Alcazar casino parking lot. You have any theories as to how said vehicle could have got itself so vandal-ized? I sure as hell hope not."

Gant looked out to sea. "So we'll just never know, will we?"

Monroe said, "Traile."

Gant turned. "I see no trail."

"Ephrum Traile."

Gant scowled.

"I have his ID," Monroe seethed. "He was sitting there in the lounge getting his balls squeezed by—"

Gant raised his hand. "Please, Lou, I have enough on my plate—"

"He was there!" Monroe shouted.

"—Without you making me too sick to eat."

The techs in the spacesuits turned around and looked at them. Gant smiled, then said in a low voice, "I'm gonna have to eat this one. Cops are supposed to go crazy when it's one of their own. But not this time. We have to give up on this one, you hear me?"

"No," Monroe said. "I don't hear you."

"Deegan was into enough stuff—"

"He won."

"The machine was found to be defective," Gant snarled. "The Division of Gaming Enforcement inspected the machine. The DGE is an arm of the state police. Got it all explained to me in a call from Commander Zimmer this morning. Answer me this, Lou. Before Deegan walked himself into the ocean, he give you any-thing? A picture maybe."

Monroe looked at the top of the Alcazar. "No."

"Did your casino-sleaze chum inform you that Zimmer and his state police unit, as well as a sequestered witness taken to driving around the town in a black-ass jeep confiscated from some drug dealer, were staying on the very same floor that Deegan was put on?"

Monroe looked back at the corpse. "He didn't kill himself."

"You don't understand the function of the ocean as it applies to Atlantic City government," Gant said. "This goes way back, long before Uncle Sam Claymore was mayor and his sons Reuben and Larry used to take folks that didn't cooperate for a little trip down by the sea."

Monroe clenched his fists. "What did Reuben do to him?"

"I can't say who did what to whom. Nobody can. The function of the ocean is as follows: anything you toss in will come back at you, but by the time it does, it'll be changed enough so nobody will know how it got there."

Gant observed the bruises on Monroe's body. "You shouldn't be running about in your condition."

"It takes the pain away," Monroe said.

"One professional to another, son, *nothing* takes the pain away, though I have had occasion to believe that women were invented for that purpose."

"When I left Deegan last night, he had no reason to kill himself," Monroe said. "What happened last night—"

"Has had the final benefit of taking you out of the trouble you were in," Gant said. "Nobody's calling for your head anymore."

Monroe could not believe what he was hearing. "Why?"

Gant pointed to the corpse. "In getting himself off the game board, this man made some people happy."

"You?"

Gant turned away as the front door of the Mobile Crime Lab swung open. Inspector Ephrum Traile ambled up, his arms folded over the breastpocket of his brown sport jacket, where the regs required that his ID be clipped.

"Good to have you on the scene, Detective," Traile breathed, his voice slightly louder than the waves.

Monroe saw Gant frown and wander quickly away.

Monroe said, "Uh, hi."

"Wonderful morning, isn't it?" Traile said, beaming.

"I found something you lost last night," Monroe said.

Traile took in Monroe's bruises. "Nothing that can't be replaced."

He gave Monroe the squinty eye of a man who sees in another

man a taste for similar vices. "Incredible woman, isn't she? Strong, assured, irresistable, beautiful . . ."

"You really think so?"

"You're asking me questions again." He nodded, though. "She was . . . incredible. Still is. You might be interested to know that she was a runaway. Blew into town, God knows why. Fell in love with the ocean, wanted so bad to be a redshirt—a lifeguard—but the Beach Patrol didn't take women then. She'd come down here and skim clamshells with the best of them. I was a lifeguard. I had all the women I wanted except her. All she cared about was taking my rescue boat. She'd jump in and row out until I had to yell at her to come back and even then, she wouldn't return until she was damned ready. She wouldn't give me a glance. I was unworthy of a woman so strong and tall and astonishingly beautiful."

Monroe told himself the man was nuts. "Fatsie Morgan, real runway material."

"Faith," Traile gently corrected him. "Her name is and always was and always will be Faith. Faith Morgan. And she was runway material. *Sensational* in a swimsuit. She won all the local beauty contests."

The air around them became steamy enough to carry odors of the corpse their way, and Traile was lost in the land of beauty pageants. "You should have seen her in the parade. She had power over every man, even Sam Claymore. Uncle Sam didn't deserve her. No man did."

A picture flashed in Monroe's mind, a photo in a book he owned, a book of pictures from Atlantic City's past. One of those pictures was of the Miss America Parade.

"That wasn't . . . it couldn't be—she didn't win," Monroe said.

Traile sighed sadly. "Miss New Jersey never does."

CHAPTER
17

The Maestro

A security guard wouldn't let him into the Alcazar. Monroe had slipped through the revolving door in the Boardwalk entrance and found himself in front of a wall of beef that said, "Sorry, sir. You gotta have a shirt on or we don't let you in. That's the rules."

"I have to speak to Dan Raleigh," Monroe said. "I'm Louis Monroe, a detective with the Atlantic City Vice Squad and I have to speak to him, now."

"What are you, going to be a problem and I have to call the real police?" The security guard unfolded his arms.

"Call Mr. Hadruna, then," Monroe said. "He knows me."

"Oh, the Haddilac knows you?"

"Hadruna," Monroe said. "His name is Hadruna. He'll definitely remember me."

"We call him the Haddilac 'cause all he needs is fins." The security guard raised his portable radio and called Hadruna. Monroe glanced out, through the green-tinted glass and saw a procession of vehicles, led by the Mobile Crime Lab, rolling north across the beach toward Utah Avenue, where the Boardwalk is high enough over the sand to permit cars to ride beneath it to the street.

Hadruna arrived, his nose sheathed in a white bandage. "So it's Mr. Problem."

"I have to see Dan Raleigh."

Hadruna gave him a weary look of hatred. "Normally, anybody sees him should at least make himself decent."

"He'd make an exception—"

"Only he didn't show up today," Hadruna continued. "Office says he called in sick but, his kind of job, you never call in sick. You gotta be here all the time or you're on the road and he ain't on the road, and he ain't here which means he's on the way out."

Raleigh was being fired?

Hadruna put his hands on his hips, as if to say whatever happened last night would *not* happen again. "All I know is you don't got a shirt, and you don't got a person to see, and you ain't carrying any money so you don't got to be in this building, which means your name is Mr. Problem until you want to leave. Now, you want to leave or you want me to change your name?"

Monroe smiled his Boardwalk smile.

"Something funny to you?" Hadruna growled. "Laugh at this."

Hadruna hauled his right hand back into a punch. Monroe saw it coming. He also saw that the punch was just a feint—that Hadruna was coming with a left hook aimed at the side of Monroe's head.

Monroe waited until the hook was committed, then stepped quickly to the right. The hook brushed past his face and continued into the green-tinted glass near the casino's revolving door.

The glass didn't break, but banged loudly as Hadruna's fist hit on its edge. Hadruna continued, the momentum of his punch pulling his body forward, his shoulder hitting the glass with another bang. The man was tough, Monroe noticed. Instead of letting the impact daze him, Hadruna pushed backward and spun himself toward Monroe, both hands out to grab Monroe's throat.

Monroe stepped back, but let his right foot catch Hadruna's left leg behind the ankle. Monroe swept his foot to the side. Hadruna suddenly didn't have a leg to stand on, and down he went again, this time falling forward on his knees, gut, chest and, finally, nose.

Hadruna let out a roar, as if the laws of the universe did not permit the same person to put him on the floor twice in twenty-four hours. He pushed himself up and flung himself at Monroe, who obligingly stepped aside as Hadruna hit the glass, hard.

The glass didn't break, but Hadruna did. His face hit the glass first, jolting his jaw up into his skull a half second before his forehead landed slightly off-center on the pane.

For a second Hadruna hung on the glass like a blob of wet meat. Then he went down, falling backward off the glass with his head making a thump as it hit the carpet.

"Damn!" the other security guard said.

"Call first-aid, now," Monroe said. "Right now."

The guard smirked. "The first time I ever seen anybody knock himself out. He'll come around."

Monroe glared at him and the guard complied. "What's happened to this man is serious," Monroe said. "He could experience short-term memory loss, nausea, vomiting and internal bleeding." He checked Hadruna for other injuries, saw the man's eyes begin to flutter and then open.

"Wha—?"

"Stay down, don't move, relax for a minute," Monroe said.

The medical team—two security guards with a first-aid kit and an oxygen tank, rushed in as Hadruna blinked. "What I . . . what I do to get down here?"

"Nothing," Monroe said, backing away. "Nothing at all."

Monroe ran back to the Boardwalk. There was something he wanted to look up in a book of photos from Atlantic City's history. He had a copy of this book in his apartment in Clam Creek. His favorite was a picture of Jimmy Durante draped across a rolling chair. The big-nosed comedian had his feet up, a happy-as-a-clam look on his face, as if there was no place in the world that he'd rather be than on the Boardwalk.

Before Monroe could get to that book, he would have to do something about his wife's birthday.

He thought of a man sitting in a wheelchair holding a silver spoon in his mouth and everything, as they say, fell into place.

* * *

"Always pleased to assist," the Maestro said as Big Mike attached the metal arms to the wheelchair. He pressed a button on the door and the Maestro and his chair rose into the back of a dark, mean, Cadillac stretch-limousine. "This will cost you."

"Anything you want."

The Maestro waved Monroe into the plush, white-leather salon. "Anything?"

He sat surrounded by peculiar steel and plastic tubings, levers and controls below his chin. He waited until Big Mike shut the door and started the car. Then he hit a button that raised a glass panel, sealing the salon from Big Mike's ears.

"Start by telling me why it is you are so sure I am this Fugari character? There is no Tommy Fugari."

Monroe felt the leather upholstery stick to his skin. "Ramona Drew thinks there is," he said.

The Maestro made a sucking motion with his lips. He threw his head back, tongued a contraption that delivered a liquid into his mouth.

"Miss Ramona is losing her mind," he said. "Skin cancer, I believe it is. From being in the sun too long. I hear it got into her brain."

"Why doesn't she go to a hospital?"

The Maestro regarded Monroe's bruises. "Why don't you? Similar reasons. She'd rather suffer than be helpless. The medical profession likes to make you helpless before it tries to cure you."

"She said you were a drummer, and that she found a baby—"

He tilted his head noncommitally. "How many years ago was it? Too many."

"I want to be sure," Monroe said.

"Of what? That Tommy Fugari may have done a bad thing in handing a baby girl off to a rookie Boardwalk flatfoot named Marty Gant *exactly* thirty-two years ago today?" He called his driver. "Michael? Take us around Mount Rushmore Street. Thank you."

They moved in silence down Atlantic Avenue. Big Mike took a

hard left turn on to Mount Rushmore. "Slowly," the Maestro said, peering out the window until they passed a boarded-up, two-story brick rowhouse on the right.

"Pause here, would you, Michael? We're just looking. Tell me, sir, what is it you see?"

Monroe studied the rowhouse. It was one of three adjacent buildings, all abandoned. "I see an old house."

"You're being kind. It's a ruin. I see it more as a story that needs to be told. But sometimes you listen to these stories and you find something you'd rather not know.

"This used to be one of a few locations in the city in which a woman who did not want to have a baby could get an abortion."

He directed Michael to keep going. They passed the white concrete columns of a casino parking garage and the Maestro again commanded the car to stop. "Now right here was the Cabana Club, a nightclub with a gambling den around the back. If they got raided the customers could run out to Mount Rushmore before the cops came. I used to hear the music from the room I had in Number 18. It was hot jazz music. Made me want to play it. Used to hit on sticks and ash can lids and any damned thing. Some of the cats let me sit in.

"I was drumming then. On my own, shackin' and crackin' with this hot little dancer named Ramona Drew. Things had sort of fallen along the rest of the street by then. A beauty queen could have her baby here, and no one would know it. One did, thirty-two years ago, today."

"Today?"

"My memory is sharp."

"That was the one Miss Ramona found?"

The Maestro closed his eyes. "She found her. I saw her. Beautiful little girl. She said some guy was putting her out with the trash. We took her in and I checked around—"

"With Marty Gant?"

The Maestro paused. "City Hall was involved. Gant was sort of on the outside of things, but not so far he wouldn't know."

"Know what?"

"Who the father might be."

"Who was the father?"

The Maestro shook his head. "Sam Claymore. The mayor. He was so sure he was the father. Had his sons take me down by the sea because he wanted to know where the baby was. They rounded up Marty Gant and had him watch. They took me down to Brighton Pier, put handcuffs on my wrists, hung me from one of the piers by the tideline. I remember thinking then, please, don't touch the hands. I need my hands to play drums. They asked me where the baby was. I honestly didn't know where the baby was and Gant, if he knew, kept his mouth shut, even after I was in pain and was begging him to tell them. By then they were hitting me because it seemed to please them."

The Maestro sipped some liquid.

"You asked me what it was to go down by the sea. The plan is to take you to the edge of death, and then bring you back. One is awake and aware during the procedure. One is aware of the person or persons doing the work. The purpose, one discovers, is to give in to the point of view of those who are beating you. If you do, you get to live. If you don't, or if you just ain't got it in you to live, they let the ocean take you out. By the time you wash back in, it's anybody's guess what happened to you."

Monroe closed his eyes, saw Deegan's twisted form on the jetty.

"They broke a lot of stuff, and my back. Gant carried me to the hospital. Michael here, was an orderly who worked in the hospital. Treated me nice. Told him, if I ever made it big, I'd take him with me. And I did that, ain't that right, Michael?"

"It is, Mr. Fugue," Michael said from the front seat.

The Maestro drank again.

"I admit, I was feeling rather low when I was told I lost my arms and legs and my dick, and that I'd have to get somebody to wipe me everytime I took a crap. A doctor told me that my tormentors had been merciful. Any higher on my spine, I'd've been dead. I wished I was dead. But Mike, here, told me not to lose faith. Michael saved me, isn't that right, Michael?"

"If you say so, sir."

"You see, Michael grew up in the projects. Michael learned the hard way that we're all greater than we can imagine, but that we must imagine greatness, if only to survive what others will do to us. All directions point up, though it takes a while to learn that."

The Maestro thrust his face forward, nudging another contraption that had gently scratched his face. "Reuben Claymore is the only one I have ever wanted to kill. I could've paid to have it done but, having saved the life of a baby girl thirty-two years ago, I came under the impression that lives are worth saving, all the time, for no reason other than the fact that as long as we're alive, we can make things better."

The Maestro took a long, noisy breath. "And you wonder why nobody cared about all those begging tickets you wrote me."

When Monroe bounded up the steps of his apartment it was way past lunchtime. He found Ellie in the bathroom, the wrapping in which her birthday gift had arrived was scattered around the living room.

On the kitchen table, next to the list of wedding supplies, was a card. "E—Here's to you—Z."

Monroe waited until he heard the toilet flush and went out to the living room window, where the wooden fire escape (a *wooden* fire escape? Only in Atlantic City) acted as a small balcony overlooking the street.

He heard the loud, nasty, *blug-a-blug* roar of the last of the clam boats returning to the docks along the Absecon Inlet. When he first found the Clam Creek apartment, Monroe had hated the arrogant, unmuffled diesels of the clam boats, made even louder by their steel hulls. It was impossible to sleep when the clammers left at 3:00 and 4:00 A.M.. The fishing fleet's presence, among the more civilized *rum rum* mumble of the creamy fiberglass pleasure yachts was a reason the rent at 221 Clam Creek was comfortably low.

Against his will, he had found himself growing accustomed, and gradually appreciating, the noise and the briny stink of the clam boats. It was the rude, uncomfortable sound of reality, of having to wake up early in the morning, on good days and bad, and go out on the sea and earn a living, not knowing until you returned if you'd be well off from a good catch, or poorer than when you started.

From talking to some of the clammers, Monroe learned that once or twice a year a boat went down in a storm and the crew didn't come back. Clamming was almost like being a cop, Monroe decided, only you were in business to feed people, not to enforce a series of contradictory, confusing sets of laws that weren't protecting taxpayers as much as they were supporting a system that had very little to do with keeping the peace.

He heard Ellie shouting at him. "Are we going shopping? We need to go shopping." He saw she was wearing the robe, saw that it looked rather good on her.

"Come here for a second," he said.

"Why?"

"I want you to see something."

"I've seen enough."

"If you can step out onto the fire escape—"

"Louis, I am *pregnant* and I will not go stepping *anywhere*."

He stood, helpless again. "Please. Just do it."

"Do *what?*" She went into the kitchen. "Honestly, we have to go shopping."

She came out and faced him, hands on her hips and Monroe saw something in her face, the way the anger shaped her mouth. "Some things are very important to me," she said. "When it was different, when I was working, they would remember these things. They always remembered."

"What's important to you is important to me." Monroe said. "To all of us."

She touched her middle. "Her, too."

207

"Not just her," Monroe said. He waved and brought her toward the living room window.

The first thing she heard was the creaky, buzzing, burbling strains of "Happy Birthday" played on badly tuned guitars, glass jugs, cardboard boxes, a xylophone and fifty-seven kazoos.

The first thing she saw was the limousine, the Maestro's big black stretch Caddy with the spoon-monogrammed flags floating above the fenders. The limo had stopped in the middle of the narrow lane of Clam Creek. In front of the limo sat the Maestro in his chair, with Big Mike behind him. Crowded around them were bums, panhandlers, former and current PARAtroopers that Ellie had counseled, friends of Jimmy the Geek and anybody hanging around the Rescue Mission, the Salvation Army, the Holy Mary the Redeemer Shelter for Young Women, anybody who, in the words of Monroe, "wanted a free limo ride to help make somebody feel needed."

Ellie covered her eyes, put her hands in her hair and, realizing it was a mess, looked around for a place to hide. Then she broke down and smiled, and cried, and said that there was nothing in the refrigerator to give these people to drink.

Monroe said, "It's been taken care of."

After playing "Happy Birthday," the assembled revelers sang a creaky, sour verse, then went around to the back of the Maestro's limousine, to which was attached the hot dog cart of Farsi "Buns" Asanawalli.

Monroe found his wallet and came downstairs, following Ellie in slippers and her robe. After Farsi Buns assured her that his frankfurters were "a hunnert percent natch," she had three.

Monroe tried to pay the Maestro for kazoos and the gas spent in ferrying the assembly in his limo. The Maestro said, "I never handle business matters."

Farsi Buns pushed Monroe away. "For thirty years I had to give away so much food to the bastard Claymore," Buns said, imitating the Maestro's tone, "that to give some more to the friends who took away the bastard is an extinct pleasure."

As soon as the Maestro wheeled himself to the motorized lift that moved him and his chair into the limousine, Big Mike loomed in front of Monroe and said, "That'll be forty-seven twenty-nine for the gas and kazoos."

"A business matter," Monroe said.

"Just makin' change," Big Mike replied.

Monroe paid.

Twenty minutes later the Maestro and Big Mike began driving the revelers back to their shelters, motel rooms and begging corners to prepare for what they hoped would be a busy Friday night. It was over almost as fast as it had happened.

Watching the limousine go, Ellie hugged him as best she could, kissed him better than ever and asked Monroe to forgive her.

Monroe asked her about a book he was looking for. She had put it by the toilet seat. He found it, took it to the kitchen table and thumbed past the photos of the grand hotels, and Boardwalking men and women in fancy dress, to a layout of four photos, three of them of Mayor Sam Claymore.

He saw a shot of a confused, bewildered Sam Claymore entering a courtroom, surrounded by lawyers and bodyguards, beside a smaller shot of a sad, depleted mayor, a cluster of television and radio microphones below his face, as he announced he would not run for another term.

"Though Uncle Sam Claymore's administration was no more corrupt than any major East Coast city," the text read, "what brought him down was not corruption as much as it was Claymore's failure to understand the changing nature of loyalty in the twentieth century. 'He trusted his own people,' commented New Jersey Attorney General Nathan Essene on the day Sam Claymore died in Trenton State Penitentiary, 'and his people betrayed him.' "

In a corner was a small picture of craggy, crew-cut Nathaniel Essene in profile speaking with a smaller youthful fellow. Both men were aware of the camera. Essene had arched his profile like a Barrymore—resolute, dramatic, triumphant. The other had raised a small, delicate hand that covered most of his face, obscuring it from the camera's view.

The caption said that Nathaniel Essene, who later became assistant director of the U.S. Department of Justice, was discussing the investigation with aide W. Zimmer.

Then he turned the page and saw the photo he remembered: A huge shot of a round, beaming, fat-cheeked man with a mouth of jagged teeth, decked out in a top hat and tuxedo, with one arm draped lecherously around the narrow waist of a tall woman in a high-necked gown and a Miss New Jersey sash. His other arm waved at spectators who were watching him on what was evidently a Miss America parade float.

Monroe checked the caption but found it identified the woman as "a Miss America contestant." The resemblance was there. An old Sam Claymore had his arm around the woman who, many years and many pounds later, would become Fatsie Morgan.

So why wasn't she in the Miss New Jersey annals? Was she disqualified, so her runner-up would take her place?

Monroe stared at her face and had to admit she was beautiful, in a familiar way. Then he almost dropped the book. Change the hairstyle and he was looking at his wife's face.

18

The King of Hanky-Panky Town

Dan Raleigh's home answering machine said that Dan Raleigh was not capable of coming to the phone right now, but . . .

Monroe dialed the Alcazar Casino Hotel, asked for the room of Wayne Zimmer.

"Lieutenant Commander Wayne Zimmer, State Police Special Investigations Division. How may I help you?"

"Uh, hi."

Zimmer's voice was low, gruff and direct. "I've been expecting your call, Detective."

"You *have?*"

"Excellent work you did procuring Reuben Claymore for us."

"He wasn't supposed to be for you," Monroe said.

"He has the potential of being very useful, an ideal witness once we remove some psychological difficulties. We let him out every once in a while in a silly little vehicle that used to be owned by a drug dealer. No doubt you've seen him."

"He's seen me," Monroe said.

"So he has. And he injured himself, physically and psychologically, which has forced me to delay some of my plans."

"I had nothing to do with that."

"Perhaps. I must cope with the fact that a witness in a neck brace is visually unappealing. Unlike some injuries, those involving the neck imply weakness and helplessness. It's important that Mr. Claymore appear to be strong, so that his conversion from sinner to penitent informer will seem an act of conviction, rather than an attempt to escape punishment for past crimes. This gives us the time to stage a little birthday celebration for your wife."

"Us?"

"I hope the robe fits. She was expecting it. I called last night to reopen the ties. There are several, you know. Ties."

"You're not going to have anything to do with my wife. Whatever it is that's in the past is going to stay there."

"I'm sure you're aware that the past never stays put."

"I'm aware that you're going to leave my wife and me alone."

"Not possible," Zimmer said. "You're both very important to me." He changed his tone. "My research—I do very thorough background checks on everyone I use—indicates you were born in Galloway Township. You had to travel to the ocean. I grew up in sight of the ocean. I would spend long hours on the top floor of the Windermere Hotel, looking at the sea. The sea itself is unknowable. It's what happens on the edge that becomes significant. You were there this morning. You helped rescue a poor creature that washed in. I was touched. I really was."

A silence passed between them.

"Mr. Zimmer, I called because I think you had something to do with my partner dying last night."

"As the highest-ranking officer on site, I approved the findings of DGE investigation of the slot machine," Zimmer said. "Presumably Sergeant Deegan was disappointed."

"That's all?"

He chuckled. "No. In the course of his career as an Atlantic City police officer, Sergeant Deegan approached me many times attempting to be useful. He also claimed to be a threat. He could never decide if my activities were, as they used to say, part of the problem or part of the solution. I found his illegal activities rather petty, though he did, like you, provide me with a witness who proved very useful."

"So it was you who decided the machine wasn't going to check out."

"I approved the report."

"It was a lie."

"You don't know that for a fact. Besides, the so-called truth is not as important as the scenarios that a peer group, or the media, judges and juries are willing to accept. I could, if I wished, create a scenario, complete with witnesses, documents, recordings and material evidence, that would show that you were more responsible for your partner's death than the workings of an inanimate machine."

"Are you threatening me?"

"Of course not. Most married men will become jealous of their wives' old flames if those flames are richer, more powerful or more successful than they are. Given your relationship to my star witness, and the fact that my star witness is still a work-in-progress, and that I have sentimental attachments to your wife—"

"You do anything to my wife—"

"Louis—and I do hope I can call you Louis—what is significant between us is not what I might do, but what you think I'm capable of. I assure you, when it comes to achieving desired results, I'm capable of anything, and I do mean *anything*. So, before we become lifelong enemies, let's get to know each other. Tell Ellie to wear something black. She was always so striking in that color. Dinner at eight. Try to arrive on time."

Monroe slammed the phone down, stomped out of the kitchen and was about to take a shower when he saw, through the open bedroom door, the future Mrs. Monroe taking a black gown out of the closet.

"It's cut really large, and if I get it to a dressmaker in a hurry, it just might work" she said. "Do you think Wayne'll like it?"

Monroe came into the Vice Squad office early, wearing a stained and faded sweatshirt and the rattiest pair of bluejeans he owned. Coming in early was arriving anytime before 5:00 P.M., when the department's Bravo Company shift officially began. Monroe ambled in at 1600 hours because he had won the first big argument he and Ellie ever had. His face was still flushed from yelling and he didn't feel as if he'd won anything.

He sat at his dented, green steel desk and tried to forget what she had said to him. He failed.

She had told him that Zimmer had asked for her, specifically, which wasn't so surprising because clients would be able to ask for girls based on photos, or word-of-mouth. Ellie always had an excellent reputation in the service, and she never developed any feelings for her clients until Zimmer, and even then, it wasn't anything major. Zimmer came into her life when she had needed somebody who didn't treat her the way the clients treated her. They would go for rides in rolling chairs. He was very loving, and very generous, almost as if he were her father and she was his daughter.

"Except," Monroe had said.

"Except *what?*"

"You said he was like your father but—"

"He didn't fuck me, okay?"

He sat at his desk and stared at the television set. As long as he had no partner, no tour-of-duty and no way of spending the night at home with his wife, he could at least get some information about Zimmer. He called the state police administrative offices in Trenton, identified himself, mentioned he was running down some rumors. He opened with an intentionally ignorant question. Was Wayne Zimmer still on active duty?

Of course Lieutenant Commander Zimmer was on active duty, the clerk to the state police assistant administrator of personnel said. "He's on the biggest case of his career right now."

"He hangs around Atlantic City a lot, doesn't he?" Monroe said.

"He was born there," the clerk said. "Hates the place so much he can't keep away."

"Does he have a wife?"

"Ha. If he did, would she let him work so hard? His file isn't that thick. It says that he was born there. He's listed as a participant in a half-dozen Atlantic City political corruption investigations. He was in his twenties when he put Sam Claymore away. Old Nate Essene took the credit, but it was Zimmer's operation. Says so in his file."

"I'll bet," Monroe said.

"Got the file right here. I can't tell you what's in it, but Zimmer, well, when I seen it in the newspapers, I couldn't help but notice the one thing the newspapers didn't get . . ."

Monroe waited.

"There was a woman involved."

"So," he said, trying to be casual. "What about this woman?"

"She was a looker," the clerk continued. "Beauty queen. The story was, she had Claymore's kid."

"Claymore was the father."

"That's the gossip."

"That's what brought him down?"

"Gossip? Nah, not Sam Claymore. You're talking about the king of hanky-panky town. Anybody that wanted hanky-panky did it in Atlantic City, and Sam kept track of that so if Sam wanted something done, it got done."

"You sound like you've been around . . ."

"The state police has always been a political organization. Only one way to survive in politics: keep your ears open and your mouth shut. Me, I had the mouth problem, you know? So I sort of stayed where I was. . . . You mind telling me why you need this stuff?"

"Just running down some rumors. Sure he doesn't have family anywhere?"

"Now there you go. This is a confidential file, which you need all kinds of clearance to get to."

"I guess I would."

"If he had a family, you think we'd let that kind of information out?"

"You can tell me what *isn't* in the file."

"There's nothing in here about him ever being married or having kids. Parents are deceased. No close relatives. Anything else, you should go to him. He's a real open kind of guy, considering he's the top special investigator for government corruption in the state. He's the kind, he likes you, or has a use for you, he'll take you with him. He pays his team higher than any other in the organization. There are people fighting just to get near him."

"I can imagine."

"You don't want to go up against him, though. He's the kind, you just can't win against him. Nobody can knock him out. He's got enough influence, he can just keep hammering at you until you throw in the towel. If you're up against him, I'd raise the white flag now."

"Thanks for the warning."

"My pleasure."

Monroe called the Alcazar. Nita Ivas was off-duty tonight. He tried to get the home telephone number of Nita Ivas but none existed. He got one for Ramona Drew but no one answered.

Another phone rang. "Vice, Monroe."

"Traile, Internal Affairs. You haven't called me today."

"I thought I was off the case."

"You're never off the case until I tell you you're off the case. You're supposed to call the number I had you memorize every day."

"I forgot."

Traile was silent for a few seconds. "Lieutenant Commander Zimmer invited you and your wife to dinner tonight. You will go and find out as much as possible about what is being planned and who the targets for Operation Long Spoon are."

"Sir, I have a huge, enormous conflict of interest regarding Wayne Zimmer that should disqualify me from—"

"Go anyway. That's an order. And bring your wife. The dinner's in her honor."

"My wife is not—"

"You wife *is* involved."

"Then why don't you take her there yourself?" Monroe roared.

"You will do as I command as long as you are a member of this police department. Failure to obey a direct order will result in suspension, which—"

"You're going to have to answer a question first. One of mine."

"I don't make deals with officers under my command and I don't answer questions—"

"It's about Faith Morgan. Sam Claymore thought he was the father of her baby. Was he?"

"It should have been me," Traile said. "But she wouldn't have me until later, when she went off."

Monroe had the history book photo in his mind. There was no way in hell Ellie could have had Sam Claymore for a father. There was absolutely no physical resemblance.

"So who was the father?"

Monroe heard Traile breathing warily. "She was a wild woman, very seductive. The mayor did sleep with her, but—"

"Who else?"

"I can't—"

"You can."

"I refuse."

"Why?"

"You'll think this is all about jealousy and revenge. It isn't."

"What is it about then?"

"Love. She's been hurt enough." He hung up.

Monroe showered, shaved, let Ellie put some goop in his hair that gave it a shine, some makeup on his face where the yellow bruises were turning purple. Then he jumped into the white, Italian-cut suit he was married in, uncomfortably aware of how tight it was around his waist. Where was his gut coming from?

"The dry cleaners must have shrunk it," Ellie said as she squirmed into the gown. She stood in front of the mirror and told him where to put the pins in.

"I'm sorry about—"

"Just don't stick us," she said.

"Us?"

She rubbed her belly.

Later, an unusually haggard Dan Raleigh shook Monroe's hand and gave Ellie a polite but hungry once-over. "I have *never* seen the two of you looking better," he said. His eyes rose to evaluate Ellie's drastically scooped neckline.

"I hear you're on the way out," Monroe said.

Raleigh mouthed the word "later" and led them to the gilded palm fronds at the entrance of the Coco Loco, the Alcazar's new Caribbean restaurant. He stepped back, permitted Ellie to go first into the restaurant. The maitre d', dressed in a loud shirt and white pants, took them down what appeared to be a sandy trail going into a stone cave. The sand was carpet and the cave was painted epoxy. It opened onto a cluster of tables on what resembled an island lagoon. On a rocky outcropping, a steel band played "Claire de Lune." Just offshore, imbedded in glistening, glassy, fake water, was the hull of a galleon. Waiters in pirate garb scurried up and down the ship's gangplank, with wooden casks on their shoulders.

"The ship is actually the service bar and wine cellar," Raleigh said with obvious pride. "The kitchen is behind the volcano."

Another pirate, or piratess, intercepted them and led them to a table at which was seated a pale, gray-haired man in a black blazer, and Nita Ivas in an indigo pinstriped suit open to her waist.

Monroe felt Ellie pause, tighten her hand on his arm. He turned to the man, whose watery eyes flickered behind severe black horn-rims.

"Lou," Raleigh said, "I think you're the only one who hasn't met Lieutenant Commander Zimmer."

"I prefer to dispense with rank when I'm off duty," Zimmer grumbled and extended his hand.

Monroe kept his arm around his wife.

Zimmer withdrew his hand, turned to Ellie and soundlessly kissed her cheek.

"Oh, Wayne," Ellie said, careful to keep her hand on Monroe's arm.

"Just a sign of respect," Zimmer said, his voice deep, but dry and vaguely raspy, as if something inside needed lubrication, quickly.

Nita Ivas put a cigarette in her mouth. As Zimmer fumbled with the matches Raleigh whipped out a gold Zippo. Ivas blew smoke at Zimmer as if she had studied every Bette Davis movie and then practiced, practiced, practiced for this one moment.

Monroe sat heavily in a creaky wicker chair and said, "I don't know if it's good for the baby."

Raleigh gestured toward the glowing peak of the epoxy volcano jutting up against a wall a few tables away. "This *is* a smoking section," he said helpfully. "A perfect place for old flames and new, eh, Lou?"

Then he took off.

Zimmer spent a few seconds eyeing Monroe. Then he said, "Ellen, though wine isn't good for you and the baby, I'll take your recommendation."

"I want the best," Nita said.

The piratess said, "There are several white burgundies that I could recommend."

"The best is never on the list," Ellie said. The piratess glanced at Zimmer who nodded at Ellie.

"If you want something off the list, then," the piratess began, "may I suggest a Montrachet Laguiche 1969?"

"I'll take it whatever it costs, as long as it costs," Nita said.

"We can do better than that," Ellie said. "Much better. You should have at least three bottles of Bitouzet Corton-Charlemagne hidden down there. One is a 1978, two are 1986."

The piratess looked confused. "I don't think we have that—"

"You do," Zimmer said with obvious annoyance. "Those are my private reserve and you do have them. Ellen has always had a superior memory, as have I. The question before us is if we should have the '78 or '86?"

"I'm not touching a drop," Ellie said. "But I'd love to look at the bottle again. It's been so long."

"The older one's the more expensive, right?" Nita snapped.

"Some things mature as they age," Zimmer said testily.

Monroe said, "I'll have a Diet Coke."

"Oh, will you?" Zimmer said, delighted. "I respect a man of simple tastes, but simple tastes can only get you so far."

Nita stabbed out her cigarette. "Will somebody order something before I scream? Honestly."

"The '86," Zimmer said, giving his softest gaze to Ellie.

"Cancel the Coke," Monroe said. "I'll have what my wife isn't drinking." Ellie found his hand under the table and squeezed it.

Cherry tomatoes in the Salade St. Croix were cut to resemble roses. The butter pats were carved into leaping dolphins. Nita Ivas blithely lopped the head off hers and mashed it into a hard, burnt roll shaped like a turtle. Monroe's Swordfish Bonnaire was floating in a sweet yellow sauce with flecks of almonds in it.

Monroe ate too quickly and then pushed his plate away. Zimmer cut off tiny pieces of his braised grouper, eating with a mincing precision. He said almost nothing during the meal, letting Nita chat rapidly about the singer who was in the Alcazar's showroom that night. The two women kept checking each other out, eyes flicking to hairstyle, clothing, jewelry, pregnant middle or lack of it.

Monroe wanted to ask Nita about Deegan and knew that he wouldn't get that chance while his wife and Zimmer were at the table. So he watched the two of them talk about themselves. Ellie and Nita weren't exchanging information as much as they were playing one-on-one. When Nita mentioned seeing some casino show or going to New York to buy clothes, Ellie countered with stories about pregnancy and feeling the "little thing" kicking.

"Little thing?" Zimmer said, pulling on his nose.

"That's what we call her," Monroe asked, trying to sit higher in his wicker chair.

Ellie opened her purse and showed Nita an ultrasound image of the baby in her womb.

"Oh, my, I can see a face," Nita said, her eyes filling with tears.

"Oh, my, she's so . . ." She paused, regained her composure. "Small."

"Starting small is the rule of life, eh, Louis?" Zimmer said. "I'm five foot three myself, so I sympathize."

"If you say so," Monroe said, aware that he and Zimmer were also playing one-on-one, but a predominantly voiceless version, in which one man finds himself exchanging what appear to be random, accidental glances with the other. Zimmer gave Monroe the eye every time Ellie did or said something that Zimmer thought was wonderful. The eye he gave was not one of jealousy, more of pride of former ownership, as if he had just sold a car to Monroe and was delighted every time the car performed.

Monroe couldn't understand what his wife saw in this man. The wine he sampled gave him the excuse to inform Zimmer, with glances and gestures and the occasional spoken comment, that, as soon as Ellie has had enough, they were leaving. This seemed to delight Zimmer even more.

So Monroe stayed out of the conversation, enjoying what was left in his glass of the best wine he had ever tasted. He studied the bottle's dull and dusty label. It looked like any wine label he'd seen in a store: French words and numbers, and a handwritten Z in the upper right hand corner.

The wine had an easy, seductive way of slipping from his lips to his throat, tasting a half-dozen different ways. It was so easy to drink. Ellie herself tasted it only once, savoring it as if she had been reunited with a long, lost friend.

Which may have caused Nita to knock her glass over with her cigarette holder. After a band of pirates mopped up the liquid, she switched to a mixed drink called a Goombay Smash.

The piratess emptied the bottle into Monroe's glass. "Another, sir?"

Ellie wistfully shook her head, displaying a moment of sadness. Monroe realized suddenly that she missed the high-life, just a little bit.

"Another '86," Zimmer said festively. "Anything for family."

"We're *not* family," Monroe said.

Zimmer gave Ellie a fatherly look and Monroe wanted to strangle him. But the second bottle, and Nita's Goombay Smash, brought an alcoholic truce to the table. Nita began to laugh at everything, and Ellie settled back in her chair, a warm, satisfied glow on her face. Zimmer ordered a round of "Bananas Flam Bay" that the piratess prepared tableside. The dessert seemed to be a few bananas, a mound of brown sugar, three dolphin-shaped butter pats and a half a bottle of rum, stirred together in a copper fry pan, set on fire and served with blue flames still licking the plate.

The rich, candied, syrupy mess wasn't that bad, and with the volcano-shaped birthday cake and the strong coffee that followed, Monroe felt his spirits rise until Zimmer checked his watch and pulled out a comp slip.

"I don't want you ladies to miss the show," he said. The entertainer about whom they'd been gossiping was doing a "ladies only show," which had sold-out weeks ago, but he had Raleigh get a pair of tickets "down front, king's-row center. Just show this to the maitre d'—"

"I know how it's done," Ellie said, plucking the comp slip out of his hands, examining it. "Just two?"

"I have been told that it is the sort of act that appeals mainly to the female element," Zimmer said. "The high-roller wives go to the show so their husbands can hit the tables. In this case, your husband and I need to say some things to each other."

Ellie glanced at her husband. The glance said, *be polite.*

"Whatever you want to do is fine by me," he said to her.

"He's jealous that he isn't the one on the stage," Nita said putting her arm in Ellie's. "You'll love it. I brought along some extra-large underpants we can throw at him."

Monroe watched them go. Zimmer held up his finger and the piratess brought the check. He signed it.

Monroe finished the last of his wine and said, "Whose idea was it to bring Nita?"

"Mine," Zimmer said. "Nita has undergone quite a transformation that Ellen helped along. I wanted Ellen to appreciate the result."

"I don't see much of a result."

"I do. Nita wants to be for me what Ellie was. She thinks she's playing me along. I like being played. So does Ellen. You didn't see the rivalry? Ellen dropped out of a Class-A call girl operation to become a middle-class housefrau. Nita has to show Ellen that she is ever much the better for staying in the game."

"As a cocktail waitress?"

"As an assistant to the investigation," Zimmer said, taking a sip of wine. "I permit her her indulgences to the extent that she's useful. Nita has been very useful. More than you can imagine."

"More than Deegan?"

Zimmer admired the wine in his glass. "*Much* more." He put down his glass. "More wine?"

Monroe shook his head.

Zimmer folded his hands. "I have three things to say to you. The first concerns Ellen." Zimmer looked at the *trompe l'oeil* tropical-blue night with its tiny twinkling light bulbs as if God lived somewhere above, and could look down and sympathize with his fate.

He said, "Since you've met her, how well do you think you know her?"

Monroe sat up straight. "Well enough."

"The woman was once in love with me. I am not the most lovable man around. I do terrible, terrible things to people. I make bad people suffer horribly. But she loved me because I was nice to her. She accepted me for what I did to her, and just to her. She has a fascinating innocence that is rare in adults, a sustaining innocence that survives no matter how cruelly it is used or how painfully much it suffers. So, I ask you, do you have any idea of what she really wants from life?"

"She wants to be a mother."

"Can you honestly say that that's all she wants, Louis?"

Monroe hated the condescension in Zimmer's tone. "She can do anything she wants," he said defensively.

"Let's be realistic. How many cars do you have? I found only one registered in your name. You live on a marginal street surrounded by ghastly slums. I'm pretty sure that Ellen still remembers a time when, for all the wrong reasons, she was on top of the world. I wouldn't be surprised if she has occasionally asked herself why can't she be on top of the world again, for some of the right reasons?"

"What reasons?"

"The reasons you married her. She is a very rare person, Louis, in that she knows how to motivate people, encourage them, influence them, make them happy. I want her employed here, at this casino. I have my reasons—"

"No way," Monroe said. "She's not working for a casino. She's my wife. She wants to be a mother."

"As I said, I have my reasons. I have a sense of tact. I didn't attend your wedding because I did not want to create a disruptive presence. And I can't offer Ellen the job. She won't take it as a favor from me. She's already aware that an opening can be made. In her previous situation, she had relationships with some very significant individuals, many of whom I may want to reach in some capacity. By positioning her here, by having them visit the casino to see her—"

"She is not going back to the service," Monroe said, raising his voice.

"Calm down, tough guy. They won't come here to fuck her. Most probably won't come back at all. But enough will want to *see* her, at the very least."

"I told *you*," Monroe said, "No."

Zimmer ignored him. "The second concerns you and Mr. Claymore. There is some unfinished business between the two of you and it may have to be finished if he is to be the star witness I want him to be. It's important, psychologically, for him to reach a level of equivalence with you, so that he can forget about you defeating him and focus his energies. I am going to create a scenario in which the two of you are going to bury your differences and become friends."

"No way," Monroe said.

Zimmer took out a cigar, clipped off the end. "It will be good for both of you." He lit the cigar carefully, studied the smoke and resumed, "A reconciliation will put you on better footing with your fellow police officers. They will interpret your actions against Claymore as a mistake of youthful idealism, which they were. It will also serve to create one more avenue of communication between the Atlantic City Police Department and my investigation. I already have Ephrum Traile, you know. It's amazing what a man will do in order to wipe out his gambling debts. He going to meet us upstairs, and he'd be happy to listen to your daily report. His love *bucket* is already waiting for him. They were *made* for each other. As for Reuben, you must see for yourself."

Monroe said, "I don't need to."

Zimmer waved his cigar. "Suit yourself. I got into investigative enforcement when I discovered that I could change the fundamental beliefs that motivated the most repulsive, odious politician this city ever had. I've become even better at it over the years. I will make you and Reuben reach an accommodation. It's just a matter of finesse."

"Whatever it is, it's not going to work," Monroe said.

"Tough talk—I love it. I'll put it a different way. I don't want Ellen to suffer. You don't want her to suffer. You have a child on the way. Even if the child isn't yours—"

Monroe stood up.

"Sit down. I told you, I do background checks. More than that, I've kept track of Ellen over the years. I know more about her than you ever will. You're a saint for marrying a woman who is carrying someone else's child. Most men would let jealousy interfere with their love of the woman. I admire your love for her. So I'm asking you to do the admirable, intelligent and . . ." he searched for a phrase, "morally *correct* thing, which is to accept the possibility that Reuben Claymore could change his ways. Isn't *your* ultimate goal to be an example to those you protect, those you arrest and those you work with, so that everybody respects the law?"

Zimmer leaned forward. "Why can't you let Claymore respect you?"

"Me?" Monroe didn't expect this.

"He does, you know. He respects, and fears you so much, he can't make the moral change—he can't go through the psychological stages of redemption that he must go through in order to be a fully realized individual."

"You mean to recite the things you want him to say in front of a grand jury."

Zimmer puffed on his cigar. "It probably won't go that far. In the old days a special investigator would gather evidence, pump the grand jury, release an indictment, hand it over to a prosecutor and assume that justice would take its course in a court of law. We now live in an age in which justice is much too time-consuming and expensive—and risky. There's always the possibility that a good defense lawyer could skew the case. Why take risks? We want to eliminate the mayor, we let him know that we can ruin him so severely by manipulating information—"

"You mean lying?"

"That's a simplistic way of looking at it. I told you—I create believable scenarios. We have the technology to invent anything—documents, recorded sounds, videotaped images, physical evidence, as well as that most convincing weapon—the human witness who seeks redemption by bringing down a higher power. Anything can be forged, faked, invented, doctored so that people will believe it. The media makes it easier. I don't control the media. I just make it easy for their various overworked, overpaid professionals to believe what they really want to believe, that the worst criminals can be turned into heroes; that heroes can have tragic, if not perverse, flaws; that all politicians are corrupt. People need to be able think that the bad will be punished, and that dedicated law-enforcement personnel, such as myself, will punish the bad.

Justice is a matter of getting enough of the right people to believe what you want them to believe. The rest takes care of itself."

"All this because the mayor wants to limit low-income housing?"

Zimmer smiled. "You must have got that from Deegan, or maybe even Gant. Believe me, I am doing far more than merely assuring that the gravy train of state and federal funding continues to sustain the state and federal bureaucracies that consume these funds, without interruption. Low-income housing funding is not for the poor. It never was. It creates jobs for middle-class people who are supposed to look after low-income housing. We need those jobs. If the state maintains the current low-income housing structure, *as it is,* it can divert the billions of dollars of casino tax revenues that were supposed to rebuild the city to other portions of the state. Of course, there was a time when the state didn't have as much control over Atlantic City as it wanted. Some of the old-timers still call Uncle Sam Claymore the king of hanky-panky town."

Zimmer stabbed out his cigar. "I crushed him."

Monroe suddenly felt cold, and it wasn't due to the air conditioning. As he listened to Zimmer gloat about his triumph over Sam Claymore, Monroe didn't hear the boasting of one dubious officer in law-enforcement, but instead saw Zimmer as one more force that shaped Atlantic City's history. While some have argued that the Boardwalk Babylon was founded on scams, schemes and shady deals, Atlantic City's existence could not be blamed exclusively on lawbreakers and corrupt politicians like Sam Claymore. It was also law-enforcers like Wayne Zimmer, who self-righteously bent and broke the laws they were supposed to uphold, and showed the people of Atlantic City that justice was just a matter of giving up, or giving in.

"The third and final thing I want to tell you concerns me," Zimmer said. "I mentioned to you that I will do anything to achieve the results I desire. I mean this quite seriously. When I first ran up against Sam Claymore I was a minor official in the county government. I was frustrated with my position in Sam Claymore's city and had already made contact with some of his enemies. When they learned that Claymore was having a child out of wedlock with his beauty queen, they told me to have the child killed. I was young then, and though I had the ability, I couldn't do it. As it turned out, in not killing this human being, I inadvertantly created the scenario that so obsessed Sam Claymore that it brought about his political end. He gave up, pleaded guilty to income-tax evasion, and died in jail."

Zimmer took out an elegant leather case, opened it and showed his gleaming State Police badge. "Of course, I was inspired to go into law-enforcement, but on my own terms. And those terms demanded complete and profound dedication. I had to ask myself, what would happen if sometime in the future I again had to kill an individual, for the common good, as I perceived it. But the more I thought about it, the more I thought that killing was not . . . extreme enough. I have men working for me who would kill for me if I asked them, and they wouldn't consider this an extreme or untoward act. I have men who are adept at creating scenarios in which accidents happen, fatalities happen, people perish due to apparent acts of God."

He admired the badge, moved it in his hand so that its highly polished surfaces sparkled and gleamed. "But killing is a crude application of force that can create unforeseen complications. Then I became fascinated with an old Atlantic City custom that, incidentally, predates Sam Claymore and his sons, of bringing an individual to the edge of mental and physical endurance, and then backing off, permitting that person to choose life or death. The person undergoing this custom understands that, in choosing life, he must acknowledge that there are forces greater than he, and that one must bend, or give in, to these forces."

He closed the case, put the badge away. "There is much wisdom in this, but there is also the possibility of evil. It's a tough job," Zimmer smiled, "but someone has to do it."

Monroe wanted to tell Wayne Zimmer that he was the sickest,

most demented individual he'd ever met, but he found himself incapable of movement, as if this revelation of the truth in Zimmer's being was more powerful and mesmerizing than any of the threats or commandments that had preceded it.

He finished the last of his wine. "Now you will meet people who will tell you terrible things about me. And your wife will admit to you that she loved me once. It doesn't matter if what these people say is true or not. What matters is what they believe, and how they act on their beliefs."

He folded his hands. "I want to leave you with this thought: what I do, I do thoroughly, and enjoy it immensely."

He smiled. "And I am certain now that no one, nowhere, nohow, can stop me from doing the right thing."

CHAPTER
19

Officer Roo

He was watching a baseball game on the Alhambra Lounge's wide-screen television, his neck rimmed in a foam brace, one of Zimmer's assistants stationed a few chairs behind him.

"You'll forgive him if he doesn't get up," Zimmer said.

"I can get up. I can get up." Reuben Claymore put both hands on the chair, pushed himself into a crouch, tilted himself forward, turned his eyes toward Monroe.

"Jeese," he rumbled. "The little guy. Would you look at that."

With the exception of the neck and back, Reuben Claymore looked better in the flesh than on video. His face was tanned, the skin clear, eyes bright and alert. He had dropped thirty or so pounds and almost—almost—appeared happy to see them.

"Howdy do," Claymore said.

Monroe couldn't speak. He was thinking of dates and places, and the fact that his wife's birthday was today.

"You want to be rude, that's okay with me." Claymore attempted a shrug and returned to the television screen.

Zimmer took a seat beside him. "Who's winning?"

"Somebody," Claymore said. "Somebody's always winning."

"Where's Eph?"

"Downstairs," Claymore said, his eyes and his mind on the set. "Getting undressed."

"Tell him to leave his wallet in the room," Zimmer laughed.

Claymore laughed with him. "I told him, I told him. But he's been lettin' her do him all these years, he's got to do it his way."

They laughed again. "I hope you noticed," Claymore raised his voice slightly, indicating that he was speaking to Monroe, "that I ain't pissed that you and that smacked ass Deegan almost killed me last night. A man's got the right to go out for a drive and not be fucked with. But I ain't pissed."

He rose, turned as far as he could to catch Monroe's eye. "I don't carry grudges no more."

Monroe said, "Oh."

"I been changed."

Zimmer added, "Transformed."

He sat down. "I'm a victim now. Victim of forces I can't understand." He started to laugh and Zimmer laughed with him.

Then Zimmer turned and said, "Would you have believed it, Louis, that old enemies would become such good friends?"

"I wouldna," Claymore said. "You would've asked me, a year ago, a month ago, that I would be best buddies with the bastard that done in my Dad, I wouldna believed it. Look at me, I never lived so rich. For what? You asked me, a year ago, that it would end this way, me on the top of the world, sittin' on my ass, watching the tube and beating on broads."

Zimmer frowned.

Claymore frowned back at him. "We went over that. Some people has been put on this earth to be smashed, and some people has to do the smashing. And you ask me, there isn't a broad born that ain't benefitted from a man lettin' her know who's in charge."

Zimmer glanced at Monroe, as if what Claymore was saying was so *ridiculous*.

Claymore said, "You should've seen Zim and Deegan last night. I wouldn't've thought it. Way back when my Dad was mayor and Zim was taking slices out of the Solicitor's Office and dating Deegan's mom, we all thought you were after her yourself."

"That's *enough*, Reuben." Zimmer said and, at that moment, Monroe saw, Zimmer would have killed Claymore. But Zimmer merely tightened up, as if it was beneath his dignity to respond to anything so preposterous.

But, as he looked at Zimmer, Monroe caught a glimpse of something in the small man, a hint of the furious urge to hurt, and hurt the kind of people who could not fight back.

How could *anyone* spend one minute in that man's presence?

"There are sick people and there are sick people," Claymore said.

"And then there's you," Monroe said.

Claymore paused. "Zim, I think we just been insulted."

Zimmer pushed his chair back so he could take in Claymore and Monroe in a single glance. "I don't know, Roo. Have we?"

Claymore shifted uncomfortably. "You ask me, I think the little shit needs a reminder of respect for his elders. I wasn't wearing this goddamn brace, I'd . . ."

"Try," Monroe said.

"I should. I could do it. I'd have to be careful about my arms. It's amazing, you fuck up your neck and every little thing you do, you get reminded you have a fucked up neck. I could beat the shit out of you, Monroe, with or without a fucked up neck."

"But you've been transformed," Zimmer said. "We may have skeletons in our closet, bad deeds in our past, indiscretions, mistakes and problems, but we can better ourselves."

Claymore downed something that looked like bourbon, coughed, shuddered. "Fuckin' ay."

Zimmer added, "We don't have to be what we used to be."

"Like hell I'm not," Claymore groaned. "You put a woman in front of me, I'll show you what a man is. That Nita chick. How come she's off tonight? What a goddamn tease. You're the one that wanted the chicken," he said to Zimmer. "You eat your chicken. I want her. I get my hands on her, I swear, I wouldn't know when to stop."

Zimmer gazed helplessly at the heavens. "Roo, I see we have some more work to do before you're ready."

"All work and no play, you know what they say." Claymore muttered, focused on the game. "I gotta admit, Wayne, the way you act like you respect me but you don't, you make me wish, back when Dad was mayor, he would've let me take you down by the sea, instead of that drummer. But Dad was a shit. You were a shit. Everybody's a shit. Except—" he tried his body toward Monroe. "Some shits is littler than others."

Zimmer shrugged, turned to Monroe. "She's in the salon. You might want to knock."

Monroe put his hand on the doorknob, twisted it, found that it was unlocked.

He shoved open the door, saw the smooth plain of the massage table, a shower and whirlpool tub against the far wall, a desk against the near wall with a telephone on it. Leaning against the desk was the largest, widest, fattest arm Monroe had ever seen. The arm was connected to a huge, smooth, gelatinous shoulder, framed by a tent-like black tank top above elephantine black shorts.

She turned and Monroe found himself looking into the wide, creased and furious face of Fatsie Morgan.

They stared at each other for about a second. Then Monroe said, "There's something I have to know."

He was close enough to her to see in her eyes the unsettling strangeness of genuine insanity. Her voice was sharp and broken as she said, "Dipshit."

"You know who I am. I'm also married to—"

Morgan placed two enormous fists on her enormous waist. "I'm workin'. Get the fuck out."

"What I want to know is—"

She peered at him. "You're in Vice? How long you been in Vice?"

Monroe paused. "A few months."

"You gotta lot a fucking nerve." She squinted at Monroe's ID. She said, "Monroe. Louis Monroe. You must be nuts, comin' round to a place of business, askin' for a slice."

"I'm not getting any kind of slice," Monroe closed the door. "I don't take anything from anybody and I want to make that clear."

"So you got a charity that wants it now? Widows and orphans of vice dicks? You come in here, you say you want something. Ain't never been a vice dick that didn't need to get himself slammed."

"You, uh, already did that."

"I'll do it again."

"This isn't about me," Monroe said, searching the ruined folds of her face for signs, similarities, resemblances, and finding them. "A long time ago, you had a baby—"

Half her face smiled. "Listena this? Would ya listena this? A dwarf vice dick is playing choirboy in front of my face. In front of my face, he's doing it. If my asshole could cry, it'd be shedding tears right now."

Monroe put his badge away. "Look. I have to know what happened to your baby."

She opened her arms, put her right hand on his tie, hooking one finger under the knot, and then lifted him toward her. Monroe felt his collar buckle, the blood constrict in his neck, his feet slowly leave the floor. He put his hands on the fist or rather, around it, trying to remember the wrist releases he'd learned in Sergeant Vinnie Almagro's bump-and-thump classes when he felt his collar fly open, the tie snag his windpipe. He saw her bring her left hand forward, felt another finger hook over the knot, watched her tremendous arms draw back.

His tie came off and he was flat on his ass on the floor, looking at the broad, veined slabs of her feet imbedded in extra-wide black patent-leather sandals. His eyes moved up the sagging, white columns of her legs, saw knees as large as knots on a tree trunk, the grotesque black spandex shorts and tank-top squeezing the projecting bulk of her stomach, thrusting it out over his head like the prow of a tanker in dry-dock.

"I'm taking your necktie," she said.

He kept his eyes on her, backed away until he felt the door behind him. "Tell me," he said.

Morgan ignored him, put the necktie in a wide, black patent

leather purse, hoisted the purse on her shoulder and reached for the door knob.

Monroe locked the door and clamped his hand on the knob. "You're going to give me back my tie and you're not getting out of here until you tell me if Marty Gant gave your baby to Carlton and Annmarie Meade of Dunn's Hollow, West Virginia."

Morgan put her hand on his, squeezed it until he winced, pulled his hand off the knob and pressed the button on the knob that unlocked the door. She was about to pull it open when Monroe pulled out his gun and held it with both hands, pointing it at her chest.

"I don't want to use this, but—"

She put three fingers on the snout of Monroe's Smith-and-Wesson thirty-eight special, turned it around until the gun was twisted back in Monroe's hands, the sight pointing at his nose.

"You left the safety on," she said, pushing the gun toward him until the sight on the edge hooked Monroe's right nostril. "That's good. You shouldn't hurt yourself. Little prick vice dick can get himself hurt, messing in he don't know what he's doing."

Monroe strained and couldn't move the gun, or himself. She was leaning against him, her body flowing around his, crushing the air out of him.

"I . . . know . . . what . . . I'm . . . doing," he gasped, stifled not only by her weight but by an odor of industrial bathroom air freshener.

She said, "Don't matter."

Behind him, someone was banging on the door. Each bang went through the door and into Monroe's spine. "Lou, are you in there?" It was Raleigh's voice. "It's Dan. Open the door."

She unlocked the door, stepped back and Monroe collapsed like wrinkled laundry, the gun falling to his side. She frowned at him, as if he was a greenhead fly she had just squished between her fingers.

"What a waste," she said, sighing so heavily that the room seemed to shake.

Raleigh continued to bang on the door. "Lou, you'd better let me in. It's your wife. She's in an ambulance going to AC General. She's having your baby."

Morgan picked Monroe up by his jacket collar, ripping it as she hoisted him out of the way. She dropped him against one of the legs of the massage table. Monroe glanced up and saw panels in the table that could be taken out to hide drugs.

Then she pulled open the door.

Raleigh saw her and said, "I hope I'm not interrupting?"

She said, "Nahh," gave Raleigh a look that sent him scurrying beside a wide-armed, barrel-chested security guard.

She glanced at Monroe. "Hope it's a girl." She threw Monroe at him and slammed the door.

CHAPTER
20

Serendipity

Louis Monroe's first words to his wife, as he rushed into the delivery room with a hospital smock thrown over his ripped suit jacket, were, "I'm sorry."

Ellie Monroe, in a similar smock and a loose plastic cap over her hair, sat with her legs wide in the tilted throne of the birthing chair. Her first words to her husband were, "What happened to your necktie?"

Nita Ivas, her plastic hair cap tilted to her right side, her smock gathered fashionably in a knot on her left said, "Stand over *there* and hold her *hand* and don't do anything unless she tells you. Or I tell you."

Ellie's hand was wet and cold. Monroe said, "There's something I have to ask you."

Then she tensed and her eyes bulged out and she said, "Shut the *fuck* up." Monroe flinched. Ellie so rarely swore. She swore again and Monroe flinched again.

Six hours and forty minutes later Ellie stopped swearing. The obstetrician handed Louis Monroe a whimpering baby girl, eight pounds, six ounces.

Monroe was again afraid to move. He had seen the messy miracle of the girl's birth, watched in terror and astonishment as she made her weak, helpless, vulnerable entry into the world.

"She's early. Oh my, she's early," Ellie said, her eyes dazed, her face flushed and drenched in sweat. "*I* was early. My mama said I was early. Is it still Wednesday? Is it still my birthday."

"It's tomorrow," Monroe said.

"It's her birthday," Nita Ivas added. "Her own birthday."

Monroe began to apologize again. "I'm sorry I forgot your birthday. It was a mistake. An accident."

"That's it!" Nita squealed. "You're going to name her Serendipity. Like the slot machine."

Monroe was tired, weak, and so thoroughly drained that if it wasn't for the fact that all he did was stand beside his wife and tell her to push, he would have been content to collapse on the floor, roll up against the wall and go to sleep. But he couldn't do that because he had a baby in his arms.

So he got mad at Nita Ivas, who had been obnoxious to him throughout the birth. "I'm not naming her something nobody can spell."

Nita put her hands on her waist. "She can always call herself Sere if she thinks it's too weird. What do you think, I don't know what it's like to have a dumb name? You think they don't call me Neat, or Juanny boy?"

Ellie looked at the screaming baby in her husband's arms, said, "Sere," and immediately began to sob.

"Give it to her," Nita said.

"Give what to her?"

"YOUR DAUGHTER!"

Sere quieted for a second, then screamed louder. Monroe became afraid to let the small thing out of his arms. He had a silly thought that if he let go of Sere, she would break, or he'd do something stupid and drop her. He felt Sere moving in his arms.

"She's crying," Monroe said stupidly.

"So are you," Ellie said.

"I'm just standing here," Monroe said, aware suddenly of water droplets falling off his chin. He sniffed, summoned all his strength, and gave Sere to his wife.

"Oh my," Ellie said, to weak to do anything more than clasp her daughter. Monroe put her hands around Sere as she said, "Oh my, oh *my*. Wait 'til all the people at the casino see her."

SERENDIPITY

* * *

Captain Marty Gant arrived later that morning with a pot of red geraniums and a pair of pink infant's socks in a gold-foil wrapped box.

He found Monroe in the maternity ward, staring at his infant daughter sleeping in a cloth-lined bassinet, one of twenty or so similarly wrapped newborns, some of whom were crying, wiggling, squirming through their first hours of life.

Gant had his cowboy hat on, and a light tan sports jacket covering the holstered, long-barrel Colt six-shooters he wore western style around his waist. "You gonna tell me which one she is, or do I have to use the process of elimination?"

"Front row, fourth from the right." Monroe said.

Gant said, "Ain't she the cutest thing. Lucky for her she doesn't look like you."

"She looks like who she is," Monroe said.

"Don't she ever. You watch the birth? When my wife was having ours, the husband's attendance wasn't the fashionable thing. The men were supposed to read magazines in the waiting room, pass out stinky cigars. Then we had our second at home—couldn't get the wife to the hospital in time. She put up a fit, kept me up for the entire night and the day after. One time, I heard her screaming, I thought she was going to die, so I rushed in, past the doctor and half the female population of the neighborhood and saw this little head coming out. Made me lose it, right there, in front of all those women. Grown man crying, that was me. The sight of that little head developed in me a powerful appreciation for what the so-called weaker sex has to do to keep this dumb-assed show on the road."

"Women are not weak," Monroe said.

"Now there's a man speaking from experience," Gant said, fingering Monroe's ripped jacket collar.

Monroe said nothing.

"Seems you lost your necktie."

239

Monroe looked at his daughter and felt nothing but pride. "Can I be honest with you, sir?"

"Make it a habit."

Monroe chose his words carefully. "You said a long time ago that there was a reason that Ellie was working for you as a youth counselor."

"I did. She was good at what she did."

"And that was all?"

"Anything else should come from your wife, not me. She's allowed to have secrets. We all are."

Monroe watched Sere move in her sleep, delighted in the way her little fingers crawled to her mouth.

"I'd like it to come from you," Monroe said finally.

"It had to do with keeping her out of trouble."

"What trouble could she get into?"

Gant shook his head. "Wrong question, Lou. You should ask me why I should give a damn about her."

"I love her. I don't have to ask that."

"You have a blind spot then. Just like . . . just like Deegan used to have."

Monroe turned to him. "Why didn't you let him go after Zimmer?"

Gant took a deep breath, let the air out slowly. "I would have loved it if he had something, but he didn't."

"He said he had a witness."

"Ms. Ivas, an underage street hooker who would do anything and say anything to get off the street. I have spoken to Ms. Ivas on many occasions and her character remains consistent. It is possible that she had been treated badly when Deegan found her, but it is unlikely that she had the liaison that Deegan described. Ms. Ivas merely said what Deegan wanted to hear."

"How can you be sure about that?" Monroe asked. "The man was serious about her."

"The man had what we call a blind spot. That's when an officer becomes so obsessed with going after his suspect that he loses

making up stories about herself, as runaways will. Then I hear about her entering the local beauty pageants, and winning.

"It takes a few years for a girl winning the local pageants to make it up to Miss New Jersey. Faith started going to the right parties, hanging out with older men, then I'll be goddamned I didn't see her on the arm of the mayor.

"Now Sam Claymore was everything they say he was, and he was also getting to that stage where a man can look back at his life and wonder where it all went. And Faith, well, she wanted some guy to turn her into Cinderella. So, when Sam hooked up with Faith Morgan, it was electric to see them together. Every man was jealous. Every woman was scandalized, but jealous, too. Sam pulled the strings to get her into the Miss New Jersey Pageant, and it was no miracle that she won."

"But she got pregnant again," Monroe said.

Gant nodded. "Sam thought he did it, but she told me it wasn't his."

"Why would she tell you that?"

"Because we were friends." Gant rolled up the napkin. "I married young and I had my daughters young and what's wrong with keeping something going with a woman that you would have married in an instant, things being different? Faith was a strong, wild kind of woman who could with sleep a different man every night of the week and not care. My Regina, may she rest in peace, would've left me if there was even the whisper of me thinking about another woman."

Gant took Monroe's napkin and started making half-moons.

"One day she tells me she's pregnant and what's she going to do? She says Sam Claymore wants to have the baby and he didn't give a damn what anybody would say. He was going to fix her up in a nice apartment in the Windermere Hotel and when her time came she'd deliver in some fancy Philadelphia hospital. I told her that was just great, that say what you like about Sam Claymore, he had the power to do what he said and that she shouldn't worry. But she was starting to worry the way women will when they have a child in them. And soon I saw what it was she was worrying about. There were plenty of people out there that didn't like Sam Claymore and they were making the kind of threats around Faith that she did not like hearing.

"Then Sam did the dumbest thing ever. He found this punk in the Solicitor's Office named Wayne Zimmer and told him to see after Faith. Why he trusted Zimmer, I don't know but . . . I heard rumors."

"Such as?"

"That he really, really liked children."

Monroe was amused. "Zimmer, a family man?"

"Pedophilia is the kind of liking I'm talking about. You see, one of the ways Sam Claymore got the kind of loyalty that he did was his way of finding out about sins. Zimmer liked to be seen with ladies and was quite the swell when he took a ride in a rolling chair, but Sam must have found out what he really went for."

"Children?"

"The story I heard was that he liked them around ten, twelve years, and that he could get rough with them. Boys or girls."

Monroe grew weak. When he remembered the drugged up twelve-year-old girl he became nauseated.

"Now, I'd volunteered to squire Faith Morgan and see her through her pregnancy, but I was just a cop on the Boardwalk beat. Sam picked Zimmer. And there was talk of Sam divorcing his wife and marrying Faith, which just wasn't done back then. People began whispering that Sam had lost it over this girl, and that the city would be better off if Sam was replaced."

He turned half-moons into circles.

"The upshot was the baby came two weeks early, while Sam was out of town. Zimmer didn't take Faith Morgan to some fancy Philadephia hospital, but to a wayward girls home on Mount Rushmore. The rumor was that Zimmer paid the doctor to botch the job so that the baby would die. The doctor delivered the baby perfectly. Faith lost a lot of blood and was unconscious when, according to what I could piece together, Zimmer had the doctor kicked out and put the baby in a plastic bag and threw it in a trash heap a few minutes before the trash truck was coming. It was an accident Miss Ramona was on Mount Rushmore Street just ahead of the trash truck. She took her—the baby—to Tom Fugari, who talked to me about it. We figured that as long as Sam was away, the baby was in danger. Tom was playing a date at one of the nightclubs and overheard this couple talking about how they wished they could have a baby. They were from West Virginia."

"Carlton and Annmarie Meade," Monroe said.

"And I made them promise never to come back. It was a foolish thing, I suppose, but from the moment I held her in my arms, I wanted nothing bad to happen to her. And there just seemed to be too much bad stuff that could happen to her here.

"Sure enough, Sam comes back and Faith was already going off the deep end, Wayne having told her the baby died. Sam wants to bury the child, but Wayne says he had it cremated and Sam, who took a slice off all the undertakers in this end of the county, starts smelling the rat. He rounded up everybody ever had anything to do with babies and he narrowed it down to a few people, me and Tom Fugari among them. He and his sons rounded up me and Tom, and Wayne Zimmer, and took us down by the sea. Sam acted as if it was a toss-up, which of us was going to get it, but I could tell, the way Wayne smiled at him that, no matter what Sam would do to him, Wayne would just enjoy it. So it was down to me and Tommy. They strung Tommy up under Brighton Pier and I had to watch them break his back."

Gant put down his pen.

"He told me," Monroe said.

"And he told you I didn't say a thing. I just kept seeing that baby's face in my mind, and I didn't want nothing to happen to her, and I promised myself I'd get Sam one day for what he did, but I didn't have to. He'd been losing his grip even before he met Faith. He lost it totally after that. Both of them did. I didn't see Faith for almost a year, then I saw her under the Boardwalk, living with the bums, giving herself to anyone and anything. She looked a mess and I tried to talk to her but she never saw me, never heard me. Turned herself into this thing and Eph Traile, who by then had joined the department, started carrying on with her. I ran into her once and I tried to tell her about the baby *but she didn't want to know.*

"Before that Sam got this know-nothing Nate Essene on his back. Zimmer was part of Essene's investigation team. Sam had had the best lawyers in the state working for him, and he also had associates in organized crime, who would have murdered any informant or witness willing to testify. Add to that potentially damaging information on dozens of politicians in New Jersey, many of who would have stomped Essene's investigation if Sam had wanted it. But Sam didn't want it. Losing the baby had done him in. He just gave up.

"When that baby came back here, twenty-two years later, as a grown woman, I didn't know she was Faith's girl. I was in Vice then, and it was only when I heard there was a new woman working in the service, and that she was from West Virginia, I still didn't know it was her, until I saw them together. Zimmer turned to me and he gave me a look that told me he knew exactly who she was and exactly what he was doing and it was goddamn awful . . ."

But Monroe was thinking of Sam Claymore and tried to see his wife's face in his. He couldn't.

Monroe hadn't spent much time in hospitals and, beyond the weirdly unnatural clean smell, what most unsettled him was how insulated they were from the outside world. Inside, down long, functional, cheerless corridors, lights burned day through night, and unless you were up against a window that wasn't shrouded in opaque curtains, you could never be sure what time of day it was.

The insulation, and isolation, forced a strange introspection on him. Even when visiting, the bleary, eternal light of the halls, the shrouded claustrophobia of the rooms, disarmed him, dismayed him, gave him a feeling of helplessness that hit him when he came in. As he struggled to find the right combinations of switches that would turn out the lights over his wife's hospital bed, it hadn't left him.

He couldn't turn off enough lights to bring on what he really wanted—darkness, so he could be with his wife without seeing her blotched face, the weariness around her eyes and mouth, her lips chapped and cracked, her body empty and deflated, wrapped in faded blue cotton pajamas under the bland, white sheets.

In the dim light he watched her sleep, her mouth closing occasionally, the rolling movement under her eyelids that signaled she was dreaming. She had passed out a few minutes after she held Sere, and had been asleep through Gant's visit.

Some time later, a nurse told him he could come back in the morning, and that even husbands had to go home for security reasons. If it hadn't been his wife he was sitting next to, Monroe would have informed the nurse that, inasmuch as he was a police detective, a hospital with him in it couldn't be more secure.

But he didn't say that because he was waiting for Ellie to wake up and look at him. He couldn't take his eyes off her until she did. He told the nurse, "in a minute." He told her that five times during the last hour.

He wasn't sure when it was that she turned on the bed, rolled over on her stomach and woke up.

"Where is it?" she said. She touched his hand and clung to it.

"Where's what?" he said quietly.

"Oh." She put her other hand over her middle. "My stomach. You know. What I've been carrying around all these months."

"Sleeping," Monroe said. "In the maternity ward."

"She's got to be fed. My whole body is telling me she's got to be fed. Tell them. Tell them to bring her to me so I can feed her. It's a she, right? You're going to think I'm crazy but, for a second I wasn't sure."

"She's a she. Serendipity Monroe, if you like that name."

"I do, I guess. I mean, it's okay, right? She won't hate us when she grows up with a name like that. A name is just a name, and if it means something, that's not so bad, is it?"

"No, it's fine," Monroe said, aware that he was waiting for something, but not quite sure what it was.

"Louis, I need to hold your hand."

"You're holding it," Monroe said. "You've been holding it since you woke up."

"Oh. Sorry." She looked down at his hand. "So . . . so she came out a little early."

"Sere's healthy, that's what counts."

She paused. "Louis, you're not concerned that . . . that she's not yours?"

"No. Not at all. I thought we'd been through that."

"I had to ask because she's a real person now. We're *both* going to have to provide for her. As soon as I'm done nursing her, I'm starting part-time in the Alcazar's marketing program. You can resign from the department. You can stop getting yourself hurt."

They were silent for a while, and then Ellie asked him about the baby and Monroe told the nurse to bring Sere for her feeding. He watched Ellie try to figure out how to make Sere figure out how to feed. It was messy and awkward and he felt helpless, watching it and unable to do anything to make things better.

After a few minutes, Sere got the knack.

"Oh my, she wants all of me," Ellie said. "I can't believe this. It's so . . . *new*. I wish I could tell you how it feels. Oh, my, she's greedy. She's such a little thing and she wants the whole world."

"She's not a thing," Monroe said. "She's a person. A little person."

Ellie began to cry. "Oh, Louis, I'm scared. I'm scared of . . . so much can happen. She's so precious. I need you. I'll need you forever."

"I'll be around," he said. "No matter what."

He slept badly, aware that he was alone in his bed, not liking it much. A nightmare that he couldn't remember woke him too early.

On his way to the bathroom he saw Nita Ivas snoring on the couch, bundled in one of Ellie's robes. She was like a child, this girl. He watched her for a few minutes. Then she turned and one of her breasts popped out of the robe and Monroe reminded himself that this was no child.

He averted his eyes. He was a married man and this woman was. . . . She turned over, curled up into a fetal ball and Monroe saw his daughter, there, curled up and asked himself how it was possible for anybody who had seen a baby born, who had witnessed the pain, or had felt that pain—how could anyone who had experienced all of that do any harm to another human being?

She opened one eye. Monroe watched that eye start on his face, move down as it scanned his chest and settle somewhere on his crotch. He realized he was naked. He said, "Oh my God, excuse—" He grabbed a cushion, covered himself.

She laughed. "If I had a thing like that I wouldn't be so quick to cover it up."

Monroe backed into the bedroom, shut the door, fell onto the bed and waited for the room to stop swimming.

He remembered a conversaton with Ellie about Nita staying with them, to help look after the baby.

He was going to have to talk to Ellie.

CHAPTER
21

The Horseshoe

From her hospital bed, Ellie Monroe handed Louis Monroe a list five pages long. She said, "I'm coming home tomorrow, so we'll need the baby's carseat then. Nita will help you find one. The stuff on the first two pages you also should get tomorrow. I'm going to nurse her part of the time, but we should have a case of formula on hand, and some four-ounce bottles with infant-sized nipples. We'll need the other stuff by the middle of next week."

Monroe nodded. "About Nita."

"She's offered to pitch in, and I'm going to be something of a cripple for at least a week, and you'll be grateful for every minute she's with us."

Monroe nodded glumly and then he saw the flowers, a small, discreet little grouping in a shallow tray on her bedtable.

"Who sent those?"

"They came this morning," she said. "Aren't they lovely?"

He shrugged. "I guess so. It looks like there should be more in the middle. What did they do, run out?"

"They didn't run out. That's called *ikebana*. It's a classical Japanese arrangement and it's supposed to suggest an emptiness that the young blossom will rise to fill. See the young blossom there? That's supposed to represent Sere."

It was just a bunch of flowers. A rather thin bunch. "If that's Sere, where's you?"

"Oh I don't know. I'm not an expert."

Then he saw the card next to the arrangement. He picked it up, turned it over. Written on the side that had been facing down, in blue ink from a fountain pen, was "Congrats—Z."

Monroe tapped the card on his fingers.

"Shhh," Ellie said. "Don't wake your daughter."

Monroe sat down, saw his daughter stir and felt a hot blush crawling up his face. "I don't want you to take anything more from him," he said quickly.

"Oh, he's just some old guy who likes me a whole lot," she said, fussing with Sere. "He wants the best for us, he really does. Frankly, I'm a little bit flattered by it."

"I think it's more than that," Monroe said carefully.

"Then maybe you should stop thinking and just accept him for what he is."

"I'm not sure what he is."

"We made a promise, you and I, to keep what's in our pasts, in our pasts, right?"

"Yes!" Monroe said, too loudly. Sere squirmed and Ellie held her close.

"Wayne was the first cop I fell in love with," she told him. "You're the second."

Monroe wanted to ask her what she saw in him, but he was distracted by his daughter rolling around in her mother's arms.

"I think she's awake. Do you want to hold her?"

Monroe took her and he felt as if he held the world in his arms. He looked at her small, plump face and felt his eyes grow wet.

"Serendipity," he said, bouncing her gently, tracing his finger through her wispy hair. "My happy accident."

Nita was singing in the shower when Monroe came home.

"You should lock the front door," Monroe called to her through the door.

The water went off, the bathroom door opened and Monroe caught a glimpse of her naked.

He looked away.

She opened the door wider.

"You shouldn't do that," he said.

"Do what?"

"Stand there with the door open like that. You could . . . catch a cold."

She wrapped a towel around her waist. "I'm letting out the steam. You can't see yourself in the mirror with the steam."

Monroe wandered into the kitchen, tossed the mail on the kitchen table. Nita called after him and said that before they run errands, they should pick up some of her stuff.

"I keep my things with Miss Drew. Her kids will let you in."

Monroe made himself a sandwich and waited. She emerged in a shredded white leather jacket, tight white spandex shorts and gleaming white aerobic shoes.

"We're going to the malls," Monroe said, trying not to let his eyes wander down her tanned, smoothly muscled legs. "You don't dress like that for the malls."

"Since when do I gotta dress for a goddamn mall?"

"Since you're going with me."

"So I won't go with you. I know what Ellie needs. I'll get it myself."

"Fine with me," Monroe said, pretending to study the water bill.

"Bullshit it's fine with you." She pulled a chair out, sat down and leaned over so that Monroe noticed she was naked under the jacket.

"You got serious problems. Just like Deegan."

"Would you just let me alone for a while?"

"I thought you said we got all these errands to run."

Monroe got up, went to the cabinet, dumped a spoonful of instant coffee in a cup and ran the hot water.

She said, "I'm bothering you."

"You're not bothering me."

"Then why are you trying not to look at me."

Monroe banged his hand on the kitchen counter. "Because I don't want what you're selling."

"I'm not *selling*. Maybe you're in the market?"

"Just leave me alone."

She leered and licked her lips. "I'm just sitting here, minding my own business, and you start telling me what to do."

He sipped the awful coffee and the taste distracted him. "Look," he said. "You're Ellie's friend."

"I'm not her friend. I just helping out."

"And I'm Ellie's husband."

"I know what you are."

"So stop showing off. I'm not interested."

She shook her head. "Then you and Ellie got problems. Only men who didn't want me were faggots, and that Zimmer asshole."

Nita put a foot on the table, rocked her chair back, folded her arms under her breasts and pushed them up until the nipples rode just under the open zipper over her jacket.

"He never raped you?"

"That was some bullshit Deegan put on me. Deegan was all crazy to get me to say bad things about this Zimmer, and I never met no Zimmer until now, when he checked into the hotel."

"Never?"

"Never. They put me up in the Alhambra, and I see this Zimmer, and I could tell he's into the kinky shit. But not with me. I'm too old for him, but he likes it when I tease him. Him and the fat cop, Claymore. That fat cop wants me bad, but I tease Zimmer and it makes the fat cop mad. He goes on about how he wants to show me who's boss. 'I'm the boss,' I tell him, and he gets madder."

"You should be careful with Claymore. He likes beating up women."

"I don't need you to tell me what I should do," Nita said. "Only reason I get the promotion to the Alhambra was that Zimmer heard Deegan was hot for me, and he wanted me, as he says, 'on his team.' He keeps asking me if Deegan gave me anything."

"A picture?"

"Deegan gave me bullshit. He was all messed up about Zimmer. Bunch of assholes, both of them."

She pulled the jacket over her head, threw it down, stomped out of the kitchen and returned, bouncing her breasts in a purple-and-green lettered Find Your Luck-E-Star at the Alcazar T-shirt.

"You like me better in this?"

Because he grew up in Galloway Township, on the Atlantic County mainland, Monroe found comfort and familiarity in each trip he made to the mall. The mall brought back to him the precious time before his parents divorced, when running errands and spending money became a family adventure that always began and ended inside an automobile.

Now he was inside his rattling Datsun 280Z on his first errand to the mall as a father. Beside him Nita Ivas had her shoes off, her bare feet against the windshield.

"You're not wearing a seat belt," he said.

"That's not the only thing I'm not wearing."

"Put the seat belt on. It's the law. I can get a ticket if I get stopped and you don't have the seat belt on."

"You won't get a ticket," Nita said. "If the man stops you, I'll say I don't know how to put the belt on, and the man will want to show me how. He'll bend over, get himself a feel, maybe pinch my ass, and he'll walk off like he's having a great day."

"And he'll write me a ticket," Monroe said. "So put the belt on."

"You put it on."

"No."

"You want to touch me. You admit it. Say to me, 'Nita, I want to touch you.' "

"Nita, you might be Ellie's friend—"

"I'm not her friend. I just helping out."

"Then if you want to help, help me."

"Help yourself."

Monroe swore under his breath.

Nita laughed. "Did I make you say a dirty word? I make men do a lot of things."

"Stop teasing me."

"What are you going to do if I don't want to be what you want me to be? Spank me? You'd like that."

"What I'd like is for you to act normal."

"Just like Deegan. I tried to get him to fuck me, and look what happened to him."

Monroe glared at her. "What happened to him?"

She winked at him. "I'll tell you. Tonight."

The Horseshoe Bar was one of several dives used by the Pacific Avenue Regular Army. It was nestled in the U-shaped "corral" of the Wagon Wheel Motel, a Pacific Avenue quick-sheet accommodation located two blocks south of Convention Hall.

Way after 9:00 P.M., when they had bought most of what was on Ellie's list and unloaded it in the apartment, Monroe called Ellie, who was sleeping. She yawned and told him to meet her at the hospital tomorrow at 11:00 A.M.

Then Nita insisted that Monroe drive her to the Horseshoe. She put on another shirt, and Monroe got out a winter jacket for the uncharacteristically chilly August night.

"You sure you want to go out in this cold?" he asked her.

"I'll warm you up," she said.

He didn't bother to explain that he would not be drinking, and there was no way in hell he would do anything more than listen to her and then take her either to his apartment, or to Miss Drew's, or wherever she was spending the night. He eased his car between two highly ornamental pimp-mobile vehicles adorned with holographic decals, running lights, chrome intake vents and boomerang antennae.

He locked the car door, followed her into an even colder horseshoe-shaped bar where the girls sat. Just off the bar were a row of booths where pimps played cards and talked about their mutual funds. Cheesy pop tunes tumbled from hidden speakers,

and a huge, wide-screen television was showing "Gilligan's Island."

"This is the best place you want to watch the Miss America
Pageant," Nita said, hopping on a pink leather barstool. "It's
really wild here. The girls try to guess which one of the contestants
is a man in drag."

She patted him on his leg. "You like music?"

"I'm not in the mood," Monroe said.

"You want to be the nice guy." She reached out a slender hand
with long, red nails and played with his hair. "Ellie told me all
about you. You want to be a nice guy, so be a nice guy. So you
pretend you're the nice guy, and I'll be your nasty girlfriend. How
long has it been since you had some fun?"

"Tell me what happened to Deegan."

She ordered two Long Island Iced Teas, then leaned back and
rubbed her leg against his. "You feel that muscle? I carry that
fucking tray, I'm on my feet ten goddamn hours a day. Gets me
great legs but it's no fun."

Her glance swept over him. "You look all stiff. Nervous. Whatever you're nervous about, I can make it go away. You should let
me. This is your last night out before you got the baby. Then you
got to be real smart about sneaking out."

The drinks cost ten dollars. Monroe took the Iced Tea that was
put in front of him and slid it toward Nita. "I'm not drinking and
I'm not letting you do anything to me that I wouldn't want my wife
to know."

She downed half the first Iced Tea and shuddered. "Okay. You
want to know about Deegan. He got into the room with me, and
I shut the door, and I had on my uniform, with the three pairs of
pantyhose they make us wear, so first I have to take off—"

"Stop trying to tease me, or I will leave you here," Monroe said.

She put her hand on his thigh. "How you ever going find out
what you're missing?"

Monroe stood up. "You want to help out with the baby, meet
me at the hospital tomorrow at 11."

She held his arm and he saw a tear, darkened by mascara, roll down her cheek and make a blotch on her white leather jacket. "Look at me, okay? You're no fag. You want me. Deegan was no fag. Before he won the money, I didn't give a shit about him. So now he's got three million dollars, I wouldn't mind getting on his good side. So I took off my pants, real slow, and then I took off—"

Monroe took a breath, shook his head. "I don't have time—"

"So why *didn't he give a shit?*" she yelled loud enough to cause a brief dip in the background conversation. She grabbed the cocktail napkin under her drink, knocking the glass over, and dabbed at her eye. She checked her reflection in the bottom of an ashtray and wiped her cheek.

"It was like the part of him that was crazy for me was dead. He just wanted to give me something. He was crazy. He called it the ultimate insurance policy."

She gulped Monroe's Iced Tea. As she drank, he took the cocktail napkin, paused uncertainly, and then wiped the darkened tear off her jacket.

She put the glass down gently, wiped her mouth on her sleeve.

"What did he give you?" Monroe asked.

She nodded her head wildly, the drink beginning to loosen her. "A picture."

"Did you—"

"Sure. A man and a boy playing on the beach."

"The man was—"

"I didn't care who the man was. I took my clothes off. I stand before him. I take his head and I put it on my chest and then I push it down and he starts crying. I figure he's the kind that likes to cry so I put him on the table like I'm his mother. He says, 'He never wanted my mother.' And then he curls himself up in a ball and he won't let me go near him."

She finished the drink, set it down with a loud pop and asked for another. "I been with a lot of guys but, the way he did it, it was like I was *nothing*. It was an insult to me, and I tell him and he asks me about the first man I ever do it with."

She crossed her legs. "Now, this question, I know how to answer. Some guys, they ask you these things, because it turns them on to hear you describing how you became a woman. They want to hear about all your boyfriends and what they did to you so they can do it to you, and then you can tell them they the best you ever had. So I start in, tellin' him about this tall, dark handsome stranger, and he says, no, he wants to hear the truth. So I tell him about a big black man, and he says, no, he wants to hear the truth. So he starts to piss me off and I tell him it was my father. I was four years old and he did me so much I didn't know what he was doing until he did me in front of my mother. Then my mother tried to kill herself and that's when I went to Miss Drew . . ."

Her eyes were shut tight. "And he lost it there. He fell off the table and opened his mouth and couldn't say anything. I tried more things. I tried everything. I kept seeing three million dollars in front of me. I think I was in there for an hour, trying everything."

"Did you look at the picture again?"

"He had it in his hand, and he was holding it so tight he almost ripped it. He was terrified. His face was all messed up, like he was about to be hurt worse than he'd ever been. Then he said, 'I want to go to the beach now.' "

She put her hand around her third drink, opened her eyes to make sure she had it in her hand, took a sip. "He bent over, on his hands and knees and, because I had his clothes off, I could see the scars on his back and on his legs, and I figured out that the stuff he wanted me to say was done to me, had been done to him.

"That's when Zimmer knocks on the door. He has this happy face. He gives me that look like I shouldn't be there, and I take my uniform and got the hell out. I put on my uniform in the lounge and I started to lose it, it was so . . . sad. I told myself I was sad about him getting rich and not wanting me, but it wasn't that. I don't know what it was. I've seen a lot and I've done a lot, and a lot's been done to me, but to see Deegan like that . . ."

She began to cry.

THE HORSESHOE

The background noise became still and Monroe thought he saw a dark shape emerge from one of the booths.

Nita covered her face. "All my life men want me, and they do me and then they don't want me until they want me again, and it's like that. I learn, I learn, you want a man to do for you, you make them want you, then you don't give it to them, so they do for you. You think I want you to do me, man? I get sick thinking of any man doing me. But if I want something, and I can get if you do me, then it's okay. Deegan, he just wanted Zimmer to hurt him."

Monroe smelled the odor of air freshener, but he didn't move. "Nita," he said, "you don't have to go on. I'm sorry I asked."

"Don't be sorry!" she glared at him. "I don't want you sorry for me. I don't want Deegan sorry for me. I'm glad he killed himself. I hate him. I hate Zimmer. I hate you, trying to pretend you don't want me. I hate your wife. She thinks her stupid life is so good, but it's just bullshit. She don't—none of you knows what it feel like when you let them do you, and then they don't want you, and you become nothing. You become less than nothing. You become a mistake, a somebody shouldn't've been born, like you gotta pay for the rest of your life."

Then Monroe heard the voice: "Nita, this prick bothering you?" The enormous shadow on Monroe's left moved into the light and he felt her hand clamp around his shirt and hoist him off his seat.

"He's not bothering me," Nita said, choking back her sobs. "He's making me sick."

Faith Morgan wrapped an arm around Monroe and squeezed him so hard he couldn't breathe. Then she carried him out and threw him into the parking lot. Monroe touched asphalt and managed to break his fall, ripping his pants and his jacket sleeve. He turned and faced her.

"Ms. Morgan!" he called. "I have something to tell you about your daughter."

She stopped, turned slowly to look at him, her face impassive, the chill turning her words into mist as she said, "I don't have no daughter."

"But Sam Claymore—"

"She didn't belong to him." She turned, hesitated, shook her head. "She was never his."

She moved to stand over him.

"But, I think, I mean, I'm almost certain you have a grand-daughter. Her name is—"

He gagged when her hand tightened around his throat. She raised him up until he saw that her eyes were wet. "I don't have nothing," she said.

She tossed him backward and he fell against the side of a pimp-mobile, hitting the ground on his left foot. The pain in his ankle climbed up his spine. It wasn't broken but it was certainly sprained. He grabbed the fender of the pimp-mobile and dragged himself to his feet, staggered back into the Horseshoe and found neither Faith Morgan nor Juanita Ivas. The bartender, a thin man with painfully close-cropped hair, sneered at him with disgust. "Next time," he said, "pick on somebody your own size."

22

Retirement

He drove aimlessly for a while, trying to master moving a clutch pedal with a sprained ankle. He thought of visiting his wife in the hospital but remembered she had been sleeping when he called her. He thought of other friends. He remembered the room full of people at his wedding. Now, in a city with a summertime population of nearly a half million, he could think of no one he wanted near him.

Back in his apartment, the message light on his answering machine was blinking. He shoved aside some of Nita Ivas's clothes, sat down on the couch and listened to Dan Raleigh, telling him that he wanted Monroe to "assist on a project of mutual interest" and not to call the casino because he wasn't there, but he'd call back later.

Thanks but no thanks. He turned on the television, listened to a news report about "tightening the noose on the state police probe of corruption in Atlantic City's City Hall, with the possibility of an indictment being served against the mayor and many top officials as early as tomorrow."

Monroe turned off the set. The big news was that Serendipity Monroe was coming home tomorrow. Anything else was just. . . . He sighed. He tried to sleep. When the phone rang he tried not to answer it. Failed.

"Lou."

"Dan."

"I want you to tell you that I'm disgusted."

"You're not the only one."

"I'm resigning from the Alcazar." He waited. "Aren't you shocked to your shoes?"

"I assume you have a good reason."

"I told you, I'm disgusted."

"It'll pass. Then you'll regret it."

"It won't pass and I'm getting a better deal in six months. I get severance, bennies, stock, and I get to do nothing for six months."

"What kind of deal is that?"

"If you've been in the industry and you walk away with your legs unbroken and you don't work for six months after that, you can work in government."

"You shouldn't be in government."

"No more than your wife shouldn't be in the industry. She'll be great."

"She's not getting into the industry."

"She is. That's part of the deal."

"Zimmer set this up."

"The way it's coming down, the marketing department is getting split into these five different fiefdoms and there are at least two high-level positions in VIP development, and she's getting one of them. You'll be able to quit the department and be a housewife."

Monroe held the phone hard. "I'm not quitting."

"You should consider it."

"Dan, tell me the real reason you called, or I'm hanging up."

"Sorry, Lou, it's just that, it's just that there are too many mirrors in the Alcazar, and every time I look in one I don't see myself. I see Ray Deegan when I went up to tell him the machine was defective."

"*Was* the machine defective, Dan?"

"The Division of Gaming Enforcement—"

"Inspects the machines and the Division is an arm of the state police," Monroe said. "And Zimmer is the highest-ranking state police officer in the city, so if he wanted the machine to be defective, it was defective, right, Dan?"

Raleigh paused. "I'm resigning because I don't like what's been happening on our property lately and there's not much I can do about it as an ex-employee, but at least I'll be able to see myself in the mirror."

Monroe was astonished. "You're chucking a six-figure salary."

"It's seven, if you count the bennies and stock options."

"A million-plus job because you don't like this guy?"

"I don't mind people who rip off other people. I don't mind people who try to cheat me. I can tolerate people with weird tastes and mixed-up values. But when I told Deegan—you have to understand that I had to tell him in person. You can't just pick up the phone and say to someone that the three million they thought they had they don't have anymore. Our very own Mr. Hadruna was standing in front of the suite I'd given Deegan. I told him I had to get in there and he says he's not moving.

"Then I hear Zimmer's voice. He says, 'It's under control, Mr. Raleigh.' I just push myself past Hadruna and Zimmer is at the door in one of the hotel bathrobes, his face pink, like he'd been scrubbing it."

Monroe sat up in his bed. "Where are you calling from?"

"Out-of-state pay phone. If Zimmer's tapped your line, I have a head start before he tries to find me."

"Why would he do that? You see anything else in the suite?"

"Nothing. Zimmer looked at me like everything is so *ridiculous* and told me to leave."

"And you left?"

"I went down to the fly's eye, that's where all the security cameras are monitored, and I have them put the ones in front of Deegan's suite on full. I see Zimmer come out of the room, in clothes now, and I see him and Hadruna get Claymore. They go into Deegan's suite and it takes a while but then Claymore and Hadruna carry Deegan out. He's—"

"Were his clothes on?"

"Yeah, but it was like they put them on, and badly. And he can't walk. His legs won't work. So they carry him to the service elevator. I switched to the service elevator camera and it's aimed right at Deegan's face and he's just *gone,* Lou. It's like he's given up and there's nothing left of him. They take him down to the loading dock and out somewhere. I swear I didn't see a car pull away. I don't know where they took him and Hadruna won't say a thing to me."

"I think we know where they took him," Monroe said.

"Good. Then you can do something about it."

"I don't think so. I need more. I need . . . I don't know what the hell I need."

"Do something, Lou."

Raleigh hung up and Monroe looked at the phone and said, "What?"

On Friday morning at 8:37 A.M., Vice Squad Commander Captain Marty Gant emptied his desk drawer into a cardboard box.

The old war dog was in uniform, with his shoes shined bright. After thirty-five years of service, Gant had to clear out his stuff before 9:00 A.M., when a flunky from the City Administrator's office changed the locks on his office door.

Gant appeared happy to make the change. "I got a nice, safe nine-to-five waiting for me in private industry. Going into management. The Unlimited Security Agency: dedicated to the protection of warehouses, abandoned buildings, concrete slabs, the occasional human being."

Monroe found himself the only officer to see Gant during his last hour on the job.

He watched as Gant lifted the doodled, ink-smeared blotter off his desk. Gant scrutinized the geometric doodles to see if any names, dates, addresses or telephone numbers were visible beneath the scrawl. He tore the green paper into small pieces and was about to throw them in the garbage can when he changed his mind and emptied them into the box.

"When I started with the department," Gant said, "a police officer couldn't root through a man's trash without a warrant.

Now the Supreme Court said once a man throws something away, it don't belong to him no more. The FBI could carry out my trash, put it all together, find out all kinds of nasty shit. Like where I get my pizza from."

"Sir," Monroe began. "I'm almost sure Deegan and Zimmer were together on the night Deegan died, and that Zimmer had something to do with him dying."

Gant had his back to Monroe. "I told you not to fight him, Lou."

Monroe said, "Faith Morgan told me last night that the father of her baby wasn't Sam Claymore."

Gant pulled an F-111 jet fighter poster off his wall, rolled it into a tube, stuffed it into a corner of a box. He emptied the last drawer into a box.

"It would be wonderful if we could forget about him, or come up with something so we didn't have to know the truth. But we can't, you and me. That's the curse of this job. There ain't a cop in this department that hasn't seen something or heard something or found out about something that he'd be better off not knowing."

He put his hand on Monroe's shoulder. "Lou, we've been through a spell, you and me. I feel like I raised you in the department. There've been times I've gone to bat for you on the fifth floor, times I even bucked the Foambutts."

"Sir, you *knew* about Deegan and Zimmer."

Gant sighed. "I heard that there was a possibility that Zimmer was dating Deegan's mother for reasons more than her company. But I was a rookie on the Boardwalk and—"

"Who'd you hear it from?"

"You hear a lot of things. Mrs. Deegan went to the captain of the juvenile unit. Shortly afterward Zimmer fired her from her job."

"And what did you do about it?"

"There was nothing to do, Lou. My beat was the Boardwalk."

"Your beat was this entire city."

Gant shrugged. "I looked out after Deegan when he joined the department. I helped him where I could."

"But when Deegan wanted to get Zimmer, you told him he had no case."

"He didn't."

"He had a picture of himself with Zimmer. He said it was ultimate insurance."

Gant took a final glance around his office, his eyes resting on Monroe.

"Take the last piece of advice I hope I ever have to give you. You have a wife now. You have a child. Be smart, play dumb. Do as little as possible, as often as possible. No matter what you can do, evil is going to keep happening. You owe it to your wife and child to stay alive, and keep them out of harm's way. Everything else is bullshit. If you can't leave well enough alone, if you don't play along, if you end up fighting them, you'll make it harder for people who love you and don't deserve a life any worse than the one they already got. My advice, Lou, is keep the peace."

So saying, Gant put on his captain's cap, hoisted the boxes of personal belongings out of his office, and left without saying good-bye.

It was still cold from last night's chill so Monroe went home to get jackets, a blanket and the infant carseat for Sere. He wasted a ridiculous fifteen minutes trying to secure the seat in his car, gave up and roared down to Atlantic City General.

Nita wasn't there. Ellie was in a wheelchair, holding a wide-eyed, pink-faced Sere in a white receiving blanket. She said nothing about him being late.

"What a gal," Monroe said, cradling his daughter in his arms.

"I signed all the forms," Ellie said as Monroe nudged her out of her room. "You have to pay eighteen dollars cash for my color TV."

"Your what?"

"There was a color TV in my room and they charge extra for a color TV."

"Did you watch the thing?" Monroe said, suddenly exasperated.

"I never found the remote control."

"You didn't call a nurse—"

Then Monroe heard a sound unlike any uttered on the planet. Sere said, "Awk."

Monroe stopped.

"Why did you stop?" Ellie demanded.

"She was talking to me," Monroe said. "Sere wanted to say something." He looked at her dark eyes, wondered if they were looking at him, or at the light in the corridor above her.

"She's going to want to be fed soon and there are some things I forgot to tell you and Nita to get. By the way, Wayne called me this morning. He said Nita didn't show up for work last night and he wants her to be part of his investigation for a while. It seems she's seen or heard some things that he's concerned about. He said he wants to send some documents to Nita's home so he can sign her on to the state police payroll. But her employee file didn't list which room she is living in at Sea Park Plaza."

Monroe could almost hear Zimmer's voice. "And you told him."

"Those papers have to go to the right place."

Monroe was certain that papers were last thing Zimmer would send to Sea Park Plaza. He began to push the wheelchair just a little too fast.

Hours after he dropped Ellie off at their apartment and lowered Sere into her bassinet, Monroe shivered as he bounded down the hall of Sea Park Plaza. It was as if the chill from the night before hadn't left.

All the rooms around 1G were silent. Monroe didn't hear any sounds, no music, no television, no voices. He remembered all the kids Ramona Drew lived with. He knocked on 1G.

The dented, chipped brown enamel door was locked tight. He squatted to peer through the crack in the threshold, and saw a rug had been rolled up against it, sealing the room.

Monroe asked himself why would anybody want to seal off a room? People staying in places like this didn't care if the world smelled what they were smoking.

Then Monroe remembered last night's cold weather. If this building had any kind of heating system, it was shut down for the summer. Those who needed heat would have to close the windows and then maybe boil hot water on the stove, or turn the oven to broil and open the oven door.

The ovens in low-income housing projects were notorious for losing their flame and flooding apartments with gas. Monroe had read about entire buildings blowing up because of sparks made from electric alarm clocks going off in rooms filled with gas.

He took a pen out of his pocket, crouched down and pushed the rug out of the way. Then he pushed his nose forward. He hoped that he wouldn't smell gas. That would require him to call the fire department, and he didn't want to wait around for the fire department to show up to a place like this.

He caught a faint whiff of something stale and metallic. It reminded him of the faint musty, chemical odor from a car's tailpipe exhaust.

Then he caught another odor, and he jumped back and put his hand over his mouth to stop from gagging. And then he was on his feet, running out of Sea Park Plaza to the street. Then he ran around the building to the back, finding garbage cans, a rusted box spring, anything that would lift him high enough to peer into the tightly closed windows—the only tightly closed windows on the southeast corner of the building.

He smeared away the grime on the window and saw Nita's stars, or rather, walls papered with huge posters of pop singers and actors and celebrities crammed together so tightly that they weren't pictures as much as a mass of preening faces and perfect bodies.

Below the posters Monroe saw what appeared to be a pile of dolls, but was actually a half a dozen children of various ages, sprawled in a heap on stained mattress.

They weren't moving. Their mouths were open, as if they had been caught yawning. Their cheeks were bloated, their eyes closed, the skin on their faces was a terrifyingly bright, angry red. One had reached stiffly toward a poster. A leg stuck up at an odd angle.

Monroe tried to push the window open. Then he dropped down, found a chunk of masonry that had fallen from the walls, climbed back up and broke the window. The bitter, revolting stench of death engulfed him. He felt his breakfast coming up, let it come up and out of him until he stood gasping. His head drew up to see a black, battered, dented, four-by-four jeep pulling away from the alley, onto Mediterranean Avenue and out of sight.

CHAPTER
23

The Smoking Gun

Unlike the smashed, battered and rusting pay phones along the Boardwalk, the pay phone on Mediterranean Avenue was in perfect condition—free even of graffiti. In the poorer sections of the city, drug dealers used pay phones to monitor their operations and while you can vandalize the phone company, you'd better not mess with a drug dealer.

After calling the Homicide Unit, Monroe dialed his home number, told Ellie that some people—he didn't say who—at the Sea Park Plaza had died last night and would she make sure that if Nita came by, that she stayed there so he could talk to her when he came back?

Ellie assured him that she would.

Monroe then spent four-and-a-half hours with the Homicide Unit, License and Inspections Unit, the fire department's Atlantic Red Rescue Squad, and five hundred and twenty residents of Sea Park Plaza who had to be shoved out of their apartments while Licenses and Inspections did what was probably the first top-to-bottom inspection of the place since it was converted to low-income housing ten years ago.

Milling among the displaced persons, of which only three hundred and ten were registered with the Atlantic City Public Housing Commission, were sixteen parole violators and an additional twenty-three fugitives with standing bench warrants. Arrests were made and overtime racked up.

Monroe followed Inspector U. O. "Flash" McTeague into the

basement. McTeague's flashlight beam played over a forest of dust-encrusted gas water heaters, until it rested on the top of one of the water heaters.

"That's it," said McTeague, a paunchy, white-haired, leather-skinned City Hall survivor, to the half-dozen acolytes, assistant inspectors, deputy assistant inspectors and worshippers of mighty Flash. "That's your smoking gun."

"I don't see no smoke," one of the acolytes muttered.

"You never do in carbon monox poisonings." McTeague dropped the beam, began to hunt the filthy concrete platform on which the waterheaters stood. "When it's cold, and there's no heat in the building, these shitheads shut all the windows, seal up the cracks in the doors and turn on the ovens and run the hot water in the sinks and the tubs. Anything that's hot that they can pull in, they figure is better than no heat at all, which makes these damned, dumb, cheap, badly installed waterheaters—"

An acolyte waved a hand. "Excuse me, Mr. You-Oh—"

"I am to be referred to at all times as *Inspector* U. O."

"Yessir, Mr. Inspector sir, but I was wondering because you said that the waterheaters are badly installed. Since we're supposed to inspect them, does that mean the city's liable—"

Inspector U. O. McTeague glowered at the acolyte, who shut up only when the flashlight beam went into his eyes. "That's enough out of you." His flashlight lowered to a faded, crinkled label. "Well, it seems here that whoever was *supposed* to do the inspection here hasn't recorded that the inspection has been done since . . . damn, but it looks like near ten years."

He turned the beam off. "But, in answer to your question, *yes*, we must inspect buildings under municipal management. But this building is *not* under municipal management. The Low-Income Housing Authority runs this place, and is responsible for Class A through C inspections, which might include waterheaters. We're only involved after significant structural changes, changes in service or deployment of utilities, or before a sale of premises, or at the request of the building's owner. Personally, I wouldn't come a hundred yards near this place without an armed escort. The people here would as soon as kill a man for his pocket change. They're all scum."

Inspector McTeague waved the flashlight again. "Worse, they're stupid. They burn a lot of gas, which makes carbon monoxide that is supposed to go up into that exhaust manifold you see up there, which is nothing but open metal pipe which can get itself loose from time to time, which this one did."

McTeague aimed the light on an eight-inch length of tubing lying behind the water heater, then shot the light at the octopus-assembly of similar tubes above the water heaters. The tubes gathered into a single, large exhaust pipe that ran into a crumbling brick chimney.

"A piece dropped out up there, the carbon-monoxide that was supposed to go up the flue went up through this flooring here, which is also falling apart, into the apartment which had all its windows and doors closed, the gas range going full blast, sucking up oxygen, and Mom and the kids started to yawn and figured they was just tired from such a long day. At least they died in their sleep."

He brushed the dust off his maroon suit jacket, took out a pen, stuck the pen into the fallen tube and raised it in the air as if he were Sherlock Holmes with a major clue.

"Accidental death," he said. "You can see here where the section came loose. And there's a dent where it hit the floor."

Monroe saw what appeared to be a second dent, deep, in the center of the pipe section. "Maybe that dent came from somebody knocking it off."

McTeague didn't look at the plainclothes police detective. He assumed that this was another contrary remark made by one of his acolytes.

"You can read it any way you want," McTeague said. "We counted five hundred people living in a building that's only supposed to have three hundred, too many of them ex-cons, fugitives, juvenile offenders, junkies, drug dealers, sex offenders, child abusers, wife beaters, welfare cheats—miserable scum that never should've been born and wouldn't even be here if they had responsible jobs and didn't sit around all day eating and watching TV and fucking so they make more of themselves. They come down here and they hide drugs and needles and it's just a waste."

Monroe hadn't seen a single needle in the basement. While waiting for homicide to arrive, he discovered that every door leading to the basement had been locked, tight.

McTeague crouched down and turned off the waterheater. "No, it's accidental," he said, spelling the word for one of the acoloytes. "I'd probably have to cite the owner for code violations concerning these floorboards here, but inasmuch as this is an *inquiry* into cause-of-death and not a formal inspection, I can only *comment* upon conditions that, in my professional opinion, can contribute to a hazardous situation. These pipes can slip any time, and accidents happen."

"But what if it *was* intentional," Monroe demanded.

"Anybody who would be deliberate about this kind of thing would have to have a reason for killing these people. He'd have to know about the bad flooring. He'd have to have a key to the premises and the guts to walk in here, which most respectable people don't, even in broad daylight. You have one good reason that somebody would make this happen?"

"If I do, I'll let you know," Monroe said.

McTeague shined his long-barreled chrome-plated flashlight past his acolytes until it landed on Monroe's face. The light dropped to Monroe's ID card, which was hanging from a string around his neck.

"I don't recall authorizing a Detective Monroe to accompany this inquiry."

Monroe shrugged. "I was just curious."

"Curious. He's just curious. I wonder, sometimes, about the priorities of some of our younger civil servants."

Monroe saw a few of the acolytes sneering at him. This was McTeague's show. He might as well play his role. "I'm here because I was first on the scene. I was the officer that called this in."

McTeague chewed his lips. "Well then, you must be a model citizen if there ever was one. We got so much drugs and prostitution on the streets, it's getting so little old ladies are afraid to leave their homes, on account of the junkies and creeps and perverts we got hanging around, and you need a reason, it's that cops like this spend more time defending the so-called rights of scum that are just weights around the taxpayers' necks, than they do with the decent people that pay their salaries. Maybe when Officer Roo gets us a new mayor, we'll throw these scum out."

Monroe turned away. "So you say this was accidental?"

"What I say, I say for the edification of my troops here, and is not for those that rat on their friends."

He turned to his troops. "I almost forgot to mention, you find a lot of rat infestations when you go into poorhouses like this, and there's only one way to deal with rats."

He smiled at Monroe. "You put out the poison." Then he laughed. His acolytes laughed. Monroe backed out before McTeague said anything more.

Nita Ivas was gone when he returned.

"She left," Ellie said, emerging out of the bathroom.

"But I told you—"

"And I just told you. She came, helped me make the bottles and left. She can leave if she wants to."

"The people she lived with were killed last night. A woman and eight kids. Gas heater in the basement leaked carbon monoxide and it went through the floor and if she had been staying with them, she might have been killed, too."

Ellie was on the couch, looked for something to put in her hands, found the remote control for the TV set and sat staring at it for a while. Sere was asleep in a cradle in the bedroom.

"She left because she had to," Ellie said finally.

Monroe went to the kitchen, filled a glass of water, stared at it, poured it down the drain. "What's that mean?"

"It means what I said. She . . . you don't understand. A girl that comes off the street, has to *want* to come off the street and sometimes she has to go back."

"Go back where? Even if they decide it was accidental, that room is a sealed crime scene for the next 48 hours. She—"

"She's not going *home,* for the Lord's sake. She's going back to whoever she feels safe with."

"Safe? She say who this guy is? I have to find her."

"She didn't say who it was. And don't go looking for her. Not now. She has to understand that she has choices, that she is acting under her own free will. If you start looking for her, she'll run away."

Monroe opened the refrigerator, saw a row of bottles with cans of formula behind them and slammed the refrigerator shut. "Look, I don't care if she runs or walks. I think she's in trouble."

Ellie glared at him. "I could sense that Nita is scared. But she's not scared of being hurt. That's already happened, do you hear me?"

Monroe said, "Tell me where she went."

She said, "I don't know."

Monroe sat at the kitchen table, stared past the air conditioner through the narrow slice of window below the yellow curtains that Ellie put up that he couldn't stand. He stared at the fishing boats and pleasure yachts chopping up the Clam Creek inlet, going places, going goddamn *fishing,* and none of them having to live with the sight of dead kids with their eyes half open, and their skin lobster-red, and the mother face down on the floor with blood around her head where she fell down, smashed her chin and was too weak to get up so she may have died from breathing in, and choking on her own blood.

"Maybe she has a protector," Ellie said. "A person who is not a pimp, who reminds you of the parents you never had. A protector is somebody she can *love,* Lou."

Monroe said, "Excuse me," and ran down the steps, got into his car and took off for Pacific Avenue.

*   *   *

It was dark when he parked in front of the Horseshoe. Nita wasn't in. Monroe went to the pay phone near the lavatories and called the Alcazar, asked if Nita Ivas had arrived for work and was cut off. He called again, was put on hold. A man answered and said the computers were down, it was Friday night, all the gamblers were coming in and who has the time to check the time cards?

He hung up and stomped out.

That left one place.

He drove down Mount Rushmore, shining his flashlight on every surface, checking every door. She wasn't hiding anywhere he could see.

In front of him was the King Arthur Motel. Faith Morgan was not on her corner, perhaps because it was early. Or maybe because she was with someone.

He drove three blocks up Pacific, put his car into an abandoned lot, and trotted back to the King Arthur. He pushed open the glass door, wandered through a dim lobby cluttered with a ripped brown oilcloth sofa over which hung a chromed plastic suit of armor. The lobby stank of mildew and cigarette smoke. He went to the desk, where a withered woman sat, watching a portable TV.

"I'm looking for Faith Morgan's room," Monroe said.

"She ain't here," the woman at the desk said. "Ain't no one here."

Monroe showed his police ID. "I need to know her room number."

"You got business here, you come in with a warrant," the woman said, not taking her eyes off the set. She handed him a card. "My son-in-law's my lawyer. You talk to him."

Monroe ran past her, past a flight of dingy, sticky steps to a frayed-carpeted corridor leading back. He heard other televisions, smelled burning food odors. He ran to the second floor. At the very end of the corridor, leading to a room that would be facing the ocean, was a door that he thought exuded an aroma of bathroom deodorant.

He knocked. He heard nothing. He put his eyes to the crack under the door and saw nothing. He ran back through the lobby, up three blocks to his car, got the flashlight, went down a narrow alley between the King Arthur and the Heart of Palm Motel next door. The alley dead-ended with a row of garbage dumpsters.

He stood on the lid of a dumpster that had been shut. He put the flashlight in his mouth, jumped and managed to cling to the rusting, weatherbeaten edge of an air conditioner. He pulled himself up, grabbing a piece of aluminum window molding, holding tightly to it until he could put a foot on the sill of the second-floor room. He had to hold on to the molding, his fingers pulling himself up. He wasn't high enough to peer in the window. He figured that if he jerked himself upward, he might have a few seconds to see in.

He hung there and heard the sighing of the ocean. He smelled the salt brine and felt the evening breeze tickling his neck. He counted to three and groaned, and strained, and pulled his head up and saw into a darkened room. He saw in the wash from his flashlight an enormous rounded bed. On the walls around the bed, shimmering in the silvery light, were thousands and thousands of neckties.

His fingers cramped and he dropped down, his elbows taking the shock as his body slammed against the bricks below the window. He forced himself not to let go, to look down and think—he was going to fall so he had to put his feet somewhere. He saw one of the dumpsters was open. He saw something in the dumpster. It looked like an arm.

Then he heard it, a voice, or *almost* a voice. His fingers gave out and he fell down with a bone-jarring jolt in his ankles that worked its way up his spine, and then to his skull. He wasn't aware that he was on his side until he pulled himself up and went toward the open dumpster. He picked up his flashlight, and saw a line of white along the top edge of a dumpster, moving. It seemed to be crawling, moving. He drew closer and suddenly it dropped—an arm, a pale arm hanging down, a purplish bruise over the wrist, the hand open, three of the small, fragile blue fingers on the hand were twitching to that beat. The little finger and third finger on the hand weren't moving because they'd been snapped back, the broken knuckles dark and swollen.

Monroe tried to keep calm, couldn't, tried to look into the dumpster but couldn't, dragged empty garbage cans to the side, held the flashlight high and saw the girl, twenty to twenty-five years of age, brown hair, clothing torn, signs of recent physical violence from fists or blunt object; jaw broken; four teeth on left side pushed in; left eye closed and blackened; bruises to the face and left temple; cut in left ear still bleeding; shortness of breath indicating possible broken ribs. Monroe yanked off his jacket, pulled it over the girl, searched for the portable radio that was supposed to be clipped to his belt. It wasn't on his belt because he wasn't on duty.

But he had found Nita Ivas. And she was still alive. He looked up at the window and realized she had been put here so that when Faith Morgan went to her window and looked down, this would be the first thing she'd see.

"Don't die," he said, knowing it was stupid, knowing she probably couldn't hear. He touched her skin, which was clammy and much too cold. He wondered if she was under the influence of some dumb drug, wondering what kind of world it is that can have this happen to anyone, especially a girl, a woman who starts life as an infant—small, helpless, like his new daughter Sere.

He had to leave to get help, but he thought that if he left her then all that was left of her would be gone when he came back.

As Monroe stared at her he could see the hands of Reuben Claymore moving over her, doing things to her. This wasn't a blind spot. He'd seen enough of Reuben Claymore's victims.

But, just to be sure, he'd have to get a statement from Nita when she regained consciousness. There were procedures to follow. He had to build a case.

Nita Ivas failed to regain consciousness and died, four hours later. The coroner judged her a victim of an unknown assailant.

CHAPTER
24

Blind Spot

The next morning Monroe awoke groggy, having sat in the emergency room as Nita Ivas's life drained from her. After that he had held his wife as she cried herself to sleep, only to wake up an hour later for Sere's 6:00 A.M. feeding.

He put on his running shoes, a shirt and shorts and drove his car to the King Arthur Hotel.

No one answered when he knocked on the door. He thought he heard plumbing noises inside but couldn't be sure. He waited for a few minutes, knocked again.

He took out the note he had written, about how Ellie was her daughter and that Faith should call him to see the baby. He asked himself if maybe he should talk to his wife before he invited relatives home, especially this one.

So he put the letter back in his pocket, returned to his car, drove off to buy the hundred or so other things that Ellie said they needed. Somewhere along the way he put the letter in a trash can—one more bit of waste created by human beings living on New Jersey barrier islands, to be taken to unknown landfills that might, just might, transform it to something useful hundreds of years from now.

At home Ellie taught him how to change a diaper, make a bottle, hold Sere, hold the bottle, hold Sere and the bottle, hold Sere, the bottle and a cloth diaper to mop up what dribbled down Sere's chin. It was a wonderfully easy thing to do, except when she cried, and then Monroe felt helpless, his world falling apart because someone so small, so important was unhappy.

He could see himself doing this for the rest of his life. He could see himself secure, a good father, enduring the suffering and salvation of bringing another human being into the world.

Then Ellie said to him, "She didn't have to die."

Sere was sleeping. They were sitting on the fire escape, taking in the breeze and its odors—diesel fumes and dead seafood—as it rolled off the commercial fishing docks of Clam Creek.

"She should have lived to see this day," Ellie said. "And the one after it."

Monroe sipped his Diet Coke.

"She had a lot done to her, a lot of terrible things done to her, but she wanted to make something of herself," Ellie continued, drinking orange juice. "She deserved that. She deserved another chance."

Monroe nodded.

"Sometimes I ask myself, how it is that I get to be so lucky, when people like Nita, who deserve all the help in the world, never make it."

"People care for you," Monroe said.

"People cared for her," Ellie said.

Monroe looked at his wife. Her face was still pale and bloodless from the childbirth. The skin around her eyes was dark and puffy from lack of sleep. "You bring someone into the world and you learn how much a life is worth."

Monroe stood and asked her if she wanted more juice.

"Wait," she said. "How come you're so distant? What aren't you telling me?"

"About Nita?"

"About all of this. It has to do with Wayne, doesn't it?"

Monroe looked down. "I'm just tired, that's all."

"You're lying to me. I can always tell when a man's lying."

"Oh?"

She nodded. "You don't do what I did for as long as I did and not develop understanding of people."

"I guess not."

"You remind me of him. Of the way he would handle me, protect me from things that he thought I was too fragile to understand. I am not fragile. If I ever needed proof, I got that now."

Monroe kissed her forehead.

"He'd do that, too, when he thought I was so sweet or precious. I am not sweet or precious."

She gazed east, at the casino towers sparkling in the sun. "He's a bad man, isn't he?"

Monroe nodded.

"But he was always good to me. Wonderful, in fact. The kind of man that girls dream of. When I met him, I was so delighted. He cared for me, Louis. He brought me the finest things. He never asked anything of me. It was easy to like him."

"But he was good to you on his terms," Monroe said. "He was in control of your relationship at all times. He was using you, paying for you."

She looked at him. "I didn't like thinking about it. I guess I fell in love with him because I didn't want to think about it. I spent so much energy not thinking about it that, for a while, I could pretend that it was like a dream coming true."

"He was in your blind spot," Monroe said.

"It wasn't the love I feel with you now."

"What's that?" Monroe asked.

"Lucky. Lucky to be alive."

He put his hand on hers. "Stop that," she said.

"He used to do this, too?"

"When he didn't want to listen to what I was saying."

"I want to . . . I am listening."

"But something's in the way. Just as it was whenever Marty Gant would talk to me. Something's in the way. What is it, Lou? And don't you say 'nothing' because I will not be able to live with you if you lie to me. I have had every man who is important to me, from my father on down to you, lie to me and I am sick of it. I left my parents because they wouldn't admit to me that I was adopted. We had neighbors. They told me that my folks came back with me after a trip to Atlantic City. Why do you think I was drawn here? Could you stay away from the place where you were born, where your real parents are?"

"I guess not."

"You had better guess not. I admit, I made some mistakes, but I never lost sight of the fact that if I met my parents, I wouldn't think of why they didn't want me. I would just love them because they gave me life. They gave me this day with you. They gave me our daughter."

Monroe hoped the agony inside him wouldn't show.

"Louis, if you're jealous of Wayne—"

"I'm *not* jealous, believe me."

"You are. You're jealous of the power he has. I've never seen you so defeated. I didn't marry a man who gives up so easily."

He turned so she wouldn't see his face.

"I remember I asked Marty Gant how to find my parents, and he said he didn't rightly know. But his assistant, Ray Deegan, he helped me."

Monroe sat up.

"We went back into the old record room behind the Solicitor's Office. We went back there and dug, and dug, and dug. We found all sorts of interesting stuff about babies, wills and deeds. But he didn't find anything about me.

"Then I just went out and started talking to people. On my days off, when I wasn't working, when I'd come in after running the Boardwalk. I sat and talked to people. It became an obsession. I had to know about the history of this place. Because I had the feeling that, from being born here, I was part of that history, and somewhere there would be someone who would remember. I found folks that remembered a man you'd see on the Boardwalk if you wanted to adopt and you didn't want a hassle with the government. That's when I was sure that Gant was lying to me."

"He—" Monroe stopped himself. "What did he tell you?"

"He said that there was a lot he had forgotten and there was a lot he couldn't be sure of. But then he said to me many women had to give up babies because they were prostitutes. He asked me how I would deal with it if I found out my mother was somebody like a prostitute. I said to him, 'Marty, I was a prostitute, and I'd love and respect any woman who was my mother, no matter what she'd been through.'

"That's when he put me on as a youth counselor. And he acted as if the fact that he was paying me a salary was enough I should shut my mouth. I had a job to do and for a while, I looked at every girl that I counseled as somebody who could have been my Mom. And I could tell, some of them were just using me, or thinking they were fooling me, or ripping me off to buy drugs, but what can we own that's so valuable, that's so significant that it's more important than a human life? I said to myself I didn't care how low somebody's sunk, there's decency and dignity in everyone and if it was my job to remind people of that, then I was going to be the best damned reminder in the world."

She frowned. "But I never met my mother. I'm sure of that. If I had, I would've known. I can't tell you how, I'm sure of it. I'd have had a feeling, like what the players are supposed to get when the slot machine is set to pay off."

"You never got that feeling?" Monroe asked carefully.

"Never. No. That's not true. I did once. I was driving into town, back in the days when I was in the service and earning enough to have a car, and the traffic was bad on Missouri Avenue, so I took a turn down some street next to it."

"Mount Rushmore," Monroe said.

"And I felt something then. And the only other time I got it was when I first met Marty Gant. I remember looking at that broken nose of his, and wondering why, even with it squashed so flat, it looked like mine. I figured then that he would be important in my life. And he was."

"Gant," Monroe said. "Gant."

"So now I figure that if my father and mother are out there, they just might walk into a casino hotel one day. So, as soon as things get into a routine with Sere—"

"I know where your mother is," Monroe said.

Ellie stared at him for a minute. "I figured you did. Or that you could find her."

"We will find her," Monroe said. "Tonight."

"Here," Ellie said. "It was right here."

The car had stopped in front of Number 20 South Mount Rushmore Street.

Monroe looked at the carseat in the back. Sere was still sleeping.

"Keep going," Ellie said. "This night is so beautiful. This night is so, so beautiful." He brought the car to a halt just at the mouth of Mount Rushmore.

For several minutes Ellie stared at the woman standing under the awning of the King Arthur Motel. "I drove past her so many times and I felt nothing," Ellie said. "I didn't even see her. Of all the girls on the street, she was invisible to me. Why is it that I never had the feeling for her? Why, Lou?"

She turned on the dome light and looked at the picture of Faith Morgan standing beside Sam Claymore. "She was so beautiful then. See the way her eyes are, and the way her jaw comes down like so. Those are my eyes. That's my jaw. And you say she used to row boats when she was a kid? There weren't any boats in the hill country, but I was always a tomboy, running around, climbing trees, trying to beat the boys. When I moved here I took to running the Boardwalk, and I ran past that motel and I didn't feel a thing. Not a thing."

She looked up from the book, and then back at the picture. "I read this book when I bought it for you, and I never saw myself in her, or anybody."

She turned the page. "And there's Wayne."

"His role in this isn't clear," Monroe said awkwardly.

She closed the book. "My mother will know who my father is," Ellie insisted. She grabbed his hand. "When I signal, you bring the baby. She has to see Sere. She has to know the gift she gave me has been passed on to someone else."

"You sure you don't want me to be with you?"

"Positive. She has to see me alone." She checked her reflection in the rearview mirror, smoothed her light cotton dress, then kissed him. "I love you so much for doing this."

He watched her walk across the street. She was very weak and sore from childbirth and she wasn't supposed to be walking much. He saw that it took a while for Faith Morgan to notice her. Monroe couldn't hear conversation from where he sat in the car, but he saw Morgan stop and turn and saw Ellie take Faith's huge hands and put them on her face. Then he saw the hands fall to Ellie's shoulders and those great arms come down into a hug.

Then he felt the snout of a gun in his ear.

"This you shouldn't have done," Reuben Claymore said.

CHAPTER

25

Down by the Sea

"Easy," Zimmer said as he told Monroe to leave the car. "Roo, take the baby."

"I don't want nothing with a baby," Claymore growled.

"So learn," Zimmer sighed, removing Monroe's gun. "We'll give the baby to Gant. He's down at the pier with Hadruna. Man's raised two daughters."

"You're not going to do this," Monroe said.

"I will," Zimmer said. "Because you value the baby over your own life, you're going to endure everything we do to you. If you don't, you'll die. But we want you to live. We want you to think about what will happen to this dear, sweet, sleeping baby if you die." He sighed. "Give up, Lou. I got you."

"Ellie's coming right back here," Monroe said. "She's going to find me and the baby missing and—"

"She'll call the cops," Claymore laughed, slipping handcuffs on Monroe's wrists. He took the baby out of the carseat and then shoved Monroe up Mount Rushmore toward the dark bulk of the jeep.

"Get in," Zimmer said.

Monroe didn't move.

Claymore handed Sere to Zimmer, grabbed Monroe by his jacket collar and slammed his face into the side of the jeep, once, twice, three times.

"I think I maybe broke your face," Claymore laughed. "Oh, it

286

feels good to do that. Like what I did to that Nita cunt, but better. She I just wanted to fuck. You, I want to kill."

"But we're not going to kill you," Zimmer said. "We're going to give you a choice. You can die if you want to. Or you can live. We're just going to put you right on the edge and let nature take its course."

"My baby," Monroe said, the blood running down his face. "Gimme my baby."

Zimmer said, "You don't want to bleed on her, do you?"

Claymore hoisted Monroe up and tossed him into the back of the jeep. Then he got in, started the engine, began to back the jeep out.

Sere began to stir. They she began to cry.

"Gimme my baby," Monroe moaned.

"Maybe I should put on the music," Claymore said. "Some kids shut up when they hear music. My father used to play it when he'd beat us so the neighbors wouldn't hear."

"Good idea," Zimmer said. "Sinatra?"

"There is anything else?" Claymore boomed.

They were driving to the Utah Avenue ramp that went under the Boardwalk when Monroe pushed himself off the back seat and brought his handcuffs down on Zimmer's head. He felt the skin rip open, he felt hair snag the cuffs and he heard a scream, and he felt blows to his face and neck, and hands.

But he didn't hear Sere cry, so he figured he did something good.

They rode with their lights off over the sand up to the wooden pilings of Brighton pier. There was enough light coming off the Boardwalk for Monroe to see Claymore put Sere in Marty Gant's handcuffed arms. "Wayne, you can't be serious," Gant said. "This is the man's child."

"She isn't his child, Gant," Zimmer said. "Enjoy the show."

Hadruna and Claymore pulled Monroe out of the jeep and dragged him face down in the sand to the edge of the water.

Zimmer shoved Monroe's head into the water, held it under for a few seconds, then yanked it out by his hair.

"Hope you don't mind," Zimmer said. "I didn't have more of a crowd assembled. Most of my assistants would have difficulty understanding the need for this. I thought it better to keep it among friends."

Then they lifted him high enough to hang his handcuffed wrists on a rusting boathook imbedded in one of the piers.

Monroe felt pain in his shoulders. He was hanging with his back to the wet, slime-encrusted wooden pilings, the oddly warm water tumbling in over his knees. The waves would push him against the piling, putting strain on his arms. The tide appeared to be coming in, so he expected the pull to grow lighter as the water-level raised.

"Listen to him, no sound," Claymore observed gruffly to Hadruna. "We did Deegan, he was making all kinds of sounds."

"He'll be singing soon enough," Hadruna said.

Zimmer stepped into Monroe's line of sight. "The ocean will drown out any sound you make, and I do mean any sound. In addition to whatever internal damage, there is the added delight of the seawater coming in. The salt will make any skin lesions absolutely excruciating, and the waves will keep you moving, so whatever broken bones you have will scrape up against each other and work their way through your skin, which will increase your pain until you pass out. *That's* when we take you down, take off the cuffs and throw you in the water."

"Or maybe we don't," Claymore said, hoisting a length of rubber hose. "Maybe we just party all night long and leave you for the sharks."

"Wayne," Gant called. "Let's stop this now. There's no reason he has to suffer."

"He's a pain in the ass, you're a pain in the ass," Zimmer said. "You'd think you were related."

"We are," Gant said, his voice choking up. "He's my son-in-law."

Zimmer's head snapped around.

"Ellen's mine, Wayne," Gant said. "She always was."

Monroe managed a brief smile.

"None of this matters . . ." Zimmer said.

"It does to the man you got hung up there. It does to me, who had to see you hang him up there before I had the guts to say it."

"Hey," Claymore growled. "We gonna do this guy or not?"

Zimmer touched the back of his neck where the blood dripped. "Do him."

Then Claymore started whipping him with a garden hose, the metal end ripping his skin through his clothes. When Sere started screaming her wet-diaper cry, Monroe wanted to die, quickly.

His ears were roaring with pain, and it seemed the sound of the water itself was rushing through his bones, punishing him, pushing him to the edge of awareness.

But as soon as he reached what he thought was the end, Claymore would shift to the baseball bat again, or take him off the hook and turn him around, so that he hung with his face in the piling and his back exposed. And suddenly he was awake, alive and aware again, feeling every ache and agony.

He realized he was looking death in the face again, but this time he wondered if he would ever recover.

He heard Sere crying for him and he knew he would, and that scared him. To be disfigured, to be crippled, to be less than a father to her, that was terrifying and more painful than his wounds.

And then he heard another shot. A third, a fourth. He recognized the sound of the gun. It was his gun.

Zimmer had his gun out. Zimmer was firing it. It went off a fifth time. Monroe twisted until he could see him firing it at Faith Morgan and Ephrum Traile.

He saw her collapse on the sand. Behind her Ephrum Traile was facedown, motionless. Behind them, off to the side, Monroe saw Hadruna holding Ellie, a gag in her mouth, the garden hose going around her arms. Monroe would live long enough to kill that man, he decided.

He saw the blood pouring from Morgan's sides into the water that tumbled over her back. He remembered from a Police Academy weapons and ballistics class that large areas of fat on obese people could deflect bullets away from vital organs. She might survive her wounds. She might not.

Then he saw her put her hands on the ground, press down with her big arms and rise. Zimmer moved toward her, put the gun near her head and she sprung forward and fell on him.

Zimmer was making gasping, gargling noises as the sea rushed over his face. Reuben Claymore stood around, trying to pull Morgan off, but she was too heavy for him. He stood back and started kicking her in the ribs, the arms, the face.

Monroe saw Zimmer's face become a foamy blur under the water. He saw Zimmer's mouth open into a scream that he could not hear. He saw Claymore raise his foot to stomp Faith Morgan's head. He saw Faith Morgan roll away the second before Claymore's foot came down, so it went on Wayne Zimmer's neck, and Zimmer's feet and arms shot out at once, and then were still.

Then he saw Claymore raise his foot to stomp Morgan's head again. He managed a broken cry. "Roo—"

Claymore stopped.

Monroe said, "Fuck you, Roo."

Claymore turned and Monroe, once again, looked death in the face. Claymore waded in the water toward Monroe. He stood, his hands on his hips, the neck brace framing his head, thrusting his chin forward.

"I'm going to kill you," Claymore said.

Monroe said, "No."

He smiled, and the smile must have pulled something in his neck because it made him flinch. And as he flinched, Monroe summoned his last bit of energy, the last smoldering flame within him, and pulled up his legs, screaming as the pain ripped through his stomach and arms, while the tips of his shoes hit Claymore's jutting chin and nose, and knocked him backward into the water.

Then Monroe hung, spent, exhausted, in such excruciating pain that he began to sense himself coming loose from the part of him that was feeling. If there was an edge between life and death, this was it. Nothing seemed to matter anymore.

Claymore rose from the water, a dripping, roaring monster and then Monroe seemed to leave his body, float above it, look down. Monroe watched his legs come up again, hitting Claymore even harder, right straight into that open mouth, snagging teeth, pushing deep until he could hear Claymore gag, pushing deeper, pushing Claymore backward toward a piling.

Claymore's head made a popping sound as it smacked against the piling. He landed facedown in the water and didn't move.

Faith Morgan lay in the water for a while. Monroe heard Hadruna say, "I'm getting the fuck out of here." He heard the engine of the jeep roar and then Gant was bending over Faith Morgan, and Ellie was next to her husband, the gag still in her mouth, a squalling Sere in one arm, her other arm holding him.

Then Morgan struggled, rose to stand and reach, and pull Monroe down. She clamped her hands around his handcuffs and broke them free.

"Faith," Gant said. "We gotta get you to an ambulance."

"Mom," Ellie said, ripping off the gag, "you got to—we have to—"

"No ambulance." She was on her knees, the water billowing around her chest, when she grabbed Gant's cuffs and groaned, twisting them loose.

"Listen to me," she said, breathing heavily. "I'm not good enough to be with you. Maybe, someday, I come back. Maybe not. But, I can't be with you now. You gotta—" she put her her hand over her chest and collapsed. "You gotta make me . . . you gotta see me as I was."

"We *need* you as you are," Ellie wailed. "We need you. We all need you."

"You need me to go . . ."

Monroe tried to raise himself from the water. "Uh, hi," he said, the words sputtering out with blood. "Mom."

She closed her eyes and her face seemed to shrink, her body contract. She slowly pushed herself to her feet, staggered painfully toward an upended, beach patrol boat, stood on one side and pushed it over. The boat hit the wet sand with a thump. With one hand in the bow, she dragged the boat to the tideline.

"You need . . . a hospital," Monroe said. "Both . . . us."

"Don't like hospitals," she wheezed. She grabbed Zimmer and tossed him into the boat. She heaved Reuben Claymore over the gunwales. Then she went up to the sand, where Ephrum Traile lay dead. She let out a single cry, cradled his body, fell down, rose on one knee, then the other, and placed him gently at the stern.

"Faith, don't do this," Gant said.

She didn't hear them. She was murmuring to Traile. "Come on, Eph. We got one more left. One more life, you and me. We gotta go, you and me. Gotta leave this place. It ain't our place no more. It ain't our place."

She set him down gently in the boat, then gathered the bow rope over her shoulder, pulled the boat forward into the surf. Waves smashed and leaped around her. She tried to heave herself into the boat but fell backward, letting go of the boat and sending up a great spray of water.

Monroe discovered he could crawl, or at least drag himself forward into the water. The waves crashed into his face, pushing foaming brine into his mouth and nose. He let the water move him toward the boat and the woman hanging on its side. He pushed his head above the foam and said, "Wait."

A wave rocked both of them up and down, shoving Monroe below. He felt a hand on his neck, the fingers tightening around his collar, lifting him up, out, where he grabbed the air with his mouth.

He clung to that arm, to the boat and then felt a reasurring numbness as his knees touched the bottom. He planted his hands.

"Hold on . . . me," he said, his head hanging inches above the water.

Her voice, from above. "I'm doin' that."

"And—" the wave caught his throat, washed over him. He choked, coughed, spat out water and said, "Climb . . ."

She said, "I'll kill you."

"No," Monroe said, sensing the rhythm of the waves enough to lift his head out of the way of the advancing sea. "You won't kill me. Put your knee on my shoulder."

He grabbed some shells in his hands, clenched them into fists and looked up into her face, seeing age and decay, and unbearable grief.

"Do it," he said.

"I'll kill you."

"Try," Monroe said.

He could keep his elbows locked straight for only a second as the impossible weight descended on his left shoulder and then his arms bent and he felt his face slap the water.

Though his legs felt dead he found he could sit and lean his body against the movement of the water. He was aimed toward the dim shadows of the pier. He turned his head and saw the boat twenty feet away, floating free, apparently empty. No head or torso could be seen over the gunwales. He felt immediate, incredible sorrow, thinking that she had slipped off and was drowning somewhere, as he had been.

Then he saw a hand on the gunwales, followed by her broad, thick arm. She rose awkwardly in the boat, painfully turning her back to the bow. He saw one oar slap the water, and another. His sorrow turned to wild, giddy joy as he saw her lean forward and the oars dip into the water. She leaned back and the oars pushed the boat. It tipped and crested over a wave as she leaned forward again, the slow rhythm of the oars pushing the boat out to sea.

Gant and Ellie pulled him back to the sand. He lay for a while with his head on Ellie's leg and his hand touching Sere's cheek. She was sleeping again. Why was she sleeping?

Ellie was saying something about Gant going to get help, and that Faith had seen them take Monroe out of the car. The reason it took so long is that Lou had taken the keys to the car, and they had to call Ephrum Traile . . .

Monroe tried to nod, and with Ellie at his side, holding Sere, he saw the edge slipping away. He looked at his daughter and saw life, a new life that was also his life, and realized that, no matter how painful, dangerous or stupid it can be, there is something wonderful and magnificent to be said for anyone crazy enough to keep life going, to stay with a game, no matter how dangerous, hopeless, no matter how terrible the odds, and play it through to the end.

Afterword

Maximillian Hadruna was arrested on the New Jersey Turnpike when he tried to run a tollbooth at Exit Nine. He was convicted of kidnapping and is currently serving a life-term in Trenton State Penitentiary, which is, coincidentally, a few miles from New Jersey Turnpike's Exit Nine. He will be eligible for parole some time during the next century.

An empty Atlantic City lifeguard boat ran aground near the Longport jetty. Marine police found bloodstains inside the boat. Laboratory analysis revealed that the blood came from four people.

Operation Long Spoon was disbanded following the disappearance of Special Investigator Wayne D. Zimmer and former Atlantic City Patrolman Reuben Claymore.

Moby the pygmy sperm whale was released into the ocean after a two-week stay in a hospital tank in Brigantine. He was never seen again.

Captain Marty Gant returned from retirement as temporary head of the Atlantic City Police Department's Internal Affairs Division.

On the September night of the televised Miss America Pageant, the remains of Ramona Drew, Nita Ivas and eight children were cremated in a Mays Landing funeral home.

In November, Atlantic City Mayor Bernie Tilton was reelected to a second term.

That same month, Ellen Monroe became a part-time marketing

executive at the Alcazar Casino Hotel, Inc. She was recently profiled as one of the "Ten Gals With Clout" in *Rolling Chair Magazine*.

With the coming of cold weather, Tommy Fugari, aka the Maestro Toccata N. Fugue, left for his vacation home in St. Martin. He plans to return in the spring.

Jimmy "the Geek" Doochay remains under the Boardwalk.

In December, Detective Louis Monroe emerged from Atlantic City General Hospital to complete his disability leave at home. Between physical therapy sessions he found that he could change diapers, fill bottles and otherwise attend to the needs of Serendipity Monroe. He wants to return to active duty as soon as possible.

He is confident that his family will provide him with a moral anchor with which he can ride out the storm of greed, corruption and self-interest that has roared through Atlantic City for far too long.

No way, José.